A Fear of Seaside Heights

Also by Jane Kelly

Meg Daniels Mysteries
From Plexus Publishing

Killing Time in Ocean City
Cape Mayhem
Wrong Beach Island
Missing You in Atlantic City
Greetings from Ventnor City

Writing in Time Mysteries

Swoon '64
Pretender '56

Widow Lady Mysteries

Widow Lady

A Fear of Seaside Heights

By Jane Kelly

Benday Publishing

Phoenixville, Pennsylvania

Disclaimer

This is a work of fiction. Names, characters, places and incidents either are the product of the author's imagination or are used fictitiously. Any resemblance to actual persons, living or dead, is entirely coincidental.

ISBN: 978-0-9963340-1-3

To Dennis

Acknowledgments

Thank you to Barbara, Beth, Bill, Carole, Carolyn, Deb, Debbie, Linda, Marilynn, Maureen, Rick, Suzen and Victor who fit into one or more of these categories:

*For walking the boards, riding the rides and tasting the delicacies of Seaside Heights so that I could experience all the town had to offer – including lots of Skeeball.

*For sharing their memories and offering their expert advice.

*For reading and re-reading many versions of the manuscript.

To Maureen Stoddard whose affection for Seaside Heights helped me see the town through a child's eyes.

CHAPTER 1

Where was it? Where did it go? I can't figure it out. And then, when they saw the roller coaster protruding from the ocean waves, they said the same words: I can't believe it.

I, too, said that sentence. I'd seen the sight dozens of times, on the front page of newspapers, on the cover of magazines, as the lead story on the evening news. Photos were all over the Internet. Yet, seeing the roller coaster rising out of the waves, the last amusement standing, brought home with a wallop the reality of how hard Seaside Heights had been hit.

Superstorm Sandy had swept away the Boardwalk in the last days of October 2012 so the following April tourists had to walk the streets of Seaside Heights instead of the boards. Concessions driven from their Boardwalk locations lined the pavement but the compulsion to win a stuffed animal was not as strong without the sounds of the amusements, the sight of the surf and the feel of wooden planks under our feet.

Andy and I, like many others, bypassed the makeshift stands and cut through a pizza joint to a platform overlooking the beach and the roller coaster beyond. That was as close to the ocean as we were going to get. We could see the foundation of the reconstructed Boardwalk but no section was ready to accept vacationers. "It will be back by Memorial Day," the authorities said.

"It's going to be a tough job," Andy observed. "They've got six more weeks."

"I don't know why I feel so disoriented. I can see we're near the wide part of the Boardwalk, but how many blocks to the Heavenly Dips shop? I just don't remember."

"That might not all be the storm's fault."

"Are you saying that I am old?" I asked with faux horror, refusing to admit that I was approaching the age when expressing concern about my memory might no longer be play-acting. I'd heard stories about forty.

"I am saying it's been a lot of years. Jersey Shore hadn't even hit MTV when you worked on the Boardwalk. Snooki grew up and had a baby since you were last here."

"Well, she had a baby, anyway." I led us back to the street. "I don't know why it is so hard to identify the Heavenly Dips store with the sign gone. I did go in and out the backdoor and I didn't need a GPS to pick out the right one."

"We didn't have a GPS in those days," Andy answered, deadpan.

"I was making a point. I remember that you would drop me off by the water park." I pointed across the street. "And I would walk up onto the Boardwalk." I made a show of surveying the area. "I don't quite remember where the store was."

"Perhaps because you worked so hard to get the memory out of your head."

That was true. I hadn't been exactly thrilled by my undercover job scooping ice cream. "Remember how hot that summer was?" Despite the cool weather, I used my hand to fan myself at the memory.

"Living on the Maggie May before I got the air-conditioning fixed wasn't fun." That summer he had moored his sailboat on Long Beach Island at a dock behind the bay-front Beach Haven home of a friend, but that wasn't the plan. We thought we would be staying, at least for a few weeks, in Oliver Wilder's guest room. However, Oliver— a good friend who had stuffed into his mailbox a warm letter of greeting, a sheet of instructions for every electronic gadget in the house, a complete list of the refreshments in the kitchen, and a calendar of cultural events in the county—had forgotten to leave the key and the code to the burglar alarm. Luckily, the neighbors on the left, a kind couple in their eighties, knew that we were coming and understood our predicament. The house on the right had been taken over by kids for the season. They wouldn't have cared, or noticed, if the QM2 had docked at Oliver's deck. "Maybe we should have broken in." Andy reconsidered many years too late.

"If only that summer's weather had been like today's. Working on the Boardwalk that summer was not what I would call pleasant."

Andy tried to defend my job. Tried. "Heavenly Dips had those awnings shaped like clouds. They might not have worked in the morning but they did provide a little shade in the afternoon."

"A little. I remember waiting for the temperature inside the booth to plummet into the low nineties."

"Bit of a breeze came off the ocean, right?"

"If it did, it didn't make it across the beach and up onto the Boardwalk. And, even if it had, the air would have been warmed by the heat of the refrigeration units. I kept telling you that the ice cream business was not as glamorous as it looked."

"Well," Andy continued to search for the bright side, "if all the summer days were like today you might have been comfortable, but business would have been bad. Bright sun and blue skies but a little cold for the beach and ice cream."

Of course, we both knew that summer had not been about the ice cream business. "What a moment of weakness. Were you actually that charming that I agreed to go undercover in an ice cream store?" I infused my words with a heavy dose of amazement.

"Are you saying that I am no longer that charming?"

We both knew that there were things I had been willing to do to help my then-brand-new private-investigator boyfriend that I might resist after all the years we'd been together. “I guess going undercover to chat up employees made sense.”

The topic had been the whereabouts of Jonas Angel, the heir to the Heavenly Dips ice cream fortune. My job was to gather information that Jonas’s peers were unlikely to give to his parents or a private investigator hired by his parents—who in that case was Andy. I agreed to take a job at Heavenly Dips in Seaside Heights before I saw the store’s uniforms. Even I, who believed that a flannel nightgown tucked into a pair of jeans made appropriate daywear, felt that outfit sank below my standards.

I continued before Andy got the impression he was off the hook. “That is not to say the job wasn’t horrible. It was. All I did was watch the clock. I swear it took three hours for the second hand to make a single sweep. And, don’t forget that being the oldest person in an angel getup gave me an edge in the battle for the title: Most Ridiculous Person on the Boardwalk.” In Seaside Heights, that was going some. “You should feel lucky that no one I knew ever saw me.”

“You didn’t even know anyone from Seaside Heights.” Andy waved off my concern.

“The town did not post guards at the borders. Just because the town is small . . .”

“3.3 square miles,” Andy interjected.

“But I worked on the Boardwalk, by the Sky Ride.”

“Which runs twenty feet above the beach.”

“But it runs . . . ran right along the Boardwalk. Offering,” I paused for dramatic effect, “an excellent view of the Heavenly Dips store and the people employed there. I lived in constant fear that someone would see me.”

“Give me a minute.” Andy forced a pensive expression. “I’m trying to think of an upside.”

“The work was boring, the pay was lousy and my boss hated me from the get-go.”

“Which is hard to believe because you looked so cute in your uniform.” Andy teased.

I did not tease back. “Andy, there are some things that are best forgotten.” If only I could. “Did I ever tell you how Big Al slammed his fist on the bathroom door to get me to come out on my first day?”

“Many times.”

I stared at him until he met my gaze.

“However, I would be happy to listen to the story again.”

I didn’t hesitate. “You see I had gone into the bathroom to get into my uniform, the one you didn’t warn me about.”

“Gee, you never mentioned that before.”

I glared at him.

“Go ahead. I’m all ears.” He feigned an apologetic tone.

“That’s okay. I am actually feeling nostalgic. This is our first visit to Seaside Heights since that summer. Looking back the entire experience doesn’t seem so bad.”

At the time, however, it seemed pretty painful. I felt no guilt making Andy listen to my story one more time.

CHAPTER 2

"Planning on coming out today, Ms. Daniels?"

My new boss, Big Al, and I had not exactly hit it off. Sure, when I reported for work at the Heavenly Dips ice cream store his words of greeting were polite enough. "Meg Daniels. They just told me this morning you was coming." Only his intonation added, "You, plague, and pestilence." That welcome had pretty much been the high point of the encounter.

Identifying the low point would be the harder task. I would have bet on the moment Big Al showed me the royal blue angel gown that was the Heavenly Dips uniform, but that horror paled in comparison to the instant he stood on his toes, pulled a quivering handful of faux gold from the top of the cupboard, and handed me the shimmering mass. A halo. A halo he expected me, a woman on the far side of thirty, to put on my head. And wear. In public. I knew that I could not stay in the bathroom all day, but I did not feel ready to face the world in a Heavenly Dips costume, excuse me, uniform. Not the one I saw in the mottled mirror.

"Move it, Ms. Daniels." On the other side of the door, Big Al's voice lowered into a growl. "All this commotion to rush you in here. Why was they in such a hurry to get you started? Normal, we send new hires down to New Gretna for a real orientation." Big Al snickered at the mention of they and the town where Heavenly Dips was headquartered. "Not that they need to. I know all there is to know about this company. This year I celebrate twenty-two years here on the Boardwalk. Last ten, I'm in charge. Don't know why those corporate types think you gotta go to no home office for training."

I didn't respond. I stood on my toes to study as much as I could of my reflection. Accessorized with the halo, the mini-dress would have been appropriate for many occasions—most of them in the late 1960s and all of them on Halloween.

What would it matter if I quit? From what Andy told me, Jonas's father believed that his son had, because of a surfeit of alcohol, drugs, or romance, simply failed to notice the weekend reach its conclusion. It wasn't the first time. There had been many Mondays that Jonas did not appear at school, at work, wherever he was expected. Sooner or later the June graduate, who despite his new management position in the family business, apparently still fancied himself a hard-partying college boy, would show up whether I scooped ice cream at Heavenly Dips or not. Maxwell Angel, the founder of the company and Jonas's fed-up father, had hired Andy simply to make sure his son's return came sooner. Locating an AWOL playboy wasn't a matter of life and death. I could walk away with a clear conscience. Okay, a clear conscience but no cash. And, there were financial issues. Andy had taken the proceeds of an earlier investigation and I, an unemployed marketing executive, had misspent funds designated for graduate school to finance a sailing expedition from Antigua to New Jersey. Our financial future had looked bleak when a friend of Andy's recommended him to Maxwell Angel. Andy needed this job and I needed to help him.

While I pondered my options, Big Al cleared his throat but couldn't dislodge years of smoke with a single snort. A croak in his voice didn't stop him from launching into his orientation script. "Remember, you must be in full uniform at all times because you represent Heavenly Dips at all times."

I wanted to ask if that meant I got paid at all times but Big Al did not pause to take a breath. "You owe a $75 deposit on the uniform. We'll deduct it from your first week's pay or if that isn't enough from the first two.

Whatever it takes. You get paid weekly. We divide up tips daily. They go in the cup. Don't let me catch you pocketing no tips."

I doubted that the gratuities at Heavenly Dips would drive me to a life of crime.

"You work first shift today. After that, we'll figure it out. You fill in where I need you, when I need you. You make an extra twenty-five cents an hour for the late shift. Not bad, considering you're already making two bits more than minimum wage." Big Al made it clear that I would work hard for my not bad pay. "No goofing off. Your title is Little Dipper. Things go good you move up to Big Dipper and get rid of your blue wings and get white."

Wings? What wings? Had I declared a low point before reviewing all the evidence?

"Every shift has an Angel or an Archangel working. I'm the store's only Archangel. An Angel or better opens and closes. You'll recognize the Angels; they have gold wings. Remember, Big Dippers have white wings. You can tell the Little Dippers like you because they have blue wings. I got yours out here for you."

Yes, it was true. I had wings. Not only would they make a strong fashion statement—

I am a dork—they would be exceedingly practical for working in a confined space.

Big Al sounded perplexed as he continued. "You're an oddball here in Seaside Heights. We don't usually get no blue wings in this store." Again, his fist hit the door. "We open in fifteen minutes, you know."

I stared at the pathetic image in the mirror. Waiting. Hoping. For what? Word that angel gowns and halos were popping up on runways in Paris and Rome?

Big Al twisted the door handle. "Ready to come out?"

Not really but what choice did I have? It wasn't as if I'd taken a real job with a long term commitment. I'd only have to wear this outfit for one day. Maybe two. Just until Andy found Jonas and dragged him home. I could tough it out. I straightened my halo, pulled back my shoulders, and began my life as a Little Dipper.

CHAPTER 3

Moving around the small ice cream stand would have been difficult if I had been the lone employee wearing two large, feathery protrusions on my back. I wasn't. Four pairs of wings were working that shift. Only Big Al, as the store's Archangel, had his emblazoned on a bright blue badge.

The white sets belonged to Sharmaine DeAngelis and Hilde Bossick. Sharmaine had warm brown eyes speckled with gold set in a face that still retained most of its baby fat. Combined with her curly blonde hair, the similarity to the older Shirley Temple or the younger Sally Struthers was overwhelming. She greeted me with a big smile. Her preternaturally white teeth gleamed against her deep tan. If Jonas deigned to hang out with anyone in this group, she was the one. If I could befriend her and get her talking, I might be able to quit before the lunchtime rush.

I didn't expect to get a smile out of Hilde let alone any gossip. I didn't know what her generation called the look Hilde affected—unnaturally black hair, unnecessarily thick-framed glasses, unpleasantly dark expression—but I got the message. I got it, I just didn't buy it. I suspected her nose ring was fake. The tattoos of angry mythological creatures, however, appeared real.

The single set of gold wings on duty belonged to Ed Brickmeyer to whom Big Al entrusted my training. Ed claimed to be twenty-one although in the masculine interpretation of the Heavenly Dips uniform he resembled an overgrown twelve-year-old.

I tried to get Ed talking about Jonas Angel right away but he had no time for idle chit chat. He had much to teach me about the ice cream biz before the store opened or as Ed explained, commerce commenced. "Within moments, we must be ready to greet our customers at the Pearly Gates." He waved an arm towards the store's façade where happy cherubs, each floating on a cloud named for one of the forty flavors, clustered around golden gates festooned with plastic pearls. "Be sure to welcome each of them with the standard Heavenly Dips greeting."

My stomach turned. This could not be good. It wasn't.

"'Welcome, and what heavenly delicacy can I serve you today?' Can you remember that?"

I probably could, but I preferred not to. I grunted.

Ed took the noise that came out of my mouth as an indication of agreement and went back to his lecture. "Customers come first. Employee ingress and egress are through the back door. Be sure you hit the clock." Although I'd been in the store for half an hour, Ed punched my timecard for me. "There's much to do, but always address the needs of our clientele first."

As we headed for the front of the store, Big Al called from his strategically positioned desk beside the time clock. "Tell her, Ed. She got free time I don't wanna see her hanging around yapping. There's counters to clean. Floors to mop. Napkins to restock. Show her the ropes. You make sure she knows, Ed. We expect a full day's work for a full day's pay. After all, we're paying her good money."

Big Al saw no humor in his remark but curly-haired Sharmaine smirked. Ed frowned and lowered his voice to a whisper. "Watch out for Big Al. He tries to live up to his sobriquet."

My new boss wasn't big enough for the nickname to be accurate or small enough for it to be sardonic. "Why is a five-foot-ten, 185-pound man called Big Al anyway?"

Ed shrugged. "I don't know. As far as I know, he's always called himself Big Al. He likes to act belligerent and pugnacious. Just do what he says. Otherwise, he'll castigate you." After a nervous glance to the rear of the store where

Big Al slumped over his desk, Ed whispered. "The good news is that he makes about ten trips a day to the bank." His speech returned to a normal tone. "Now, as you know, Heavenly Dips offers a plethora of gustatory sensations."

The pride in Ed's voice pegged him as the quintessential company man, or at least company boy. Considering the money he made and the getup he had to wear, his fervent devotion to Heavenly Dips struck me as stupefying—although not as stupefying as his vocabulary. I felt confident that I'd identified the owner of the GMAT prep book I'd seen in the communal locker.

"We will start you off on ice cream only before we move you up to toppings."

I guessed if someone requested one, I would tell them I am not certified for marshmallow.

"I conjecture you are cognizant of all the flavors. What's your predilection?"

I didn't want to shock or offend Ed, and admitting I'd never been to a Heavenly Dips store would certainly have done both. I glanced up and spotted the words Angelic Anise and declared it my favorite before learning the flavor was a bitter-tasting concoction in a uniquely unappetizing charcoal shade of gray.

"Hmm. Unusual choice. Ranked thirty-eighth out of forty flavors. Right ahead of Uranus Raisin and Pluto Plum. I'm a Celestial Chocolate aficionado myself. Consume all the Angelic Anise you want but ring up your scrumptious delicacy as a comp so we can track our inventory. We do not masticate in front of the customers."

I heard a snicker that I believed originated with Sharmaine.

Ed bristled. "Chewing in front of the customers would be rude."

The job's best benefit, unlimited ice cream consumption, slipped away. With the exception of the unisex bathroom, in which I did not plan to consume any edible item, the store didn't offer a single spot to get out of the customers' sight, not even behind the walk-in freezer since the restroom, communal locker, and time clock were crammed into that space along with Big Al's desk.

I'd had enough of Ed's training. I tried not to anger him by appearing at all impatient or to encourage him by appearing overly curious, but I was anxious to finish my investigation and quit my job. "So do the Angels, the real Angels, the owners, ever come by?"

Ed didn't even acknowledge my question. "Let me show you our state-of-the-art freezer." Ed patted a heavy metal door with a level of affection most people reserve for family members and beloved pets. When he pulled the freezer door open, I enjoyed the rush of cool air—for about fifteen seconds. After that, I felt happy to go back to the counter—for another fifteen seconds until my body adjusted to the heat. I again tried broaching the topic of Jonas.

According to Ed, however, I still had much to learn, but not about Jonas. Ed wanted me to learn about the business. And Ed? He wanted to learn about me.

His tone was tentative. "I don't mean to criticize, but aren't you a little old to be doing this?"

"How old do you think I am?"

Ed shrugged. "I don't know. Out of college. Twenty-four?"

I tried not to let my relief show. "Yep. Twenty-four."

"You realize that you're old enough to drink."

"Yeah?" My intonation asked him to make his point.

"You could find a job at one of the bars or a good restaurant. A job like that would help you in your banausic efforts."

Was he talking about money?

"One of my roommates waits tables. He makes great tips. Sometimes a hundred bucks a night, sometimes more." Ed turned our tip cup upside down. One quarter fell out. "I put that in to encourage others but we won't have accumulated much more in the way of cumshaw at the end of the shift."

I didn't exactly know what banausic or cumshaw meant. Actually, I didn't know at all. But I got Ed's drift. I wasn't going to get rich at Heavenly Dips, and adults my alleged age, twenty-four, could get better pay at places where liquor was served. How could I explain my presence at Heavenly Dips? I didn't. I answered his question with a question. "I thought you were already twenty-one. Now that you are will you work in a restaurant?"

"Oh no. I've labored for Heavenly Dips since the age of sixteen. This is my third summer on the Boardwalk. It's quite an honor to work in the first store Maxwell Angel opened thirty-three years ago. I worked assiduously to merit an assignment to this store. Maxwell Angel, himself, worked here for ten years after he founded the company. I find working where it all began so exciting. I'd never relinquish this job."

"Never?"

"I mean until I finish business school and embark on my career."

"Do you want to move up the ladder at Heavenly Dips?"

"That's not likely—not with Jonas Angel set to inherit the whole enchilada."

I detected bitterness in Ed's tone. "Are you and Jonas friends?"

Ed's eyes narrowed but I knew the Angel heir wasn't the focus of his thoughts. He answered my question with a question. "How did you get this job anyway? We hardly ever use Little Dippers in Seaside Heights. I think you may be the first."

Again, I ignored Ed's question and asked about a subject he liked, the cash register. Ed patted the machine with almost as much affection as he'd shown the freezer. "Have you operated a register before?"

I felt the constellations bobbing about as I shook my head. I wasn't worried. Surely running a cash register would be like running any computer. I could learn in a minute. Apparently, I was wrong.

"You can stick to scooping." Ed's tone sounded soft and consoling as if breaking the news that I wasn't going to the majors but back to the Triple-A team ten states away. "Don't worry. The register is hard."

The sympathy in his smile, meant to console, offended me. Hard? A cash register? I wanted to protest. I had managed multi-million dollar budgets. Large staffs. Major projects. But the truth was I couldn't make that register perform for me. I consoled myself that it hardly mattered. In a couple of hours, I'd have gathered all the information I could from the angels of Heavenly Dips and be on my way back to planet earth.

Ed hit a button and the dulcet tones of an angelic chorus flooded our little stand. Heavenly Dips was open for business.

CHAPTER 4

Less than a minute after the choir began its chanting, I faced my first customer, a smooth-skinned, slick-haired, blue-eyed blonde leading a pack of ten-year-old boys. I didn't know him, but I knew the type. He smirked as he placed his order. "I like all the planets on your halo." My limited experience with ten-year-old boys told me he wasn't finished and he wasn't. "But I can't see Uranus."

And just when the world had despaired of finding the next Noel Coward.

The cones that I produced for his gang were the same size in the sense that the dunes in Seaside Park and Mount Everest were the same size. The kids complained. Hilde snickered. Sharmaine jumped in and helped. "Big Al goes ballistic if he sees a cone that's too small or, God forbid, too big." She shared her tricks for constructing a uniform cloud (plain cone), black hole (chocolate cone), and cup (cup). She also shared her tricks for extricating a head topped with a halo from the freezer. I thanked her and wondered how I had sunk so low that my job required training on deely bopper control. I had to find some key information fast and quit.

"Kid was pretty funny don't you think?" Sharmaine whispered as she scooped Cloud Nine Cinnamon from a bin adjacent to the one where I was scooping Hazelnut Heaven.

"Yeah." I wasn't laughing.

"Don't let something like that bring you down. Some kid pulls the Uranus joke on me once a week. It happens to everyone." Stars and planets bounced above her head. "Well, not Hilde. The customers don't mess with Hilde."

I could see why. Hilde was the anti-Sharmaine. Whereas Sharmaine radiated enthusiasm and openness, Hilde might as well have worn a No Trespassing sign.

She had no more in common with Ed. His physical presence was expansive; his arms and legs seemed to flail in all directions. Hilde occupied a tiny amount of space in the stand, not necessarily an easy task for a five-foot-eight woman wearing wings. Ed's big and bright blue eyes were open wide to welcome the outside world. Hilde's eyes, so dark they were almost black, were small and narrow as if judging everything they saw. Harshly. She followed company regulations and told customers to have a nice day, but I didn't believe her and I doubted the customers did either.

What I found out about Hilde I learned from Ed. He said she was not big on badinage which sounded like first aid to me but which apparently meant small talk. Nineteen that summer, she had graduated from high school at sixteen and had only one year of college left. She'd been transferred to the Seaside Heights store in July of the previous year—Ed suspected because her father had connections to Maxwell Angel.

"She go out with the kid? You know, Jonas?"

Ed's eyes told me he found my question odd but he answered. "In her dreams."

Before I could ask a follow-up, an order for the very popular Orion Orange sherbet drew his attention away from my inordinate interest in Jonas Angel.

Given the choice of pumping Sharmaine or Hilde for information, I bet on Sharmaine. Hilde would be a tough nut to crack, but Sharmaine had no shell. Ed had described her as "A ditz but I mean that in a nice way."

Ed's view confirmed my first impression of her as warm, friendly, and loquacious, without a critical thought in her head. Whenever I saw the crowd thinning I worked my way to her side for general chit chat. Although I tried to turn the topic to Jonas Angel, our conversation assumed an unproductive pattern. I'd learn a couple of pieces of personal information about Sharmaine—she had just graduated from high school, had transferred to the flagship store only weeks before, and had no plans beyond a fun summer at the beach. Then, rather cleverly I thought, I would say something like "tell me about the company" or "tell me about the Angel family" or finally, in an act of near desperation, "tell me about Jonas Angel." Her responses were always similar. "The things I could tell you about this company. Excuse me, I have a customer." "The Angel family is pretty interesting. Excuse me, I have a customer." "Jonas isn't as bad as everyone thinks he is. Excuse me, I have a customer."

I considered Andy's plan and how easy we thought it would be for me to breeze into the store, chat up the staff, and find Jonas. Yeah, right. This would really work.

CHAPTER 5

I was quizzing Ed on Jonas Angel's view of our get-ups, and multitasking by restocking napkins when Big Al came to the front of the store to tell Ed he was in charge. Big Al had to run to the bank which Ed described as an hourly event. Why, however, did he have to pick that moment? After spending six minutes maneuvering the conversation to the point where I could ask about Jonas, Big Al's departure threw Ed into a frenzied display of managerial efficiency. I'd have to start over.

I could still see the trail of smoke Big Al left in his wake when Sharmaine said she had an errand to run. "Let Ed know." Ed, busy scooping for a family of eight, never saw her duck out the back door with a double-dip of Celestial Chocolate.

I figured this would be a good time to chat up Hilde, or would have been if I could have forced her to make eye contact with me. When she failed to respond to my direct question—"Have you worked here long?"—I dug out a taster of Saturnian Spearmint and sprawled across the top of the Orion Orange display case in hopes of getting cool and drawing a reprimand from Hilde. Even violating the company rules failed to get her to acknowledge my existence.

Hilde was ignoring me and I was humming along with the Heavenly Dips choir when I saw them, a news team rushing up the Boardwalk. A microphone, in the hand of a familiar TV personality whose helmet hair even 90% humidity couldn't budge, led the charge. The group probably would have made better time if the reporter hadn't been wearing four-inch heels. I felt grateful for the lead time.

"Ed, where is that news team going?" I had a sick feeling I knew.

Ed appeared thrilled as he pushed the cash register drawer shut. "I think they're coming here."

"Why would the press be coming here?" I asked.

"Probably another heat wave story. The hot weather puts a spotlight on ice cream." Happy anticipation overwhelmed him. "I can get on television."

True panic rose in me as I dropped to the floor. "I have to get out of here."

"They are coming here. We can be on television." Ed was excited, in a happy way.

I too was excited, but not in a happy way. Oh, please God, no. I can't be on television. Not in this outfit. "Are they still coming?" I crouched so that only my halo was visible above the counter.

Hilde stared down at me with cold, dark eyes. "Why are you acting so silly? It's only a local television station." She redirected her serious gaze at the approaching news crew but made no move to attract their attention.

Ed, on the other hand, waved and called out to the lead newswoman. "Celeste."

"What are you doing?" Panicked, I crawled through globs of Nutty North Star, Venus de Vanilla, and Space Shuttle Sundae towards the nearest corner. The move, in retrospect undeniably bad, left me farther away not only from the press but also from the only opening to the back of the store.

"No problem." Ed smoothed his forelock. "I'll be the frontman. Go get us more Cherubic and Celestial."

"Right away." I would have agreed to move the pyramids from Giza if the offer got me away from news people.

Ed puffed the sleeves of his angel shirt. "I'll converse with the press. Probably pursuing a new angle on ice cream sales during the drought."

I peeked over the counter and saw a crew from a competing station approaching. "And that story warranted two teams?"

"Whatever it is, I'll handle it." He straightened his halo.

Crouching, I scurried towards the freezer where I could hold the heavy door ajar and watch the action through the small glass window. Cameras were trained on Ed's face and microphones were shoved in front of his mouth. I couldn't quite hear the conversation but I heard the name Jonas Angel. Repeatedly. This could not be good news.

I stuck one ear around the corner of the door and heard Ed explaining that Jonas often visited the Seaside Heights store but not since the previous Tuesday. The reporter asked if Jonas had seemed worried or concerned. Had he mentioned anything unusual going on in his life? I didn't hear Ed's answer because Hilde chose that moment to inform me that I should get back to the counter. She was taking her break early. Like Sharmaine, she slid out the door before Ed missed her. Her departure left the front of the stand empty. Not that it mattered. The gathering crowd wasn't interested in ice cream—only a chance to appear on TV.

I left the freezer just in time to see Big Al, back from the bank, fighting his way through the mass of onlookers that was expanding faster than my stomach would if I could get to the free ice cream. Even on a Boardwalk jaded by years of hosting the MTV Beach House television cameras still drew a crowd.

Our boss reached the front of the throng and, interrupting Ed mid-sentence, introduced himself to the press as Big Al Braddock, store manager. His first step was to move the news crew so their shot could capture the entire cloud bank that decorated the storefront. Big Al understood there is no such thing as bad publicity. Unfortunately, he didn't understand that a comb-over might not stay combed over with an opposing breeze. Big Al began his interview with his red hair standing straight up, a great look only for the coolest rooster in the hen house.

I grabbed a tub of Celestial Chocolate and, struggling to hold it at face level, staggered to the front to meet Ed. He was beaming. “Did you see me talking to them? I’m going to be on television.”

“What happened?” I dumped the tub into his arms, grabbed a rag, and wiped a large spot of Venus de Vanilla from the floor.

“Well, Celeste asked me to stand with my back to the storefront . . .”

“No.” I interrupted. “What happened to Jonas?”

The broad smile on his face contrasted with the news he delivered. “They found his abandoned car this morning. I can tell that they think maybe something awful happened to him. That’s why they’re here. They wanted to know all about him. Did you hear me? Did I sound good? Do you think they’ll use my shot?”

What twenty-first-century news organization could resist broadcasting an interview with a man with a constellation of golden doodads orbiting above his head? Unless that man insisted on saying that Jonas was “inexorably drawn to the ocean air so redolent of his childhood years” which Ed did. On top of that, he had competition. Big Al did have that rooster thing going for him. Ed’s chances of getting on the air were not good but I kept my opinion to myself. What did I know? I was only a Little Dipper.

I worried that the cameras would turn our way when they were done with Big Al. Reporters weren’t being too fussy about their sources. They were putting microphones in front of customers who had never even met Jonas for their insight into his disappearance.

Ed grew despondent. “I bet they show Big Al, not me.”

“We’ll see.” I feigned casualness. “Well, it’s time for my lunch.”

“No, it isn’t. It too early. Besides, I take lunch first.” Ed sounded almost grouchy.

“If you leave now you may miss a chance to get on TV.”

"We can get on TV? I saw the crowd. What's up?" Sharmaine had returned and no one but me had ever missed her. "Can I get on television?"

"Not if you take lunch." My answer puzzled Sharmaine but not Ed. In under five seconds, he agreed that I could take his lunch slot. I moved fast – before he realized that Hilde had also gone. I hit the time clock and left the stand through the back door like a good Little Dipper.

CHAPTER 6

Seaside Heights is a colorful town with a colorful population but not so colorful that a woman wearing wings and a halo blends. In the hopes of fitting in, I removed my Heavenly Dips accessories, but, since few vacationers wore royal blue angel gowns, my hopes were not exactly fulfilled. Better to stay out of sight.

I took the back alley north for a few blocks before I returned to the Boardwalk where I chose a bench with a view over the sand to the ocean—not so much for the vista as for the privacy it offered. At least for three minutes. That was when a meticulously groomed young woman in nicely pressed khakis and a starched blue shirt slipped onto the bench beside me. Her smooth, cropped, auburn hair didn't seem to mind the humidity. Instead of aluminum painted gold, she wore tasteful accessories that I pegged for fourteen-karat. Based on her neat appearance, undercover-me had nothing in common with this woman. Yet, she seemed to be speaking to me.

"Sorry?"

"I was saying that I saw you run. Why did you flee? What are you afraid of?"

I didn't even ask who she was. "I'm afraid of looking like an idiot on national TV."

"The Angel story won't make the national news. Besides, why did you think you looked like an idiot?"

I responded with the hard stare I generally reserve for Andy, the defending world champion at asking questions with obvious answers. I slipped the halo on top of my hair. She seemed puzzled so I explained. "I have a halo on my head. A halo with a universe of faux stars and planets unknown in our galaxy bobbing above it. I'm working at Heavenly Dips to earn money for graduate school and I don't want . . . . Oh, let's face it, I don't want anyone to see me in this getup. I don't even like the customers seeing me but," I heard my own chatter and didn't find it appealing. "I don't think I want to say anything else. Who are you?"

"Bridget Simkus." She flashed her press credentials. "I write for the Asbury Park Press. Occasionally. Or I'm trying to. When I saw you run, I said to myself 'there is a woman with something to hide'."

"Only my head."

If she recognized my feeble attempt at humor, she didn't let on. "Would you like to give me your name?"

"No."

"Would you like to give me a scoop?"

"What flavor?" I glimpsed no trace of a smile on Bridget Simkus's lips. "It's a joke. You know, a little ice cream humor."

"Good humor."

Was she making a joke? I believed she was. I snickered. "Give me your card. If anything comes up, I'll call." Maybe Andy could think of a way to use the reporter. "Truth is I don't know anything. I never even met Jonas. Did you?"

"Nah. I never even heard of the kid until this morning. Know the father. He's a real piece of work. Energetic. No. Frenetic. He loves the press. He needed us to build that business. He needs us now to find the kid. I'm thinking this story might have legs. You know, be good for my career—if it turns out there was a crime committed. I'm betting on foul play. Although, from what I hear, the crime scene unit didn't find much. That doesn't mean they won't. Forensic tests take time." She studied my face for a reaction and, when she did not find one, changed the subject. "How do you like working for Heavenly Dips?"

"I don't want to comment. On any topic."

"Then give me your name and number and I'll keep in

touch."

"I have your number. And you know where to find me." I lied. That woman would never see me again. Jonas Angel's car had been located. At the end of my shift I, along with my halo, would retire.

CHAPTER 7

Two hours later a somber Andy came up the Boardwalk. I started to greet him, but he signaled me to stop with an almost imperceptible move. I understood the message; go to our agreed-upon meeting spot. He vanished behind a crowd of boisterous preteens, and I hit the time clock. Without a word to my co-workers, I followed. What would Heavenly Dips do, fire me? I should be so lucky.

Sweat flooded my forehead by the time I reached the arcade. Stepping inside I felt comforted not only by the cool air but by the bells, whistles, horns, and electronic simulations of shootings, crashes, and other mayhem. The sounds I usually found overwhelming and annoying drummed the chanting of the Heavenly Dips choir from my head. In one morning, I'd heard the same sixty-four bars so often I feared the store's theme song was now encoded in my DNA.

I ran down the stairs to the batting cages and found that Andy had the area to himself. He dropped the metal bat as soon as I arrived. "Nice outfit."

"Andy, did you know about this . . . this uniform before I agreed to work at Heavenly Dips?"

"They're in every store. In all the ads. It's no secret."

It was from me. "Thanks a lot, Andy. I appreciate the opportunity to appear on national television in an angel costume."

"The story won't go national. Besides you look cute in your angelic little gown."

"You really think I am gullible enough to believe that?"

"It's not horrible."

"State one way in which it is not horrible." I challenged

him.

He made a great show of trying to come up with an idea and then let his expression explode in a burst of excitement. “Your name isn’t on it. No one will know who you are”

“Number one, if I have the misfortune to encounter someone I know, I can’t be sure of this, but I suspect that they might figure out who I am without checking the name on my uniform.”

He considered my words. “Probably true.”

“Although I no longer have my own identity. When I walk into that booth I become a generic little dipper. Meg Daniels, as you knew her, no longer exists.”

“Actually, that might be a good thing, given that you’re undercover.” His raised eyebrow asked me to agree. When my glare told him there was no point in waiting for that outcome, his tone lost its playful edge. “I am worried that this story is not going to have a happy ending.” He curled his fingers through the metal fencing and I moved forward to place mine over his. “We found Jonas Angel’s car this morning. I spotted it about twenty-five yards into the woods on a dirt road off Route 9 that heads towards Gloucester County. As far as I could determine, no one had seen Jonas after he left a bar on Friday night. He didn’t tell anyone where he was going or meet up with any of his usual cronies. So, I drove up and down all those roads below Tuckerton on the way to New Gretna hoping for a clue.”

Many roads intersected Route 9, however, I never turned onto any of them. Not many people did. Civilization encroached every year, but few of the unpaved roads were heavily traveled.

“The car was stashed behind a sand berm with a row of pines on top. Even though the woods aren’t that thick, his convertible wasn’t easy to see. It’s black. With its top and windows down there was no glare. I missed it on my first pass. It appears that someone went to a lot of effort to hide that car.”

"And Jonas?"

"He wasn't inside. Or anywhere nearby."

"You don't believe Jonas ditched his car there?" My statement took the form of a question, but I knew what Andy thought.

"And left the top and windows down, his cell phone turned off on the front seat and the keys on the floor? No way." Andy shook his head. "From what I've heard, the kid is careless. Daddy fixes everything for him. But everyone says he loves that Porsche. The pine branches did a job on the paint job. Why would he drive through a clump of trees? And then? I can believe Jonas leaving the car unlocked with thousands of dollars' worth of golf clubs in the back and not worrying about them. Clubs are easy to replace. But to leave the car with the keys in it?"

"You've heard that Jonas is arrogant and thoughtless."

Andy chuckled, one of those rueful sounds that hints at despair. "That's with people, not with German sports cars."

As I ran through a string of positive alternatives my theories sounded unconvincing—even to me. "Maybe he was in a hurry and thought he'd be back right away." I disregarded the holes in my theories. "Maybe he left the phone so no one could track him down."

Andy's cool green eyes gazed over my shoulder. "I saw Maxwell Angel's face when he arrived at the scene. He believes the worst. I can't disagree. He went public in an effort to bring in any leads, but there's something else." His intonation suggested something else wasn't good. "I sneaked a peek at Jonas's golf clubs."

I stared into his eyes.

"No seven-iron."

I knew what that suggested but I again tried for a positive spin. "Maybe he doesn't use one."

Andy shook his head. "A seven? I'd believe that of a three or a four. But a seven?"

"Maybe he lent it to a friend. Maybe it's getting repaired.

Maybe he used it as a walking stick." I stopped. My suggestions were veering toward the absurd.

Andy shrugged. "Maybe. Max is organizing a search party to walk the woods. He's prepared for the worst."

I stroked his fingers gently. "I would feel terrible if something bad happened to the kid, but I must say that quitting Heavenly Dips will bring me great joy."

"Quit? Why would you quit?"

I flipped on my halo. "Andy, check out my head. What did I say about hats?"

"It's not a hat."

"It's a hat."

"Meg, you were quite clear. You said that you would do any job that did not require you to wear a hat. If you meant any form of headgear, you should have been more specific." Andy caressed my fingers. "Maxwell Angel asked me to keep you on the job." His voice softened. "Now that I suspect this is no longer a matter of fun and games I am hesitant, but this is the time we really need you to stay. Then I thought if we kept in touch . . . ." He pulled out a flip phone. Back then everyone did not carry a cell phone, especially people who didn't work, people like me. "I'd like us to communicate on an ongoing basis. Just note anything you overhear. Promise that you won't probe too much. Tell me what you find out and I'll do the follow-up. We don't know what Jonas might have been involved in. Just pass the information to me when you feel no one can hear." He dropped the phone in my pocket. "Keep in touch but be discreet."

Yeah. Discreet. That pretty much described me at the moment.

CHAPTER 8

By the time I said good-bye to Andy, my break had been over for five minutes. I rushed up the steps and froze. On the Boardwalk sucking on a cigarette, squinting through the window, searching the arcade, stood Big Al. I averted my eyes. If I didn't see him, he couldn't see me. Not that he was watching for me. He wasn't able to track everyone who returned late from a break, was he? I answered my own question. No way.

Big Al couldn't know that I was inside, but, if I didn't get out of there fast, he would. I glanced towards the entrance and saw him charge into the arcade with a stride as belligerent as his expression. Apparently, I wasn't the only person Big Al didn't like. From what I could see of his face, he didn't particularly like the person whose deeply tanned hand, long and thin but definitely male, emerged from behind a video game and fell onto his arm for a reassuring squeeze. And when I say fell, I mean fell. The hand must have been weighted down by the big gold square that someone found an appropriate size for a ring. Others might find it an appropriate size for a bowling bowl.

I plopped the halo on my head. Although I couldn't quite maneuver into my wings, I was at least three-quarters in uniform when a family of four ran out of quarters and abandoned a pinball machine, just in time for me to mingle with them as they passed behind Big Al and out the door.

Big Al had only treated me like a child for a few hours and already I was behaving like one. But that wasn't the only reason my heart felt as heavy as my feet when I limped back to work. Like Andy, I had a strong feeling that Jonas Angel was not going to walk into the corporate offices of Heavenly

Dips anytime soon, if ever. Sure, I felt bad about that but I felt worse that my tenure at Heavenly Dips would go on longer than I hoped. After four hours, it had already gone on longer than I hoped.

"What happened to you?" Ed made a big show of being annoyed.

"Female emergency," I whispered.

I detected a slight blush on Ed's cheeks as he backed away nodding.

Back at work, I had only scooped two Space Shuttle Sundaes, three Pisces Pistachios, and one Cloud Nine Cinnamon when my new cell phone vibrated. I held the receiver between my ear and my shoulder as I dug out two scoops of Big Bang Bubblegum. I whispered, "I've got a customer. I have a job you know."

"That's why I'm calling." Andy was brief. "You're about to get a surprise." And then the phone cut off.

"What surprise?" I raised my voice as if yelling could bring the connection back. "What?"

I handed the cone to the perplexed customer and hit redial. Before Andy picked up, I saw my surprise coming across the Boardwalk. The smooth pale skin. The sultry dark eyes. The brilliantly white teeth. The smirk. Petino.

CHAPTER 9

I could figure out why we were getting a visit from the Ocean County police department. What I could not figure out was why that visit came in the form of Detective Petino. The last time I'd seen Petino, the detective was investigating a homicide.

The cop smirked as he walked towards the Heavenly Dips stand. His expression betrayed nothing. He had smirked almost every time he looked my way and he had looked my way quite a few times in the course of a murder investigation on Long Beach Island several months earlier. I couldn't recall if Petino worked exclusively on homicides but I steeled myself for the news that Jonas Angel was dead. That, however, was not the message Petino conveyed.

"I'd like to see Al Braddock." If Petino recognized me, he didn't let on.

"Big Al?"

"That's what I've been told." The expression in the detective's eyes matched the smirk on his lips.

"He's in the back. You can go around and I'll let you in. Or, you can move fifteen feet to your left and slip under the counter."

"Thanks. I'll do that. And by the way, don't go away. I'd like to interview everyone here. Tell your buddies." He nodded at Ed, Sharmaine, and Hilde.

Petino flashed his badge at Ed and ducked under the counter. No need for me to relay his message. Everyone knew the cops had arrived. I went back to scooping.

After ten minutes of mumbled conversation at his desk, Big Al came forward to send us, one by one, to meet with Petino. I went last. Before I was summoned, Ed emerged looking excited. Hilde emerged looking perplexed. And, Sharmaine emerged looking worried. No one explained why.

Big Al introduced me to Petino. “Our most recent hire. She don’t even know the kid, but you can talk to her if you want.”

Petino wanted.

“Hi,” I said in a friendly tone but Petino did not respond, even after Big Al returned to the counter.

“Your name?”

“Meg Daniels.”

He gave no sign that he recognized me or my name. He must have. Did he handle so many cases, suspects, and witnesses that he had already forgotten me?

“Date of birth?”

“Date of birth?” I repeated a little too loudly.

“Yes, date of birth.”

I glanced over my shoulder to make sure no one was listening and leaned close to the detective. I stated the month and day clearly, and then mumbled the year.

“Didn’t get that.” Petino smirked.

I repeated the year nervously and he jotted the four digits down.

“Occupation?”

That was the first time since going undercover I’d been asked. I stumbled through my reply, “I . . . well . . . I guess . . . I’m an ice cream scooper. Little Dipper is my title.”

He didn’t seem surprised. Nor did he push for an explanation. He simply made notes on the yellow lined pages of a small notebook with a green cover. “How long have you worked for Heavenly Dips?”

“Well . . . I just . . . today is my first day with the company.”

“Not usual starting in the flagship store. You got connections?”

Why was he asking? Didn’t he know? He smirked but since he always smirked I had no idea if the expression was meaningful.

"A friend of mine hooked me up with the job."

The detective accepted my explanation but with another smirk. "Do you know Jonas Angel?"

I shook my head. "I've never even met him."

"Have you heard anything in your work here today that would give you any idea where Jonas Angel might be?"

Again, I shook my head.

"Are you planning to leave any time soon?"

"You mean quit Heavenly Dips? I'm only here for the summer. I begin graduate school in the fall."

"Ah, right." His smirk became more pronounced. Yep. He remembered me. "You know, you're old enough to drink. You could find a job in a restaurant around here. Make good money. Have you ever thought of that?"

"I'm committed to the ice cream industry."

His lips moved, almost into a smile. "Well, Ms. Daniels, here is my card. Call me if you hear anything you think I should know." And then, of course, he smirked.

CHAPTER 10

By the end of my shift, my dream of endless free ice cream was dashed. I had managed to taste only six flavors—Astronutical Butterscotch was my favorite. I paid for those tasters with blood, sweat, and tears. Okay, sweat. Plus, my feet, back, and right arm ached from the rigors of bending over and digging in vats of ice cream. I was developing into a fairly competent Little Dipper but I was pretty much of a failure as an investigator. The customers keep interfering with my real work. I had little to report when I met Andy for a ride back to his boat, the Maggie May, where I sprawled across the cockpit bench and waited for the sun to go down.

"Don't you think you should take your uniform off so it looks good tomorrow?" Andy sounded genuinely concerned.

"There is nothing I could possibly do to make this uniform look good tomorrow or next week or next year." I glared at Andy with a hard stare intended to challenge. The expression would probably have been more intimidating if I'd remembered to take off my sunglasses.

He shrugged. "As long as you're comfortable."

I felt comfortable. Well, almost comfortable. As comfortable as I was going to feel. In the shade from the neighbor's tree, the evening felt bearable but not cool. Humidity still hung in the air. The Northeast was in the midst of a drought, the longest in over a decade. More than a month had passed since the last sign of rain – not a good follow-up to a dry winter and spring. The temperatures were high. The woods were scorched. The reservoirs were low. The airwaves—full of "I Wish It Would Rain," "Baby the Rain Must Fall," "Walkin' in the Rain," "Laughter in the Rain," "Kentucky Rain," "Purple Rain," "Fire and Rain"—

told the story. Andy drove off to pick up dinner with "Have You Ever Seen Rain?" playing on the radio. As I waited for his return, the sounds of "Raindrops Keep Falling on my Head" drifted across the lagoon. I sang along as I perused the file Andy had compiled on Jonas Angel.

While I served ice cream Andy, the professional private investigator, had visited all the clubs—country, sport, and night—that Jonas frequented and the library, which, as far as I could tell, Jonas had never been inside. Most of the web pages that Andy had printed out at the local library were from the Heavenly Dips corporate website. The photos were shot from a low angle that failed to make the headquarters look impressive. I didn't blame the photographer. Ansel Adams couldn't have done much shooting the dull red brick building behind a chain-link fence topped with razor wire. The photo screamed maximum security prison, not ice cream. The only thing that appeared at all modern was the metal console that I assumed was a card reader. No pearly gates, no St. Peter, not even an automated facsimile, stood at the entrance to serve as greeter. How did the marketing department miss that opportunity?

Behind the sheets about the corporation, I found Andy's notes on a number of interviews with Jonas's friends and family. His childhood friends from Mantoloking and Spring Lake, two affluent Jersey shore towns north of Seaside Heights, said they hadn't seen Jonas lately and when they did it was mostly by accident. Nonetheless, the four that Andy spoke to all described Jonas as a great guy. Andy's margin note asked FOR REAL? None of them had seen Jonas last week. None of them had any idea where he might have gone. High school friends reported pretty much the same thing. In the margins, Andy had printed in large block letters COOL CROWD. WHAT ABOUT OTHERS? Jonas's college buddies were scattered across the country. Andy interviewed the only one in the area. He hadn't seen Jonas in weeks. "When I don't run into him for a while, I figure he's met some new honey." Next to that quote, Andy wrote LECH. I assumed the comment referred to Jonas but another printed note asked WHERE TRENT? If Trent was a person, not a place, it might have applied to him.

Among the female friends Andy interviewed only one, Schyler Devereaux, said she had seen Jonas a few times within the past two weeks. She had tried to catch up with him on Friday night but by the time she reached the bar, he had left. Schyler described her relationship with Jonas in glowing terms. Next to her comments, Andy had printed, MOM SAYS NO. WHY SCHYLER NO CELL PHONE NUMBER 4 JONAS?

Andy's other notes were about the Angel family. Before Jonas's car was found, Andy described Maxwell Angel as fed-up. Jonas's brother, Edwin, younger by eleven months, appeared indifferent. Andy's margin comment was NO LOVE LOST.

According to Andy's notes, Amanda Angel felt concerned even before the Porsche turned up abandoned in the woods. She worshipped her oldest son.

Photos told the family's story. Maxwell's physical appearance was average in every way—height, weight, coloring. Amanda's appearance was in no way average. She was beautiful with a smile that could be measured in megawatts. Jonas was the fortunate son who inherited his looks from his mother and, apparently, his disposition. Jonas failed to grin in only one portrait where he displayed a sultry expression for the camera. In that photo, taken on a beach at dusk, he had his arm wrapped around an almost-pretty blonde in a long white gown. I turned the photo over and saw the notation: Jonas and Schyler, spring formal.

In every other picture, Jonas flashed a broad smile with dazzling white teeth. His brother Edwin's expression was always sullen. If he had teeth, Edwin wasn't going to let the photographer see them. Unlike his brother's serious pose that I read as sultry, Edwin's attitude came off as sulky not seductive. Whereas Jonas and his parents huddled together in the pictures—often with arms wrapped around each other—Amanda's arm reached out for Edwin but he always held himself a bit apart and stared into the lens with an emotionless stare. Andy hadn't made any notes on the photos but the pictures spoke volumes. At least to me.

CHAPTER 11

When Andy returned, he found me engrossed in the files. He plopped opposite me and served dinner from three plastic bags bearing Wawa's logo. Since the chain of convenience stores computerized ordering, rustling up anything else to eat seemed like too much effort. We were eating our way through Wawa's menu.

"So what did you find out today?" Andy tossed a bag of chips my way.

"I found out that royal blue polyester should not be worn over white underwear on a hot, humid day."

"I thought you were working in a cool environment."

"Only the ice cream is working in a cool environment. The rest of us are working in an area heated by the refrigeration system. You can take my tip about white underwear to the bank."

"Interesting but not what I was looking for." Andy passed me a can of Coke.

I made a great show of propping up my feet but found minimal relief for my aching lower extremities. My right arm was sore but, with great effort, I lifted the Italian Shortie sandwich in search of a taste that wasn't sweet.

I explained what I had learned, all about the core staff, nothing about Jonas. "Big Al made six trips to the bank during my shift and if my arms weren't so tired, I'd put air quotes around to the bank. I think he's just going out for a smoke. He seems to have a heavy-duty habit. His desk is way in the back where no natural light reaches but he's out of the booth so often he puts on suntan lotion several times a day. Of course, he is a blue-eyed redhead, who, by the way, had the misfortune to give a TV interview during the only fifteen-minute interval when there was a breeze on the Boardwalk."

"Misfortune?"

"He has a comb-over. A modest one, but the wind really did a job on it in front of the cameras. He's a miserable man, but I actually felt bad for him."

"Anything else?"

"I hear that he brings in a constantly rotating staff for extra help on the weekends and nights, but I met the core day staff. And by the way, they think I am twenty-four." Before Andy could comment I added, "And, yes, they believe it."

Andy finished eating and pulled my feet onto his lap. "That's all?" He massaged my right foot which appeared marginally more swollen than the left. After initial resistance, my muscles relented and let his fingers call them back to life.

"Big Al fraternizes with men who wear really, really big rings."

"And that means . . . ?"

"That he knows at least one man who wears a really, really big ring. I don't interpret the news. I just deliver it."

"Anything else?"

"Could you do the other foot?"

"Anything else related to the case?" He clarified and began work on my left foot.

"We were so busy I didn't get much time for conversation. Ed seems to like me okay. I can probably find out anything he knows about Jonas but I'm not sure that will be much. Sharmaine is an open book. If we ever get an opportunity to talk, I predict she'll spill everything she knows. On the other hand, I think getting information out of Hilde might require a thousand watt light bulb and a cattle prod. She seems tightly wound and a little odd."

"She fraternizes with men with really, really big rings?"

I ignored his comment. "I don't think she'll confide in

me. She doesn't seem to like me very much, which doesn't make me special. Her main interaction with other employees is staring at them as if they had second heads growing out of their shoulders. Sharmaine is probably my best source. I think she actually likes me. Admittedly, I think she likes everyone. Except Big Al, of course. From what I can tell, no one likes Big Al. For good reason, from what I can see. He's a bully."

"Ignore him. You don't have to pump him for information. One, I doubt that he and Jonas hang out together much. Two, Max Angel has been in touch with him."

"None of those kids seem like the type to socialize with Jonas. They were more thrilled by the thought of a TV appearance than they were alarmed by, or even curious about, Jonas's dilemma."

"All I know is that Maxwell Angel suggested you work in the Seaside Heights store because Jonas went there the most. He visited it just about every day."

"That's odd. When Ed talked to the reporters I am sure he said he hadn't seen Jonas since last Tuesday. "

"Was Ed at work every day?"

"Given what I've seen of Ed, I'd have to say yes. I can find out."

"Don't worry. I can get that information. Do you think Jonas has been avoiding the Seaside Heights store?"

"As I said, I was scooping not snooping. I didn't get much time to probe."

"Well, maybe we'll find out tonight?"

"Tonight?"

"You don't feel like dancing?"

I didn't feel like sitting up. I had a plan: an hour under the strong spray of hot water in Oliver's outdoor shower followed by bed. "You want me to go out tonight? I thought you didn't want us being seen together."

"Not by the people you work with. I might have to speak

with them at some point. Tonight I want to check out one of Jonas's haunts in Point Pleasant Beach. We won't run into any of your coworkers up there."

Andy was right—theoretically. Most visitors to the Jersey shore didn't routinely travel a half a dozen towns north, or south for that matter, to go clubbing. At least if they had opportunities nearby and Seaside Heights offered plenty to do. What harm could come of tagging along to PPB?

CHAPTER 12

The crowd in line at Jenkinson's on the Point Pleasant Beach Boardwalk appeared a lot younger than I was. Actually, the crowd appeared a lot younger than I was pretending to be. I aspired to invisibility as I calculated the average age of the folks waiting to pay the cover charge. Andy didn't seem to mind that we looked like geezers. He surveyed the mob for contacts. I searched for people older than we were and found a few. A few.

The bouncer studied my driver's license for an eternity or, more likely, five seconds but I knew he wasn't admiring the picture. The woman at the DMV had pressured me to let her retake it. He handed my license back without comment and I followed Andy into the night club. The interior was vast with bars scattered around the space and a large dance floor ahead. I couldn't see the band but it was in the house. At least music was in the house. Whatever the source, the sound overwhelmed a geezer like me.

Andy said, "Lenny's a fink" or maybe "let's get a drink" since he headed for the nearest bar. He ordered a beer for him and a Coke for me. "You seem sixteen," he shouted in my ear. Or maybe he said, "you need caffeine." Probably the latter.

We sipped our drinks and watched the dance floor packed full of young and fit people most with tans that, if obtained naturally, would have alarmed the Surgeon General. Romance was in the air. Maybe romance was overstating the situation. The term getting lucky popped into my head.

I asked Andy what was next. He said he was "withering his left shoe" but I think he was considering his next move. His next move turned out to be mine. "Gawk at the sky over there."

"Whaaaat?"

His lips brushed my ear as he enunciated each word. "Go ask that guy if Jonas is coming here tonight." He pointed at the only individual in the building who had not been touched by the sun, a tall, emaciated twenty-something male with shoulder-length hair that was dirty blonde—in color and condition. A heavy coating of tattoos provided the only color on the man's skin if you did not count the black eye that was really more of a magenta shade. A split lip provided the perfect accessory to the burnt-out rocker style.

Andy said something that I would later learn was Lynyrd Matuchek. "Why would he talk to me?" My lips touched Andy's ear. He gestured that he couldn't hear me. Then I realized if he couldn't, neither could the guy. I didn't need a good story—just Jonas's name and a few hand gestures. With any luck, the guy would shout loudly enough or gesticulate clearly enough for me to understand his answers.

I assumed a confident posture and headed out on my mission. My target didn't see me coming. Probably good. In a black t-shirt, matching slacks, and no makeup, I couldn't imagine that, even if I were ten years younger, I would be the woman he'd waited for all his life. He didn't even glance my way when I stopped beside him and called out, "excuse me." He was very into something. It might have been musical or it might have been chemical. Whatever the cause of his distraction, I had to tap him on the arm to get his attention. He seemed amused as he gazed down at my five feet six inches from his eight-inch advantage. Amused but not particularly pleased.

I held up my hand in an effort to convince him that my interest wasn't romantic. I gestured that I wanted to ask him a question. His gray eyes were cold and hard but they didn't turn away. I had to stand on my toes to get my words within shooting distance of his ear; the rocker dude wasn't going to make it easy for me.

"Is Jonas Angel here?" I screamed.

The man furrowed his pasty white brow and shook his head so that his straggly locks twirled in the air. I interpreted his response not as an answer, but as an indication that he couldn't hear.

I waved for him to bend down and reluctantly he leaned forward so I could yell directly into his ear. "Is Jonas Angel here?"

He stood straight and studied me before he again bent down – this time to shout in my ear, "Who wants to know?" He turned his head for an answer. If he'd heard the news about Jonas's car, he gave no indication.

"A friend of mine asked me to find him." That statement was actually true.

"He's not here."

I not only heard him, the surrounding fifty people heard him. The song had ended. The applause had died down. Now, I needed a reason for asking.

He lowered his voice. "I can probably help you. What do you need?"

An adequate cover story was my first thought, but I couldn't come up with one. I copied his approach and answered with a question. "What do you mean?"

"You said you wanted to find Jonas. I heard something about his car on the radio. He's like missing or something."

"What happened to him?" I played dumb.

The rocker dude shrugged. "I don't know but I doubt he's gonna show up here tonight. I might have whatever you need." Before I came up with an answer, the guy shrugged. "If you want to wait for him, fine. That's your choice." His tone indicated my decision meant nothing to him. "But, I haven't seen him in a couple of days. Let me know if I can help you."

With that, the tall skinny man waved towards the bar indicating he was going for another drink. I was dismissed. Just as his Lynyrd Skynyrd T-shirt disappeared into the crowd, a male voice whispered into my right ear. "They do random drug testing."

CHAPTER 13

I spun around and found myself nose-to-nose, actually nose-to-chin, with Ed Brickmeyer. His eyes were as big as ever but not as bright.

"They do random drug testing at Heavenly Dips. Don't think because you passed the initial test that you're safe."

"What are you talking about?"

Ed shrugged. His wide blue eyes narrowed into a sad expression.

"Clarify. Please. I'm hot, I'm tired, and my feet are killing me. I don't have time for guessing games. What are you talking about?"

The way he forced his words through clenched teeth left no doubt in my mind that he was angry. "I saw you with that guy."

For a moment I feared he meant Andy, but he had to mean the rocker dude.

"I know who he is. He and Jonas work together."

"At Heavenly Dips?"

Ed infused his sigh with disgust. "Don't play coy with me. I know why you were talking to him."

I raised an eyebrow to encourage him to continue.

"Drugs. Jonas isn't around so Lynyrd over there is the next best source."

I relaxed. He was talking about the rocker dude. "Jonas deals?"

Ed turned his back on me but didn't walk away. "I was so wrong about you." He twirled to face me. "I thought you were a nice person."

"I'm nice."

"No, you're not. You're one of them."

"Them?"

"You know." He waved off my question.

He was right. I did know. He meant the cool, the hip, the careless. But he was wrong in believing that I was one of them, that I had ever been one of them. I positioned myself to block Ed if he tried to flee. With my head tilted back to catch his eyes, I pleaded. "I'm not part of any them. I'm just me. A graduate student who needs to make a few bucks to keep her head above water. Even if I liked drugs, which I don't, I can't afford them." I begged Ed to believe me, to like me.

"What about the old guy I saw you talking to?"

"Old guy?" Even as I asked, I knew. This time he meant Andy.

"Yeah. I saw you talking to a guy. He must be thirty or something. He pointed out Lynyrd. I figured he sent you over to buy drugs."

"Ed, you are so wrong. I was just talking to that . . . that . . . old guy. I had seen him around so I asked him about a bar in Seaside Heights. He didn't know it but said that skinny guy did." I felt shocked, and a little uneasy, at how effortlessly I lied. "I didn't know about any drugs."

"Did you come with the old guy?"

"Him? No way. I came with my friend. Stacy." I had no idea where the name came from. In my entire life, I'd never met a Stacy. "You know, she's seen Jonas around and kind of has a crush on him. She's younger than I am." I clarified quickly. "I better warn her about the drug thing. Tell me about Jonas's drug business."

Ed shook his head. "Business is overstating it. He likes to supply a little Ecstasy for his buddies. And I've heard him talk about some other drug, HPC or GNP or something. It's not like Jonas is a drug kingpin or anything. He just takes care of his friends."

"How do you know all this?"

Ed's features registered his disgust. "I hear him on his

cell phone, and he wears a pager. Sometimes he gets paged and makes jokes like 'time to do my good works'."

"Do the kids at the store use his services?"

"Kids? No."

"Big Al?" Why did I sound shocked? I didn't know Big Al.

Ed shrugged. "I don't know what's going on between Jonas and Big Al. For a while, they were best buds. We call them the badge boys and the wingless wonders. They like to flaunt their superior status. I bet Big Al showers in that badge. And Jonas." His face registered bewilderment. "Geez, Jonas even wears his badge out clubbing. Like anyone cares about that disgusting blue piece of crap." He shook his head, but I knew Ed cared.

"Something happened between Big Al and Jonas?" I tried to get Ed back on the track I wanted.

"Those two were like peas in a pod but something happened. I don't know what and I don't care." Suddenly he shifted gears. "What bar?"

"What?"

"What bar in Seaside Heights were you interested in?" His eyes were devoid of their usual earnestness. Was he testing me? I hoped not because I would fail.

I waved off his question. "Oh. It doesn't matter. Not if those kinds of guys go there."

Ed seemed, if not satisfied, at least appeased by my answer.

Out of the corner of my eye, I saw Andy chatting with two scantily clad women who didn't see him as the old guy. I wanted to get back to his side but couldn't risk Ed seeing me with the PI. Besides, winning Ed's confidence marked a big step toward fulfilling my mission, and he seemed willing to be my friend. Freed from the constraints of Heavenly Dips business he volunteered the key facts of his life in the way that many Jersey residents do—by turnpike exit number—his bright blue eyes sparkled. Ed grew up at Exit 10, went to school at Exit 9 and in the winter worked part-time at another Heavenly Dips store at Exit 12.

What exit did I hail from? I told him I grew up in Philadelphia but now lived in Manhattan. Ed asked which New York exit. I lived uptown at 16E.

"Do you like working at Heavenly Dips?" He asked.

A question for which I had no straight answer. "I've only worked one day. And today was such an odd day. What do you think happened to the Angel kid?"

"I wouldn't know. Jonas and I are not exactly best buds." There was no missing the touch of bitterness in his tone.

"Why not?"

"Have you seen Jonas?"

I nodded. Big mistake. Would Ed question where I had seen Jonas? Maybe he would think I'd caught the news before coming out. The broadcasts about a missing person had to include photos. The gloom on Ed's face suggested he wasn't focused on how I saw Jonas but on what I thought when I did. I would have found it hard to explain only because I couldn't identify the right adverb to modify cute when it came to Jonas Angel. He was astronomically cute. Fabulously cute. Staggeringly cute. With a smile that could light up the island of Manhattan and a bone structure that could support the city's skyscrapers. His profile brought to mind the classic movie stars of the silent era. He was, in short, both the cutest and the most handsome young man I'd ever encountered outside the pages of GQ.

"Well, you've seen Jonas and you've seen me."

"So?"

Ed looked cute in baggy khaki shorts, an oversized navy blue T-shirt, and sandals. Cute and skinny. He needed to eat more free ice cream. His loose-fitting shorts made his scrawny legs seem even thinner, his arms were like twigs hanging out of the voluminous shirt, and his head seemed oversized sticking out of the wide neckline. That every visible body part was in some way disfigured by bruises from his rampant clumsiness didn't improve the general impression. Still, there was something appealing about the boy.

So what if he wasn't adorable in the way that Jonas Angel was adorable. Few people were. Ed lacked Jonas's striking coloring, eerily light blue eyes, and lustrous brown hair. What hair Ed did have was a dull brown that appeared resistant to summer highlights. Okay, maybe his chin was a little pointy. Maybe his face was a tad on the long side. Maybe his nose was too prominent. But his big blue eyes could sparkle—at least when he smiled—which he was not doing while discussing Jonas Angel.

"I knew . . . or rather didn't know . . . kids like Jonas in high school. The kids who have it all. Money. Looks. Maybe not smarts. Who needs smarts when Daddy's going to give you a company?"

Under other circumstances, I would have liked to discuss Ed's self-image, but finding out about Jonas was my job. "I take it you don't care if Jonas ever comes back to the store."

"I should be so lucky. He'll be back. Over fifty locations in the tristate area and he likes Seaside Heights best. Like I told you, it's an honor to work there. You have to earn it." Suddenly his gaze met mine, his brow furrowed, but he kept silent, probably wondering how I landed my cushy job at the flagship store.

CHAPTER 14

"I have to find Stacy." I spoke quickly before Ed could ask too many questions.

Ed insisted on walking with me until I located my imaginary friend whom I dressed in imaginary white pants and imaginary red top. It promised to be a long search.

"She must be going from bar to bar." I apologized. "She probably moves every time we do. So if you have something you need to do . . ."

But Ed didn't. "Don't worry if we can't find Stacy. I'll take you home. I came with a friend but I have the keys to his car."

"Great." I didn't even try for enthusiasm. I felt hot and tired with feet that screamed at every step. I wanted the night to end. Immediately.

"Where do you live?" Seemed like a fair question since he'd just offered to take me home.

"With friends." I made a great show of peering over his shoulder. "I think I see Stacy."

Oddly enough the woman in red and white wasn't Stacy. After circling the bars a few more times, I had to admit that I couldn't find her. "Guess she got lucky."

"What kind of car does she drive?"

"You know, one of those bright lime green VW bugs." Again, I experienced alarm at how quickly and easily I lied.

"Let's see if it's still in the lot. You know where she parked don't you?"

"Sure." Why wouldn't I?

I procrastinated until I felt certain that Andy saw me going outside with Ed. Then I began my search for the fictional Stacy's fictional VW bug. I felt guilt-ridden. Maybe

I wasn't cut out for PI work. I didn't mind deceiving rotten people to discover that they had done heinous deeds, but I hated lying to a sweet guy like Ed, or at least like Ed appeared to be. That didn't stop me from claiming the imaginary car had been parked in the spot now occupied by a Jaguar convertible.

"So what are you going to do?"

I explained that Stacy did not have a cell phone. She and I had a plan. My imaginary friend with the imaginary car had her own imaginary friend with an imaginary house up the Boardwalk. Ed insisted on taking me in his friend's car that was definitely not imaginary. Ed had driven fewer than a dozen blocks north when I yelled stop. "It's right down this row. Don't turn in. It's too narrow. I'll walk down the lane."

I thanked Ed and jumped out of the car before any further explanation was required. I backed down the walkway waving. Ever the gentleman, Ed insisted on watching until I was safely inside. Hoping the neighborhood watch was not on high alert, I ducked between two houses and waited. Finally, Ed drove away. I gave him time to get out of the immediate area and then, with an increasingly painful and decreasingly speedy gait, headed south on the Point Pleasant Beach Boardwalk. If my feet and back hadn't been aching so badly, I might have appreciated the beautiful night. A gentle breeze off the ocean provided a modicum of relief from the relentless heat and humidity. The moon laid a path of silver to the beach. The surf rolled in low and languid. Yeah, it was all pretty nice but I didn't care. My feet hurt.

CHAPTER 15

Before I reached Jenkinson's—and the danger of running into Ed again—I discovered Andy on the Boardwalk chatting with a kid who might have been the most handsome male person I'd seen in recent years if it weren't for those photos of Jonas.

Hanging back, more to keep a low profile than to avoid interrupting Andy, I caught only snatches of his conversation with the kid whose name I could not catch. I heard him tell Andy that when he last saw Jonas on Friday night he had been wearing Ralph Lauren khaki pants, a blue Abercrombie shirt, brown Gucci loafers, and a stainless steel Rolex watch. The kid, who claimed he had met Jonas "just around," knew that Jonas had visited the brand new Heavenly Dips store on Long Beach Island on Friday afternoon. Then he had met a group of guys at a bar and restaurant they liked on Route 9. The place, just north of Tuckerton, was central enough that friends from different shore towns could meet there.

"Usually, Jonas would have gone on with the gang for a full night of partying but he didn't even hang around until the entire group showed up."

"Was he going out with anyone else that night?" Andy asked.

"Not that he told me."

"Did he talk to anyone while you were there?"

"Only the guys in our crowd. I didn't see him speak to anyone outside our group. Schyler Devereaux arrived minutes after he left. She hadn't run into him on the way in so I assume he headed right out."

Andy nodded. I had seen in his notes that Schyler claimed to have missed Jonas.

"Was he meeting another woman?"

"If he had any plans, he didn't tell me, and I think he would have. He knows I'm not a big fan of Schyler." Andy asked why and the kid had no problem explaining. "She's a predator and absolutely no fun. Doesn't like Jonas hanging out with his friends. She wants him all to herself. I'm telling you she's got a ring on hold, a wedding dress in her closet, and monogrammed christening gowns for the kids. That's nuts. We're only kids ourselves."

"Does Jonas view Schyler the same way?"

"He feels sorry for her. They went out in high school. He never meant for it to drag on. He never meant to hurt her. Under his cool surface, Jonas is actually a nice guy. He tries to let Schyler down gently. She just will not be let down, gently or otherwise."

"Did Jonas talk about that on Friday?"

"He never mentioned Schyler. I was surprised when she turned up. When she saw Jonas wasn't there, she didn't stick around. She told us to let Jonas know she would be home all night."

"Did Jonas feel okay on Friday?"

"If he didn't, he didn't mention it."

"Did he seem worried or preoccupied?"

The kid shook his head. "No. He seemed fine. Just Jonas. He claimed he had work to do. Lately, he's been really into his job. I assumed he was headed back to the office in New Gretna. He still had one of those bright blue Heavenly Dips IDs on a chain around his neck, but he never said where he was going." The kid simply made an assumption since the office was not that far away. "Where else would he go?"

Not to Heavenly Dips' headquarters. Andy explained that to gain access to the grounds Jonas would have used his badge as a key card and the card reader showed that his had not been used. The kid shrugged. "There are lots of stores where he could do some work. When you're in New Jersey you're never far from a Heavenly Dips."

"Did he happen to mention anything about the Seaside Heights store?"

"No." He grew animated. "And, he loves that store. He goes there just about every day. I don't know why. He just likes it. He likes the Boardwalk. He likes Seaside Heights."

Hearing the town's name reminded me: I had to get back into that angel gown in eight hours.

Almost as an afterthought, or what he wanted to appear to be an afterthought, Andy asked the kid if he knew Trent Barlow. He did. Had he seen him around lately? He hadn't. Did he have any idea where Trent might have gone? The kid stared over the waves into the night sky and feigned deep thought. "No. No." He did not. Even I, watching from twenty feet away, knew he was lying.

CHAPTER 16

After we left PPB Andy and I had different plans for the remainder of the night. Both of us planned on getting horizontal. I planned on going to sleep immediately.

When we reached the boat, Andy went off to Oliver's outdoor shower and I dove into the V berth. I expected to be unconscious within minutes but the cabin was too hot. I stripped off my t-shirt but that didn't help. The heat was unrelenting, even in the middle of the night. The soft breeze I'd felt on the Boardwalk wasn't making it into the Maggie May's cabin. I felt happy that Andy had a case—and an income—but I would have been a lot happier if he accepted the job after he got the boat's AC running.

It didn't take me long to give up on sleeping below deck. Wearing as little as I thought legally viable, I pulled a cushion off the cockpit bench, stretched out on the bow, and began the countdown. If I go to sleep now, I can get more than six hours sleep. If I go to sleep now, I can get almost six hours sleep. At that point, I realized Andy had yet to return from his shower. I peeked over the top of the deckhouse and could make out his figure standing on Oliver's patio. He wasn't alone.

I couldn't identify the person Andy was talking to except to say it was a male. Sadly, the figure appeared too short to be Oliver's. Our missing host remained missing. I could barely see but I couldn't hear a thing. The two spoke in hushed tones that were completely appropriate given the time of night. As I watched, they crossed the lawn towards the Maggie May. Good thing I had hidden. Good thing the boat's bow faced away from the house. I flattened my stomach against the cushion and buried my head in crossed arms. Even if the man spotted me, he wouldn't see anything he couldn't see on the average beach.

I listened as Andy told his visitor to wait on the dock while he retrieved his notebook from below. He didn't turn on the light as he headed down the companionway. I heard him bumbling around in the cabin but couldn't see what he was doing through the port. Suddenly the light went on. I stole another peek. Andy was wearing a towel and a look of concern. He knew I had left the V berth. He just didn't know where I had gone.

I tapped lightly on the glass and pressed my face close. He nodded, slipped on a pair of jeans and stuck his head up the companionway. "Karl, would you mind coming down here?"

Through the port, I saw a buff man in stiff jeans and a tight white t-shirt. His carefully maintained physique was at odds with his general appearance. Everything about his face was soft and unexceptional. His thin hair and small eyes were the same shade of brown, dull to match his expression. I hypothesized that Karl had developed his physique to fend off bullies that had plagued him since grade school. According to my best estimate, that would have been over thirty years of bullying.

Andy made a note for himself, jotted a few words on his card, and handed it to the visitor. As Andy led Karl topside and escorted him off the boat, he blocked any view the man might catch of me. Another ten minutes passed before Andy dropped a cushion beside me and fell onto it with a groan. He gave me a quick kiss, but either Karl's visit or the humidity had put Andy off romance. We didn't touch as we lay on our backs staring at the stars and listening to the sounds of "Summer Rain" waft across the water.

"Who was Karl?"

"Karl Elkins. His wife worked for Heavenly Dips before she left him. He wants me to work for him, to find her."

"Does he think you have office hours between midnight

and 6 AM?"

"He's a tad on the desperate side. I told him that I had no time. I'd rather not take a domestic case if I can avoid it but I feel sorry for the guy. I took his number. If, I mean when, we find Jonas maybe I'll check it out for him. But even then I'd rather not do the job. I gave him a couple of referrals."

"How did he find you?"

"When I visited Heavenly Dips headquarters yesterday, he was there too, asking around about his wife. Maxwell Angel's assistant wouldn't give him my information. Instead, she left a message for me. When I didn't call back, he thought he'd drop by."

"But you said she didn't give him your address."

"You." His pause for effect was meant to charm me. "You are a natural investigator. She's new, the replacement for Karl's wife. I don't think she understood what information she could give Elkins. She told him that I didn't have an address because I was living on my boat in Beach Haven. Somehow he got the name, Maggie May, out of her. At first, he gave me some cockamamie story about going fishing and seeing the name on the stern by accident. But he abandoned that story even before I could confront him with the fact that I'd turned the boat around to do some work. He sobbed when he explained that he'd spent all day searching for the Maggie May."

"But the bow . . ."

"He saw the name on the flotation device. He then took his boat home, drove back to locate the house, and found that we were gone." He paused and I wondered if he had dozed off. He hadn't. "Make that I was gone. Even though his ties to Heavenly Dips are tenuous, he shouldn't see you with me."

"But didn't he see us come in together?" I assumed he had been waiting for Andy.

"No. He works nights. He took a chance and came by on his way home. He said he can't sleep anyway. He's awake all night missing his wife." Andy shifted onto his side to face me. "He scared me to death. I stepped out of the shower and found him peering at the boat. He's lucky I don't take my gun with me when I bathe."

"So what's the story with his wife?"

"Poor guy works two jobs. On Friday, he felt a cold coming on so he decided to blow off his night job. Ever since he got laid off from some large company, he's been doing custodial and maintenance work third shift so he figured he could make up the time over the weekend. He didn't have much to do since he works at schools and summer classes don't make much of a mess."

I pulled myself onto an elbow and stared at the chatty PI. "Andy."

"What?"

"Could you cut to the chase?"

"Just telling the story like he did – although I did cut about twenty minutes on the unjust nature of his firing. Why do you think I was gone so long?"

I asked for a synopsis and Andy continued. "He came home from work and found that his wife was gone."

I waited for more information but none was forthcoming. "Andy?"

"You said to cut to the chase."

"Did she leave a note?"

Andy shook his head.

"So how did he know she was gone?"

"He didn't at first. He said she worked late a lot at the end of the month. His Bunny. His wife's name was Bunny, but he kept referring to her as my Bunny. He didn't want to call and disturb her. He wasn't worried. He took some cold medicine and went to sleep in the spare room so he wouldn't give her his cold."

"So he realized she was gone in the morning?"

"Not exactly. He figured she got up early and went out. Her bed was made but she always made it before she left.

So, again, he didn't worry. He went fishing. He assumed she'd be home when he got back."

"And she wasn't?"

Andy yawned. "That's when he got worried. He called all her friends. They said they hadn't heard from her. He called the police but, according to him, they weren't interested in what he had to say. Then on Sunday one of his wife's friends had the pleasure of telling him that his wife had left him, that she had been planning to go for months."

"Good friend. Why didn't the wife just leave a note?"

"I have no idea." At least that's what I think Andy said. His yawn sabotaged the message.

"Why did she leave him?"

"He hasn't got the foggiest."

"The good friend tells him what but not why?"

"There are things you can't ask a friend to do for you."

"His wife worked at Heavenly Dips. She left Friday. Do you think she ran off with Jonas?"

"Not likely." His tone mocked me.

"Why not?"

"For one thing, they would have driven his Porsche. Her car is a ten-year-old Toyota sedan." He yawned.

Andy's persistent yawning served as a sedative for me. I closed my eyes but continued my questioning. "Those things run forever plus there would be more room for her clothes."

"I don't think that would be the key factor in the decision. Besides, she's at least fifteen years older than Jonas."

"That is not such a big difference. Age doesn't always matter."

"In this case, I think it might. Karl showed me his wife's picture. It kind of reminded me of your driver's license photo."

I carried a license that might have been stolen from a sad, yet intimidating, prison matron thirty years my senior.

"He said hers was a good likeness." He paused only briefly before realizing he'd better clarify. "Which yours, of course, is not."

Of course. I got Andy's point about Bunny's driver's license. "We've heard that Jonas used drugs . . ."

He cut me off. "They don't make drugs that strong." I heard him say something about Bunny not liking Jonas but I didn't quite understand what her feelings had to do with George Clooney. I asked.

"What did you just say?" Andy seemed confused.

"You don't have to wear a hat on Easter."

"You're asleep."

"No, I'm not."

"Then you should be. You're not making any sense. I'll fill you in later. Go to sleep."

I did.

CHAPTER 17

After a dozen hours on the clothesline, my angel gown felt not a lot dryer than it had after we showered together the night before. It, and I, felt clammy as Andy's car inched past diners, stores, and a car dealership that bore an eerie resemblance to Oliver's house. Actually, to the orange and turquoise color scheme at Oliver's house, an homage to the Miami Dolphins. I had a lot of time to study the decor. The line of traffic was going nowhere; we moved ten yards in three minutes. "I'm going to be late."

Andy checked the dashboard clock. "Bridge is probably open."

He was right. In those days, the draw bridge over the bay opened every half-hour—on the half-hour and on the hour. We were stuck in the 10:30 opening. "I hope we get through this time."

Andy appeared amused. "What's with this sudden display of zeal?" When I didn't answer he guessed. "Are you afraid of Big Al?

"Afraid? No. Unwilling to be subject to his rudeness? Yes."

The truth was that given the possibility that Jonas was in real trouble, I felt motivated. I planned to attack my private investigator duties, i.e. unlicensed private investigator duties, with a vengeance. I would find out all I could about Jonas Angel. Bringing up his name would be easy, even natural. I would crack this case and then I would quit, with any luck before noon.

Andy's mind focused on the case. "The cops are playing along in deference to Jonas's father but they still think the kid just took off. I'm sure they're not rushing any forensic material through the system but they did collect it. You read my file so you pretty much know everything I found out."

"What about the guy I talked to last night?"

"Lynyrd Matuchek."

"He doesn't look like a Leonard."

"He isn't a Leonard. He's a Lynyrd. Lynyrd as in Skynyrd which explains his T-Shirt. His father was a huge fan and totally devastated when Ronnie VanZant and the other Lynyrd Skynyrd crew were killed in that plane crash. His father called him Lynyrd. He called his son Ronnie."

"So Lynyrd is a big fan too."

"Even though his dad deserted his mother when Lynyrd was about ten."

I stared at Andy with a perplexed expression that asked how he'd uncovered all this information.

"One of Jonas's friends knew about Lynyrd. He told me the guy's life story in such detail that I thought he was doing it to hijack the conversation. I felt sure he was hiding something—until he related his life story with the same level of detail. Anyway, he suggested I check Lynyrd out."

"Why Lynyrd?"

"Right now Lynyrd deals a small amount of drugs out of a motel back on Route 9. Apparently, he is the sole support of everyone he lives with: his girlfriend, his five-year-old son, her four-year-old daughter, their one-year-old son, and a teenager who I heard is his girlfriend's sister."

"So he can't be dealing too small an amount of drugs."

"He works at legitimate jobs too. He's a very minor player in local drug distribution."

"And he knew Jonas?"

"Jonas used his services on occasion but then cut him out. He started getting drugs directly from Lynyrd's supplier."

"I can see that would create a problem."

"But that guy didn't think that Lynyrd cared that much. That's why I wanted you to ask him about Jonas—to see how he reacted. From what I saw and from what you say, he didn't appear to have of much of a reaction at all."

I agreed. "He did seem copasetic with the topic of Jonas. What did you expect? That he would turn to me and say, "That creep Jonas . . . I hate him so much that I locked him in the kitchen closet in my house at 123 Main Street?"

"That would have been nice."

I eyed the halo in my lap. "Yep." I agreed. "That would have been nice."

CHAPTER 18

I hit the Boardwalk just as the food stands, souvenir shops and arcades were coming to life. My stomach balked at the aromas of the specialties being readied for the day, but in another hour I'd be responding like Pavlov's dog to the scent of pizza, hot dogs and heavy grease in general. When I heard the chanting of the Heavenly Dips angels, I knew that I was late. I knew by the big hand on the time clock that I was two minutes late. I knew from Big Al's orientation that I would be docked for fifteen minutes. Nonetheless, I punched in and bounced to the front of the store as if I were reporting to work at my dream job. Hilde was at the counter and I hadn't given up on ingratiating myself with her.

"Any word on Jonas?"

She shook her head.

"I heard Ed tell the press that he hadn't seen Jonas recently. Any idea why he hasn't been around?

She shrugged. "Heavenly Dips opened a new store on Long Beach Island. I think he's spending a lot of time there."

"Jonas told you that?"

With an intensity that suggested that I had asked her to calculate the square root of 7468, Hilde stared at me through small panes of glass surrounded by heavy black plastic frames. "Sort of."

Just my luck! A woman who needed to test ten flavors before concluding that she wasn't very hungry showed up at the counter and lingered until Hilde no longer appeared in a mood to talk, at least about Jonas. She pointed to her halo. "We think these heavenly bodies are just anonymous stars and planets. Did it ever occur to you that one of them might be a satellite?" I could not come up with an appropriate response. Given two years I don't think I could come up with an appropriate response. Hilde elaborated. "A spy satellite."

I detected a smile on her lips. She was joking. Wasn't she? I seized the opportunity to make the conversation serve my purpose. "Did Jonas tell you that?"

I suppose Hilde could have injected more condescension into her response, but I didn't see how. "Don't be ridiculous."

She was right. That effort had been just short of ludicrous. No wonder I'd struck out. Now, Hilde wasn't interested in talking to me at all, let alone about Jonas. Maybe Schyler Devereaux would be. I recognized the young woman headed for our stand from the spring formal photo in Andy's file.

Schyler belonged to a small group of women that, to my knowledge, held a disproportionate percentage of the world's wealth: blondes who look good in white slacks. Schyler looked very good in white slacks. She'd accessorized simply: black, short-sleeved T-shirt, black leather flip-flops, Gucci sunglasses, and a Burberry baseball cap that cost more than I would clear that week. Hell, the Burberry scrunchie on her arm cost more than I would clear that week.

Schyler worked at the classic-blonde style and almost pulled it off. She had the hair – pulled into a ponytail that protruded from the back of her hat. She had the jewelry – simple gold worn on neck, wrist, and fingers. What she didn't have was the beauty. Her features were angular, but not in that patrician don't I resemble my horse sense. The angles on Schyler's face gave her a hard don't I resemble my bookie look. She slipped off her sunglasses as she approached the counter and I saw that her eyes were uninteresting, a dull green flecked with gray. Since I was the only server free, they were focused on me.

"Has anyone heard from Jonas?"

I broke the news to her that no one had. Schyler gazed into space, bit her lower lip and, after many deep sighs, confided in me. I wasn't surprised. I have one of those faces. "You heard the news about his Porsche?"

The sad expression on my face as I nodded was real. I just exaggerated it a little.

"I know that something horrible has happened to him. I mean Jonas has run off in the past and not shown up at work or home when expected, but he would always call me. I mean we're . . . well practically—I mean it's not official—but Jonas would call me whenever he could. He worked so hard. He couldn't always find time." So she didn't expect calls from his cell. I wanted to ask her why, but was afraid to interrupt. "It's getting close to a week since I talked to him. I tried to see him on Friday afternoon but I missed him. He must have left the bar right before I arrived. And then, well, he hasn't called. That isn't like Jonas."

From what I'd heard from Andy, this was exactly like Jonas.

"The police aren't taking his disappearance seriously, you know. They say they're working on Jonas's case because of his father but they aren't. If they were, wouldn't they have talked to me? I mean we are practically engaged."

I would have reminded her that 24 hours had not yet passed since his car had been located but she never took a breath.

"I know that money is not an issue for people like us, but why would anyone leave an expensive car in a place like that and go away? Why? It makes no sense." Schyler's voice grew gentle. "You know Jonas always had a soft spot for the Seaside Heights store. This was his favorite store and Cherubic Cherry was his favorite flavor." Her voice broke. I took the hint and scooped one pink and red dip into a black hole. She closed her eyes and licked the ice cream sensuously as if I had handed her Jonas in a cone. I was a little creeped out.

CHAPTER 19

While I served Schyler, Sharmaine reported to work—ten minutes late for her shift and two minutes after Big Al returned from the first of his many excursions. We all had to spend the next quarter-hour listening to his ranting about her tardiness. Sharmaine let his tirade roll off her back, but Hilde developed a headache. She hung out a virtual No Trespassing sign and sulked in the corner massaging her temples for half an hour before Big Al gave in and said she could leave.

Sharmaine expressed delight when Hilde punched out. "Odd one. Very odd, that one. I haven't met her twin but Ed says she's fairly normal."

"Hilde's a twin?"

"So I hear." Sharmaine spotted someone or something on the Boardwalk. I upgraded her usual cheerful expression to elated. When I turned to identify the source of her joy, I saw Lynyrd Matuchek—the same Lynyrd Matuchek that I'd approached the night before at Jenkinson's. He headed our way. My stomach did a quick back-flip. I thought of hiding. Instead, I gambled that Lynyrd would not recognize me. Turned out to be a good bet. He didn't acknowledge me on his first trip to our stand. Or his second trip. Or his third trip. By his fourth visit, I felt comfortable that Lynyrd was not going to recognize me. Ever.

The very sight of Lynyrd in the hard light of day depressed me. He was thin but not fashionably so. His appearance suggested more than a passing relationship with chemicals not approved by the FDA, but no relationship whatsoever with soap. Lynyrd's voice sounded raspy and the smell of nicotine escaped through his pores and across the counter. He dropped his cigarette only when Sharmaine passed him a double scoop of one of his favorite flavors. He had a lot of favorite flavors. Sharmaine's bright eyes said she believed his frequent visits were driven by love. I agreed—love of ice cream. Lynyrd acted as if he were doing her a favor letting her fawn over him, check his wounds, and give him free cones—a move that threatened her employment. Okay, she wasn't risking a fantastic career, but she did have white wings to lose.

I might have been pretending to be twenty-four but I wasn't. I was old enough to see through Lynyrd. I wanted to leap over the counter, chase him away, and warn Sharmaine to dump him before their life story became the basis for a TV movie. Okay, I made up most of what I concluded about Lynyrd but I believed it fervently. Lynyrd was living off his youthful beauty, well not quite beauty. He was good-looking in a tormented young man way or would be if he got rid of the bruising and decided to eat or bathe. He wasn't Jonas Angel handsome but attractive enough to appeal to adolescent girls or girls with adolescent fantasies. The sulky expression that endeared him to Sharmaine constituted his most significant attribute.

Sharmaine saw Lynyrd with completely different eyes. For one thing, hers glowed whenever she glanced his way or mentioned his name, which basically meant whenever she opened her mouth. "Can you believe it? Some guy who doesn't like Lynyrd just jumped him last weekend for no reason. Who wouldn't like Lynyrd? Lynyrd said the guy was drunk."

"You're not serious about Lynyrd, are you?" I tried to sound unbiased.

"I'd like to be." Sharmaine couldn't suppress the exhilaration in her voice. "So far we've only hung out a few times. He has so many jobs it's hard for him to find time. It isn't as if he actually can ask me out or anything. He has a girlfriend but she isn't nice to him. She just wants him for his money. Lynyrd has to stay with her for a while because of their baby."

I nodded. Supporting a child I understood. What I couldn't understand was Sharmaine's infatuation. With her kewpie doll looks and carefree personality, Sharmaine could have done much better than Lynyrd.

"Lynyrd and I go to the same clubs a lot and if we run into each other, sometimes he'll stay with me for a couple of days. We always have a good time together."

I didn't ask for her definition of a good time but apparently Sharmaine felt the need to explain. She told me the great things Lynyrd could do in bed. Or as I saw it, the great things Lynyrd would let Sharmaine do to him in bed. All I could hope was that she would use everything she learned to land a decent guy someday. I vowed to take her romantic well-being on as a project but first I had to find out what she knew about Jonas. I asked if they were friends.

Sharmaine gazed into space for a full moment before speaking. When she finally responded, her thoughts were well organized and her tone was controlled. Her eyes did not glow. "He isn't my type. I mean he's cute and all. He likes playing at being cool but he really isn't. He's just waiting to be his father." She sneered. "Jonas wants everyone to think that he's a wild one but . . ." A shake of her head said she didn't buy his act.

"Drugs?"

Again, she hesitated. "Sometimes he provides stuff for his friends' parties. Usually Ecstasy. You know Ecstasy?" Her question confirmed just how old twenty-four seems to an eighteen-year-old. "He likes to think that makes him cool. He isn't a professional dealer or anything. I'm not sure he does the stuff himself. Jonas likes to act like a big deal. He doesn't ever seem to lose control. Maybe he just gets off on seeing other people lose it so he can feel superior. I don't know. I just think he wants people to like him. He feels like he has to impress them or something."

"How so?"

"Jonas is not all that mature. He's not a bad guy but he doesn't think things through. He's getting better. I don't hate him. He's just not my type of person. He thinks that everything is okay between us and I guess it is. I mean I'm not like being two-faced or anything." Sharmaine punctuated her comments with a toss of her voluptuous curls. "When he talks to you and he's like all charming, you can't help but be friendly back. Even though he knows he has to be nice to me, I know that he doesn't like me. Not really."

"Why not?"

"Not his type." The woman Sharmaine went on to describe as Jonas's type would be any guy's type. The difference between Jonas and other guys, however, was that Jonas could land the long, lanky, cool goddesses and pretty much any other type he felt like having. According to Sharmaine, Jonas proved that time and time again. "He has to have them all, everyone he meets. You'll see when you meet him. After he gets a girl, he blows her off. Every one of them. Except Schyler. He tries to get rid of her, but she won't go. Schyler thinks that she's special, that she is his soul mate."

"How do you know all this? Did Jonas talk to you about this kind of stuff?"

"No way. I see him and Schyler around. I watch. I listen. Schyler always comes by when Jonas is here. You were waiting on her when I came in. I'm surprised she didn't tell you above their great love."

I didn't share.

"If you give Schyler a chance she'll go on and on about Jonas and how close they are, how many years they've been together." Sharmaine sounded apologetic. "It gets really boring. It's a long story. Jonas went to high school with her. He took her to the senior prom. They date on and off. They didn't go to the same college but her school was close to his. Jonas probably does see her more than any other girl, but that's only because she's constantly showing up wherever he goes. She told me they're getting married."

"Are they?"

Sharmaine chuckled. "In her dreams. Schyler thinks she is some sort of sophisticate but she is so naïve. Jonas isn't about to settle down, not for years."

If I wasn't on a mission I would have challenged Sharmaine's view that Lynyrd was different. However, I was on a mission. I didn't interrupt.

"He could marry her eventually. After a decade or two. But why would he?"

"Because Schyler is special to him?" I answered the rhetorical question.

"No one is special to Jonas except Jonas. Not even Schyler. Although he's probably afraid to tell her."

"Why?"

"Did you ever see that old movie with, you know Cruella DeVil, when she tries to kill the guy who married Catherine Zeta-Jones?"

"Glenn Close in Fatal Attraction?"

"Yeah, when Schyler finally realizes that Jonas isn't planning on walking down the aisle with her, she's gonna make that lady seem like a pushover."

"Excuse me." The voice was male. The tone was angry.

Darn those customers. While Sharmaine and I were chatting I hadn't even noticed the fortyish couple with scowls that, according to the depth of their matching facial lines, they had been perfecting for years. Why did these two succumb to a craving for ice cream just when the conversation was getting good? I developed a scowl of my own.

After the couple, still frowning, moved away with their cones, excuse me their clouds, I tried to get Sharmaine back on the topic of Jonas but failed miserably. Here are a few examples of conversation with Sharmaine

Me: Do you have any idea why Jonas hasn't been coming

around?

Sharmaine: You think he would come here what with the sunny weather and all. Lynyrd likes working at the beach during the heatwave. Lynyrd . . . .

Me: Do you know the girls that Jonas dropped?

Sharmaine: Some girls are not easy to get rid of. Lynyrd's girlfriends are always holding on. Lynyrd….

Me: Do you know anyone with a grudge against Jonas?

Sharmaine: Guys! All these disagreements they have. Can you believe that someone had enough of a grudge against Lynyrd to beat him up for no reason? Lynyrd….

I stopped asking. I expected no more news of Jonas Angel from Sharmaine in the immediate future, and I didn't think I could bear any more details of Lynyrd's life.

CHAPTER 20

When my lunch break came I set off in search of nutrients from the salt food group to balance my day's diet. I didn't have to travel far along the Boardwalk before the aroma of heavy grease lured me to a stand that offered to fry and salt any item I could imagine.

I was picking up napkins by the fistful when I felt eyes on me. I glanced up but didn't see anyone watching—which was actually odd. In under forty-eight hours, I'd learned that if I scanned the crowd while walking around in wings and a halo I'd always find at least one person sneaking a peek my way, if not blatantly staring—even in the middle of the eclectic Seaside Heights population.

I found an open bench facing the ocean and dug into my lunch. An odd feeling, and not a good one, compelled me to check over my shoulder. There he was. Big Al. Standing across the Boardwalk smoking a cigarette and faking interest in the prizes available to air-rifle sharpshooters. But I knew. He was watching me. I pretended I didn't notice him. I had nothing to fear. My wings were in place and my halo was clearly visible.

I finished eating, checked my watch, and decided no way would I return to the Heavenly Dips stand early. I called Andy and he picked up on the first ring. "I met Schyler today. She came seeking news about Jonas. She appeared very upset."

"Why did she talk to you?"

"Just because I was at the counter. Schyler claims to want a stronger official reaction to Jonas's disappearance. I know you've already talked to her, but if you express your ongoing interest in the case, you might be able to get more out of her."

"If there's anything to be gotten. Anything else?"

"Hilde went homesick, so I had a chance to talk to Sharmaine. She insists that Jonas planned on breaking it off with Schyler, but she wouldn't let go. Schyler would never admit anything was wrong between them. That would destroy the myth of her great love. If someone could convince her, however, that being open and honest about their relationship would bring Jonas home . . . . I just wanted to report in."

"Thanks, Maggie. Love you. Gotta go."

"Love you too."

I tossed my trash into a can and strolled south to soak up the Boardwalk atmosphere. I watched a father fail to win a stuffed animal, even the tiniest frog, for the preschool daughter who, with admirable loyalty, cheered his questionable pitching skills. As the uncoordinated dad missed time and time again, I heard the sounds of an escalating altercation behind me. There he was. Again. Big Al. Conversing in heated tones with a woman in hot pants and a halter top.

From what I could gather, she was angry because Big Al had failed to apologize for a collision that, according to her, he caused by stopping in the middle of the Boardwalk for no apparent reason. In return, Big Al delivered an expletive-seasoned tirade about watching where she was going. I couldn't hear every word but my grandmother would have claimed the ones I could make a sailor blush.

Before my boss noticed me I slipped across the Boardwalk into the Magical Carousel Shoppe. The store represented a great choice for several reasons. It felt cool and I needed a break from the heat. It sold souvenir items and I wanted a memento of Seaside Heights. More importantly, Big Al didn't strike me as the type who bought miniature lighthouses or carousel horses and that was what the store sold.

Although I yearned to avoid my boss, I appreciated that the store's wide windows allowed me to keep an eye on him. As I browsed for a souvenir, I watched Big Al extricate himself from the argument, or try to. He waved his arms wildly in the hopes of dismissing the woman who did not appear to feel the discussion was over. She barked what I could only surmise were insults at his back as he headed across the Boardwalk directly towards the shop where I feigned shopping.

I waited for Big Al to storm into the building but he stopped short of the glass doors. His face was as red as his hair. Both were soaked in sweat. He gazed north. He gazed south. He cupped his face in his hands, pressed them against the glass of the display window, and peered into the shop. I jumped behind a rotating jewelry display hoping my halo would appear to be just another doodad among the store's offerings. I hated to sound neurotic but I didn't think there could be much doubt. Big Al was following me.

This guy would make a great case study for bad management techniques. Did he follow all the employees to make sure they stayed in uniform? I bet he did. Why wouldn't he? Why make a rule if you don't take steps to enforce it? I had nothing to fear. I was in compliance with his ridiculous edicts—in danger of being late from lunch, but still in compliance.

I stepped out from my hiding place only after confirming that Big Al no longer stared through the window. I rushed onto the Boardwalk and spotted my boss wandering north checking left, checking right, probably searching for me. A wake of smoke from yet another cigarette made him easy to track. When he took the right path through the cluster of stands in the center of the Boardwalk, I took the left. And ran. I arrived back in the booth, via an illegal slide under the counter, two minutes before Big Al returned from one of his alleged trips to the bank. Okay, I hadn't seen him every minute he was out of the booth but I hadn't seen him go anywhere near a financial institution. I concluded that he'd left the booth only to tail me.

CHAPTER 21

I'd been back from lunch for an hour before Big Al deigned to make eye contact. Another hour passed before he spoke and when he did I felt more than a bit perplexed by the topic. He was working the register and I was dipping Comet Cherry Sorbet from the case next to him when apropos of nothing, he posited, although I'd never actually heard anyone posit before, I felt certain that he posited, "I'm this store's Archangel, the only Archangel. I'm our store's link with corporate. I got the badge. The only badge." His emphasis on the word, badge, underlined the pride he took in wearing the bright blue laminated card around his neck. "I'm the only one in this store who talks to the boys in New Gretna. The only one." His tone indicated that there was no fooling Big Al. He knew I had been secretly calling the home office every fifteen minutes since I'd walked in the door. "You have any problems you go through me."

"Well," I ran through a list of appropriate responses and decided on "Thank you. That's good to know."

"And while we're chatting, do something about that hair, would ya? The color's okay. Personally, I like blondes. But it's all over the place. Get hair gel or something. You can't have that mess hanging over the freezers."

I didn't get up on time for jobs that paid ten times as much; I wasn't going to rise with the sun for twenty-five cents above minimum wage to create a hairstyle that Big Al found appropriate. Again, I ran through a list of appropriate responses. I couldn't come up with one. Luckily, Big Al didn't expect a reply. He'd moved on to berating Sharmaine and her curls.

Blood flooded my face as I watched Karl Elkins approach

the counter and not just because I was fanning myself with my skirt. The last time I saw the man I'd been naked. That he hadn't seen me made no difference. I blushed.

"Excuse me, miss, my name is Karl Elkins." He addressed Sharmaine. "My wife works at Heavenly Dips or did until last week. I wondered if she had stopped by at all. Do you know her? Bunny Elkins."

"Sorry, I don't know her." Sharmaine shook her head and the planets above whirled. The forlorn expression on Karl's face probably compelled her to ask, "Is she okay?"

"I don't know." He paused for about three seconds before spilling the beans. "She left me. I have to find her."

"Have you talked to Big Al?" Sharmaine was all cheery solicitousness. "He might know her."

"No, I wouldn't want to impose."

Of course not. He'd probably wait until after midnight and drop by Big Al's house.

"I just thought while I was here I would ask." Elkins used a bright blue Heavenly Dips napkin to wipe the sweat from his brow as he surveyed the ice cream display. "Could I have a Cherubic Cherry in a black hole, please? That's my Bunny's favorite."

While Sharmaine dipped, I studied Elkins. In the daylight my impression was the same as it had been when I spotted him in the dark: his head sat on the wrong body. If I weren't viewing him in the flesh, I would have thought he had pasted a photo of his face above a muscle-builder's body. The man was in good shape with a slim physique with well-defined muscles, but the features on his soft face totally lacked definition. His bland coloring didn't help. Neither did the profuse perspiration. He glanced my way, probably because he sensed my stare. I flashed a brief smile, turned away and faked great interest in a couple necking their way north on the Sky Ride. Those two would never sense my stare.

"Poor man." Sharmaine's big eyes were full of compassion as Elkins walked away. "Did you hear that? His wife left him. Hard to imagine anyone leaving a nice man like that."

"You know him?"

"Just now from serving him."

"How do you know he's nice?"

"I could just tell." Sharmaine's smile added Silly.

I'd never convince her that she might be the silly one. I didn't even try.

CHAPTER 22

When I heard Big Al grumbling on the telephone I figured something was up. I also figured something wasn't good. He walked to the front of the stand and snorted while he studied the current staff. He made a big show of deliberation but I suspected he knew what he wanted all along. He crooked a finger in my direction. "Daniels." With that, he turned on his heel and took the few steps back to his desk. I assumed he meant that I should follow him.

Knowing that he was going to fire me, I trailed him into the small space behind the freezer. My heart soared but then plunged back to earth. I was about to be fired from a job that a trained monkey would accept only when the organ grinder business hit a slump.

As it turned out my employment had not been terminated. I was simply being sent away for three hours so I could come back and help on the night shift. I had a lot of questions. Why? Why me? Why couldn't I work through to the night shift? I didn't ask any of them. I clocked out, and, without saying good-bye to any of my coworkers, slipped out the back door to kill three hours.

Newspapers claimed that northeastern cities were boiling. Shore towns like Seaside Heights might have been cooler but not by much. No breeze provided relief. Even the surf seemed lethargic. I certainly was. At the northern tip of the Boardwalk, I claimed a bench that faced the beach and called Andy to leave a message telling him when to pick me up. Then, waving my skirt in a futile attempt to create a breeze, I alternated watching the surf patting the sand and the people exiting the Sky Ride.

"Do you work at Heavenly Dips?" The words came from

the far end of the bench. I turned and discovered a thirtyish man lounging opposite me.

"Are you talking to me?" A dumb question. Even if I hadn't been the only person in the area wearing a psychedelic angel outfit, I was the only person within earshot.

"I wondered if you worked at Heavenly Dips." The guy's voice, nasal and harsh, did not match the bright smile he offered.

I shook my head so that my galaxy of heavenly bodies made a quick orbit reminding me I wore a halo on my head. "No, I just think this is a cool look."

As his large display of teeth became huge, I realized how threatening the stranger's preternaturally white teeth appeared against the leathery skin tanned to a deep brown. I found the effect creepy but suspected the guy found his look awesome. The tan complemented a slick style characterized by a dapper wardrobe and topped by blonde hair pasted back with a severity I viewed as a bit passé. But, what did I know? I hadn't seen a fashion magazine in months.

The man seemed vaguely familiar. He might have been a customer once or twice, although I couldn't connect him with a flavor. Maybe I had noticed him passing on the Boardwalk. He was the type of person I would have noticed. Slick. Smarmy. And overdressed. In deference to the heat, he had his shiny suit jacket slung over his shoulder. However, he didn't seem uncomfortable in a long-sleeved starched shirt that, had he slipped out of it, would have continued to sit upright on the bench without him. The stranger extended his arm across the back of the seat. His fingers were only inches from the hard polyester rim of my right wing giving me the opportunity to see the band of slightly lighter skin that, I assumed, his wedding ring had recently covered. A minute ago? An hour ago? A month ago? I didn't know. I didn't care.

"You're right. On you, the look is very cool." His brown

eyes flirted with me.

Was this guy for real? Could he possibly be interested in a grown woman in an angel costume? Or had he, in a burst of religious fervor, mistaken me for a real angel? I felt relieved to feel a vibration in my pocket. I pulled out my cell phone. I explained to Andy that my shift had been changed.

"You're resourceful." Andy put a positive spin on the development. "Entertain yourself. After all, you're in a resort town."

"Dressed like a clown."

"You can easily play Skeeball for three hours. There's no dress code in Skeeball."

Down the bench, the stranger studied me and listened unabashedly. I tried to encrypt my conversation. "Not enough C A S H." The guy wouldn't have to be a master code-breaker to figure that one out.

Andy's tone grew kind. "I'm sorry. Do you still love me?"

"I remember thinking that I did but at the moment I can't quite conjure up the feelings."

"You will." I heard a smile in his voice. That tone made me smile as I hung up.

"Boyfriend?"

I turned and fixed the stranger with a stare intended to ask: Are you still here? Apparently he believed the expression asked: Why don't you slide down here and make mad passionate love to me?

His voice sounded sad, soft, and suggestive. "Don't tell me you have a boyfriend." The intonation that might have aimed for intimate seemed slimy to my ears.

"No problem. I won't tell you."

Again he flashed those teeth in a tight, forced smile. "Really, do you have a boyfriend?"

Did I? The real me did. But what about the undercover me? "That was my brother." I dodged the stranger's question.

“Really?” He didn’t seem to believe me.

“He’s having problems.” I provided an explanation for my loving tone. “Tonight we’re going to talk about it, but I have to work late.” I sighed with a theatrical flair. “I hope I can help.” I let my features form a mask of concern for my imaginary brother.

“I couldn’t help but hear." He lied. “It seems you have some dead time on your hands. May I buy you a drink?”

“That’s very kind of you . . .” I responded to his lie with one of my own. “I have a million errands to run. Nice chatting with you.” I felt the man’s eyes on me as I walked away.

CHAPTER 23

I carried a credit card to work just in case of an emergency. In my world spending three hours in a Heavenly Dips uniform was an emergency. I went shopping to find something—anything—to camouflage my royal blue gown. The selection of casual clothes on the Boardwalk was broad. It just wasn't what I would call me. Short-shorts with the word NASTY in block letters across the rear? Not really me. TROUBLE seemed marginally better but not quite my style. And, since I was not born in New Jersey I didn't think I had the right to be a JERSEY GIRL or a JERZ GIRL. Despite all the time I'd spent in the state, I'd never even had a New Jersey driver's license.

In the end, I charged a T-shirt, white with Seaside Heights tastefully imprinted over the left breast. The sleeveless top promised to hide most of my angel gown. I returned to the municipal bathroom at the north end of the Boardwalk and, in what could be construed as a violation of the no-changing signs, pulled the shirt out of the bag and hid the halo and wings inside. I slipped my new purchase over my head. Just what I needed during a heatwave—more clothing. The bottom of my t-shirt almost reached the hem of my gown. Heck, the armpits almost reached the hem. Or at least I suspected they did. To discourage folks from changing in the restroom, there were no mirrors. Probably better that I couldn't see myself before I stepped back onto the boards.

My first instinct? Play Skeeball. Even years later when I had a Skeeball app on my phone, I still welcomed the opportunity to bounce a real ball into a three-dimensional circle. My funds, however, were limited. In under five minutes, I'd invested four quarters in four games. I had to make a choice if I wanted to stay away from my credit card. Food or Skeeball. A tough decision. Reluctantly, I pocketed my prize tickets and cut myself off.

I used some of my lunch money to buy a one-way ticket on the Sky Ride and waited for the car to swoop me up and lift me above the beach. Before long I knew I had made the right decision. Twenty feet in the air I detected traces of a breeze and felt the coolest I had since I last stuck my head into a freezer with Apollo's Apple Pie.

The Sky Ride offered a new perspective on Seaside Heights. Not only did I get a better view of the rows of color—chairs, towels, and umbrellas—stretched across the beach from the water's edge, I could see the line where the surf hit the beach – a sight hidden from me at Heavenly Dips by the curve of the sand. I could peer into the distance, instead of the slice of Seaside Heights visible from the store. I could observe the rooftop establishments along the Boardwalk where rooftop meant second floor. That was where the man I'd met on the bench worked his charm on a waitress. Or tried to.

Apparently, the slick stranger had a weakness for women in uniform. He stood at the bar chatting up a blonde whose tan would have appeared deep had she been standing next to anyone else. I was so busy studying him that I almost missed Big Al at a table along the railing. Big Al faced west, an odd choice for a man sitting alone at an Atlantic Ocean-front bar. An odd but fortuitous choice. He had his back to me as I rode by with bright blue sleeves and traces of my blue skirt flapping gently in the breeze and no sign of wings or halo to be seen. Was this the bank our Archangel left the store to visit so many times a day?

As my car passed an arcade, I saw a familiar blue dress, white wings, and gold halo. Along with Sharmaine's curls, they were all flailing wildly about on an amusement that required total involvement by the player. The game was new to me that summer. Demonstrating a marked lack of imagination, I'd dubbed it the dance machine. Sharmaine had described the game as the reason she so often arrived late for work. Now I could tell that her flushed appearance was not simply the result of rushing to the Heavenly Dips stand. Sharmaine was working hard and looking good. A small group of passers-by had stopped to watch her obey the game's prompts.

A few minutes later my car passed the Heavenly Dips stand where Ed scooped alone. If he minded, his annoyance didn't show. He had his usual professional grin plastered on his face. I noticed that the planets on his head bobbed in time to the Heavenly Dips theme as he rang up his sale.

Shopping, Skeeball and the ride killed over an hour. At Casino Pier, I watched the carousel spin it had been doing since 1932 and would continue to do after Superstorm Sandy's attempt at destruction. Like three generations before mine, I hummed along with the Wurlitzer organ music. When that activity grew old, I sauntered down the boards ignoring the uninhibited barkers who offered me overstuffed animals in return for a modest display of skill and a slightly less modest investment of funds. I watched typical American families, no longer WASP blonde but now in the more prevalent tones of tan and brown, play touch football, Frisbee and badminton on the beach. My viewing was interrupted by a loud cheer at the paintball stand across the Boardwalk. A player had just landed a particularly good shot on a living target that had more to fear from the costume than from the paint. What was the temperature inside that suit? Did anyone not handling bio-level 4 contaminants need that kind of protection?

When the shooting stopped, the players wandered away and the target started a well-deserved break. He pulled off his helmet. Lynyrd. If I had known Lynyrd was the human target, I would have fired some paint his way myself. Or would I? No wonder the guy's hair looked so dirty. Maybe I misjudged Lynyrd. At least he was ambitious. Maybe ambitious was the wrong word, but he was industrious. I wouldn't want to work dodging blobs of paint in ninety-degree weather. I admired someone who would.

I shook my head. Was I having sympathetic thoughts about Lynyrd? What was wrong with me? It had to be the heat and the sun, the relentless sun. The thought reminded me of my thirst. I headed for a cluster of food stands on the pier and succumbed to what Ed would have called aromas redolent of childhood outings to the Boardwalk. I did what I normally do when I have time on my hands. I ate.

CHAPTER 24

"Do you usually come here for lunch?" Ed plopped onto a chair across from me. I don't think he actually meant to take that particular seat, but he tripped over a table leg and landed on the nearest flat surface. To his credit, Ed didn't spill a drop from the tall cup he balanced in his hands along with a mass of greasy paper and a plate of butterfly fries. I averted my eyes and stared out over the ocean. I didn't think I could face whatever was hidden in the wrapping. Not after a half-hour of uninterrupted food consumption, including 2,000 calories from both the sugar and salt food groups, but nothing with any nutritional value.

"No. I'm killing time. I thought watching the amusements might be fun."

"But you're not paying any attention to them, although nothing wrong with an ocean view, not that you seem very interested in that either." Ed inhaled melodramatically. "I love the sea air."

I assumed he meant sea air blended with the smell of hot grease, spun sugar, and my favorite aroma of the hour, caramel popcorn. I didn't ask.

He was still waxing poetic. "Don't you just love the cacophony of the Boardwalk? The tapping of the feet on the wooden surface. The roar of the surf pounding the beach. The churning of the plane engines towing banners."

Ed didn't mention the calls of the barkers and the sirens from the game stands. He left out the organ music, gongs, bells, and whistles that accessorized the amusements. He missed the screeching of metal wheels on the big rides' tracks and the screams of human riders that accompanied them. I could have waxed poetic on the items he overlooked but I was in no mood to play along. I shrugged.

"Why so glum?" Ed pushed his butterfly fries under my nose.

I waved them away and fanned myself, ineffectively, with a paper napkin. "Did you notice there's a heatwave? It's in all the papers."

"No, seriously. The aura you are projecting is hardly indicative of a happy state of mind." Ed bit into a cheesesteak. Sauce, onions, and a stream of unrecognizable commingled condiments overflowed the bun and dribbled down Ed's chin.

Having failed to create a breeze with the increasingly limp napkin, I donated it to Ed's cause. "Big Al gave me a rotten schedule. Now, I have to hang around here filling three hours. Okay, maybe now it's only one hour." My sigh asked for sympathy. "I don't think Big Al likes me."

"Big Al doesn't like anyone. He's a misanthrope. At least no one could call him a misogynist. He's an equal opportunity hater. He hates everyone." With his next bite, Ed progressed halfway through the oversized sandwich.

"But I never did anything to earn his disapproval," I pleaded, ignoring the instances when I sneaked under the counter, extended my breaks, and wore my gown sans halo.

Ed didn't nitpick. He claimed my behavior didn't matter. "You will never win Big Al's approval. Never."

"Why is he like that?"

"From what I hear he was okay until his wife died. Then he . . . like . . . he went nuts. Got crotchety."

"When did all this happen?"

"Before I came to this store. I'm not sure exactly, maybe five years ago. So see, he doesn't like any of us."

"I get the feeling he likes me less."

Ed had something to say but he wasn't going to say it. His reluctance had nothing to do with the handful of fries he shoved in his mouth.

"What?"

Ed shrugged.

"Come on, Ed, you can't tease me this way."

I waited while Ed chewed the remaining fries. "I heard him on the phone yesterday. He didn't know I was in the freezer. He was talking to someone. I don't know who. Big Al said he didn't understand how you landed this job. He thinks you're a plant."

"Like a ficus tree?" My grin was feeble.

"That isn't funny."

"It's not supposed to be." I didn't tell him what the comment was supposed to be—

a quick answer to cover my fear and concern. "What other kind of plant could I be? That's ridiculous. Just silly. Dumb." I fought to control my mouth. My level of denial was becoming suspicious. At least to me. Ed didn't seem to notice.

"I think he's worried that Maxwell Angel sent you."

"Why would Big Al think the owner of the company sent me?"

"Well, you know there is bad blood between Jonas and Big Al."

"You told me that but you said you didn't know what the issue was."

Ed squirmed in his seat. "I was being discreet. Big Al claims Jonas has been skimming from the daily proceeds. Not a lot. Just enough to give him a little extra money. and to make Big Al look bad. Jonas couldn't have pilfered that much. He didn't come by to pick up the cash every day. Big Al claims the little bastard, his description, set him up to take the fall. He thinks you're here to entrap him."

"Did Big Al tell you that?"

"Not exactly. I listen. I keep my ears open."

I didn't know how to respond except to issue a denial. "I never ever suspected there night be an embezzler in the store. And why would I care if there were? If you get a chance, please communicate that to Big Al."

"Right. I'll find it easy to drop that nugget into a casual conversation. 'Meg is not here searching for a peculator'."

"Be discreet, Ed. And, I assume that a peculator is an embezzler, but if you do get a chance to speak to Big Al, promise you'll speak English not GMAT talk."

Ed didn't promise. He took the last bite of his sandwich and told me to stay put. When he reappeared he was carrying tickets for the rides. "We've got to cheer you up. It's bad for tourism to have someone with your morose visage hanging around the Boardwalk. You still have close to an hour before your shift resumes. Let's use the time wisely. There is much to disport oneself with in Seaside Heights."

Even without a dictionary, I figured out that he wanted to show me a good time. "Not the Tower of Fear." Even as I spoke I heard the screams of fun-seekers dropping down—straight down.

"You won't?" Ed sounded disappointed but not surprised.

"Not that ride. Besides, don't you have to get back to work?"

"I'm an Angel. Remember?" He pointed over his shoulders to his gold wings. "When I have to stay late to close, Big Al cuts me a little slack on my mealtimes. What would cheer you up?"

"I like the Ferris wheel."

"So does my grandmother." Ed shook his head. "Meg, you don't want to get old before your time. Live a little."

"I could have said merry-go-round." I stared into his blue eyes and repeated my preference. "Ferris wheel."

Despite his disdain for the tame amusement, Ed seemed to have clout at the Ferris wheel.

The attendant gave him one of those guy handshakes and a greeting. "How ya doing, man?" The operator's ebullience struck me as odd simply because he never shot so much as a glance in our direction.

Once he had locked us into our car—so spacious it could have held six people—I had Ed trapped. I went to work. "I met Schyler today. She's kind of pretty. Sharmaine didn't think Schyler and Jonas were going to make it as a permanent item. Were they?"

Ed stared at the horizon. "Sharmaine doesn't like Schyler. She thinks she flirts with Lynyrd. She says that Schyler is cutesy and Sharmaine thinks that cutesy is disgusting."

Sharmaine, who made a Barbie doll look like an offensively strident feminist, didn't like cutesy? That was a thought to ponder but not then. Ed was on a roll.

"But Schyler is cute. At least I think so. Very cute. She could have any guy she wanted. I don't know why she is hung up on Jonas. A lot of girls are. We sell more ice cream when he's in the store than we do all week when he's not. Especially small scoops of Rain Cloud, the fat-free vanilla. His admirers don't want Jonas to think that they might get fat."

"Does that make Schyler jealous?"

"I don't know. Maybe. Probably. But she thinks that she and Jonas are the real deal. She is so caught up in the myth. She thinks that she and Jonas look good together. She thinks they'll have a gorgeous wedding. She predicts that they'll have the most incredibly beautiful children. You would think seeing Jonas's brother Edwin would have tipped Schyler off to genetic problems among the Angels."

I didn't say a word. I wanted Ed to keep talking. Mission accomplished.

"I don't know why she chases Jonas that way. She wants him but for all the wrong reasons. I don't mean to criticize. I kind of, like, admire her in a way. She has that sort of steel magnolia thing going."

"So you and Schyler are friends."

He slid down his bench to the south edge of the car. "Not really. Sometimes when she's hanging around the store we talk. That's all." He pointed a finger through the grating. "You know, I can see my house from here."

CHAPTER 25

Just after 9 PM, Andy's bland white sedan pulled alongside the water park where I waited. The vehicle with absolutely no identifying marks served a private investigator much better than the classic Mustang convertible Andy now relegated to a recreational role. Even I wasn't sure that Andy was inside until he pushed the door open. "How was the split shift?"

"Don't ask." I plopped onto the front seat with a groan.

Andy dropped something into my lap. "A present."

"A roll of dimes?"

"Next time you have three hours off on the Boardwalk I want to make sure you have Skeeball money."

Andy's gift was a truly thoughtful gesture. I felt like an ingrate telling him it took quarters, sometimes two, to play a single Skeeball game.

"Only if you're in it for the prizes. If you are playing for the love of the game, as I know you are, there's an arcade where you can play for a dime. Takes forever to win a rubber snake, but what do you care? It's at your end of the Boardwalk. Check it out. You'll see."

My mood improved immensely. I had Skeeball and a boyfriend who was nice enough to provide access to it. What more could I ask for? I had a big, inappropriate, smile on my face as Andy described his day.

"I had to stop at the police station with Maxwell Angel. He wanted me to tell the cops everything I had discovered. The police still aren't convinced the kid didn't run away, but Angel carries enough clout that they are pursuing his disappearance." Andy's voice sounded solemn. "I overheard something. I think the crime scene team found traces of blood in Jonas's car. I don't know what they mean by traces. I don't know whose blood. I don't think the cops do either. If I heard correctly they found blood on a tiny snippet of a trash bag. Those findings aren't necessarily bad. Jonas is active. He could have cut himself. There are a lot of possibilities."

I was listening but I appeared more interested in making sure the air-conditioning vents blew directly on me. "So it's okay with the cops if you stay on the case." I leaned forward and held my gown away from my body to let the cool air blow onto my damp skin.

"The cops are never happy if a PI stays on any case, but Maxwell Angel insists. The cops will use me if they want to. I'll stay out of their way and just keep doing what I'm doing."

"And me?"

"Just keep on doing what you're doing."

"Do the cops know I'm working with you?"

"Not exactly."

"Not exactly?"

"No."

"Shouldn't they?"

"The fewer people who know the better. We don't have to tell the police everything, especially since you don't actually have a PI license. Petino knows you're on the Heavenly Dips payroll. He knows that I am working for Max Angel and probably assumes I got you the job. That won't strike them as odd. They don't know the reason Max hired you. Besides, why should they care? Any information I get, they get."

I didn't argue. "What else did you do today?"

"Talked to more of Jonas's friends. That kid I mentioned, Trent Barlow, hasn't been seen lately either. It would be great news to hear that the two of them are off on a binge."

"Has it happened before?"

"Not the two of them together, but each separately. It

seems logical that eventually they would join forces."

I agreed. "Should I ask around about Trent?"

Andy didn't pause before he said no. "We don't want you asking too many questions."

"Do you have a picture of him? I could keep an eye out for him at the store."

"I can't get any information on him let alone a picture. He went to school in Ohio, so he doesn't show up in Jonas's yearbooks. Just make a note if anyone mentions him like you would about any of Jonas's friends. He has a lot of them, some unsavory. He can cross all sorts of social barriers and fit in. A great skill if he puts it to better use." His tone suggested he found that unlikely. "How was your day?"

"Big Al doesn't like me," I spoke in a tone familiar to parents of three-year-olds worldwide.

"Why?" Andy replied in the tone used by those same parents.

I filled Andy in on what Ed had told me. "Ed has turned out to be my friend. Of course, I feign incredible interest in the ways of Heavenly Dips. Tonight, I asked him for an in-depth tour of the freezer, and he was ecstatic. Anyway, we spent enough time together today that his lips loosened up so he provided some dirt on Big Al."

Ed told me and I told Andy.

"Maybe we should pull you out."

"Nah. Big Al isn't dangerous."

"You don't know that. We don't know what happened to Jonas. What if Big Al is lying to Max? What if Big Al did harm Jonas? What if he figures out that you are there for information about Jonas's disappearance? You should quit."

I couldn't believe that the following words came out of my mouth, but I heard them. "No. Not now. Not after I finally came up with something."

Andy considered his options while I considered crawling into the air-conditioning vent. "I'll let Max know what you heard about Big Al's feelings towards you." I noticed the familiar way Andy used the name Max as if he had a new best friend. "Let me know whatever you hear about any financial irregularities but don't push. Don't make anyone suspicious about why you are working there. Promise?"

I promised but Andy remained unconvinced that staying at Heavenly Dips was my best choice. "If Big Al makes one bad move, you're outta there."

I nodded my agreement but changed the subject. "So what else did you do today?"

"I talked to your friend, Hilde," Andy offered.

"Hilde? How did you find Hilde?"

"I went to the door and knocked."

"Very funny."

Andy ignored my sarcasm. "I found her a bit weird, kind of shy. There's something odd about her."

"Really? I hadn't noticed."

Again, Andy ignored my sarcasm. "I saw her at her parents' house. They have a big oceanfront place in Mantoloking. I didn't get inside. Her mother opened the door but instructed me to wait on the porch and sent Hilde out. She was nervous talking to me. Almost scared. Her behavior broadcast that she was hiding something."

"What?"

"I have no idea. She was hiding it." He paused to give me time to sneer and then continued. "She had a lot of little stories about Jonas. I wondered if she heard them legitimately. By that I mean, I wonder if Jonas told her—or if she knew a bit more about Jonas than he realized. Something about her is just a little bit off. I can't put my finger on it. But one thing I know for sure. She hates Big Al. She thinks he's stealing from the store, working the register more than he has to because he doesn't ring up all the sales. She says that Jonas knew and told her."

"You don't seem convinced," I said.

"She couldn't remember when he told her or produce a credible explanation as to why Jonas confided in her. I got the feeling she wanted me to believe she was closer to Jonas than anyone realized. When I pressed, she finally claimed that Jonas told her because he hoped she would keep an eye on Big Al."

"He asked her to do that?"

"That's her story."

"So maybe she believes she is close to Jonas. Maybe he leads her on to recruit her to spy on Big Al. From what we know of Jonas he wouldn't be above doing something like that."

"Well, she's not as naive as you think she is. When it comes to Big Al, and even Ed, she is downright malicious."

"About Ed?" I knew she wasn't Ed's biggest fan but malicious? "What's her gripe with him?"

"She thinks he sucks up to Big Al. She resents that he acts like such a company man, as if he has a real career at Heavenly Dips as if he's more important than everyone else."

"He is an Angel. I mean by rank, not by bloodline. " I defended the Heavenly Dips hierarchy.

Andy glanced at me with a wry expression but ignored my comment. "Hilde thinks Ed is jealous of Jonas."

That I could agree with.

Andy screwed up his features and shook his head in amazement. "I thought she was kind of sweet and pretty until she started talking about Big Al and Ed."

"You think she's pretty?" This was a man who found me pretty. I was concerned about his grading scale.

"Yeah. You don't?"

"I don't buy that geek thing she does. With the heavy glasses, the nose ring, and the chopped hair."

"That must be her work image. Tonight she had on white pants and a navy striped shirt like a French sailor."

"Hilde?"

"Yeah. And her hair was nice. Curly and soft."

"Hilde?"

“Yeah.”

“Hilde Bossick?”

“Yes. Hilde Bossick.” He grew impatient.

“Are you sure you weren’t talking to her twin?”

“I made an appointment to see Hilde. When I arrived I asked for Hilde. Her mother seemed to think she was Hilde. No one said a thing about a twin.”

I shook my head. I wasn’t convinced. What was Hilde trying to pull?

Andy didn’t seem concerned. “Don’t read too much into her appearance. Maybe she just doesn’t want to fight the battle with her parents, so she dresses like a little angel at home and a little hellion outside.”

I shrugged. Maybe. I wasn’t so much worried about Hilde as I was about the air-conditioning in Andy’s car. “Are you sure this thing is on high?”

CHAPTER 26

I couldn't believe I was still working at Heavenly Dips. I couldn't believe I had offered to continue working at Heavenly Dips. My third day felt like my third week. Who was I kidding? It felt like my third month.

No one had heard from Jonas Angel. He'd gone missing for longer periods but never without his car. Not that anyone at the Heavenly Dips stand in Seaside Heights was worried about him. Aside from the occasions I brought up his name, Jonas Angel was never mentioned. Even basing my calculation on the minimum wage, any cost-benefit analysis would show my tenure as a Little Dipper wasn't worth the effort.

Nonetheless, I was the one who volunteered to stay in order to make friends at work—and use them. Okay, Andy suggested the approach and he didn't actually say use them. He suggested that if I couldn't wheedle information out of them during my shift I should try getting involved in the social life of my coworkers.

I targeted Ed first. I convinced my co-worker that we had a chance of earning a reward for locating Jonas. He wasn't particularly interested in the cash which was good because, as far as I knew, there wasn't any. I never actually claimed there was. I merely persuaded Ed that the person who found Jonas would certainly win Maxwell Angel's favor and that couldn't hurt an angel's career. Once that idea was on the table, Ed was in.

My plan was simple. Since Ed had heard Jonas talk about his social life, he could identify spots that Jonas might visit, places unknown to Jonas's family. We could visit them and from that point just wing it. Of course, I laid out this plan before I realized Ed would come up with a long list of strip clubs.

"You're going where?" Andy sounded shocked when I called to tell him about my plans for the evening.

"You told me to make friends."

"Can't you make friends riding the merry-go-round or eating pizza at Klee's?"

I ignored his suggestions. "Have you been to any of these places?" I named a couple of the bars Ed mentioned.

Andy hadn't been to any, or so he claimed.

"Ed said Jonas used to frequent those spots. He's taking me. "

"Why?"

"For the reward."

"What reward? There's no reward."

"Yes, but Ed doesn't know that."

"Why are you going to a strip club?"

I explained to Andy one more time that Ed claimed these were places Jonas frequented.

"Why don't you wait until later when I can go with you?"

"Because I am undercover, as you keep telling me."

"But you can't go alone."

"I'm not going alone. I'm going with Ed. I'll call you for a ride home. You're going home eventually, right?"

He ignored my question. "What are you wearing?"

"Oddly enough strip clubs are one of the few places my Heavenly Dips angel gown might fit in. I'll take off the halo and pick up a pair of flip-flops and I'll blend."

"Why would you want to fit in?" Andy sounded exasperated.

I reworded my thought. "I don't want to be conspicuous. How much can I stand out in a shadowy bar?"

"You complain that dress glows in the dark. Everyone will think you're a working girl."

"Working at what? Andy, why are you worried? Men don't go to bars to meet women like me. And besides, I'll be with Ed."

Andy protested in what I could only describe as a petulant tone. "If you wanted to go to a strip club, I could have taken you."

"Andy, I don't want to go to a strip club. I am going as part of my undercover work. What are you afraid of? That I'll decide to quit the exciting world of ice cream and take a job on the pole. I know you think I'm hot—that's one of the things I love about you—but even if I wanted a career as an exotic dancer, no respectable strip joint would hire me."

He didn't answer. "What am I supposed to do tonight?"

"I thought you were busy."

"Yeah, early on." He sulked.

"You have leads to follow. Follow them. I'll call you later to catch a ride."

"OK," he answered grudgingly. "Just don't let them take you to that dump, Club Velvette."

CHAPTER 27

By the time we set out for Club Velvette, five of Ed's ten roommates had joined the search party. Like clowns from a circus car, they tumbled out of their two-bedroom house and piled into two vehicles. Ed and I rode with a Rutgers student named Sean in a ten-year-old compact that he insisted was more reliable than Ed's vehicle. Sean's explanation that he had bought it with last summer's earnings suggested that he stood on the same rung of the corporate ladder that I did. His car barely ran.

After a stop at the ATM—my ATM—we chugged over the bridge towards Club Velvette, a spot Andy described as a dump and our navigator, Ed, described as somewhere north of Toms River. The guys promised me that I would have a great time even if I was straight. "It's like any strip joint," Sean assured me.

I did not admit that I was a first-time visitor not only to Club Velvette but to any strip club.

The parking lot at Club Velvette was as rough as I expected the bar to be but not as rough as the guy at the entrance. He sneered at us as if he were the doorman at Studio 54 in the 1970s and we were not Liza Minnelli, Andy Warhol, or the Rolling Stones. With a great show of reluctance, he let us pass into a red velvet box. There two brawny guys in clothes purchased during the Ford Administration stopped our progress. When I produced the ID the bouncer required, I kept my license, and my birth date, out of Ed's sight. The guy grimaced as he studied my license and then me. "Whoa. You oughta get a new picture." I thanked him for his concern and followed Ed and his friends into the bar.

Nervous that I would be the only female customer, I surveyed the entire room and found I wasn't. I spotted three couples with female components. Two were comprised of a man and a woman. The third consisted of two women. Having confirmed that I wasn't the only female—make that the only fully attired female—I relaxed. I caught up with the guys who were trying to find seats together at the bar that wrapped around the long, brashly lit stage, an oasis of light in the center of the narrow room that was dismal, dark, and devoid of velvet. The interior was all veneer and vinyl accented with splashes of duct tape. The floors were carpeted, but only if you used the term loosely. The cement felt hard through the thin weave.

If the clientele minded the lack of decorating acumen, their disappointment was not evident on their faces. The bar was lined with males of all varieties, some young, some old, some rich, some poor, some attractive, some not so attractive. Those who didn't have their eyes fixed on the redhead wrapped around a pole on the elevated runway were busy with dancers mingling in their midst.

Disappointed that they couldn't find seven seats together at the bar, Ed and his roommates decided on a high table nearby.

"The girls come around to the tables too." Sean leaned close to reassure me. It wasn't as if he wanted to lean close. He had to lean in to be heard over Gloria Gaynor's pulsating proclamation that she would survive.

I couldn't come up with a response. So, I pulled out money and told him to get the first round. He glanced at the bills and sneered. I gave him two more. He smirked. I gave him two more. He headed for the bar with my order: bottled soda. If soda came in a glass, bottled beer. The key word was bottle. Posh was not a term that would be applied to Club Velvette. Neither was hygienic.

The guys watched the show, I watched the crowd, and Ed watched the table. I appeared more comfortable than

Ed. “I thought you had been here before?”

“Sure. Well, not really. Not actually here.”

“But other strip clubs?”

“Not like this.”

"This?”

“Where people are like all naked and all. You know I’m only twenty-one.”

I shook my head. Ed had misled me. “I counted on you to know the ropes. If we want that reward, you have to get used to this. We’re never going to find anything out if you keep staring at the table. Do you recognize anyone? What about the girl on the stage?”

Ed glanced at the dancer and shook his head. He didn’t recognize the redhead or Bambi or Crystal or Amber who one-by-one followed her onto the stage to boogie to the beat of disco classics released before the oldest of the girls was born. He didn’t know anyone in the audience either.

“Did Jonas ever mention the names of any dancers or anyone he met at these places?”

“I’m sure he did. He liked to brag but I don’t remember the names. I never thought there could be money in listening to his bragging. I mean braggadocio.”

A woman came onto the stage dressed in gold if wearing a G string can be considered dressed. She danced to Maniac if not with skill at least with enthusiasm.

“Why do guys like this stuff?” I shook my head.

Ed didn’t answer. He simply turned his eyes towards the woman who executed a split while hanging upside down. Watching her gyrate in a fashion that clearly appealed to the patrons, Ed, at last, became enthralled by the entertainment.

Sean slipped a warm can of Coke in front of me. I was still trying to sanitize the top with a Heavenly Dips napkin when he stuck an elbow in my ribs. “I didn’t think Ed would ever notice that there were naked women around here. But these girls aren’t his type. Any guy who could spend all his time pining for Schyler Devereaux isn’t interested in an exotic dancer." He shook his head. "Any guy who would spend all his time pining for Schyler Devereaux probably isn't interested in sex."

"Ed likes Schyler?"

Sean whistled. "He knows he's not in her league, which in my opinion is the good news. But the guy is smitten." He snickered, not a kind sound. "He doesn't want anyone to know. From what I hear of that Jonas dude, he would go ballistic but not because he likes Schyler so much. He just wouldn't want Ed thinking he was in the same league."

"I didn't know you knew Jonas."

Sean shook his head. "I have never even seen the guy, but Ed talks. I fill in the blanks. Trust me, I am right on this one."

What kind of undercover agent was I? I never picked up on Ed's feelings for Schyler. Ed, the coworker I knew best. Allegedly.

Having finished her act, Crystal was trying to mingle with Ed and getting nowhere. He may have grown more comfortable with watching scantily clad women on a stage, but having a half-naked woman next to him was a step he was not prepared for. Ed was trying hard to focus on the small area of shiny lavender material that Crystal wore for mingling. Her outfit was a gown in the sense that a postage stamp is a quilt.

I pulled a twenty out of my pocket and caught Crystal's eye. "Can I talk to you for a minute?" I held out the bill and Crystal lost interest in Ed. Immediately. She rubbed her less-than-ample breasts against my arm. I suspected she was telling me to slip the twenty between them. So, I did. After that, I had a tough time convincing her that I only wanted to talk.

"You know, Crystal, those are lovely but I have a set of my own. What I'm seeking in a relationship is what I don't have as part of my own anatomy."

Crystal shrugged and pulled a lavender satin robe around

her—at least as far as she could. "Suit yourself. What do you want?"

I told her we were Jonas Angel's friends. "We're trying to find him. It's been in the news. He's missing. Has anyone been in to ask about him?"

"No. Why would they?"

"You know Jonas?"

"Sure." She tried leaning close once more. Was it force of habit?

"You know you don't have to do that. Really."

She backed off. "The Heavenly Dips kid. I knew him. Real charmer. Thinks he can get away without a cash investment. I don't think he's as charming as he does."

"Did he get in trouble here?"

She didn't answer.

"Like with a bouncer?"

"Nah, he never did nothing out of line. The girls didn't like him much 'cause he was cheap. 'Cept for Randi. You could ask her about him. She comes on next. After that she'll be on the floor."

"Can you send her over?"

The woman glanced at my pocket. Twenty bucks merited a little conversation but wouldn't get a referral. I didn't figure the referral was worth another twenty. I gave Crystal a ten and she seemed satisfied if not happy. "I'll tell her." She leaned forward so her breasts were brushing my arm. "I could spend time with you until she comes out."

"Thanks. I'm fine."

Luckily, the DJ picked that moment to announce Randi's appearance. Randi was a long, extremely lean woman in her twenties with purple spikes on her head that, although short for hair, were long for spikes. Randi had a little talent, with the emphasis on little. I surveyed the audience. No one seemed to mind. Not the loners. Not the frat boys. Not Andy. Andy?

Andy had positioned himself across the bar from our

table. His eyes were riveted by Randi but his attention was focused on me. I felt it. Eventually, he let his eyes meet mine to show me that finding me at the one spot he advised me to avoid amused him. Beside me, Ed didn't notice a thing except Randi.

As Crystal had promised, Randi came to our table after stopping to wrap a small portion of herself in a dressing gown with a total length of about sixteen inches. I didn't think of her as Jonas Angel's type but if this investigation taught me anything, it taught me that everyone was Jonas's type. "I heard you were asking about the Angel kid. He's not here. He hasn't been here in a couple of weeks. I think he got religion."

"Religion?"

"Well, not real religion but something happened. I used to see him sometimes, you know, when I wasn't working. The last time I saw him, he didn't even come to watch me dance. He met me after work. He was different. He hasn't been back here since."

I slipped the last of my twenties into Crystal's robe. Her hands were fast. I yelped at her touch. "Not me. There's a guy over there in khaki pants and a yellow shirt with the sleeves rolled up. Go tell him what we were talking about. That's important, okay? Tell him I sent you."

"Whatever turns you two on."

I watched out of the corner of my eye as the woman approached Andy. He didn't see her coming and jumped when she ran an arm over his shoulder. A few seconds later Andy peeked around her maroon spikes. I raised my Coke can in a toast. "Come on, boys. It's time to get out of here." Only Ed and I stood up. The guys from the other car wanted to stay and Sean decided to travel with them. He threw Ed his keys. I didn't know if Ed's lack of coordination or newfound interest in the dance caused him to miss the catch. I picked the heavy key ring off the table and, thanking Sean, guided Ed to the exit.

He wanted to drive me home, but I told him that I'd promised to give my imaginary friend, Stacy, a call although when speaking to Ed I once again left out the part about her being imaginary. "Drop me at the next Wawa," I asked before we got back to Seaside Heights. His expression made me explain. "Stacy and I use it as a meeting place."

Ed still seemed perplexed but he pulled into the parking lot. I waved good-bye to him and called Andy. He had parted from Randi but was on his way to an appointment. "Take this number and ask for Jim. He'll pick you up and take you home." Jim did, after we stopped at another ATM so it could fork over a week's pay. Unless Maxwell Angel was willing to advance expense money, I couldn't afford to make friends at work.

CHAPTER 28

I didn't hear Andy come home but the ringing of his cell phone woke me before the sun rose high in the sky. Andy knocked his phone to the floor, retrieved it, and grumbled "hello." He swung his feet over the edge of the V-berth and leaned forward as he listened. I rolled close and waited for the bad news. No one calls that early to tell you anything good.

I felt Andy's body slump as he listened. "Oh God, Max, I am so sorry. Sure. Sure. Right away. Sure."

Andy didn't have to tell me, I knew. I stroked his back as he sat silently for a few minutes before speaking. "I've got to go. They found him."

A battered body, believed to be that of Jonas Angel, had been located two miles from his Porsche on the same dirt road. Although the cause of death could not be confirmed until the autopsy was finalized, the assumption was that he had been beaten to death. The police did not know, or would not say, if he had been killed in that spot or dumped there. Jonas had been found not by a search party but by a passer-by who had walked from his car into the woods to relieve himself.

"I didn't know what to say to Max. He's sort of a blowhard but he loves his family, especially that wild boy." Andy took a deep breath. I reached over and grasped his hand. He squeezed hard. "I've got to go. I'll leave cab money for you to get to Seaside Heights. Get to work early and watch how everyone reacts. Let them tell you the news. Pretend you didn't know." He planted a light kiss on my forehead and slid out of bed. He threw on his clothes and didn't speak until, as he climbed up the companionway ladder I heard him mutter, “I hate my job.” Andy and I had one thing in common.

Andy had left me more money to get to work than I would earn that day, but making a profit wasn’t my goal. I grabbed my clammy angel gown and was forcing myself to pull it over my head when I heard a male voice calling Andy’s name. I peeked out the port. The visitor’s long, languid strides across the lawn identified him. The visitor was no visitor. He was Oliver Wilder, Andy’s longtime friend, and our host. I rushed to greet him. Oliver lifted me off the deck and deposited me on the dock. He held me at arm’s length. “Usually, I am wearing the worst outfit. What’s with the Moby grape attire? You know your dress is a little damp.”

I explained that I hadn’t gotten the angel gown onto the clothesline until almost midnight the night before.

“Why did you hang your laundry outside? Why didn’t you use the dryer?”

I broke the news that Andy and I hadn’t been inside the house yet. “Oops.” His hand went to his pocket and extracted a clump of keys. “I guess this is a bit heavier than it should be. I didn’t mean to take the extra set of keys with me. Sorry.”

“Andy and I were comfortable on the boat.” I almost said perfectly comfortable but that would have been a lie.

“I have a cell phone. I should have called or at least I shouldn’t have turned it off. But, I’m not sure you could have reached me out in the wilderness. I have been up north in Canada for a romantic interlude with a woman who is still speaking to me after almost three weeks alone.”

“Oliver, I’m proud of you. Can we go inside where there’s air-conditioning and talk about the remarkable, make that miraculous, improvement in one of the most abysmal love lives on record?”

Oliver’s arrival relieved all of my physical discomforts. While my angel gown tumbled in the dryer, I, in one of

Oliver's Miami Dolphin jerseys, lounged on his leather sofa and cooled off courtesy of his central air that had been humming tantalizingly the entire time Andy and I had been locked out. I cradled the remote control in my hands and, starting with Oliver's default selection ESPN2, ran through hundreds of selections before I found the local channel. I waited for news of Jonas's death. When the story came on the segment was brief, still in the category of breaking news. Reporters were pictured in front of the Heavenly Dips offices and a large Victorian house that I assumed belonged to Maxwell and Amanda Angel. The press knew less than I did about Jonas's death.

"You should have just broken into the house. I assume Andy knows how." Oliver chuckled.

"He worked on getting in but he didn't want to do any damage, or summon the police."

"Staying outside was the crime. I left food, drink and look," Oliver pointed to a garish vase of dried-up flowers. "I even left fresh flowers."

"In the Dolphins' colors."

"Actually they are the colors of the car dealership. I got the flowers as a thank you for buying my car. I love the car. Wait until you see it." Oliver flopped into an oversized baseball glove/chair that epitomized his decorating style. "I hate to think of you sitting out there hot and dirty and bored. You should have broken a window to get in. After all, the cops know you around here." He snickered and then checked my expression. "Isn't that funny yet?" He referred to my decidedly negative experience with Detective Petino on LBI several months earlier.

"It's getting there, but not quite." I explained my job, and my outfit, as I drank a Coke from the case that Oliver had stocked for my morning beverage. What had been fresh fruit and baked goods had long since passed their prime. Oliver pulled a box of Pop Tarts out of the cabinets and made breakfast.

"How long did it take you to get here from Antigua?"

"We set out in early May. We meandered up the intercostal waterway and got here about a week ago. We'd barely seen anyone when the Angel case fell into Andy's lap. Speaking of which, I need to get to my job. I'm reluctant to ask a man who just drove home from Newfoundland, but could you give me a ride?"

"You can see my new car!"

Oliver had the engine running when I reached the driveway. "Isn't it great? I saw it on the highway and just had to have it. I didn't need a new car but I bought it. This is a standard color."

I understood. The tone was almost a perfect match to the standard orange of the Miami Dolphins, the football team Oliver loved most, the football team whose colors Oliver had used when selecting furniture for the interior and paint for the exterior of his house. No other residents of his street had taken such care in color-coordinating their home and car. I could only imagine what the neighbors were saying about Oliver's latest decorating effort.

Oliver hit a button and music filled the car. Just in case I had been lulled into a sense of well-being by the air-conditioning, Martha and the Vandellas sang "Heat Wave" for the thousandth time that summer.

CHAPTER 29

The press arrived at work before I did. Not a huge number or the A-team as before. I knew from the morning broadcasts I'd caught at Oliver's that the bigwigs were at the police station and the Angel home, along with their cameras. I would have to remain alert but I saw no imminent danger of an unplanned media appearance.

"Did you hear about Jonas?" Ed didn't bother with hello or with taking his head out of the display case. He yelled his question from the vicinity of the Taurus Tofu Temptation.

"What?"

"They found his body." Assuming Ed was not aroused by the cone he was scooping, he must have been excited by the news about Jonas. He barely noticed the loud thump when his skull caught the metal edge of the glass case. "You didn't know?" A broad smile accessorized his question although I'd heard the impact five feet away.

I shook my head. I had less difficulty delivering nonverbal lies.

"The story made the news on every station. I didn't see my interview used yet but I bet I get on. We haven't had any television crews this morning but I hope they come." He handed the cone to a teen-ager and turned to serve her friend, a regular customer that I feared had an addiction to Marshmallow Cloud. When he finished, his eyes were still bright. "What do you think?"

"I think it's tragic that a twenty-two-year-old kid is dead. What do you think happened?"

Ed handled the register before answering. "Schyler caught him with another girl and finally gave him what he deserved. He crossed Lynyrd in a drug deal. He picked up the wrong hitchhiker. He screwed with some tough guy's woman. He sold bad drugs and made someone mad. That's the thing about Jonas. He annoyed enough people that anyone could have done the deed." I could tell Ed was calming down when he dropped a few GMAT words into the mix. "Allow me a few more minutes to cogitate and I'll produce a myriad of scenarios. I mean even I hated him. Of course, I won't divulge that on TV."

"Don't kid, Ed. This is serious. You don't seem to get that. I didn't see you have much of a reaction, certainly not a genuine one, to his death. You knew Jonas. You worked with him."

"He didn't give a damn about me. Why should I care about him?"

I spoke from the heart. "Because he was a human being. He had a family, including a father you idolize, that loved him. Someone took his life. Like him or not, I thought you would have more of a reaction."

"No, you think I should have more of a reaction. I hear it in your voice. You want a reaction, talk to Hilde."

"Hilde?"

"Yeah. She called in sick today. Some coincidence. She's not sick. She's in mourning. You know she's nuts about Jonas Angel."

Or just nuts. "She doesn't speak to me at all. I doubt she would talk to me about Jonas."

"She was never nice to any woman who worked here. Notice she doesn't talk to Sharmaine. She sees all women as competition for Jonas."

"For Jonas? Me? Competition? For a guy I never met?"

"But if you had, he would have worked his charm on you."

I shook my head. "I'm too old."

Now it was Ed's turn to shake his head. "No one was too old. You must have heard how he was. He flirted with everyone. He even flirted with me. I mean he was straight and all, but he just had to win everyone over. Everyone had to buy into the Jonas Angel myth. And poor Hilde bought in."

"So Hilde isn't nuts to have a crush on him if he hit on her."

"But he didn't hit on her. He charmed her. There is a big difference." Ed grew thoughtful. "He did hit on her twin. Hilde has a twin, Heidi. She worked here for a few weeks substituting for Hilde. Heidi resembles, closely resembles, Hilde but she's prettier, smarter, more personable. Big Al hired her as a special favor to Hilde. Hilde was taking a class or something and she was afraid of losing her job. She asked if her sister could sub for her. Heidi was a good worker. Quick learner. I liked her. I mean I try to initiate interactions with Hilde but I don't think that her elevator goes to even the penultimate floor, let alone to the top floor."

That was obvious, although not particularly clear. "Hilde is a little on the eccentric side."

Big Al called from the back. "Stop yer yapping up there. We're gonna be mobbed today. Word's out. Jonas bought it. They found him. Dead." Big Al emerged in a white short-sleeved shirt with gold wings and Big Al embroidered on the pocket and a bright blue tie with the Heavenly Dips badge he was so proud of clipped front and center. His comb-over was well combed-over and, if I weren't mistaken, I smelled cologne. Big Al was ready for his close-up. "I'm going to meet the press." He smoothed the tie that had seen its heyday at least a decade earlier and pasted a somber expression on his face. Then he did what he criticized me for: he slipped under the counter.

When he'd gone I reopened the topic of Hilde with Ed. "So, Ed, tell me about Hilde. She really is as weird as she seems, right?"

"Yeah." He smirked. He continued as he moved a drum of Pisces Pistachio into the display case. "She's a little unusual." His tone suggested he was making one of the great understatements of all time. "So, anyway, Jonas lays his charm on her and she's hooked. Last summer she thinks he loves her. When he comes to the store she thinks he's coming to see her. She thinks he's too shy to tell her. I told her there was nothing shy about Jonas, but she insisted that he was shy with her because she was different. She thought he really cared for her."

"She told you this?"

"She said a few things. I kind of, like, figured out the rest."

I knew what Ed meant. He made up the story, but that didn't mean it wasn't true. "Did Jonas know how she felt?"

"The boy didn't confide in me, you know, but I think he understood. Not that he cared. He went after Heidi when she showed up. Then, after his fling with Heidi was over, he still played the charming routine with Hilde. I found it kind of odd. Hilde grew calmer around him after he dated her sister. She was out of town, so I don't think she knew what happened with Heidi. If she did, I think she would have hated Jonas but she didn't. She believed that she and Jonas had a special connection. I didn't get it. Jonas was smart about those kinds of things. He was a lot more sophisticated than the average guy his age, for example, me."

"Why didn't you tell me this before?"

"That I'm not sophisticated?"

"That Hilde's twin had a thing with Jonas."

He shrugged. "The subject just never came up. Why do you care so much?"

I shrugged. "Just curious. What with the murder and all."

We shrugged in unison and went to work.

CHAPTER 30

I felt disgusted. Did all our customers wake up with a craving for Heavenly Dips? No. They woke up with a craving for tabloid news in their neighborhood. What I found even more worrisome than the surfeit of clientele, as Ed called our increased store traffic, was the press. Every time I thought the coast was clear of people with the power to put me on television or in the newspaper, another reporter would show up at the counter. I exhausted the list of tasks that would keep me out of sight. The display cases were full and the floor was spotless even though I dripped a bit of every serving on the floor simply so I could stoop to clean it up.

Ed, on the other hand, was in a great mood. He loved the media. "Would you please stop calling attention to us," I hissed in his ear as we juggled for scoop position in a drum of Venus de Vanilla. "If you keep cooperating they will never go away."

"I'm only providing the members of the fourth estate with what they need. They need quotes. They need photo ops. I can give them both."

When Sharmaine arrived to fill in for Hilde, she was as animated as Ed. "Do you believe the crowds? If Big Al had known killing Jonas would be this good for business, he would have offed him months ago." She grinned.

Since Sharmaine wasn't renowned for her sense of irony, I asked, "Do you think Big Al killed Jonas?"

Sharmaine whispered conspiratorially. "There were plenty of times Big Al probably would have loved to kill Jonas. They were mad at each other about something. A couple of weeks ago I heard Big Al telling Jonas to keep his nose out of his business. Do you think he could have done it?" She made no attempt to hide the excitement in her voice. Like Ed, she didn't seem particularly saddened by Jonas's death.

"Can't you think of anyone else who would have killed Jonas?"

At first Sharmaine was confused. I could see that her brain was in high gear. Indignation swept across her face. "No, why would I?" She turned to greet customers with a flounce of her halo that made it clear she would no longer be available for gossip. She didn't display her usual smile again until she glanced across the Boardwalk and spotted her beloved Lynyrd.

I had the distinct impression that Lynyrd had washed his hair and possibly shaved within the past twenty-four hours. Along with the three-day growth he had also lost the sneer. I had to admit it. Lynyrd looked almost cute. Okay, he looked cute. Especially since his bruises were clearing up.

Given the traffic at the stand, Sharmaine had no time to chat or to provide free ice cream. Lynyrd leaned on the railing across the Boardwalk and watched her for as long as it took to smoke a cigarette. She gazed longingly over the counter at him. He gazed longingly at the display cases. I felt more certain than ever that he was in it for the ice cream.

As I scooped for the masses, I felt down for several reasons. One, the reinforcements Big Al had called in had not yet arrived and my dipping hand was killing me. Two, Jonas was dead and I couldn't come up with any helpful information. Three, the threat of being included in a news photo wearing a halo still remained. My feeling of dread was justified when I noticed Bridget Simkus picking her way through the crowd. She would definitely target me. I had to escape.

"Sorry. I have one of those female emergencies." I yelled at Big Al as I ran out the back door. "I'm taking my break." As I stepped outside, I ran into backup, two college girls from the night shift, white wings, who did appear angelic in their gowns and halos. They could handle the gathering throngs.

I didn't go to the bench where Bridget Simkus found me earlier in the week. I headed in the opposite direction and didn't return to the Boardwalk until I estimated I'd passed the parameters set up by the press. Unable to resist the aromas, I bought a little refreshment from the sugar food group before I picked a spot to lay low until the reporters moved on. I found no seats facing the water, so I sat with my back to the ocean and settled in for a little people watching.

"So whatta ya think about the Angel kid buying it?" Lynyrd plopped on the bench and blew smoke at me and my funnel cake.

"I think I'll never have time to eat any free ice cream again and eating all day is the only thing that makes this job bearable."

"Yeah, Sharmaine likes that."

Sharmaine liked free ice cream all right but not eating it – she liked violating company policy by sneaking as much as she could to Lynyrd.

"So the place is crazy, eh? Do they know who killed him?"

"If they do, no one told me." I tried to find a section of dough that Lynyrd had not blown smoke on. I gave up.

Lynyrd wiped the sweat from his brow with his red Lynyrd Skynyrd t-shirt giving me the opportunity to view the serpent tattoo that wound from just above his navel over a few ribs before disappearing around his right side. "Do you have any ideas?"

I shrugged and played dumb. "I didn't know him. You did. What do you think?"

"Why would I know?" Lynyrd sounded more than a little defensive.

"Well, you were in the same line of business."

He appeared confused, but only for a few seconds. "Oh. That. I only do that to get money to take care of my family and get a decent place to live. We're living in a motel 'cause we can't come up with the deposit for an apartment. Once I have those kids in a decent place I can walk away from my sales job. It ain't like drugs are my career or nothing."

"But it was Jonas's?" I worked hard to keep my mind on Lynyrd's words and off the snakes, symbols, and mythical creatures tattooed on his hands and arms.

"Hell no." He hesitated. "You ain't a cop or nothing are you?"

"No. Why would you think that?"

Lynyrd shrugged. "I mean you just show up here. And you talk about Jonas who you say you never met. And now you ask if he made a career of drugs."

"I never met the kid. I'm just curious about him. That's all." I feigned annoyance. "You've got to admit that he is a hot topic of conversation today. I wonder why he was killed. Doing drugs is one way to get yourself murdered."

"Man, are you naive." Lynyrd had only scorn for my claim.

"Maybe so, but I just wondered about how much drug action Jonas was involved in." I was determined to get an answer to my question.

"Not much. Half the time he bought the stuff and gave it away. But lately I haven't seen him around. People were asking for him but he was pulling out."

Luckily, Lynyrd still didn't remember the night at Jenkinson's when I was one of those people asking for Jonas. "Why was he pulling out?"

"He didn't tell me no secrets, you know. I think something spooked him. He got real serious and then he just didn't show up around here so much."

"But he didn't say what was bothering him?" I realized I should be studying Lynyrd's expression but I couldn't tear my gaze away from the way his hand movements made the monster-like creature on his left forearm grow more threatening.

"I hardly ever talked to him. He was a creep. A rich, snotty creep. He didn't want nothing to do with me 'less he needed cash and pawned off some of those crap drugs he sold."

"The drugs he sold weren't any good?" I decided the creature on his arm was a dragon.

"There are drugs and there are drugs. I think some drugs are crap." Flames burst from the dragon's mouth.

"Why do you hate Jonas so much?" I watched the dragon breathe fire.

"Like I said, he was a creep. All handsome on the outside, you know, like a movie star or sumpthin. But inside, in here," Lynyrd laid his hand on my chest and held my gaze with an intensity I found surprising but not off-putting, "there was nothing inside that guy. A pretty face. That's all he was. A pretty face."

A pretty face. A perfect body. A winning smile. I made the list mentally and kept quiet. Why make Lynyrd hate Jonas more? "What did he actually do or say to make you hate him?"

Lynyrd removed his hand and shook his head in disgust. "He, like, thought that he was better than the rest of us. Just because he got all the breaks. Jonas didn't earn anything. He was just born into a rich family. I coulda been born rich. If I was lucky—which I certainly ain't."

"Did he say mean things to you?"

"Yeah, he thought we were all too dumb to know, but I knew. He would tell me that my girlfriend was a real fox but I knew what kind of broads he likes. My honey is not one of those blonde bitch goddesses he goes for, like that Schyler chick who trails him around. So yeah, he's mean. He sneers when he says my girlfriend is a fox. He knows that is a word I use. He would never say fox. When he says my girlfriend is a fox I know that he is really saying: your girlfriend is a loser and you are a loser and you always will be a loser and your kids will be losers and I, Jonas Angel, am not a loser. He acts nice but he is saying—and I know that he is saying—I owe him because his dad pays people like you and Sharmaine two crummy bucks over minimum wage and he knows that is the best we will ever do because we're losers." Lynyrd took a long, deep drag on his cigarette. "You know I'm feeling okay . . . almost good that he's dead. He got what he deserved."

Lynyrd felt good. I felt stunned. Sharmaine was making two bucks over minimum wage?

CHAPTER 31

Petino didn't come that day. Another policeman, young and not in uniform, commandeered Big Al's desk to interview each of us. The officer's crisp, nouvelle preppie appearance made his surroundings appear all the shabbier. The tattered corners of the old fashioned desk pad, rougher. The coffee stains on the cardboard insert, darker. For the first time, I noticed that the calendar with the water damaged photos of classic cars was three years out of date.

Thanks to the chanting of the Heavenly Angels choir I couldn't hear the conversations. Thanks to the big freezer that partially shielded the area, I could only steal an occasional glance. The white-winged backup scoopers looked angelic. I could determine by Ed's posture during his interview that he was using his best GMAT vocabulary. I could also determine from the cop's expression that he thought Ed was from Mars. Sharmaine seemed nervous. The planets above her head never stopped orbiting. Her wide brown eyes were at their widest giving her face a cartoonish naiveté. The cop didn't mind. I got the impression Sharmaine could have told him she'd planned and executed several murders and he would have thanked her for her honesty. He thought she was adorable. He did not think that I was adorable.

"Can you tell me where you were on Friday night?"

"On Friday night I had never heard of Jonas Angel."

"Just answer the question, Ma'am." The guy's flat tone and blank stare made me miss Petino's smirk.

"I can't remember where I was on Friday night."

"Try."

Remembering wasn't easy. Without the rhythm of

Monday through Friday in your life, all the days seem to blend together. I knew that Andy and I had been at Oliver's. "I was with a friend. I know that."

"Your friend's name."

I ignored his question. "I remember now. Friday was the night we went out to dinner at Kubel's in Barnegat Light and then to a movie in Manahawkin. I remember because I don't like to go to the movies on weekend nights because it gets too crowded."

"What movie did you see?"

That was no problem. He corrected me on the full title but my guess was close enough to satisfy him.

"And your friend's name."

"We went to the 7:30 show which I hate because there are just too many people. Lots of dates. Lots of kids. Teenagers, not little kids."

He wasn't interested. "I didn't catch your friend's name." The cop had perfected an intimidating stare. I was intimidated.

I glanced towards the front of the store. Couldn't this guy figure out that I didn't want to be overheard? I leaned forward and murmured, "Andy Beck."

At least the cop's expression changed. His eyes narrowed with suspicion. "I didn't get that."

I moved forward on the seat so that I could get closer to the cop's ear. Heaven forbid he should lean forward and help me. "Andy Beck."

"Lady . . ."

First ma'am, then lady. I did not like this kid. I heard the impatience in my voice. "May I have your pen?"

He gave it to me reluctantly. Actually I pulled it from his grasp. I wrote the eight letters on a napkin and handed it to him.

"I don't understand. Who is An . . . ?"

"Please." I cut him off with one word.

He stared at me but remained quiet. His face was

expressionless. I definitely missed Petino's smirk.

CHAPTER 32

The combination of a sunny day and a juicy scandal drew the weekend crowds to Heavenly Dips like flies to, well, like flies to Heavenly Dips. The workday flew by. I didn't even have time for a dip of Marshmallow Cloud with a Copernicus's Coconut chaser. Traffic at the counter was heavier than I had ever seen it.

Ed, Sharmaine, and I scooped with the part-time weekend workers many of whom could barely remember the flavors, and none of whom could remember Nirvana. Whoever came up with the idea of sticking wings on eight people and dropping them in a ten by twenty-foot space to dip ice cream had to be considered a genius—right up there with the folks responsible for New Coke, Nehru jackets, and the Edsel.

Big Al assigned himself the job of clearing makeshift shrines to Jonas from the front of the counter. My coworkers protested that removing the monuments made us appear callous, but Big Al claimed to be worried about customers lighting up like torches from an unexpected brush with a votive light. When assured that was improbable, he admitted that he had an ulterior motive. He wasn't willing to lose customers because they couldn't get to the counter through all the crap people left around for Jonas. Personally, I opposed the improvised memorials because I viewed them as a good marketing ploy. I suspected the sales director had dropped most of them off.

Big Al cut back on trips to the bank. When he wasn't removing tributes to Jonas, he handled the register, as I had noticed him do before in times of high traffic. Considering that he thought I was a plant, I didn't observe too closely but I wondered. Was he ringing up every sale? I tried to keep an eye on him but that surfeit of customers—Ed's description—kept arriving at the Pearly Gates and interfering with my surveillance efforts.

When I saw Karl Elkins headed towards my line, I felt a knot in my stomach. Although I had seen him at the boat, he had not seen me. I reassured myself that the man had no idea who I was, that he had no way of connecting me with Andy.

When Elkins reached the front of the line he spoke softly. "All these people are here because of the kid, eh?"

I smiled, nervously, and nodded.

"You probably think that's why I'm here. Trying to get gossip about the kid. I bet you get a lot of that. You probably don't know anything anyway, right?"

Again, I nodded.

"Did they give you a canned statement to make?"

I shook my head.

"Not that it matters. Like I said, that's not really why I am here. I have my own problems. I told you or maybe one of the others." He spoke apologetically as if he suspected he might be making a pest of himself. "My wife used to work for Heavenly Dips."

"Really?" I played dumb.

"Yeah." The abandoned husband appeared wistful. I had no reason to question his emotional display. "Do you know her?"

I shook my head, shrugged and frowned, a trifecta to ask who is she?

"Her name is Bunny Elkins." A single bead of perspiration slid south from his hairline.

"I never met her. I've only been here for a few days. When did she work here?"

"Not here. In the home office." Karl explained that his wife had recently left her job. "Since this is the flagship store, I thought she might feel sentimental what with the kid dying and all. I hoped she'd come by for ice cream."

I hoped he'd nab that drop of sweat headed for his chin. I

brushed my cheek but he didn't emulate my action. The drop reached the precipice that was his jaw.

"If she did drop by she didn't introduce herself. Maybe she talked to one of the other kids." Other kids? Was I seriously viewing myself as one of the kids? I corrected my statement. "You know, one of the other employees."

He went for a kicked-puppy-dog look. "She left me." The words knocked the droplet of sweat from his chin. It splattered leaving a dark circle on his pale blue t-shirt.

My relief that the flow of perspiration had ended occupied my thoughts so completely that I almost forgot to say that I was sorry. When I did, he responded in soft tones. "So am I. You know, before this news, before they found out what happened to Jonas Angel, when they thought he was missing, I actually worried that he and Bunny had run off together. She always talked about how she disliked him, but you know that line about protesting too much."

From what Andy said about Bunny's picture, I think it would have been Jonas who protested. I couldn't tell Elkins that, and not just to avoid hurting his feelings. He had no idea I knew anything about his beloved Bunny.

"Would you like to order?" I asked Elkins. The huffing and puffing of the woman behind him could be heard over the chanting of the heavenly choir.

Elkins's voice perked up as he ordered a dip of her favorite flavor: Solar Eclipse, vanilla with a chocolate swirl. Not to be confused with Cherubic Cherry, the flavor he claimed was her favorite on his earlier visit. I felt like lecturing him—if he had paid closer attention to his wife's preferences she might not have run away.

"If you see her, if she comes by, would you tell her that Karl misses her?"

I bobbed my head several times.

"Excuse me." The woman waiting behind Elkins didn't feel obliged to hide her annoyance, or her breasts, but that was a different issue.

Undisturbed, the grieving husband gazed into the sky over the ocean. I waited for his next declaration of love for his wife. Instead, he said, “It’s got to rain. This heat is getting to me. Do you think it will ever rain?”

He didn’t expect me to answer and I didn’t. I gestured towards the woman behind him. She stepped forward and Elkins wandered away, north on the Boardwalk.

“Sorry. He . . . I was . . . .” I decided I didn’t owe the cranky customer an explanation. “What can I get for you?”

“I’d like to taste Scorpio Strawberry.”

I gave her a tiny scoop on a cloud-shaped spoon. “No.” She pulled her features into an exaggerated sneer and made a great pretense of studying the array of flavors in the display case. “How about the Capricorn Coffee.”

Proud that I managed to suppress my impatient sigh, I pulled out another plastic spoon and dug out a generous taster scoop.

She pulled all the ice cream into her mouth and twirled it around like a 1789 Chateau Lafite. “No.” She screwed up her face as if to convince me that she was taking the selection process seriously. “I’m not sure what I want. What do you recommend?”

“Well . . . .” This was a first. Maybe I could put this job on my resume. Identified customer needs and recommended comprehensive solutions to meet dietary requirements. “Do you like nuts?”

She scrunched her nose and shook her head.

“Something fruity? Orion Orange?”

“Not a sorbet. I want ice cream.”

‘Mercury Mango Mix is an amusing little flavor. Creamy yet light, with an insouciant twist of citrus.”

The customer was not amused. “Let me taste it.” She did. And five more flavors. I didn’t expect her to order. Ever. She’d eaten a meal in samples. And for her I gave up the opportunity to learn why Bunny Elkins disliked Jonas Angel.

CHAPTER 33

The air-conditioner's cool discharge that I fanned towards myself was the only good news in Andy's car that evening. Andy related what was known about Jonas's death in a subdued, flat tone. "It was brutal, Meg. Max told me. We won't know the details until the autopsy results come in but he was beaten badly. We can only hope he was dead before most of the blows were delivered. Max can't bring himself to tell Amanda. 'Her beautiful baby.' He kept repeating that. Jonas was unrecognizable."

I envisioned Jonas's handsome face and imagined the hatred that compelled someone to destroy it. "Could Big Al have done a thing like that, just because of the money?"

"I can't say, but Max feels it's impossible. I told Max I wanted to pull you out of the store, but he would really like you to stay. He was impressed with the information you got about the money issues between Big Al and Jonas. I told Max that I could not answer for you. I am concerned about your safety. So is Max. He is having surveillance cameras put in the Seaside Heights store."

"So he'll be able to see who killed me? Like, maybe, Big Al."

"Max talked to Big Al, asked about some talk he heard, said someone told him that Big All didn't like you."

"Oh great. Now I get it. He thinks I'm a tattletale with a direct line to New Gretna. He'll feel sure I complained. Now I'm in real trouble."

"Don't worry. I thought the same thing but Max told Big Al that he'd better hope that you never find out and tell your father."

"I have an imaginary father?"

"Yes, and he and Max are very close. So you could imagine how embarrassed Max would be if word got back to your father, your imaginary father, that his management was giving you a hard time."

"So my dear pretend-dad got me this cushy job because Max knows him."

"Thinks the world of him."

"And this job is the best Max could do for the daughter of a guy he thinks the world of?"

Andy didn't argue.

"Shouldn't I have known this? What if I said something that contradicted this story?"

"You're trying to keep your connection a secret, along with the real reason you needed help."

"I needed help? Why?"

"I don't know. You choose. Max was far too discreet to tell Big Al the details."

I didn't have any response except an expression that conveyed confusion, doubt and more than a smidgeon of annoyance.

"By bringing the story of what he heard out in the open Max feels Big Al can't make a move towards you. The only person in that store that you and I are worried about is Big Al. Max isn't. He is convinced Big Al couldn't have hurt Jonas. He doesn't think he is capable of hurting you. He's known that man for twenty-five years. That is a long time. Besides, Max told him about the cameras, so even if he were tempted to do anything, he won't. He'll know he's being filmed."

"Does Big Al think Max is installing cameras because he heard he was skimming?"

"No. Max told him that there were suspicions that an employee was stealing. Max will make Big Al think the two of them are on the same team although that is not true. I don't believe that Big Al is aware of every camera."

"What about my safety when I'm not at the store? Big Al

does leave the building."

"Yeah." Andy sounded pensive. "We have to talk about that." He stopped and turned to face me. "Max wants you to stay, but don't feel you need to do it for me. You could go away, maybe Philadelphia, stay with friends. This is no longer a case of chasing a missing playboy. This is murder."

"I'm not afraid, Andy. Do you think I need to be?"

He squeezed my hand. "No, but I worry. By the way," he marked the change of subject with a sly grin, "nice work today." His intonation told me my work was anything but good.

"What's the problem?"

"The cop sent to interview the people at the Seaside Heights store came back and reported that only one employee had acted suspiciously. Wanna guess who?"

I knew. "I didn't want to give your name aloud."

"I know. I took care of it."

"At least I had an alibi. Did everyone else have an alibi?"

"Of sorts. The police do not have a precise time of death. At this point, they are going on the assumption that he was attacked shortly after he was last seen. With the exception of Big Al, your colleagues are not suspects so the police only asked the question as a formality. Lynyrd is Sharmaine's alibi. Hilde says she was at home. Big Al and Ed worked until closing. With the exception of Big Al, I don't think the cops are going to check any of them out unless a new discovery points a finger in their direction." Andy pulled over to the curb. Why did he seem so happy to find a spot? We'd only driven for a few minutes. "It's a one-way street with the cops. I give them information. They don't reciprocate unless they have a motive or want to throw me a crumb to give me the illusion we're a team." He stopped talking but gave no indication he was going to explain our unscheduled stop.

"Where are we?" I knew we were on an east-west thoroughfare lined with neatly maintained houses with minimal landscaping and maximum cement between them and the street. I also knew that we were in front of a three-story building—clearly the most poorly maintained structure on the block. What I didn't know was why.

CHAPTER 34

"What is this?"

"This could be your new home."

"Why are we moving?" We both knew we were crowded on the boat, but now that Oliver was back we could move into the house.

I repeated my question, but Andy didn't answer. He came around the car, opened the door, and reached a hand in to help me out. He continued to hold my hand as he guided me up a metal staircase that climbed the side of the brick building. We stopped in front of a door made of plywood that couldn't resist an intrusion from Woody Woodpecker, let alone an intruder with malfeasance on his mind. "This will be replaced tomorrow." Andy put a key into the crusty gold lock, flung open the door with a flourish, and stepped aside to let me enter.

I stepped into a sea of gold. Not gold as in Fort Knox gold. Gold as in autumn harvest appliances of the 1960s gold. The color was ubiquitous, as Ed would be sure to say. It covered the floor, the walls, and the upholstery. Only the ceiling had been spared. "What is this place?'

"I told you. This could be your new home."

"You mean our new home." I grimaced at the cracked linoleum, sneered at the rickety furniture, and sniffed at the mildew. "I don't think so."

"You're undercover. Remember?"

"At work. I'm undercover at work, remember?"

"If you're going to make friends with the people at work, you can't simply vanish at night."

"But I make friends easily. When things slow down, I'll be able to get information during my shift."

Andy ignored me. "We were lucky to get this place so late in the season." Lucky wasn't the first word that came into my mind. "Especially since it's so close to the store. You can invite people back."

"But we don't want them to see us together."

"Actually . . . I won't be here. I'll be . . . well . . . Max . . . Maxwell Angel wants me to stay near his house."

"Which means?"

"In Mantoloking." Andy lowered his voice to name the town that as far as I knew did not have a plastic curtain or a plywood door within its borders. Andy was quick to explain. "Max was building a new house there. It's finished except for the kitchen. Given what's happened the Angels aren't planning on moving anytime soon, if ever. It's just sitting empty. Max thought I should use it but Mantoloking isn't really commuting distance for you." Andy sounded a little nervous. "You need to be near your job."

"Andy, people move to be near jobs where the benefits are great, the pay is high, and the bonus pushes it over six figures. People do not move to be closer to jobs that pay minimum wage. Excuse me, two bits over minimum wage."

"You need to be closer to make friends."

"By bringing them to this place? Who would want to come?" I leaned on the dining table. The top shifted six inches to the left.

Andy was talking as I regained my balance. "They're kids. Do you forget the places you stayed in when you were young?"

I tried to. Memories like those have a tendency to persist. The half-painted bedroom that matched mustard yellow with mint green. The hole in the ceiling that provided easy but unwanted access to the attic. The weak porch that required white-out painted caution signs on almost every board. I pulled away and plopped on the couch, a mistake I wasn't likely to make twice. I yelped, "Ouch" and rubbed my hip with exaggerated motions designed to elicit sympathy. "I hope you got a bargain on this place."

That was when Andy revealed that Maxwell Angel was paying.

I stared at him hard. "Maxwell Angel, the multi-millionaire ice cream mogul, is paying and this is the best he can do?"

"Well, it would hardly make sense for a Little Dipper to live in a beachfront mansion."

"It would make sense to me but what do I know? I'm just a Little Dipper." I rubbed my sore hip.

Andy paused and took his time surveying the apartment. "It's up to you."

I took in the details of the room. Plastic curtains from the fifties. Formica tables from the sixties. Vinyl couches from the seventies. As far as I could see no later decades were represented in the décor. I would have bet that even the room air-conditioner, which I was ecstatic to see, predated the Carter administration. "That work?"

Andy hit a button and the AC rumbled into action. It performed better than it looked or sounded. A 747 taxiing into the room could hardly have made more noise.

"This is all Angel agreed to pay for?"

"In a way. I asked for a car for you because the commute from LBI was becoming a problem. Max proposed a different solution. This place is what he came up with. He owns the building."

"He's a slumlord!"

"He's our boss right at the moment and the money he gives me will pay for whatever we decide to do next, so let's show a little respect."

"For 25¢ above minimum wage he doesn't buy my respect which is, by the way, for sale. Tell him to throw in a few more bucks and we can talk."

"Actually," Andy sounded more than a bit sheepish, "I'm billing him for your time and expenses."

"Beep." I mimicked a buzzer and raised a finger to call

for a ruling. "You're billing him for my time?"

"Sure."

"At what rate?"

"$50 per hour."

"And of that, I get . . . ?"

"Well, after I deduct administrative costs and overhead, you'll get about . . . $50 an hour."

I grew enthusiastic. "Why didn't you tell me?"

"I had to figure out how to bill your time since you're not licensed. By the time I figured how much it would be, I felt it would make a nice surprise if I gave it to you in a lump sum. Plus, I thought living on minimum wage would make it easier to stay in character."

"Andy, I'm not an actress. I don't need to starve to death in character."

"You won't starve and not just because you can eat all the ice cream you want." Andy pointed to a grocery bag on the kitchen counter. "Max sent them over. I put the perishables away but we can pack everything up be out of here in five minutes. You'll definitely want to take that thirty-pack of Coke, just in case you can't consume enough sugar at work to feed your habit." Very carefully he slipped onto the couch beside me and rocked me in his arms. He was apologetic. "I never would have gotten you involved in this if I'd known how it was going to turn out. When I first met Max, I never thought we were talking murder. I wouldn't even consider asking you to live here if I thought you were in any danger. But this is your decision, not mine."

"Jonas hadn't even visited the Seaside Heights store for a few days before he disappeared, so I don't feel menaced in any way."

"There is a question as to why he stayed away. We can't rule out that he developed a fear of Seaside Heights, although I think that is very unlikely."

"I'm the one with a fear of Seaside Heights."

"No, you're loving your stint in this town. You have a

fear of being seen in your uniform." His tone grew solemn. "I doubt that any of the people you work with will ever be considered suspects, but who knows what information they might have and not even know it. I swear that if any one of them is in anyway implicated, I will beg you to quit immediately. I can't disagree with Max that we just need someone inside, someone who hears gossip that no one will share with the cops, but your opinion is what counts."

I understood why Max Angel would want to intensify my involvement but Andy understood why I might want to extricate myself from the investigation. The choice was mine.

"I think it is safer that you do not live with me until we see how this plays out. And, not just so that no one at Heavenly Dips sees us together. I've talked to a lot of people, many of them shady. Since I can't be with you to protect you every minute, I honestly think you'll be safer here, away from me. Tomorrow we'll install a heavier door, a stronger lock, motion-sensitive lights and a very prominent surveillance camera aimed at the bottom of the stairs. It will appear to be for the business's protection."

"As we passed I thought I noticed that the business was actually an out of business."

"If you don't think this place is safe, you don't have to move in."

I thought the security was more than sufficient. It was the harvest gold that concerned me.

"When will I see you?"

"We'll work it out." Andy wrapped an arm around me and pulled me close. He kissed my forehead and reminded me that no one at Heavenly Dips should connect the two of us. "I can't live here but I'll keep an eye on you. But you do not have to do this."

"If I thought I was making minimum wage, believe me, I wouldn't. But I am a paid professional. Okay, a quasi-professional. All right, a faux-professional. Whatever. This is part of the job and I said I'd do the job."

"It won't be that bad. We'll have dates. Secret dates but dates. After we wrap this case up, we'll have plenty of time. Maybe we can even take next winter off." I didn't remind him that I was once again scheduled to start graduate school. "I have to admit that I have mixed feelings about having you live here but I do believe that when you are undercover . . ."

"Yeah. I get it."

Andy tried to be upbeat. "I put a couple of your things in the car. Just in case you wanted to test the place out. It's your call. I'll stay too. There are linens in the closet. And there's cable."

"Cable." I perked up. "Where's the remote?"

CHAPTER 35

"You look awful, like you were up all night." Ed's greeting, although not exactly diplomatic, was completely appropriate. "Your halo is crooked."

"I have my own place. Really close." I told Ed as if this explained my appearance. "It has cable and air-conditioning." Neither of which kept me up all night—that credit went to Andy—but both of which I found exciting. Since, unlike me, Ed had been living with all the modern conveniences I didn't expect him to appreciate my exhilaration. I was wrong.

We talked cable. We talked sleeping under the covers. We did not talk about Jonas. The lack of interest shocked me perhaps because I was older and closer to death, although I didn't exactly view my demise as imminent. Jonas hadn't even been buried but no one on staff appeared interested in talking about his murder. Ed wanted advice on getting to know the blonde from the arcade. Sharmaine wanted to wax poetic on Lynyrd. Big Al stayed on the phone, calling for backup to deal with the crowds. Only when Hilde came in did I think I had a chance at getting any info on Jonas.

I suspected Hilde might be in mourning. The girl was so uncommunicative to begin with, I found it hard to tell. But I swore she was even quieter than usual. So, clearly, any information wasn't going to come from her mouth. To me, that did not mean she couldn't be a source. Wherever she went, I would follow. Surveillance was the only viable investigative skill I had learned from Andy, although the way I did it very little skill was involved. I just watched and waited. I never knew what I might find out although I could generally guess: nothing. But why not give it a shot? I was not learning anything staying behind the counter at Heavenly Dips.

My first opportunity for surveillance came when Hilde took her break. I told Ed I had a female emergency and ignored his comment that I seemed to have a lot of them. Hilde went out the back door at 11:33. I went out the back door at 11:34. She had broken into a run down the alley. I waited on the small platform behind the store until I saw her white wings vanish around the corner. Then, with planets bobbing above my head and wings flapping on my back, I ran after her.

Wherever Hilde was going, she was in a hurry. I turned the corner just in time to see her head north up the Boardwalk. I ran up the ramp and tracked her by the dancing constellation above her dark hair. She was flying along the Boardwalk. I had failed to notice that my coworker was virtually all legs. Someone with my legs couldn't keep up with her wide strides. Even if someone with my legs was in shape. Which in my case, someone with my legs wasn't.

My breathing was labored by the time Hilde stopped at the end of the Boardwalk. I watched her as I caught my breath. She stood on a twenty by twenty platform that the maps posted along the Boardwalk identified as the Heiring Street stage. I hadn't been in town long enough to know what might be staged there. Hilde was poised on the edge as if she might jump. She could. No railing prevented her from leaping off the edge, but considering she was only four or five feet above the sand, I didn't worry.

Hilde gazed over the beach to the ocean. From the heaving of her shoulders, I could tell she was taking deep breaths that failed to calm her. I wanted to approach Hilde but how could I explain my presence? Then I remembered. I was on a female emergency. Maybe my fictional crisis was over.

"Hilde, I saw you when I came out of the bathroom." I found that a believable lie. After all, people in Heavenly

Dips uniforms weren't easy to miss and the public restroom was just across the Boardwalk. When she turned I saw that Hilde's face was covered with tears. "Are you okay?"

Hilde's nod didn't convince me. I pulled a Heavenly Dips napkin out of my apron pocket and passed it to her. One blow and her nose turned rough and red. Heavenly Dips had a larger budget for stuffed angels than for napkins.

"Is it Jonas?"

"Why would you say that?" The fear in her voice wasn't hard to detect.

"I don't . . . I mean a traumatic thing happened. I can't understand why everyone isn't crying.

"They were jealous. They didn't like him."

"Who?"

"Big Al. Ed. Sharmaine and she even likes that Lynyrd guy. Everyone, the weekend staff, the night crew, people who didn't really know him, they all resented him."

"But you liked him."

That statement brought tears to her eyes. "I guess I did—even though in a lot of ways he didn't deserve it. People are complex, aren't they?"

I shrugged. "I suppose. Hilde, what do you mean by 'he didn't deserve it'?"

She searched for a clean portion of the napkin. "I don't know. Everyone thought he was so cool and detached, and part of me thinks he was. But another part of me . . . ." She punctuated her thoughts with a sniffle. "Oh, I don't know what to think. And . . . ." She shook her head slowly and stopped talking.

"It's okay. You can talk. And . . . ." I prompted her.

"And?"

"You started to say something. You said 'and.'"

"I don't know." She tossed her head back so the constellation above it bobbed wildly. "This is silly. Jonas's murder has nothing to do with me. I should get back to the store."

"Are you okay to work?"

"Yes." She synchronized her nose blowing and nodding. "You go ahead." Her dark eyes grew icy. "And Meg, please don't tell anyone I'm upset."

I went back to work but not before I squeezed in two quick games of Skeeball and a call to Andy, actually Andy's voice mail. I described Hilde's behavior and let him draw his own conclusions.

When I got back traffic at the stand was heavy. Ed and Sharmaine were handling it— Ed with a forced grin. I didn't bother going to the back door. I slipped under the counter and found the next customer and returned to work beside Sharmaine. When Hilde returned I saw no sign of her earlier distress. She took a position on the other side of Sharmaine. Along with the backup Big Al called in, we lined up along the counter scooping. Every time I elbowed my way to a different vat of ice cream, I tried to ingratiate myself with the nearest dipper, "Wow, do you believe this? Did you know Jonas?" They all said, no, they didn't know Jonas; their tones said they didn't want to know me either.

The customers came in a steady stream, a steady stream in the sense that Niagara Falls is a steady stream. I had no illusions about why. "Do you think the Director of Sales killed Jonas?" I thought I'd made a joke.

"Why?" Ed's puzzled tone said he didn't have any idea what I was talking about or, despite his aspirations for an MBA, any proclivity for marketing.

"You know because business is so good."

"Oh yeah. Good one." Despite his efforts at vocabulary building, Ed wasn't much for repartee. God, I missed my friends.

CHAPTER 36

Sharmaine and I reached the time clock within seconds of each other. We were both waiting for the big hand to hit the twelve. "Got an exciting night planned?" Sharmaine didn't seem capable of sarcasm but I did detect doubt in her intonation.

"Yeah. I'm not sure whether to spend it with George Clooney, David Duchovney or Brad Pitt." Too old for Sharmaine, but I didn't know anyone younger.

"Why don't you have a boyfriend?" Sharmaine's tone made not having a boyfriend sound like a terminal condition.

I shrugged. "I'm between, if you know what I mean." The clock hit the hour and I plunged my card into the time clock.

"Tell me about it. I was between all of my adult life until I met Lynyrd."

I ignored her claim of adulthood. "You have big plans for tonight?"

Sharmaine shook her curls as she stamped the time on her card. "No. Lynyrd is usually busy on Saturday nights." She didn't add with his family. "But you know," her big round eyes grew rounder, "you should come out with Lynyrd and me some time. He has lots of friends."

Why did people always think that I was just like them? The sun would rise in the west before I would be interested in someone like Lynyrd. Yet Sharmaine couldn't see why I wouldn't love a guy just like the one she loved. I didn't argue the point. I agreed that maybe we could work out a date but, in the meantime, I was headed home. "My feet hurt."

Before I could invite her to drop by, she came up with

another idea. "Too much for a little dance machine?" Sharmaine mocked the name I'd given the arcade amusement. "Want to try it? It's truly awesome."

My feet were killing me yet I felt the urge to dance. Could I gamble no familiar faces would join the small crowd the game generally attracted? No one I knew had passed by yet. I took the chance and followed Sharmaine to the arcade.

Sharmaine went first. Her blonde curls bounced wildly about her head as she performed for a family of five and three women whose best dancing days appeared to be behind them. I peeked around her bobbing curls and read what the machine was telling her. The words were encouraging. She was Perfect. She was Great. She was occasionally Very Good but nothing less. The crowd murmured its approval but said nothing to Sharmaine when the heavy beat stopped and she collapsed against the rails designed to keep dancers from spinning out of control and into the arcade. After a minute's rest, she was ready to go again.

I took my position on the left pad and let Sharmaine take the right position. She made all the initial selections, dumbed down for my benefit. Before the entire word "ready" came out of her mouth, she began following the prompts. I fought to catch up with the heavy beat. The good news was that once my feet got going I forgot about the people on the Boardwalk. I forgot about my angel gown. I forgot about everything except the screen in front of me and my feet. I found it amazing how slowly communication passed between my brain and those feet.

Left. Right. Forward. Back. Forward to the right. Backward to the left. My eyes saw the instructions but by the time my feet caught up, the message had changed.

"Use a light touch," Sharmaine called without missing a beat. I tried to obey her instruction but I wasn't exactly the Brittany Spears of my generation. Wait, I think Brittany Spears was the Brittany Spears of my alleged generation.

"It's hard the first time." Sharmaine sounded sympathetic

as I leaned against the guard rail gasping.

"Yeah. I found that out." I leaned forward and wiped my brow with my skirt.

"But I think you were getting better. Want to try it again?"

"No way. You're on your own."

Sharmaine was dancing to a heavy rock beat when I heard the male voice. "You are very good at that."

I turned. I was, as usual, shocked by the head of a milquetoast on the body of a bully. Karl Elkins. "Thanks."

"I see you at Heavenly Dips. You wait on me."

"Leo Lime?" To dupe him into thinking I didn't remember his visit, I named a flavor he never ordered.

"No. Karl. Karl Elkins."

I laughed, a tiny insincere sounding laugh. "Leo Lime is a flavor, not a name. I thought you ordered Leo Lime. Sorry."

"Oh." I glimpsed no trace of a smile on his lips. "Do you remember me? My name is Karl. I told you my wife used to work for Heavenly Dips. In the corporate office." He didn't wait for an answer. He seized the opportunity to talk about Bunny. "She loved working for that company. She worked too hard, too much. Sometimes she didn't get home until almost midnight. I think she was more married to that job than to me." He swallowed hard and gazed over my shoulder. "Did you notice I said 'was'? I make myself do that, to force myself to accept that she left me."

"I'm very sorry."

"Did you know my wife? Her name was Bunny." He pulled his wallet out of his pocket and showed me her picture. Whoa. I saw why Andy hadn't worried that Jonas ran off with her. Not that Karl shouldn't have considered himself lucky to have her. But Jonas? No way. Bunny appeared to be a nice, middle-aged lady who didn't spend much time on her appearance. Unfortunately, in her late thirties, Bunny should not have looked like a nice middle-aged woman who didn't spend much time on her appearance.

"I've never been to Heavenly Dips headquarters. I've never even been to New Gretna. I'm not from New Jersey."

"Where are you from?"

"New York."

"New York? I was there the other day."

Yeah, you and ten million other people. I didn't say that. Karl was trying to make polite conversation. The least I could do was respond in a courteous fashion. Besides I wanted to hear more about why his wife disliked Jonas Angel. I tried to figure out how to return the conversation to the talk of his beloved Bunny, but I shouldn't have worried. Karl couldn't keep off the subject for more than a few seconds.

"My Bunny liked New York. She was a happy person." He used the back of his hand to wipe the perspiration from his brow. "She liked almost everyone."

"But not Jonas Angel." To stave off the frown forming on his brow I added, "You told me the other day that she didn't like him. Why not? He seemed to have everything."

"That was the problem. He had looks, money, and a cushy job. He didn't have to work for any of it."

I didn't need a PI's license to detect the resentment in Karl's voice.

"He won't get tossed aside by a heartless corporation after twenty years of faithful service the way I did."

I stuck to the topic of Jonas Angel. "You knew him?"

Karl said he had never met the kid but had heard plenty about him from his wife. "Bunny was Maxwell Angel's assistant. She likes and respects him. He's a self-made man, but Jonas, she has no time for Jonas. From the time he was sixteen, his father let him work in the business. Gave him every opportunity. Gave him everything. Fancy schools. Fancy clothes. Fancy cars. Spent more on golf clubs than some people spend on food in a year. And what does he give his father in return? Grief. He'd be okay for a while and then he would slip right back into his old ways. He wouldn't do what he was supposed to do or show up where he was supposed to be. It made my Bunny furious. She didn't understand how he could be such an ingrate. Like I said, she really likes the old man." He stopped and clenched his lips. "Liked. She liked him. I have to accept that she's gone. You know she didn't even tell me where she went. Bunny. She just left."

Given the pain in his face, I didn't think it would be appropriate to return yet again to talk of Jonas. I felt sure I'd have other shots at chatting up Karl. "Maybe I'll see you at the store. Leo Lime, right?"

He flashed a grin so shy I expected him to kick the Boardwalk and go 'Oh pshaw.' Instead, he said, "Maybe I'll try it."

"Great." I hoped Sharmaine caught my wave good-night. She seemed to wave back but her arms might just have been flailing around as she danced. I left Karl watching her, probably waiting for a chance to ask if she had seen his Bunny. I turned north and slammed into a four-foot-tall purple teddy bear that was heading south in the arms of a person who couldn't be seen behind his furry prize. Karl reached out a strong arm to steady me. I couldn't help noting that his weak personality did not match his strong physique.

CHAPTER 37

A cold drink, a warm shower, and a revved-up air-conditioner revived my work-weary body. I was actually feeling cheerful when I heard a knock on the steel of my new front door. I peeked through the peephole and saw an eye staring back at me. When it pulled away, I recognized Ed's earnest grin illuminated by my security lighting. It took me three tries to master the two heavy-duty bolts. Ed was still smiling when I got the door open.

"I hope you don't mind that I dropped by. Big Al said he'd close and I figured I could find your house by your description." He strode past me without waiting for an invitation, selected an observation spot in the center of the living room, and bouncing on his toes, made a pronouncement on his surroundings. "It isn't a bad place. It's much nicer than mine."

"You're kidding." I stared at Ed in disbelief. "I've seen your place. It's cute."

"Cute equals small. You have your own bedroom and all."

"Yeah, I have two." A mistake. I didn't want a roommate. Maintaining the deception for eight to twelve hours was hard enough. But twenty-four hours a day? I couldn't do it.

"Boy, you could probably use help on the rent. I mean how much is it? I could chip in." Ed tried out the couch. Actually, he tripped over the Formica coffee table and landed on the couch. "And, I could bring my music. I don't see any. I can't believe you don't have any music here."

All my music was in storage. Good news. No better way in a world turning to iTunes to give away my age than the vintage of my CDs.

Ed paused as if he realized how hard he had pushed. Too hard. He lapsed into GMAT talk. "I don't want you to believe that I am trying to inveigle my way in here. It's not as if I am living in penury or anything. You can cogitate about my moving in. If the rent is exorbitant and you'd like to share, I'd be happy to vacate my current habitation. My domicile, however, is not unbearable. I've encountered the occasional contretemps but I witness no persistent internecine conflict in that house or anything. But if I lived here I could perambulate to work. Think it over."

I promised that I would—when I had time to locate a dictionary—but I was lying. I needed downtime. Such as it was, this apartment was my escape from my undercover life. I didn't want to give that up just so Ed could walk to work.

Ed continued his verbal backstroke. "You've seen my car. It's kind of a flivver but it runs."

A flivver? Really? I scowled. I'd never heard that word. I'd only ever seen it in an SAT prep book. Not even on a test. If Ed noticed my expression, he didn't admit it. He was on a roll.

"It's not bad commuting from my communal residence. You know where it is. It's too far to walk and I don't own a bike. The tough part is finding a parking space at work, especially when I'm not on day-shift and on weekends when the town pullulates with tourists. Since Seaside Heights is set up to handle a lot of day-trippers, it offers an amplitude of parking. During the week I can find a metered space but on the weekend I can't presuppose the certainty. Plus, the parking lots hike up the rates. Usury, you know." Finally, he took a breath.

I felt like screaming Why can't you just say parking can be a problem on weekends? I didn't. I said, "Ed, you're a twenty-one-year-old guy, a very cute twenty-one-year-old guy. Is hanging out with me the best you can do on Saturday night?"

A sly grin stole across his face. "You have cable, air-conditioning, and more than one chair. Where I've been living I have to sit on the floor most of the time, even when everyone isn't home. I work all day. I work most nights. When I am off, I don't want to party all the time. Sometimes I just want to kick back."

"Don't you want to meet someone? A girl?"

Ed didn't meet my gaze. "I don't think it's all that easy to meet someone you like. I mean all the good ones are taken."

Had I just been insulted? For all he knew, I was an unclaimed female. I didn't pursue the issue. Palling around with Ed wasn't about me. It was about Jonas. And, in Ed's case, Schyler.

"You must meet some girls you like."

"I'm not exactly that guy from that Harry Potter movie." Ed focused on tossing a pillow in the air and catching it between his knees.

I needed to talk to him about his self-image, not to mention his idea of a sex symbol. First, however, I wanted to find out what he knew about Schyler. "Very few men have much in common with movie stars, but they still have girlfriends. What's your type? Do you like blondes?"

Ed eyed me with suspicion. "Of course. Everyone likes blondes. I also like redheads and brunettes."

"But you must have a favorite."

"What? Are you going to fix me up with my dream girl?"

"I'll try if you describe her." Okay, I was naïve. I was waiting for Ed to say five foot nine, one hundred and twenty pounds, blonde hair, gray-green eyes, named Schyler.

But, Ed wasn't going to tell me a thing. He grabbed my cell phone off the coffee table and bounced it in his hands. "You're phone is vibrating." He hit the talk button and handed the phone to me.

"Do you miss me?" Andy's upbeat tone suggested that he expected a positive answer.

"To whom am I speaking?"

"Ah, I see. So many men call every night saying they

miss you."

"We do get a lot of those calls."

"Wc? What do you mean we?"

"I'm sorry. We already subscribe."

Ed scowled at the phone and made a gesture I interpreted as 'I'll give myself a tour.'

"Someone there with you?"

"I am the lady of the house. The others who live here don't make the buying decisions."

"You have company?"

"Yes."

"You can't talk."

"I'm not interested right now."

"Okay, Maggie-dearest, sweetie pie, honey-bunch, lovey, doll-baby, honey-pie."

"You used that one before."

"No, I believe I used honey-bunch. Honey-pie is different."

"Better?"

He considered his answer. "No. Just different. I'll call later. Maybe you'll be more interested then."

I disconnected and switched the setting to ringer as Ed returned from his tour of the apartment. "Can I eat some of your fudge?" He held a white box in his hand.

Fudge. When I left that morning, I didn't have any fudge. I checked inside the box. All vanilla. I smiled. Andy must have dropped by to check the security arrangements and to leave a gift. I felt a surge of warmth for my missing boyfriend.

"You know your kitchen has a great view."

I stared at Ed in disbelief. As I recalled the tiny window overlooked the back of a guest house and a garage.

"But I couldn't find the beer."

"Beer?" I had no idea how Andy had stocked the house. If Ed couldn't find beer, most likely I had no beer. I'd never check for it. "I guess I'm out."

"Do you have any money? I'll go get some." Ed appeared insulted when I asked him to get a receipt. I couldn't tell him I intended to pass it along to Maxwell Angel. I told him I tracked my expenses, and he seemed to accept the explanation.

Ed disappeared out the door and I grabbed the phone. While I waited for Andy to answer, I peered out my kitchen window to check the view. What Ed liked about the sight was not found in nature. What Ed liked was sitting on the garage-top porch: a half dozen blonde preppies of the female persuasion. A half dozen Schyler Devereaux.

"Where are you?" I spoke to Andy's voice mail. "Ed is visiting tonight. Try me later. I'm not sure how long he's staying."

Pretty long according to the thirty-pack of Budweiser he carried through the door. "I figured I might as well stock up for when I drop by." Ed threw himself on the couch. Despite his claim that television was both soporific and sophomoric, he snapped open a beer and hunkered down for an evening in front of the tube. Ed found a rerun of All in the Family, the episode where Archie offends Mike and Gloria by making an outrageously prejudiced remark. No matter how often I reminded Ed we had a hundred options, he selected a rerun. After All in the Family, we watched Gilligan's Island, the episode where the Captain gets frustrated with Gilligan. Gilligan was about to redeem himself when the phone rang again. "Gee." I hit the talk button. "Now I'll never know how it turns out. Let me know if they get rescued."

Ed almost responded before he realized I'd made a joke—or tried to. He chuckled.

"You alone yet?" Andy sounded a bit frustrated.

"Nope."

"Find the gift I left you?"

"I think so."

"All vanilla."

"Yes."

"But you're still not alone?"

"That's right."

"Good. You're making friends."

"Yes, I am."

"And you feel perfectly safe with this new friend?"

"Yes, I do."

"So you can't sneak out to meet me?"

"Not at this time. This isn't a good time to call."

"I'm at Oliver's. We're heading to Spring Lake to see if we discover any info about where the elusive Trent Barlow has gone. If I can, I'll call you after."

"That would be good."

"I love you."

"I hope so."

"Do you still love me?"

"I recall thinking I did. But since I moved here? Let's just say that I'm not quite sure at the moment."

"Of course you are. I'll call you later if I can. Love you."

"Who was on the phone?" Ed bounced the remote in his hand.

"Telemarketer."

"On a cell phone? On Saturday night?"

I shrugged. "An ambitious telemarketer."

"You were too nice to him. Sometimes you just have to let people know who's the boss." He glanced at the screen. "Hey, isn't that incredible. I said 'Who's the boss' and I check out the screen and guess what's coming on?"

"Who's the Boss?" I cited the Tony Danza sitcom.

Ed appeared puzzled. "No. A Springsteen video." He regarded me as if I were nuts. We were, after all, in New Jersey.

CHAPTER 38

I'd worked an uneventful shift and was relaxing on the sofa when the phone rang on Sunday night. I found it hard to believe Andy's news. "Andy, Little Dippers don't get transferred."

"You are not just any Little Dipper. You're special." Andy sounded a bit embarrassed about asking for the favor. "Besides the Stone Harbor store is short-handed."

"Andy, I have an apartment in Seaside Heights. I am at exit 82. Stone Harbor is . . . what . . . exit 13?"

"10." He corrected me.

"Do I walk down the Garden State Parkway?"

"I'll drive. Max thought moving you around would be a good idea. The more stores you visit, the better."

"I'm working here because we suspected the answer to Jonas's fate lay in his avoidance of Seaside Heights."

"It's a possibility, but Jonas was known at all the stores. Max wants to make sure he does everything he can. Meg, kids won't gossip to cops. Or adults. Okay, people they think are adults. They talk to you. Plus, you know the ropes. The store is asking for assistance. You can go there for one day, help them out, and nose around a little."

I sighed into the phone. "Do substitutes have to wear their uniforms? I know people in Stone Harbor, Andy."

"One day. What are the odds that anyone will recognize you?"

The way my luck ran? Pretty good.

"We'll make an excursion of your transfer. I'll get a room in Atlantic City. No one will notice us together there. I'll take the night off and we'll drive down tonight. How about if I pick you up around eight? We'll have a great time and then

I'll drop you in Stone Harbor tomorrow morning. And then," I could tell Andy was thinking on his feet, "we'll go to back to the hotel for a second night and I'll drop you back at your apartment on Tuesday morning. Come on. It'll be fun. We'll have a nice dinner out. Take a walk on the beach, or the boards if you want. Get you more fudge." Fudge clinched the deal.

In the morning I reported to work in Stone Harbor, a place that never struck me as a town that appreciated vendors dressed as angels with a devilish sense of fashion. The local citizens satisfied their needs for big rides and noisy arcades in Wildwood, just to the south. Stone Harbor's citizens congregated not on a Boardwalk but in a small downtown that had bars, restaurants, movies, and shops that sold tasteful items. But most importantly, at least in the eyes of an ice cream professional, Stone Harbor was home to Springer's, a local institution that even I noticed on the Food Network and I do not watch the Food Network on purpose. I'd never heard Heavenly Dips mentioned on any television show.

Andy explained that the store in Stone Harbor was the only one in Max Angel's chain, or, as he would say, galaxy that lost money despite its prime location on 96th Street, the main cross-town drag. I wasn't surprised. Neither was Max. But Max believed in what Heavenly Dips had to offer and announced his determination to turn the location around. That was the reason that he asked Jonas to devote more time to the store and the reason I was spending what I had hoped would be my day off there.

The store's Archangel, a neatly-attired, well-groomed man whose physique suggested that he never touched Heavenly Dips products, acted very happy to see me. Bob, according to the name embroidered on his shirt, explained that I was subbing for a girl named Serena. He didn't tell me that Serena couldn't come to work because she was too distraught about Jonas. I learned that from Morgan, a bouncy blonde who actually did resemble an angel in her Heavenly Dips uniform.

"She was his girlfriend?" I asked.

Morgan nodded and I noticed that she looked good with stars rotating above her head. She leaned close to share a secret. "But no one was supposed to know because they worked together. People might think she got favors from him."

"Did she?"

"Well . . ." I couldn't tell if Morgan didn't want to speak ill of the dead or of Serena. "She did make Big Dipper." I detected a touch of bitterness in Morgan's voice. She was still wearing the blue wings of a Little Dipper. "But she deserved the promotion. She works hard."

Yeah. The competition for those coveted white wings was cutthroat. Here was a topic crying out for an enterprising investigative journalist. I needed to pass the tip to Bridget Simkus.

"She must be really upset." My tone turned the statement into a question.

Morgan's nod was barely perceptible, but it set the stars and planets above her head in motion. "The last time Jonas came to this store Serena claimed he seemed unusually serious. He said he needed to talk to her but they didn't have time to hook up. She feels bad about that." So bad she couldn't face coming to work. That I understood. I could barely face coming to work myself.

Being a Little Dipper in Stone Harbor was almost pleasant, largely because the space shuttles in the sky above us were rotating, along with uncharted stars and unnamed planets, on a ceiling fan. Plus, collecting information in Stone Harbor was easy. Compared to Seaside Heights, business was slow, and the manager wasn't always haranguing the employees to perform menial tasks that had already been completed.

On the downside, there wasn't that much information to

collect. Jonas had only dropped by once a week and usually made his schedule coincide with Serena's. "She couldn't wait until this winter when they would have more time to spend together now that he was out of school." Morgan grew pensive. "You know, I think she expected a proposal. I don't know if she was right or not but she believed it. She said he sounded different the last time they spoke. More serious. More mature. She was shattered by the way he died. I'm not sure she'll come back to Heavenly Dips."

At least Morgan, who barely knew Jonas, saw his death as a tragedy. "You know he was cute and nice. I mean, he was the boss's son so he didn't have a lot of time to fraternize, but he knew all our names. And it wasn't as if ours was the only group of names he had to learn. He visited all the stores. Of course, he used most of his time here to see Serena."

"Did Bob like him?" I asked about the squeaky clean manager.

Morgan shrugged. "He seemed upset when Jonas died. Said it was a shame. Said he always liked Jonas. Why would he lie?"

Finding out was my job.

The incentive to remove my halo and wings so quickly in Seaside Heights was to defy management. Big Al treated me like a child so I acted like one. In Stone Harbor, no one admonished me to stay in uniform, so the rebel in me didn't feel the need to remove my Heavenly Dips accessories for my break. With wings and halo in place, I carried a Marshmallow Cloud cone to a nearby bench and called Andy. I told his voice mail that Jonas had a distraught girlfriend in the Stone Harbor store. "That would give Schyler a motive but, if you ask me, Schyler would kill Serena, not Jonas. But you might want to check the situation out. Don't forget to pick me up at five." I let the line stay open for a few seconds before recording my concluding sentiment. "Just thinking it over as I sit here in Stone Harbor with wings on my back and a halo on my head but, yes, I think I still love you."

CHAPTER 39

I became confused when I returned from my break and found two Big Dippers had reported to work. I was ready to interrogate them—I mean chat with them—but Archangel Bob expressed his gratitude as if I were leaving. Turned out I was. After he thanked me for covering in Stone Harbor, he thanked me for volunteering to do the same thing at the Ocean City store. I didn't even know Heavenly Dips had a store in Ocean City but apparently I had agreed to travel twenty miles north to exit 29 to work another shift. "I'll drive you up. I know you got a ride this morning. The company will arrange to have you picked up. We really appreciate what you're doing."

Bob led me to a station wagon painted a fluorescent blue color that I felt certain Subaru management would want everyone to know was a custom job. On the ride north, Bob continued to heap compliments on me. He attributed my work ethic to my maturity. "These kids don't work as hard as we do." So Bob, whom I judged to be about my age, had spotted me.

I could fool the younger kids by avoiding any fashion statement that their mothers would make, or actually any statement at all.

Bob, however, was old enough to know better. "I admire that you're doing this. Going back to school and all. I am a strong believer in continuing education. I'm a teacher myself. This is my summer job."

I asked about his life in a Pennsylvania middle school and managed to direct the conversation away from myself until we drove down the exit ramp towards Ocean City.

"I asked the guy from the home office how we were

lucky enough to get someone like you for the summer. Not that the kids aren't great. They are. It's fun watching them learn but sometimes I wish they already knew. I watched you with the customers this morning. You'd really succeed in a service position."

Been there, done that, I thought.

He didn't wait for me to respond. "That was young Jonas's strong point. He was great with the customers. He could charm anyone. Well, given what happened, I'd have to say almost anyone. His death was heartbreaking for that family. I liked the kid but I really admire his father. Max Angel is the real deal. A self-made man. I have a lot of respect for him."

"But not for Jonas?"

Bob needed a moment to find the right words. "With the kid, it wasn't a matter of respect. He was a kid. I heard the rumors like anyone else."

"Rumors?" I perked up.

"You're mature enough not to blab the story around. There were rumors that Jonas was the life of the party if you get my drift. He had access to stimulants and shared them freely. At least that's how I heard it or, to be accurate, overheard it. One thing about kids, adults are invisible to them, so I could listen to their Jonas discussions, mostly about what they heard he got into up north. He didn't spend enough time down here to make much trouble. Except for poor Serena. Sweet girl. A little too naive to see through a roué like Jonas Angel."

"A roué?" I hadn't heard anyone use that word in years, if ever.

"Old fashioned term to describe an old-fashioned ladies man. The kid was just a natural." Too smart to slime the missing son of his boss, Bob stopped with that characterization although I tried my best to worm some details out of him. When we pulled up to Ocean City's Boardwalk at 9th Street, he apologized for not escorting me to the Heavenly Dips store. "This is my lunch break. Gotta get back and keep an eye on my little angels."

I didn't mind. The walk along the wooden walkway provided a short period of privacy to report to Andy before I clocked in. Turned out that he already knew from Maxwell Angel, the man who scheduled my alleged day off, when and where to pick me up. He thanked me on Max's behalf. I thought of the Angel family's pain and tried to adopt a positive attitude. How I felt didn't matter. I was stuck in Ocean City until Andy came to get me.

The story in OC sounded much the same as in Stone Harbor except that the girl's name was Caitlyn, not Serena. She too had called out because her boyfriend, the same boyfriend, Jonas, had been killed. I got the scoop from an elegant twenty-year-old whose English mother and West Indian father had produced an incredible genetic mix. Danielle had completely symmetrical features, smooth skin the color of cinnamon, and a warm personality that made my job as Little Dipper easier. Her cynicism made my investigative job easier.

While Danielle talked, I implemented the manager's marketing plan to woo passers-by with the sight of staff members happily devouring the product. While I ate Marshmallow Cloud in a black hole, Danielle told me Caitlyn's story. It sounded familiar, although Jonas had just met her at the beginning of this summer. She saw him whenever he was in town. The last time he visited his tone had been more serious than usual. Like Serena in Stone Harbor, Caitlyn too suspected Jonas wanted to get serious about their relationship. Danielle shrugged. "Now, she knows that isn't going to happen. Not that it ever was."

Danielle had the dirt on Jonas Angel: he had a girl in every store. She even knew some of the names. "I have a network of friends who work for Heavenly Dips," she explained. "Jonas was pretty sweet. He could get just about any girl he wanted, although I don't think he had a squeeze in Delaware. After all, there were time constraints. I don't think he had enough time to take the ferry." She paused. "Although if anyone could have pulled it off, it would have been Jonas. In his own way, he was amazing."

CHAPTER 40

"I have no idea why anyone wants the honor of working in the Seaside Heights store." I started talking before my entire body was inside Andy's car. Both managers, excuse me, Archangels—one from Stone Harbor and one from Ocean City—had thanked me profusely and said they would welcome me back at any time. Outside the Seaside Heights store, I could work the register and even make correct change. I attributed my enhanced performance to being out from under Big Al's watchful eyes. "Big Al maintains a very unpleasant environment. When this gig is over you should tell Maxwell Angel that if Big Al doesn't go to jail, he should go to management training."

"I think he has."

"Well, tell him Big Al needs more coursework."

Andy listened to me praise the managers of the Stone Harbor and Ocean City stores and berate Big Al from Ocean City through Longport, Margate, and Ventnor to the hotel in Atlantic City. He expressed his appreciation for how I'd spent my day off with gifts I found on the bed in our hotel room. Were they for me or for Andy? One present was a short, tight, dress, the kind Andy liked on me. This one was white. "To set off your tan," Andy noted. Beside the dress laid a teddy, also white and also skimpy. "When did you have time to pick these up?"

"I bought them downstairs."

I had some familiarity with the pricing in the lobby shops. "I hope Maxwell Angel is paying."

"He will. I'm not exactly sure how but he will. I wanted to thank you by getting you something nice."

"Something you liked?"

He nodded at the silky sleeping attire. "Okay, that's as much a gift for me as for you. Want to try it on?"

"After dinner, big boy. I've had nothing but ice cream to eat all day."

"You had a huge room service breakfast," Andy protested.

"At 9 AM. Let me take a shower and put on that dress so you can take me out for a good meal."

I felt flattered by the size Andy picked although the tight dress made me resemble a slut. Then again, maybe Andy planned that. Once I slipped the sheath on, I felt my personality change. I ran my fingers through my hair to get a just-out-of-bed look and slipped on my white leather flip-flops. The flimsy, flat sandals reminded me of my usual persona. I flung open the bathroom door. "Do you think Maxwell Angel could spring for shoes?"

"I think you look great the way you are." Andy wrapped his arms around me.

I continued my protest as he danced me across the room and out the door. "I'd look better in a pair of Italian pumps."

Andy didn't argue. With a promise that we could check in the lobby, he took my hand and led me towards the elevator. When the mirrored doors slid open, the car was populated with hopeful gamblers. We squeezed on. We were about to exit the elevator in the hotel lobby when I saw him.

I grabbed Andy and yanked him back into the now-empty lift. I turned him to face me, placed a hand on each cheek, and pulled his head down for a long and languid kiss that occupied us while the elevator filled up. He didn't resist. As a matter of fact, after a few seconds of confusion, he threw himself into the kiss. He seemed oblivious to the others in the elevator. He slid his hands down from my waist, gripped my hips, and drew me towards him. I had no way of communicating what had triggered my attack of romantic verve. Any signal that my affection was not what it appeared might have attracted a loud reaction from him and unwanted attention from those on the elevator. I kept my hands on Andy's face and positioned it so that mine was hidden under his. I envisioned a lot of uncomfortable people in the elevator pretending they didn't notice our display even as they shuffled out around us. But I never saw them. I never opened my eyes.

At last, I heard a jovial, "Okay, it's all yours and going down."

I released Andy, who wasn't particularly interested in being released, and let out a quick breath. "Man, that was close."

"To what?" Andy's eyes looked watery, dreamy, and confused.

"Karl Elkins rode the elevator with us. I saw him walking towards it. We couldn't have gotten past him. That's why . . . sorry."

"Don't be. Really. I enjoyed the ride. I thought . . ."

"I don't think he could have recognized either of us. I tried to cover your face with my hands."

"Yeah, I thought . . . well . . . never mind what I thought. Do you believe it's a problem if he sees us together? His wife doesn't work at Heavenly Dips anymore." Andy didn't wait for my answer. "I guess it would still be risky for anyone remotely connected to the company to know about our relationship. What should we do?"

As an answer, I hit the button for our floor.

As soon as the door to our hotel room closed behind us, I returned to the topic of Karl Elkins. "Don't you find it a tad odd that Karl showed up in the lobby of our hotel?"

"The hotel has over a thousand rooms. I didn't think we'd run into anyone here. I believed we could get lost in the crowd. I'm sorry." Andy wrapped his arms around my shoulders. "I doubt Elkins even saw us. If he knew we were on that elevator wouldn't he have said something?"

"Probably 'would you help me find my wife?'"

Andy laughed. "You were the one who turned this into a

major drama." He raised a hand to silence my protest. "For a very good reason. I think you're right. Given his connection to Heavenly Dips, he shouldn't find out we know each other." He plopped on the bed. "He's probably out and about in the casino somewhere, gambling. We can't risk running into him. We should stay right where we are. Meg, Maggie, sweetie, honey, lovey, if we're stuck in this room can't we make the most of it?" He patted the mattress.

"You mean room service?"

He didn't but he did call and place the order. I heard him ask how long service would take. "That long? No problem. That's long enough."

I had a fair idea of what he meant but I wasn't finished presenting my theories about Karl Elkins. "You know I got the impression he was with someone."

"Who?" Andy's attention had shifted away from the episode in the elevator to a potential episode in our room.

"Karl."

"When did Elkins become Karl?"

"We talk. I'm not going to call him Mr. Elkins if I run into him."

"From what I can tell, you aren't going to call him anything." Andy brushed a strand of hair from my cheek.

"Only because I was with you. I'm not certain who he was with because he was in the middle of a crowd. I was so anxious to get away from him."

"You should probably take that dress off. You don't want to get it wrinkled in case we want to go out after . . . later." Andy slid a strap off my shoulder.

"What do you think?"

Andy was brushing his lips back and forth along my shoulder. "I think you have a very nice tan. For a fair girl."

"No." I stretched my neck to encourage his affection even as I kept talking. "What do you think about Karl meeting someone else?"

"That could be good. Maybe he has moved on, met

someone." Andy wrapped his arms around me but I still focused on Karl.

"Or maybe, he is here with Bunny. Maybe she never really left him. Maybe she killed Jonas, by accident or on purpose. Then maybe she and Karl devised this scheme."

Andy released his grasp and collapsed on the bed. "I can't wait to hear. What scheme?"

"He runs around whining about how she left him to create a diversion. All the while he knows exactly where she is."

"In a four-star hotel in Atlantic City? Who's paying?"

"They might only be staying for a few days. She'd have to live somewhere more private or she'd be recognized."

Andy tried to interrupt but I had more.

"Maybe she's had a makeover, an extreme makeover." I crawled onto the bed beside Andy. "She could have used one."

"Or, maybe he wasn't with Bunny at all. Maybe he has moved on and was with another woman if he came here with anyone at all. Maybe he was alone but got pushed up against a conventioneer from Grand Rapids." Andy offered.

"Grand Rapids?"

"I picked it at random. Nice town. Michigan. I've been there." Andy pulled me close. "But the point is: we don't know. So in conclusion, I hope, let me punch a huge hole in your scenario. Do you think one day Maxwell Angel's assistant got up and said, 'Gosh, Maxwell Angel is nice and doggone it that kid of his isn't treating him right. I've made elaborate plans to guarantee that today is the first day of the rest of my life but I think I'll throw my future into complete disarray and create an elaborate plan to kill him?'"

"Maybe." I wouldn't concede. "What better time to murder someone than right before you sneak away to a new life?"

Andy shook his head and sputtered. "Max mentioned that she picked up a new Saturn the day she left. If she planned on murdering someone, don't you think she would have been smart enough to buy a new car after her escape, not before?"

"Maybe."

"Maybe?" He moved his face close to mine and stared deep into my eyes. "We could argue this point all night and never reach a conclusion or," Andy wrapped a leg around me, "we could reach our own conclusions."

We reached several conclusions that night. I kind of lost interest in Karl Elkins myself.

CHAPTER 41

Back in the Seaside Heights store, I changed my approach. Continually bringing up Jonas Angel's name felt too obvious, not to mention futile. Besides, booming business made conversation impossible. I shifted my focus to building a social life with my coworkers—which turned out to be a lot easier than I anticipated. It wasn't so much that they liked me. They liked a fully-stocked, cable-equipped, air-conditioned apartment within walking distance of Heavenly Dips. I didn't have to issue invitations. Ed did. Even Hilde tagged along. I wasn't sure why and my taciturn colleague wasn't about to say.

Tuesday night saw a sea of fluorescent blue in my living room. I couldn't believe I was entertaining this crowd. Actually, I wasn't. My television was. Ed and Lynyrd, who arrived with Sharmaine, were roaring at a rerun of Hogan's Heroes, the episode where the POWs try to put something over on the Nazis. Sharmaine kept smiling but only because she basked in what she perceived as Lynyrd's glow. Hilde just seemed content to be included in the group. None of my guests seemed to mind that the furniture had appeared dated when Hogan's Heroes first crossed the airwaves. Viewing the situation through their eyes, I saw the virtue in chairs you could prop your feet on and tables that didn't cry out for a coaster.

When my phone rang, Ed provided instructions. "If it's a telemarketer, hang up."

The caller was, of course, Andy. "How are you doing?"

"I have friends here."

"Good work. Any news?"

"No," I mumbled.

"Have you experienced one moment of fear?"

"Not one."

"Are you still feeling completely safe?"

"No problems." I peeked around the corner and surveyed the crowd. I have to admit I reconsidered my answer when my eyes lingered on Lynyrd, but only for a second. I stuck with my original response.

"Let me know. Even one uneasy moment and you're out of there." Andy told me to enjoy my party.

"I've got to go. They're calling me." I heard my name.

"Hey, Meg." The voice summoning me from the other room belonged to Lynyrd. "Ed just told me you talked to me at Jenkinson's in Point Pleasant Beach one night. I didn't remember. What did you ask me about?"

I faked a faulty memory, but Ed piped up with an answer. "Some club your friend wanted to know about?"

"Was that it?" I shook my head and moved on to the always-popular subject of refreshments. Those under twenty-one didn't even seem to mind that I wasn't offering them alcohol. "More to drink, anyone?"

"You should let Stacy know about Jonas," Ed said.

Stacy? Oh yeah. Stacy, my make-believe friend. "Ed, she reads the papers." I sounded irritable at the need to defend the cultural literacy of my imaginary friend. "She had kind of crush on Jonas." I affected a sheepish grin as I explained to Lynyrd.

"You wouldn't want no friend of yours going out with him no how. He didn't have no respect for women."

And you do? I didn't say that. I said, "How so?"

He wrapped a protective arm around Sharmaine to reassure her, and us, that he was above such behavior. "Some of those drugs he gave to his friends. They wasn't for changing your own mood. They was for changing other people's mood—if you know what I mean." I'd heard enough on the news to know where Lynyrd was headed.

"Don't be ridiculous, Lynyrd," Hilde chimed in to defend

Jonas. "Why would someone like Jonas need a date-rape drug?"

"Number one, you're naive if you think a guy like him wouldn't enjoy tricking someone just for sport. I don't know that much about him but I do know he supplied his friends. And, believe me, those guys look all nice and clean but trust me they ain't. Not at all." With that he ran a hand from Sharmaine's ankle up her leg until it disappeared under her dress. Sharmaine gasped with pleasure and rubbed her cheek against his shoulder. He pulled away and slapped her calf. Then, the man who believed Jonas Angel did not respect women, told her to get him a beer.

My guests left shortly after Get Smart. The episode where Agent 99 outsmarts Maxwell Smart but he isn't smart enough to realize it. Everyone's mood appeared jovial as I walked them and my trash downstairs. As I waved good-bye I realized that I'd had a good time. I actually felt happy. Improved weather helped. Encouraged by air that felt less sticky than on most recent nights, I strolled along the few blocks to the beach to enjoy the sight of the sky and the sounds of the surf. I wasn't the only one lingering at the north end of the boards although I might have been the only one without a mother worrying if I'd be home by curfew. To the south, I could see crowds of people on the Boardwalk. The lights sparkled and the cacophony of the Boardwalk, as Ed liked to call it, sounded reassuring. And, sad. Life moved on without Jonas Angel.

On the walk back to my apartment, I felt uncomfortable, then anxious, and, finally, downright spooked. I turned but spotted no one behind me. I repeated the action on each of the three blocks with the same result. When I reached my new home, I ran up the steps. Once behind the locked door, I turned off all the lights. I peered through the window and found the street quiet. The sidewalk was empty. Nothing moved. I jumped when the motion-sensitive light clicked off. I had to get a grip. No matter how unintimidated I professed to be, the undercover thing was really getting to me.

CHAPTER 42

Despite complaining about the heat in the store, I liked working days—and not just because the early hour meant less pedestrian traffic on the way to Heavenly Dips which, in turn, meant fewer rude stares and snide remarks. The steps of beachgoers' feet had not yet ground away the commercial logo combed into the sand each morning. The incessant patter of other feet on the wood of the Boardwalk had not yet drowned out the din of the surf and the cries of the gulls. The relentless heat and humidity had not yet calmed the morning breeze and strained the happy mood of the people on the boards. As long as the hecklers slept late, the trip to work was all good.

I had the phone in my hand when it vibrated. "Hello, Andy."

"I'm on a Heavenly Dips phone at headquarters. How did you know it was me?"

"Have you given my number to anyone else?"

"Oh. Right. I miss you."

"Are you calling to ask me a favor?"

"No, just to tell you I missed you last night. I've got a busy day so I just wanted to call to tell you I love you."

"Love you too." I didn't bother to whisper. I should have.

"You love that brother of yours, don't you?" The voice belonged to Mr. Smarmy, the deeply tanned stranger I'd spoken to on the Boardwalk. He was again overdressed, still overeager and unfortunately going my way. He fell into step beside me.

"You remembered I had a brother. Quite impressive. But that wasn't him."

"Sister?" he asked with a big smile.

“You really were listening. How did you figure that out?”

“Your sister. Really?” He didn’t believe me. Why would I care? Why would he care?

“Andrea. Andy.” I lied. Just in case he had been eavesdropping since the beginning of the conversation.

“Oh.” He seemed less than embarrassed. “I didn’t mean to eavesdrop.”

Of course he did, but I didn’t challenge him. “No problem. I understand.” I understood that a man who felt compelled to flirt with a woman in my getup could not be within forty yards of any female and not make some sort of remark.

“How come you’re working at Heavenly Dips?”

“I’m a grad student. I need the money.”

“But why Heavenly Dips?”

“You mean because I’m old enough to work at a place where I could serve liquor and make big tips?”

“Well . . .” Clearly he hadn’t seen his question exactly that way but he found my interpretation interesting.

I stopped and faced the ocean. Why lie to the guy? He didn’t know me. He didn’t know my name. But why not lie? I was undercover. He could know someone at Heavenly Dips. Besides I needed to expand my cover story. Behind my shades, I stared wistfully out to sea. I considered removing my sunglasses but I felt insecure about my acting talents. “I’m sorry. You hit a nerve. You see, I used to . . . the reason . . .” I affected an earnest tone that would have done Ed proud. “I don’t want to say if you don’t mind.” Mostly because I didn’t have anything to say. I implied that I shouldn’t be around alcohol but I didn’t actually make that statement. What I implied wasn’t true. I barely drank—except on rare occasions when I believed, always erroneously, that a drink or two would improve an unhappy situation. But the stranger didn’t know that. He never would. He didn’t know me. He never would.

CHAPTER 43

The first big event of my workday was a visit from Karl Elkins who dropped by for a scoop of his wife's favorite flavor, now, mysteriously, Gemini Grape. I'm not normally one to lecture but I found it hard not to offer advice to the grieving husband: if he had paid more attention to his wife's likes and dislikes, he might not have been alone and crying the blues to strangers working in an ice cream shop. I didn't get the chance. Sharmaine waited on him. I didn't interact with him until an hour later when he plopped next to me on a bench where I ate my Taylor Pork Roll lunch.

"Remember me, Leo Lime?"

I nodded. My mouth was otherwise occupied. I concentrated on my chewing and waited for him to comment about my make-out session on an Atlantic City elevator. He didn't. His thoughts were focused where they usually were: on his wife.

"You must think I'm kind of a pain in the neck coming around all the time hoping for word from my Bunny."

I felt kind of relieved my mouth was still otherwise occupied. I shrugged.

"I don't know if you've ever been in love but it's not easy."

I had no idea if he expected a response. Since I didn't have one, I took another bite of my sandwich.

"You know she didn't even tell me she was leaving. Bunny. My wife. I got frantic. I called all her friends. I even called the police. At first, her friends said they hadn't seen her but that was just part of the plan. I couldn't believe that she would leave me. Okay, by Sunday morning it occurred to me. So, I called the computer at the bank for the balances in our checking and savings accounts but she hadn't taken a dime. That's when I called the cops again. I felt sure she was in trouble. They came on Sunday morning and took my statement. I don't know what they did with it, but it didn't matter. In the afternoon Bunny's friend Sandy called and told me that Bunny had left me. Bunny didn't tell me herself ."

I detected more bitterness than sadness, but when he continued he appeared despondent.

"She wanted time to put some distance between her and me before I found out. She didn't want me to know where she had gone. She had been planning for months to run away to a new life. A new life! What did she find wrong with our life?" He shook his head to underline his amazement. "I loved her so much. You think you know someone and then . . ." His voice cracked. "I felt so surprised . . . so . . . so shocked." Then the moisture started down his face but this time the substance wasn't perspiration. His cheeks were covered with tears.

I wondered if Bunny had found someone else but that isn't an easy question to ask of a weeping, abandoned husband. Then again, Karl wasn't exactly reluctant to share. I imagined many visitors to the Boardwalk had heard his story—and probably more than one lamppost.

"It's a very hard thing to go through." I deemed the answer non-committal yet supportive. I could have taken up his banner if I believed Bunny Elkins was just a bad seed, a rotten person who had run out on the most wonderful husband on the planet. But, there are two sides to every story. Karl might have acted like the most vulnerable man around but maybe that's all his grief was, an act. Okay, a good act. I heard sobs beside me. Loud sobs. He buried his face in his hands. Okay, a very good act.

Two elderly women seated on the next bench stared at me with hostile eyes that asked what I had done to make this grown man cry. I tried to calm the heartbroken husband.

Great. Now I had three jobs. Little Dipper, unlicensed undercover operative, and therapist to the lonely hearts. How would I explain this on my resume?

Something was definitely wrong with my life when the second big event of the day consisted of seeing Mr. Smarmy go by on the Sky Ride. I had taken advantage of Big Al's trip to the bank and was lounging across the Libra Lemon and Leo Lime when I spotted him. He didn't seem the type to enjoy the ride. At least, he didn't seem the type in his shiny brown suit with a matching cigar, unlit, clenched between his teeth. But there he was sprawled across the double seat, back to the beach, facing the Boardwalk. I'd experienced the ride and, yes, I enjoyed the breeze up there but I didn't think a suit coat was necessary. Mr. Smarmy appeared to be a man who would suffer for his image, no matter how sleazy that image was. I found it hard to tell whether he saw me through his dark glasses or not. I hoped not. I didn't look forward to a visit at our counter.

While I worried about Mr. Smarmy's potential arrival, I had the feeling that Sharmaine had something to tell me but every time she tried to speak to me in private, those pesky customers would approach. Finally, she took advantage of a break in the traffic that coincided with one of Big Al's bank trips. She and I moved down to the corner near the Angelic Anise, which, to my amazement, was running low.

Sharmaine kept her voice low. "What Lynyrd said last night was true. There was an incident with Jonas and a girl and GHB. But, the story didn't play out exactly the way he thinks."

"You know the girl?"

She shook her head. "I don't want to be specific but I don't like the way Lynyrd talks about Jonas. I mean Jonas was no saint but he stopped with the GHB as soon as he understood. That's all I want to say. He stopped as soon as he knew. It really upset him."

"Who was the girl?"

"It doesn't matter. Jonas made amends. He was sorry. That's it, Meg. That's all I have to say. I just don't want anyone sliming Jonas. Not that way. He wasn't my favorite person but he's dead." With that Sharmaine moved away to wait on a grandmother whose grandson had gone to Disney World and all she got was her lousy T-shirt.

I had to wait on Mr. Smarmy.

"Gee what a coincidence! I never would have guessed you worked here!" He was all teeth.

I responded with a feeble grin. "May I help you?" Although not the standard Heavenly Dips greeting, Welcome, and what heavenly delicacy can I serve you today? my words sounded polite to me.

"I'm certain you could." He paused to let the lecherous meaning of his words sink in before asking me to recommend a flavor. "I imagine I'd like whatever you like."

Was this guy for real? Although my face hadn't stopped any clocks in the past week, I didn't look my best in my Heavenly Dips regalia, and he had never seen me in anything else. He could not possibly have a crush on me. Yet that was what he wanted me to believe. He smiled at me with narrow eyes that sparkled with promise. I told him I liked vanilla.

"Venus de Vanilla." He read from the menu. "I don't think so." He ordered a cup of Triple S as we insiders liked to call Space Shuttle Sundae, coconut ice cream with ribbons of blueberry and strawberry running through it. Not a bad flavor. I handed him the cup and waited anxiously for him to move to the register. No chance. No customers. No denying. I had time to talk.

We exchanged a few pleasantries, then he pumped me for my plans after the summer. Just when I needed them, those demanding customers stayed away, leaving me with no excuse to ignore Mr. Smarmy and his questions. I told him about my plans for graduate school. Still no customers. I told him about my old job in New York. Still no customers. So I lied in response to every inquiry he made until the heatwave came to my rescue. Mr. Smarmy did not strike me as the type who was willing to become Mr. Sticky.

"Your ice cream is melting. You don't want to get that suit all gooey. Ed at the register can ring you up. I'll let you go." I handed him a stack of napkins, smiled curtly, and ignored his startled expression. I got busy cleaning imaginary dirt from the inside of a display case where the temperature felt refreshing. When I extracted my head from the cooler Mr. Smarmy was gone.

"Ed, do you know that guy?"

"The man in the suit?"

"Yeah, I keep seeing him around the neighborhood. He must live near me. I run into him a lot."

"Is he a hot prospect?" Ed accessorized his question with wide eyes and raised eyebrows.

"For what?"

"You know, Meg, beggars can't be choosers. I can't help noticing that your love life isn't exactly hopping and he's kind of attractive, isn't he? For an old guy."

"Old?"

"I bet he's thirty."

"Oh." For a minute I had forgotten that I was playing twenty-four. "Yeah, I suppose he is okay for an old guy."

Objectively, Ed was right. The guy was attractive, although probably not as attractive as he believed. Good features. Deep Tan. Slim build. But the image the guy projected did not ring true.

"Ed, do you think he's my type?" I shuddered. "There's something slick about that guy. His smile isn't sincere. I told you he's smarmy."

"Not to mention unctuous and oleaginous." Ed agreed.

"Ed you might want to work on becoming more terse, succinct, to the point and possibly even laconic."

"Good one." Ed laughed. He loved GMAT humor.

CHAPTER 44

When my cell phone rang that night, Ed and I were watching Mission Impossible, the episode when the team keeps having close calls before pulling off the mission.

"Can you talk?"

I noticed an urgency in Andy's tone.

"Not really."

"Oh," he sighed, "you and Ed watching cable?"

Now I sighed, understanding the urgency in his voice. "Yes."

"Do you miss me?"

I sighed again. "Yes."

"I miss you. A lot."

"That's nice to hear."

"I mean a whole lot. Really, really a lot. Do you get my drift?"

It was hard not to. "I understand. But you arranged things."

"Can you get away?"

"I'm not sure . . ."

Andy had a plan.

"Repeat what I say."

So I did. "How long will it take you?" "Just watching TV." "If you need my help, I don't mind." "I've always liked Harry and Sally." "What time are they due in?" "Don't worry about a thing." "If it gets too late I can doze on the couch." "Hope you get out of that traffic jam soon." "No, don't send a cab. I can walk." "Really, it's not even dark yet." "I'll find it." "See you later."

I hung up and filled Ed in on the story Andy had provided. "Friends of mine in Ortley Beach have company stuck in traffic and they can't get them on the phone. So I'm going to walk over and explain what happened and help their guests get settled."

"I didn't know you had friends in Ortley Beach."

I smiled. "There are a lot of things you don't know about me."

"Yeah." Ed's tone was serious.

"And a lot of things I don't know about you. If we ever turned off the TV and talked we could learn all those things."

"I'll drive you over." Ed's finger moved towards the off button on the remote and hesitated.

"No. Stay put." The southern border of Ortley Beach, the town to the north of Seaside Heights, was within walking distance of the apartment. "You should stick around and see if the team survives to film another episode. I gotta go. I have my keys. Lock up when you leave."

Without giving Ed time to protest, I grabbed my bag and ran out the door and all the way to the corner where Andy was waiting. When I got there, the car was parked along the curb. Its engine was running. Andy's also. He didn't even bother with verbal greetings. He let his fingers do the talking.

"You don't really have any friends in Ortley Beach, do you?" I snuggled against his shoulder.

"Of course not. But I do have a job to do. I thought you might want to come along. Like a date."

Like a date was not actually a date. It was surveillance.

When every date one goes on involves surveillance, one could begin to think that maybe one is in the wrong relationship. At least that's how one feels when one has been sitting in a hot car for three hours trying not to drink too much so that one won't need a restroom.

This one was parked with Andy on a tree-lined street within walking distance of the official buildings in the center of Toms River, Ocean County's seat of government. From our spot, we could keep an eye on a small, poorly maintained ranch home that belonged to Big Al Braddock. While Andy surveilled, I took the opportunity to fill him in on the day's events. "You must know all about the incident Sharmaine mentioned."

"Max admitted upfront that there had been a problem of some sort. Jonas gave a friend a drug that he misused. I got the general idea but he did not want to discuss it. Max said the situation had been handled. He didn't give me the girl's name but told me he provided a settlement."

"Sharmaine knows but won't talk. Of course, I don't know how she heard the story or found out about Jonas's reaction. It wasn't as if she and Jonas were best buds. She might not be a reliable source."

"Max didn't think that episode was worth investigating any further. He did give me the name of the kid involved. His parents shipped him off to Europe right after it happened.

"Not the elusive Trent?"

"Nope. His whereabouts are still cloaked in mystery, but he had nothing to do with that incident." Max said he maintains contact with the girl. He won't give me her name. He swears it's under control. That's his phrasing. I hope he's right. I already did more digging in that area than he wanted. Maybe I'll find a reason to chat with Sharmaine. Maybe she'll let the girl's name slip."

"Why are we watching Big Al or should I say Big Al's home?" We hadn't observed any action in the hours we'd been sitting across the street from the ranch house. "And why are we watching it without air-conditioning?"

In answer to my second question Andy raised the windows and turned on the engine. Cool air blew across our faces. "Okay? Now, the answer to your first question is we are here because of what you heard at work, that bad blood developed between Big Al and Jonas in the weeks before he was murdered. If I discount the missing Trent Barlow, no matter what Max claims Big Al is the best suspect I have right now—although he isn't that great a suspect. He stayed at work until midnight on the Friday Jonas disappeared. But we don't know where he went after that. He could have met up with Jonas. He could have had an accomplice. We don't know who he is close to. That's what I'm hoping to find out. He owns that twelve-year-old Chevy in the driveway but not, I'm fairly certain, that Mercedes out front."

"Are the cops looking at Big Al?"

Andy shrugged. "If they are interested in him for Jonas's murder, I haven't heard. But I am not privy to the focus of their investigation."

I yawned. "Does Big Al ever leave the house?"

"I sincerely hope so." Andy did not sound convinced.

I slipped a hand onto Andy's thigh. "We could work on our cover story." Two lovers conducting an illicit affair on a suburban street that we'd picked at random.

"We could, couldn't we?" He placed his hand on top of mine.

"I don't think this dude is going out tonight."

"Dude?" Andy seemed amused. "Do kids really say dude?"

"I have no idea. Anyway, it doesn't matter. I'm impersonating a twenty-four-year-old graduate student, not an eighteen-year-old hipster."

"You're plenty hip for me." He pulled me across the gearshift.

I felt like a kid. I hadn't made out in a car since high school. Well, college. Well, a year or so ago if taxis counted. But I found the entire experience of sneaking away from Ed to go parking with Andy exciting. I enjoyed the romantic interlude right up until the moment the cop shone his flashlight in the window and rapped on the glass. As Andy slid his window down and greeted the cop, I scrambled to straighten my clothes. Technically each item of clothing remained on but tangled in a way that I couldn't figure out. I gave up on redressing and opted for trying to conceal my condition instead. I sat with my knees pulled up with my arms wrapped around my legs.

"You're not kids." The cop didn't hide his shock. Most likely we were not a lot younger than his parents. "You two live on this street?"

Andy and I shook our heads in unison.

"You two married?"

Again, we shook our heads.

"I don't mean to each other. I can tell you're not. So why are you here?"

I waited for the usually assertive Andy to take charge. When he didn't, I chirped an answer that sounded like a question. "It's fun?"

"It may be fun but it ain't exactly legal. And I can tell you for a fact the neighbors aren't gonna like it. So move along—after you zipper and button up. And, if you don't mind a suggestion, get a room."

We did. But not right away. The cop's tail lights were still visible, growing smaller in the distance when the door to Big Al's house opened. The glow from the outside light reflected off the shiny brown suit of the man who walked down the path to the big, black Mercedes parked on the street. Apparently preoccupied, he didn't even glance our way.

"It's Mr. Smarmy."

"Mr. Smarmy?" Andy was incredulous, possibly because of the name, possibly because I knew him, most likely for both reasons.

"I run into that guy all over the place. Today, he kind of hit on me at the store."

"Some suspicious character keeps running into and you didn't think to mention it to me?"

"I didn't consider him suspicious." Odd but not suspicious. "He never seemed worth mentioning. I thought he was coming on to me." I paused. "Okay, I did wonder why anyone would be attracted to a woman in an angel suit."

"His name isn't really Smarmy, is it?"

"No. I don't know his name. If I had known we were interested in him, I would have asked. But I didn't. If he shows up again, I will."

Andy made a U-turn and followed the Mercedes at a distance to Route 37, over the bridge, and towards Seaside Park. The sedan finally stopped in front of a big, once beautiful, old house in the first block from the beach. Scaffolding said that the building was in the process of being restored.

"I can't believe that Mr. Smarmy lives in such a nice place. He certainly has better taste in housing than he does in anything else."

Andy jotted down the address along with the license plate number. Almost immediately the windows went dark. Andy leaned across the gear shift. "Well, he's tucked in for the night. Now, what did that nice officer in Toms River tell us to do? The policeman is our friend and we must do what he says."

"I believe he told us to get a room."

We paid for the night but used the motel room for only a few hours. My cover dictated that I wake up at home. Andy dropped me down the street from my apartment well before dawn. As I climbed the steps, I had the strangest feeling that someone was watching. Someone who wasn't Andy. I turned and saw Andy wave a finger above the half-open window. I waved back and put my key in the lock.

A snoring Ed slumped on the couch in front of a rerun of I Dream of Jeannie, the episode where Jeannie puts Major Nelson in an embarrassing situation. In the well-lit living room, I could easily spot the damage Ed had managed in the hours I'd been gone. Nothing permanent. Spilled popcorn, crushed beer cans, fudge crumbs. I'd clean up in the morning. I snapped off the overhead light and the TV. When I went to the window I saw Andy's white sedan had pulled up to a spot across the street where it sat with its lights off. I waved to signal I was okay. He flipped on the lights and pulled away. I felt secure knowing Ed remained in the apartment. In the morning I asked him to move in.

CHAPTER 45

"Perhaps, Maggie . . ."

When Andy used my pet name I understood that I was about to receive either very good news or very bad news. Judging by his tone, and because I had just told him about the invitation I had issued to Ed, I expected bad.

"Perhaps," he began again, "I failed to mention one of the key rules of the private investigating biz. Let me be clear. I am in no way blaming you. This is completely my fault. I should have been more specific when describing your job. I should have provided some examples of appropriate techniques. It's always a good idea to chat with the suspects, play a little Skeeball with the suspects, even go out drinking with the suspects, at least those that are of legal drinking age. But, and I never did mention this explicitly, don't invite the suspects to live with you."

"Don't be a smart ass, Andy. Ed isn't a suspect. He's a source."

"So you say."

"Andy, you said. You told me that we weren't interested in the people I worked with as suspects."

"But we can't rule them out completely. Everyone who knew Jonas Angel is a suspect. And you said Jonas wasn't Ed's favorite person."

"I doubt if I am Ed's favorite person and he hasn't killed me. What's the difference if he stays overnight? He's in my apartment all the time anyway. Besides what possible motive would Ed have to harm me? If he knew we were involved maybe he'd use me to stay close to the investigation but he doesn't have a clue."

"So you say."

"Trust me, Andy, Ed just likes me for my palatial estate and I like having him in the house. I want to stick with this investigation, but sometimes this undercover thing freaks me out. You can't be with me, so Ed is the next best thing."

Either I convinced Andy or he gave up on convincing me. "Will you promise to keep your bedroom door locked?"

"I don't think that door has a lock."

"Trust me. It will." He changed the subject.

"What are you doing with your day off?"

"Andy, I don't have the day off. Thanks to you, I have to work the night shift. I'm calling from the beach. I'll probably spend the day here, dreading."

"Dreading what?"

"Everything. My uniform. Big Al. The customers. Dipping."

Andy interrupted. "You do still love me, right?" When I didn't answer he asked again.

"I'm thinking. I'm thinking. Call me later and I'll let you know."

Jonas had minimal contact with the evening crew but Andy figured working one night shift couldn't hurt and could help. The only problem? When I reported for work I found familiar faces, Ed's and Sharmaine's.

"These high school kids are so unreliable. I already put in a full day." Sharmaine, who had graduated in June, complained. "It's just the three of us with Big Al tonight."

I consoled myself. I might not uncover any news, but at least I'd gotten a day at the beach. And, I learned that inquiries about Uranus reached their peak between seven and eight when throngs of preteens were out on their own. After that, the teenage and young adult crowd included a few sinister looking types. Fortunately, Heavenly Dips didn't attract the toughest characters in town and the ones who tried to project a threatening demeanor didn't appear so intimidating while licking a Sagittarian Sherbet on a Cloud.

When I finally got to punch out, I was ready to be at

home but my over-thirty limbs were just too tired to deliver me there. Figuring a few moments off my feet would refresh, or at least lessen the pain in, my throbbing extremities I headed for the Sky Ride.

Since most of the other riders were couples and all of the other riders came in pairs, I concluded I was the only commuter on the tourist attraction. I also concluded that I might be viewed as a bit pathetic, but sore feet won over sensitive feelings. As I waited behind an extremely affectionate couple, I resisted the urge to pull out photos and explain that I did, in fact, have friends although they couldn't make it that night. As if they would care. They didn't even know I existed. The ticket taker, who knew I existed, didn't care. He made sure I was secure behind the safety bar without giving me a second glance.

I tried to keep my eyes off the car ahead of mine and the couple who should have chosen a more private spot to spend their time. I could have claimed to be offended by their public display of affection but the truth was I felt jealous. Here I was spending the first summer of my romance with Andy alone at the ocean. Shouldn't romances be, I don't know, romantic? Digging in vats of ice cream and riding home alone on the Sky Ride did not qualify as romantic in my book.

At the end of my trip, I wandered over to the Heiring Street stage at the north end of the Boardwalk, the spot where I'd found Hilde crying and the platform I'd visited for a nighttime view. I walked to the edge and admired the moon on the water. The humid air wasn't as fresh as I hoped but the sight was beautiful and what breeze wafted off the ocean offered relief if not refreshment. Yet my mood veered towards sadness. I felt homesick or would have if I had a home. My apartment in New York was sublet. My personal possessions were in storage. The only thing that I could call mine in Seaside Heights was a rather limited wardrobe of shorts, t-shirts, and bathing suits. I had fun of sorts with my young coworkers but I missed my old friends, my old clothes, my old life. I even missed Andy the love with whom I was supposedly spending the summer. As I took in the path of moonlight on the ocean, I wallowed in the realization that I was the only one enjoying the vista alone. Soon I found myself the only one enjoying the vista, full stop.

What I didn't take into account was if a hypothetical person (unknown) pushed another hypothetical person (me) off the Heiring Street Stage, the hypothetical victim (me) would disappear from sight and the perpetrator (unknown) could stroll casually onto the Boardwalk and blend in with the crowd. Should have thought of that one.

I was enthralled with the sight of the moon when I felt them. Hands. Hands that pushed me. My flailing arms grabbed for something, anything to hold onto but found nothing. I flew into the air and, believe it or not, discovered that the wings on my Heavenly Dips uniform were not actually functional. I could not fly. As I landed on all fours in the sand, the jolt knocked the air from my lungs. At the same moment a loud, plaintive sound stopped. I think it was my screaming.

I gasped and attempted to climb to my feet but found that I couldn't. I fell onto my back and stared at the sky. I was marveling that the heavens were crowded with stars, real stars, not the painted aluminum variety that decorated the ceiling at Heavenly Dips when, suddenly, a face blocked my view. A surprised face, staring down from the spot that I'd vacated as I fell. "Are you okay?" The young man with a light Spanish accent asked. I tried to answer but no words came out of my mouth.

The stranger yelled a few words in Spanish over his shoulder and jumped to the sand beside me. Turned out he was a doctor. Lucky for me, a doctor who, in a litigious society, was still willing to help. I nodded or shook my head in response to his questions. His family came down the steps in time to see me sit up. A teen-aged girl handed me a bottle of water and I drank slowly. Once my breathing was steady, I felt fine, but I foresaw what was coming the next day. Pain. Especially the pain of admitting to Big Al that I had crushed my wings— which I suspected I had.

"Can you check my wings?"

The doctor seemed confused. I didn't know the Spanish word for wing, but the translation wasn't the problem.

"Here's your halo." The doctor's preschooler daughter regarded me with wide eyes as if she believed I was, in fact, an angel.

I asked one of the older children, a boy about thirteen, to find Ed. "You'll recognize him. He's dressed a lot like me. He works down the Boardwalk." My directions to Heavenly Dips explained my attire. The entire family seemed relieved that dad was not administering to the medical needs of a lunatic or an extraterrestrial. The boy disappeared and reappeared only minutes later leading Ed to the spot where I lay sprawled in the sand.

When I commented on the speed with which he had arrived by my side, Ed explained. "Your emissary found me right away. It's not hard to find a man in an angel outfit"

At last, an upside to these getups.

"And," despite my distress, he paused for dramatic effect, "I can run like the wind."

Ed listened intently to the doctor's instructions and nodded solemnly in response.

"I didn't know you spoke Spanish," I spoke admiringly as he helped me to my feet.

"I don't, but the guy was so enthusiastic that before I could tell him he just started talking. Then, it just seemed too late to confess." Ed wrapped an arm around my waist. "Lean on me."

I resisted his embrace. "So if he told you I had a blood clot that could break free at any moment and kill me, you wouldn't know."

"I didn't hear him say that."

"You didn't hear him say anything."

Ed shrugged. "He didn't point to his head at all. Except when he gave me this."

The sight of my battered halo made me collapse against Ed.

CHAPTER 46

Ed wanted to call the police but I wanted to call Andy. Not that I could tell Ed that. I'd have to wait until I could catch a private moment and that wasn't going to be easy. The suddenly solicitous Ed manifested true mother-hen characteristics, walking me home, guiding me to my bedroom, and bringing me an ice-filled baggie wrapped in a thin, hole-riddled dish towel, the only kind available in my rental.

Ed concluded that I had been the randomly chosen victim of a teen-aged prankster and conceded that the Heavenly Dips uniform could have been a factor in my selection. "You know what kids are like. You see the bad element that comes down the Boardwalk late at night. That type would think attacking a stranger, especially a stranger in an angel costume, would be fun. It was a test – to see if you could fly."

Maybe Ed was right. My tenure at the store had convinced me that people can be cruel to angels in their midst.

"It's a good thing I'm moving in. I can stay tonight. Tomorrow I'll get the rest of my stuff." He went off to refill my ice bag.

After the cubes melted I traded the cold comfort of the water-filled baggie for the warm comfort of a hot bath. I called Andy from the tub. The level of concern in his voice touched me. "Are you sure you're safe?"

"Don't worry," I whispered. "I scrubbed the tub before I took my first shower."

"I wasn't worried about the bathtub, although you make a good point. My concern revolves around the incident on the

Boardwalk. It's a warning."

I felt more inclined to agree with Andy's viewpoint than Ed's random act of violence theory. Then again, the undercover life had been getting to me before I took the header into the sand.

"That attack was designed to frighten you and I can't think of anyone who would want to scare you off except Big Al. He's the one who thinks you're a plant. Maybe this is my fault. I should have stayed away from you. Maybe he saw you at his house with me. I don't want you going back to the store. Tomorrow we'll tell Max that you quit."

"No, let me stay." Maybe the hot water had lulled me into a false sense of complacency.

"You fell on your head, didn't you? Did you hear what you just said?"

Even I found the words I heard coming from my mouth hard to believe. "I want to stay. Whoever pushed me wasn't trying to hurt me, if they even knew me. The perp could be some sort of demented stranger. We don't know." I paused and listened for any indication that Ed was nearby. The drone of the television was broken by his raucous laugh. "But if he or she wasn't a stranger, if my attacker does know me, he or she just wanted to warn me. I only fell five feet. I was never in any real danger. The actual threat was to anyone who happened to be under me when I landed."

"Maggie, I disagree. You could have been hurt."

"Unlikely."

"If not this time, next time."

"I don't think so." If, a week earlier, anyone had told me I'd be having this argument with Andy, I would have told them to lay off the wild mushrooms. "Andy, I was alone. If someone wanted to hurt me badly, they would have. They didn't. If someone wanted to warn me, there's something they are warning me about or, should I say, something they are warning me off." Conscious that Ed was nearby, I kept my voice low but my tone persuasive. "Let me go to work at least one more time. If anyone at work did this to me, and Big Al is the obvious suspect, we might be able to catch a reaction. Why don't you drop by and observe? Get there first and decide what you think."

After a moment of silence, Andy agreed. "Okay. I'll be there but I still wish I could come by tonight. Maybe I should."

"Let's not blow my cover until we have to. I'm fine. Although I can't say the same for my wings and halo. I plan on spending what's left of the night trying to make all my planets align." I eyed the battered headpiece. I had my work cut out for me. "Besides Ed is staying over."

"Right. That makes me feel better." His intonation added the not.

CHAPTER 47

When I got to the Heavenly Dips stand Andy sat slumped in the chair next to Big Al's desk. The PI looked as if he had slept in his clothes.

"You're late," Big Al growled at me as I slipped through the back door. "I'm going to dock you fifteen minutes pay."

I didn't apologize. I clocked in before dropping the mess of blue polyester and tangled wire on his desk. Then I backed towards the front of the store so I could check his reaction.

"And," Big Al pronounced the word with a combination of rage and disbelief, "you're out of uniform. Look, half the feathers are gone."

An exaggeration.

"I can't even straighten the frame."

"You're going to pay for these, you know."

With a show of incredible maturity, I waited until Big Al turned his big back to stick my tongue out at him. "Don't you even want to know what happened to my wings?" I called over my shoulder as I made my way to the counter.

"All I need to know is that you're not wearing them," he yelled from the back.

Knowing he couldn't see me, I directed an obscene gesture his way.

"You'll get in trouble," Hilde hissed in my ear.

"I'm too old to get in trouble." I settled onto the only seat available – the stool designated for those working the register, a task I was allowed to do only when the remainder of the staff became incapacitated by medical emergency or natural disaster. Neither had occurred that summer.

"What are you doing?" Hilde asked with real fear in her

voice.

"If I'm being docked for fifteen minutes, I won't work for fifteen minutes.

"Daniels, what the hell happened to your wings?" Big Al appeared with the crumpled mass in his shaking hands. Andy was at his side.

"I had an accident."

"Well, missy, I meant what I said. You're gonna pay for these." He waved the blue wings in the air. "I'm taking it out of your pay."

Before I could launch into an argument about the purpose of the deposit for all new hires, Andy interrupted. "What happened to you, Ms. . . . ?"

"Daniels." I filled in the blank.

"Yes, Ms. Daniels. How did you damage your wings?"

"What business is it of yours?" Big Al sneered.

"Given the nature of my work, of which you are well aware, I think I have a right to ask." Andy directed a polite smile at me. "I just wondered how you happened to damage your wings."

"I was attacked."

Both Andy and I watched Big Al for a reaction. He seemed genuinely shocked and clearly annoyed as if I had conspired with the perpetrator of the deed to harm my wings. Only Hilde asked if I'd been hurt. If I'd seen a doctor. If I needed anything. Big Al's only concern was for the angelic accessory. He asked, "Someone grab you by them wings?"

After I explained, Big Al pooh-poohed any concerns about my experience. "That platform ain't that high. You shouldna rolled onto your back. I'm billing you for them wings. Money's coming out of your next check." Big Al threatened to turn into a big cry baby. I swore I saw tears welling in his eyes. "I can't believe you did this to a perfectly good set of wings." He muttered as he wandered to the back of the store.

Was Big Al behind the attack? I didn't think so. I

checked out Andy's expression. He didn't think so either. We both understood that Big Al would never risk ruining a perfectly good set of wings.

Just as I lost sight of Andy down the Boardwalk, Big Al returned to the front of the store to demonstrate his managerial skills. "I'll get a pair of blue wings sent up. In the meantime, you get to wear these white ones." He shoved them into my hands. "Just because you're wearing white wings, don't go thinkin' you're no Big Dipper and don't go lookin' for any extra money in your check."

As if. I'd been working at Heavenly Dips long enough to figure out that an oversized check was not something I would ever see.

Before stomping off to the back of the store, Big Al issued a final warning. "Don't let those white wings go to your head." He wiped the sweat from his forehead. For once I didn't blame the heatwave. Big Al could handle heat and humidity but not the untimely demise of a perfectly good set of wings.

"Don't worry," I mumbled. "I'm a little sore but okay to work. Thanks for asking." I turned to Hilde. "He really got in a snit over the wings, didn't he?" I spoke through gritted teeth.

Hilde verified that Big Al had returned to his desk. "Cops." She mouthed the single word.

"What?" I tried to whisper but I yelped. I slipped off my seat and sidled up to Hilde ostensibly to help her straighten the cups and spoons. "Were the cops here again?"

Hilde glanced over her shoulder but the hair that fell forward obstructed her view of Big Al in the back. She could hear him, however. People in the pizza place next door could hear him, even over the Heavenly Dips Choir, as he threw unidentified items around to the accompaniment of mumbled curses.

"He can't hear you that well when he's sitting beside you. He's not going to hear you while he's back there raising a racket." I encouraged Hilde to share.

"Daniels, are you wearing your halo?" Big Al had been so focused on the wing issue he had failed to note that my halo, good as new only because it wasn't that good when new, sat in place. I took three steps to the back and pointed to my head. "Lucky thing." He sneered and went back to tossing things around.

"Tell me about the police." I grabbed a rag and ran it over places that Hilde had already cleaned. "They've been here before. Why did this visit upset Big Al so much?"

"Well," Hilde took a breath so deep it set her planetary headgear to frantic bobbing. "They came and took him across the Boardwalk to talk. I pretended I wasn't watching but I was. They were not being nice to Big Al. I could tell. He was waving his arms like this." She flung her arms about in tiny little motions.

"That doesn't seem that mad."

"No." She hissed. "Like this but bigger. I don't want Big Al to catch me imitating him."

"What did he say when he came back?"

"Nothing to me but he was murmuring a lot of not very nice words. Then that investigator, Andy Beck, came by. That pushed Big Al over the edge. He tried to be polite but I was waiting for the top of his head to blow off."

"What do you think Big Al did?" I said the words as much to myself as to Hilde.

She shrugged. "I don't know." The surprisingly talkative Big Dipper sounded earnest. I figured out the reason for her new openness when she moved onto her next topic. "I think that Andy guy is cute. I mean, he's old and all but I don't think that matters, do you?"

Normally I didn't believe that an age difference created an insurmountable problem, but this was my boyfriend we were talking about. I told Hilde I didn't think it wise to get involved with an older man. My statement was almost true. I didn't think Hilde should get involved with that particular older man whom I repeatedly emphasized was old in order to discourage Hilde.

"Has he interviewed you before?"

A trick question? It was to me—whether Hilde intended it that way or not. "Yes. I think so. I'm not sure if he was the one. I remember thinking that talking to me was a waste of the guy's time since I'd never even met Jonas."

Hilde had another question but, luckily, Derek Jeter chose that moment to step up to the counter and order Venus de Vanilla in a black hole. In retrospect, I don't think the customer was actually Derek Jeter. I think he was a thirteen-year-old wearing a copy of Jeter's Yankee jersey. No matter. I provided the most courteous of service. I wanted to avoid any discussion of my alleged interview with Andy.

I felt a little guilty, as if I were cheating with Hilde's man, when the old guy called and told me to ride the carousel on my break. Big Al was at the counter so I couldn't talk. I simply stated the time that I could get away. Big Al thought that was far too much conversation. "I never said you could have no cell phone." He was right. He hadn't. Unfortunately, neither had he said I couldn't. Cursing under his breath, he shuffled back to his desk to amend the shop rules.

CHAPTER 48

When my break came, I was ready to run. I reached the carousel just as the last riders were mounting their steeds. I didn't see Andy but I followed his instructions and found a horse. Mine was named Jessie. Cursing my fall off the Heiring Street stage, I got into the saddle with considerably more difficulty and less grace than I remembered from childhood. Now that I was over thirty, no one had to warn me to hold on. I grasped the pole tightly as Jessie rose and fell in time to the organ music. After the carousel reached maximum speed, I felt my phone vibrate. I pulled it out of my pocket and answered with a health and safety warning. "You know, it's dangerous to answer the phone while riding."

"You'll be happy you did. I have stuff to tell you."

"Where are you?" I eyed the crowd as I whirled past.

"Next time around check outside the door."

I did and spotted Andy, briefly. He was standing across the street on Ocean Terrace. He raised his hand as if to wave. If he did make the gesture I didn't catch it. Jessie and I had already spun by.

"Meet me in the photo booth. The small one with the curtain. Not the open one." He gave me directions.

As the merry-go-round came to a halt, Jessie stopped in the high position. I tumbled off and headed for the booth. I peered under the curtain and recognized Andy's jeans and loafers. As I opened the curtains, he shoved a few bills in my hand. "Put those in so we can buy some time in here."

I slid the money into the slot, pushed onto the stool next to Andy, and pulled the curtain closed. "Talk fast. This seating arrangement is rather painful."

"Okay, first and most important, smile. We'll have these pictures forever."

"Luckily, you took the time to put your best foot forward."

Andy didn't miss the sarcasm. He checked out his image in the reflective glass. Wrinkles in his polo shirt and around his eyes gave him away. "Did you by any chance sleep in your car last night?"

The camera flashed as he shook his head. "No sleep involved. I thought I should keep an eye on you. I'll be fine. Smile."

How lucky was I to find a boyfriend would sleep in his car to keep an eye on me? How unlucky was I to find a boyfriend who needed to sleep in his car to keep an eye on me? I spoke through gritted teeth. "You should go home and take a nap but first tell me what's up."

"Turns out that your Mr. Smarmy is Big Al's stepson. He's been estranged from his stepfather for years until this summer. Now, the police are looking at Big Al and Bobby Briggs. That's Mr. Smarmy's legal name."

"Do the cops believe Big Al murdered Jonas?"

"If they do, smile, I haven't heard about it. But let's proceed on the assumption he did. I don't think it's a good idea for you to work there if you are on his bad side. And you are."

I spoke to Andy's face reflected in the glass. "But if the authorities are onto Big Al for fraud, he'll lose his job, right?"

"Knowing is one thing. Proving is another."

"He's not even going to be suspended?"

"Max wants to wait until the investigation is complete. We don't know when or if Big Al will go. For all we know, he thinks you're the one who fingered him."

"Andy, Mr. Smarmy doesn't realize that I know who he is. I can use that. I can leak to him that I'm not interested in fraud." The thought of fooling the man who played me made me smile.

"How are you going to do that? Casually take a walk down his street, maneuver to run into him, and drop into the conversation that you don't care what Big Al steals, you'll never tell."

I spoke to his reflection in the glass. "I'm clever. I'll think of something. Anything else?"

"Maggie, I got you into this but now I'm not so sure your involvement is a good thing."

"Don't worry. There are cameras in the store. Ed's in the apartment. I'll take steps to guarantee that I am never alone on the commute. I'll be fine."

"What if Big Al and Ed are in cahoots?"

"Ed doesn't strike me as someone you'd recruit to be your partner in crime." I dismissed my concern with a wave of the hand that the camera caught.

"That's why he would be so good. He doesn't seem the type." Andy handed me more bills. "Here's a couple more dollars."

"Yeah, you'll want some mementos in case you were right. You'll have these photos long after Ed kills me in my sleep." Later when the photos dropped from the machine, I saw that I smiled. Andy didn't.

CHAPTER 49

If Big Al suspected I had something to do with the law's interest in him, he didn't let on. He behaved the same way towards me that he did towards everyone else. Badly. We all had a rotten day, a relentlessly rotten day. Big Al didn't make a trip to the bank and Mr. Smarmy didn't make a trip to the Boardwalk. I had no opportunity to leak the news that I wasn't interested in fraud.

On the plus side, the drought provided a beautiful beach day, at least a beautiful beach half-hour during the time I took my lunch break. A little humid even near the ocean but unmarred by a single cloud in the sky. I feared I would never see a cloud in the sky again. That's why I realized no weather was involved when I felt the shade on my body. To tell the truth, the coolness felt good. I didn't rush to open my eyes. But when the sun's warmth did not return, I looked up. A man towered above me. My first reaction was surprise. The figure didn't belong to the only man I expected to find looming over me, Andy. As my eyes adjusted, I realized Karl Elkins cast the shadow.

"Hi." He plopped onto the sand beside me. "Is this what you do on your break?" He nodded at the unmistakable blue gown neatly folded at the top of my beach towel. "Your manager doesn't object?"

My manager didn't know but that was none of Karl's business. "He thinks taking a break on the beach has a salubrious effect." Big Al hadn't actually said that; Ed had.

"You shouldn't sit here under the Sky Ride. Someone could drop a shoe on you."

I wasn't worried. "You don't find a huge choice of spots on the beach at this time. Not on a day like today."

"Yeah, and they're all like this now. Every single day." He grimaced and wiped his forehead with the hem of his T-shirt. "It's gotta rain soon. How long can this go on?" He didn't want an answer. He wanted to whine. When he spoke again, he changed the subject. "I saw you and thought we could talk." He didn't specify a subject. He didn't have to. I knew. Aside from the weather, Karl had only one topic of conversation: his wife. He checked in with Andy almost daily to see if the Angel investigation had wound down so that Andy could search for Bunny Elkins.

I didn't even wait for a question. I just answered.

"I'm sorry. I don't have any news about your wife. I never hear anything. As I said, I've never been to headquarters. You still haven't heard from her?"

"No. Her friends say she left because I smothered her. I didn't smother her."

Smother? Based on my limited knowledge of the man, I would be willing to say Karl had the potential to be a first-rate smotherer.

"I loved her." He stuttered, "I still do." He lit a cigarette and gazed out to sea. "I even started smoking again, to soothe my nerves. I gave these things up over a year ago." He eyed his cigarette with disdain. I expected, I hoped, that he would grind it out in the sand. For a second it appeared he might. Then he explained, "I have no reason to quit now. I only got in shape for my Bunny." A smile, more rueful than wistful, crossed his face along with a plume of smoke.

Karl related the story of his physical makeover in excruciating detail. How much weight he pressed (two hundred and fifty pounds). How many crunches he did (two hundred at a shot). How many miles he jogged (thirty-five a week). "I've run down every road in this county. People who saw me the first day would not have recognized me a year later." Why? Because a year before Karl's nebbish face had a body to match. But he had devoted the next twelve months to developing the physique that was now, he confessed, deteriorating at an alarming rate. I gave him a pep talk with all the usual bromides about keeping fit for yourself, your health, your feeling of well-being, but Karl claimed he didn't care about himself. I didn't think he was ready for the you'll find somebody else lecture so I fell silent but my investigator's brain kicked in. If Karl had been smothering Bunny wouldn't he have pressed her for details of her job? He might have information about Jonas Angel that he didn't even know he had. How could I turn the conversation in that direction? I didn't have to. Karl did.

"Have they found anything out about the Angel boy?"

"I don't know much about that. Nobody tells us anything."

"Us?"

"The people at the store. I never met Jonas. You know more about him than I do."

"I never met him either. Didn't even know what he looked like except from those picture Christmas cards they sent. I might have seen him at a party at Bunny's office but she didn't ask me to come that often. Not at all in the last couple years." His voice quavered.

Oh, oh. The conversation was veering back towards Bunny. "But you told me Bunny talked about how she didn't like him. When did that start?"

"She thought he was a charming kid but she always preferred the younger boy, I don't remember his name. Poor kid lived in his brother's shadow from the get-go."

"So she held Jonas's charm against him?"

Karl shook his head. "No, I remember the first thing that got her ire up. She caught him doing a drug deal on the phone, her phone, when she came back to her desk one afternoon. Got her all riled up. She didn't care what he did but she didn't think he had any right to involve the company."

"Was anyone in the business mixed up in his drug dealings?"

"Only all those girls he dated and he dated a lot of them. Bunny didn't like the way he hit on all the women."

Pushing for names proved fruitless. Karl didn't know any. His knowledge of Bunny's dislike of Jonas was general. "Did Bunny ever say anything about Big Al Braddock?"

"Did she! He was a loyal employee. He worked at Heavenly Dips even longer than she did and she stayed there for twelve years."

"So, she liked him."

"No, she hated him. Thought he was rude and obnoxious. She tried to tell Max. She did get him to send Big Al to some management training but after a week or so he'd be the same old disgusting bastard he was before."

"How so?"

"He smoked in her office. He spat in the parking lot. He made off-color remarks that bugged Bunny. I told her to lighten up but she detested the guy. Good thing she didn't see him that often, although in the winter he spent some time in the corporate office." Karl drew quotation marks in the air. "Helping."

I ran out of questions. I waited for him to redirect the conversation to his wife but he didn't. He gazed over the surf with a perplexing smile on his lips and a faraway look in his eyes. "Do you think it will ever rain again?"

"Don't know."

"Man, I hope it does. This drought is making me crazy."

Karl and I sat in silence staring at the ocean doing its daily job. Maybe the gentle surf softened my attitude towards him. Obviously the guy had made some mistakes in his marriage, and now he was suffering. I had to feel bad for him. If only he'd figured out he'd been doing something wrong sooner.

"Thanks for listening." He mumbled as he climbed to his feet. "See you around."

I had no doubt. Some things were inevitable. Death, taxes, and Karl Elkins asking about his wife. "Nice talking to you." I smiled politely before settling facedown onto my beach towel. After a brief period of shade, the sun streamed back onto my back. Karl was gone.

CHAPTER 50

On the day of Jonas's funeral, Maxwell Angel closed all his stores as well as the corporate headquarters. Selected employees were asked to sing at the service—in full Heavenly Dips regalia. Since his employees wore angel gowns, Max seemed to believe we did constitute a choir. Ed, Sharmaine, Hilde, and I had, by some quirk of Heavenly Dips management, been included in the group of employees that ended up inside St. Catherine's in Spring Lake. Had I not destroyed them, I would have been the only one wearing blue wings. In my temporary white wings, I didn't stand out from the crowd waiting for the service to begin.

I discovered one good thing about being involved in the ceremony: the temperature inside the church. The air was as cooling as the Heavenly Dips freezer but not so punishing. St. Catherine's was the church in which Jonas had been christened and the church from which he would be buried. Andy told me that the Catholic church, which loomed above the lake in Spring Lake, was no longer the home parish of Jonas's parents but of his maternal grandmother who had been buried from the church only nine weeks earlier.

Three priests and three altar boys processed to the back of the church to welcome Jonas and, after a few prayers, turned and led the funeral procession down the aisle. First came the casket escorted by six pallbearers who, had they been posing with Adirondack chairs instead of a coffin, would have appeared to be modeling the expensive blazers on their backs.

The Angel family followed. Processing behind Amanda Angel's mother a few months earlier could they possibly have imagined that they would be back so soon? Could

Jonas have ever imagined that he would not be with them? I identified the man I'd seen in pictures as Maxwell Angel. He was more bald than I remembered and shorter than I imagined as he struggled under the weight of his grief. The tall skinny kid, whom I knew from family photos was Jonas's brother, Edwin, seemed glum and annoyed. Each of the men held an arm of the woman I recognized as Amanda Angel. Jonas's mother seemed composed and strangely beautiful considering that her face was contorted by disbelief and more sadness than anyone should feel in an entire lifetime.

Seeing the family in person confirmed what I'd noted in the family snapshots. Jonas had gotten the self-assurance that comes with wealth from his father but he had been lucky to get his looks from his mother. She had the same clear blue eyes and striking dark hair I had noted in pictures of Jonas. She was neatly attired all in white chosen, I read later in the Asbury Park Press, to celebrate Jonas's life.

Schyler Devereaux, supported by a couple I assumed were her parents, trailed closely behind what I assumed to be members of the extended Angel family. The Devereauxes stood out in the group as less attractive and less affluent. As I watched, a terrible idea pushed into my consciousness. The Devereaux family looked sad, but they also looked angry. Bitter that the meal ticket they had hoped would take care of their daughter had vanished? I felt guilty at the thought but not so guilty that I could drive it from my head.

Andy came in near the end of the procession and stood against the wall two pews ahead of ours on the other side of the church. His eyes scanned the crowd. Searching for the elusive Trent Barlow? I checked out the attractive assemblage and saw a lot of likely candidates to be Jonas's missing friend.

Hilde nudged me and pointed. "See that guy over there? The one in the navy sports jacket." I realized that she was pointing to Andy.

"That sort of tan, old guy with the more or less sandy blonde kind of sun-bleached hair that seems to have some gray in it?" The less admiring I sounded, the less suspicious I seemed. Right? If I had described Andy as that handsome guy with the chiseled features and the cool, penetrating green eyes, Hilde might have noticed my interest.

"He's the detective looking into Jonas's death. Don't you remember him?" Hilde sounded amazed.

Did I? Why would I? Why would Hilde think I would? "Oh." I tried to sound distracted which is hard to do when whispering directly into someone's ear.

"He's cute don't you think?"

"Isn't he a little old for you?"

"You know, Meg, you have a thing about age. I think he's handsome. He has green eyes. They are a very cool shade. Have you seen them up close?"

"I didn't really notice." I lied. That cool shade was one of the first things I noticed about Andy. Depending on the light, Andy's eyes called to mind the waters of the Caribbean, the fields of Ireland, or the emeralds of Tiffany. My eyes were also green but their color evoked Army jackets and jungle warfare. "So you'll miss Jonas, won't you?" I tried to shift Hilde's attention back to the reason we had all assembled. But Hilde's eyes remained fixed on Andy. A church full of young and gorgeous male specimens and she focused on Andy! "Do you think he has a girlfriend? I've never seen him with one . . . you know . . . for sure."

"Never?" How often had she seen Andy?

"Well, when he questioned me and when he came to the store."

"He was working. That's his job. He wouldn't bring a date to work." Actually, he would. He had. I was relieved to hear the first organ chord.

As we began our choir duties, my voice quavered. I felt shaken by the palpable grief inside the church, but beside me Ed, Sharmaine, and Hilde, seemingly unaffected, sang with strong, if not particularly accurate, tones. I couldn't chase the image of Amanda Angel's face from my mind. Until the week before Amanda Angel had been a woman with everything. If you believed the press, Amanda Kennedy had, after a privileged upbringing, married her husband for love before he built his business and a very nice life for his family. Suddenly, she became a woman who knew only grief. For years, she must have worried about Jonas but I imagined her thinking that his adolescent antics would end and, just as Sharmaine had predicted, he would become his father. I made all this up based on a fleeting moment when following her son's casket down the aisle, Amanda Angel let her eyes meet mine and allowed me to see the depth of her pain. I saw it and I felt it. I suspected I was the only one of the group in my pew that did. I alone had moist eyes as we filtered out into the summer day.

We were still on the church steps when my coworkers decided that coming to my place to watch cable was a great idea. Spending the night in front of the tube drinking non-alcoholic beverages seemed like an appealing thought but I was twenty-four. Excuse me, over thirty and pretending to be twenty-four. The others were young. I couldn't understand why they had nothing better to do but they all claimed that they didn't. They were just into hanging out. I hoped that they needed comfort because under their cool surfaces they were affected by Jonas's death and the Angel family's grief. I'll admit that I also hoped that sadness would loosen their lips. I wanted to believe that they had the emotional depth to comprehend what they had witnessed, but I didn't. Even Hilde, who had demonstrated true feelings, had now moved on to what I feared might be an obsessive interest in Andy. My co-workers simply wanted to kick back, eat my food, and watch my tube, although as the word crossed my mind, I wondered if any of them even understood the concept of television tubes.

Ed picked up pizza at Klee's—with my money. In less

than fifteen minutes the group polished off all but a few slices, even the ones with spinach that I ordered for myself. Then Ed, the only one who had changed out of his angel gear so it would be fresh for the next day, took the sofa, the entire sofa. Hilde sat upright in the middle of the floor. Sharmaine staked out the armchair. I'm not sure how Lynyrd got his invitation but he arrived from one of his many jobs and, after killing off the last of the pizza, squeezed onto the worn cushion with her. I reclined across the linoleum that was only marginally harder than the pillow I grabbed from the couch.

Once again everyone commented on the fact that I had premium channels. Then we watched reruns on one of the many basic cable stations that offered television new only to those under ten. We started with a half-hour of Cheers, the episode where Sam acts like a ladies man, Woody says something dumb, Frazier acts pompous, Norm drinks beer, Cliff pontificates, and Carla insults them all.

I poured myself a glass of lemonade that I'd made myself, admittedly with powder, not lemons, and left the pitcher on the coffee table. Ed and Hilde worked their way through the pitcher with such intensity that I should have suspected that Ed had spiked the mixture. Sharmaine, content to drink in Lynyrd's alleged beauty, didn't consume much but everyone else seemed satisfied with my offering. Lynyrd drank beer that he had carried in. I didn't card Lynyrd. Given the miles on his face, I assumed he was over twenty-one.

After Cheers, we switched to Matlock because Ed had fond memories of watching the detective show with his mother. We caught the episode where Matlock's client is falsely accused. Although Ed picked the show, he was the first to yawn. Hilde was the first to close her eyes. I felt certain I'd identified the culprit who had framed Matlock's client as I drifted off on the hard linoleum. Soon Andy Griffith's voice faded away and I fell into a deep sleep.

CHAPTER 51

The floor seemed even harder and definitely colder when the rising sun woke me. The morning sky was overcast. Although I was not generally awake to know, I understood a gray sky wasn't unusual in the early morning. What was unusual was the gray sky was directly above me. After struggling to a sitting position, I discovered that I'd been enclosed in a cage with two benches, four wire-mesh walls, and half a tin roof. If I had, in fact, awakened and was not still lost in a dream, I felt fairly certain I had just come to on a Ferris wheel.

The car resembled the one I rode on Fun Town Pier but felt considerably less spacious. I couldn't even straighten my legs. I put my palms on the cold metal bench and yanked myself up. As my eyes came level with the back of the seat I saw nothing. I climbed onto the bench. Whoa. I was on a Ferris wheel all right, but no Ferris wheel I recognized. Instead of the ocean or bay view I expected, I saw trees. Miles and miles of pine trees. Where was I?

I peered down onto the grounds of a small fair, the kind of traveling carnival that pops up periodically in a town near you. Although the portable ride wasn't high when compared to the big amusements in Seaside Heights, the Ferris wheel was the tallest of the amusements scattered across the grass. Tall enough to make me unhappy to find myself alone at the top.

How was I going to get down? The obvious answer—wait for the fair to open—did not appeal. Who knew what time these amusements got rolling? The sun was still big, orange, and low in the sky but it had cleared the horizon. I had no idea what time the sun rose, except that it happened before I got up.

Alone at the top of that Ferris wheel, I had to face the biggest fear in my life: being mildly inconvenienced. I had long ago concluded that had I ever been imprisoned in the Tower of London my first reaction to word of my morning execution would be: I hope there's no line. The prospect of hanging in a coop for hours with no food, no beverages, and no facilities gave me chills. Even the morning air gave me chills. I shivered. My bare feet were downright cold. With my luck, today would be the day the heatwave ended. This was shaping up to be one darn inconvenient situation. I slumped on the cold metal bench and considered my options. I could worry about how I got on the Ferris wheel later. What mattered was how to get off the Ferris wheel.

Didn't this carnival have a guard on duty? If the park had excellent security, I probably wouldn't have spent the night on one of its rides in the first place. Nonetheless, I invested a few minutes in screaming for help. My voice sounded weak and strangely hollow. The words came out slow and deep like voices in movie nightmare sequences. "Heeeeeeeelloooooooo. Caaaaaaaaan yoooooooooou heeeeeeeeeeeelpppppppp meeeeeeeeee?" Screaming accomplished nothing. I stopped.

My car was one of two dangling near the top of the wheel. I wasn't at all sure I should climb down. I wasn't at all sure that I could climb down. Why would I be able to move any better than I could speak? When a half-hour passed and the sensible course, staying put and waiting for the carnival workers to arrive, produced no results, descending on my own seemed not only possible but imperative.

The amusement appeared to be an old design full of heavy girders with rims that a foot could fit between and wires that hands could hold onto. I decided to test my footing but going out the door was not an option. The cage was locked from the outside.

Two slabs of tin meeting in a point covered most cars but the half of the roof that should have rested above my head was missing. I stood on the bench and tried to hoist myself up. Andy never harangued but he did hint that I might want to work out on occasion. If I had taken his advice I probably would have been able to lift myself through the roof on my first try. Since I didn't, I slipped back to the floor with a loud thud. I climbed back on the seat and, reaching over the top of the car, managed to find a bar to grab. I was swinging my feet in an effort to propel myself up when the Ferris wheel moved. My car couldn't go much farther up but that was the direction it headed. The ride seemed to take forever but I think only seconds passed before the car swept over the top and down to the platform. When it stopped, I was still dangling from the roof. I dropped to the floor of the car, failed to gain my balance and plopped onto the damp metal seat.

Standing outside the door was a man in his thirties, really more of a giant in his thirties, who I would have guessed had joined the carnival after retiring from the World Wrestling Federation. He opened only the top half of the car's door. He stood with his feet firmly planted and his massive arms crossed across his chest. "And who are you?" His emphasis on the word who communicated clearly that, whoever I was, who was not welcome.

"Thank you so much." I waited for The-Rock-wannabe to open the gate to the cage. He didn't. Ignoring the hint that I should remain inside, I climbed over the half-door talking all the while. "I am so glad you came. Did you hear me yelling? I thought I would have to climb down." When my feet were back on solid ground, I turned and smiled up into gray eyes that made Lynyrd's cold eyes resemble molten lava. The man remained immobile. All of him. Arms. Legs. Eyes. Lips. Especially his lips. This man was not going to smile.

"Well, thanks. I'll just call a friend and have him pick me up. If you can tell me where I am. I have no idea how I got here. I certainly didn't come of my own free will although this place looks great. It's just that I'm staying in Seaside Heights and we've got impressive Ferris wheels there. So I wouldn't under normal circumstances come here, wherever here is, to ride the Ferris wheel. Although if I weren't staying in Seaside Heights . . . ."

The man's face made impassive appear animated.

"So," I shifted gears. "If you could just direct me to a phone, I don't seem to have my cell phone with me. As you noticed I don't even have shoes with me."

One of us had to move. I figured the one had to be me. I thanked him for his help and tried to slip by him. Before I reached the ramp he moved a strong hand and hooked it through my arm at the elbow. "You ain't going nowhere."

I turned and stared into his eyes that didn't look so much cold as artic. Apparently breezy wouldn't work with this guy. I wasn't his type so I ruled out sexy. I considered weepy but he didn't seem like the sort who would melt at the sight of tears. There weren't many approaches left. I tried aggressive.

"Listen, buddy," I snarled. "I don't know what you're trying to pull here but when I tell my lawyer that someone managed to stick me on your Ferris wheel and send me to the top while your security . . . well, let me ask. Where was your security while I was being carried into your fair and thrown onto a ride that should have been safely secured?" I thought I was getting somewhere. The guy's eyes narrowed. Of course, he appeared even meaner than before but I suspected he was thinking over what I said. "So, listen. I sense that you are a bit miffed that I spent the night on your Ferris wheel. So you could call the police and have them charge me with trespassing. And then I charge you with negligence. That would be, as they like to say in business, a lose-lose. On the other hand . . . ."

The monolith spoke. "Just get out of here."

"Ah, sure . . . I'm gone. Could you just point me to a

phone?"

The guy snarled.

"I'll just find one. There must be one along the main road that I could see from above and that road is that way." I pointed right. He pointed left. "Thanks." I took a few steps down the ramp when I realized I had nothing to lose. "I don't suppose I could borrow your cell phone, could I?"

The man took a deep breath and let the air out slowly. I was just about to turn away when he tossed me a flip phone.

CHAPTER 52

Close to two hours after I'd reached Andy on the borrowed phone, the sound of screeching brakes and flying gravel announced his arrival. He leapt out of the car and rushed to the bench just inside the gate where I was sitting. "Sorry, traffic was horrible. I left as soon as I could. I was with Max when you called." Since Barry and I, actually Barry, took up most of the space, no room remained for Andy to squeeze onto the bench. He stood beside me stroking my hair as if I were Lassie come home. "What happened to you?"

"We wish she knew." Barry, the monolith who I had pegged as a WWF wanna-be, answered Andy's question to me. "I glance up and see this woman in a loud blue dress in one of our cars. I was ready to call the cops on her." He chuckled at the thought.

"Yeah. We didn't hit it off at first. But that was . . . ."

"Bet it was two hours ago now." Barry held a box of grocery store donuts in front of Andy. "Want a donut?" Andy didn't. I accepted my third.

Barry shook his head. "You know, I'm no PI but the way I figure it, somebody gave her a knock-out drug, carried her here, and dumped her in one of our cars. They must have had the skill to open the lock and the knowledge to work the wheel. We've been over the names of all of the people that she suspects. I don't recognize any of them. If this was some sort of a sick joke, it wasn't funny. That gag was really dangerous. I don't know what would have happened if you went ahead and climbed down."

"Climbed?" Andy sounded horrified.

"That reminds me did you bring shoes for me?"

"In the car. You climbed?"

"Didn't have to. Barry brought me, brought the car down."

Barry explained to Andy that I didn't recall a thing after I dozed off in front of the TV the night before.

I clarified. "Hilde fell asleep first. I saw Ed yawn."

"Didn't the fact that you were all passing out make you suspicious?"

"Not particularly. We were watching Matlock."

"You love Matlock."

"Yeah, but I'm in my thirties. I think even the producers would tell you that twenty-year-old kids are not the show's strongest demographic. We watched the show because . . . ."

"You're in your thirties?" Barry interjected. "I wouldn't have guessed. You could pass for twenty-three, twenty-four."

Lucky thing, I thought to myself. Aloud, I thanked him.

"Meg, can we talk about what happened to you?" Andy worked hard to keep his tone even.

"I have no idea what happened to me. I fell asleep on the floor of my apartment and woke up on a Ferris wheel. You now know everything I know about what happened to me."

"Except that I saved you." The pride in Barry's tone was unmistakable.

"Yep. I owe this man my life." Turned out that the imposing figure was actually more of gentle giant, living proof that one cannot judge a book by its cover.

Even Andy had warmed up to Barry. By the time Andy carried me across the rough carpet of pine needles and deposited me in the car, he thanked my savior profusely and apologized to me. "I am sorry I was a little hyper when I got here. I was worried and it took so long, even after I left Max. I couldn't just run out on a father telling me that the cops believe that Jonas was killed with his own golf club. At least that's the assumption since Jonas's seven iron is missing and the imprints match the model. I moved as fast as I could, but you just don't walk away when someone is delivering that kind of news."

"I understand. I was fine. I am fine." While I wanted to talk about the beneficence of Barry, Andy focused on the malevolence of the unknown perpetrator of the stunt on the Ferris wheel. "This time you're out of that job. You're quitting," he said before we'd cleared the fair's parking lot.

"And let whoever did this to me win? I don't think so. I need to be in that store every day to annoy them. Him. Her."

"We don't actually know if one of your coworkers is responsible."

I didn't get where Andy's argument was headed. "We were all drugged by a stranger? Someone who stole me from the midst of my coworkers for the sole purpose of depositing my sleeping body on a Ferris wheel? Wait." I threw my hands out. "We have to find out what happened to my guests. Barry did check the other cars just to verify they weren't there. They may have all been kidnapped and distributed in amusements across the state of New Jersey. Maybe the entire northeast. Maybe the nation. Maybe . . . ."

"Okay, Maggie, I get your point. Nonetheless, I am ready to assume this was done as a warning. After what happened the other night on the Boardwalk, I think we can safely say it is a second warning. You cannot stay at Heavenly Dips. You're in danger."

"Danger, schmanger. Nothing bad has happened to me."

"You got pushed off the Boardwalk. Then this. You don't think getting drugged and dumped on a Ferris wheel is an escalation of hostilities?"

I stared at Andy over my soda. "Was that a joke?"

He thought about it. "Could have been, but I was being serious. I am being serious. I'm concerned. You are being contrary, which by the way is no big surprise. You hate that job. All you want to do is quit. Now, because you believe someone wants you out, you won't go."

"I have to work at least one more shift so we can gauge

everyone's reactions. We have to find out who did it. Maybe when I come in they'll all laugh as if my little escapade was a practical joke."

Andy considered the proposition for several minutes before he agreed. "Okay. One shift."

I borrowed Andy's cell and called Big Al and told him I had a personal situation I had to handle. After a lecture on why I should have called in sooner, he agreed, grudgingly, that I could cover the late shift. "And get here on time." He snarled as I disconnected.

Andy had reached a conclusion while I was on the phone. "I don't see much point in bringing the local police in on this. But I think the homicide detectives working on Jonas's case should hear about it. I'll make sure they know today. Let's go to your apartment and see if anything is wrong there."

I assumed he meant something other than the decorating scheme.

CHAPTER 53

Sharmaine was the first of my guests from the night before that I encountered. On my walk to work, I spotted her on her favorite amusement, dancing – but not very well.

When the music stopped she wiped her face with the bright blue skirt of her uniform. Her face was already flushed so I couldn't tell if she blushed when she spotted me. "I am a little off today. I fell asleep in your chair. Passed out cold. I was worried when we woke up and you were gone. Where did you go? You look tired. Are you okay?"

"I'm fine." I took my place on the pad next to her. The last thing I felt like doing was dancing, but I needed to put Sharmaine at ease and get her talking. "Did everyone spend the night?"

"When I woke up, Ed was asleep on the couch. Hilde was on the floor. Lynyrd came back with coffee just after I woke up." Sharmaine held the money in her hands but did not put the coins in the slot. She bit her lower lip. I sensed tears welling inside her. "Meg, tell me. I need to know."

Now it was my turn to bite my lips to control whatever reaction I might have to Sharmaine's question.

"Did you . . . .? Are you . . . .? I mean . . . I know you and Lynyrd were chatting the other day and I know he thinks you're kind of cool. You know, for someone your age. I just wondered if . . . did you and Lynyrd leave together last night? He said you were gone when he woke up to go get coffee but . . . I mean, did you and he?"

"No way." I heard myself. I was yelling. "I would never, never do that." She didn't have to know that I would never ever do that even if I hated her. Even if Lynyrd was the last man on earth. Even if the world was going to end in fifteen minutes. Even if I hated her and Lynyrd was the last man on earth and the world was going to end in fifteen minutes. “Sharmaine, I know how you feel about Lynyrd. I would never view Lynyrd that way.”

Beside me, I felt her entire body relax. “I’m sorry. I know you’re my friend. I know you wouldn’t lie to me.”

I felt a surge of guilt until I reminded myself that I wasn’t lying about my feelings for Lynyrd. About everything else but not that.

Sharmaine was concerned about what I hadn’t been doing, but she never actually asked what I had been doing. I didn’t share.

After only one dance, a Hip Hop selection I performed with the speed of a Viennese waltz, the two of us headed to work. As we approached the store, I saw Andy on the Boardwalk. He introduced himself to Sharmaine and me and, although neither of us expressed any interest in his reason for visiting, explained that he was waiting for Big Al to return from the bank, that he had already talked to Ed and Hilde, and that he still had a few questions about Jonas Angel’s last few stops at the store.

Before I expressed false contrition for my tardiness, Hilde interrupted to confirm how worried she had been the night before. Although she spoke to me, I suspected her display of concern was for Andy’s benefit. “I stayed overnight at your apartment but you were gone when I woke up. I thought you might have gone jogging.”

Beside me, Andy cleared his throat in a pathetically insincere and patently ineffective effort to stifle a guffaw.

Ed joined the conversation giving no indication that he recognized ‘the old guy’ from Jenkinson’s. “When he asked if anyone knew when Meg Daniels would be in today,” Ed spoke with a firmness I found surprising, “I told him that I was really worried about you.”

So worried that Andy later recalled that he had not used one GMAT prep word.

Ed did his best to sound sympathetic but he came off more like Judge Judy. "If you have a secret boyfriend that's okay with me. I feel happy for you. Relieved actually. I've been a little worried about your social life. But if you feel you have to run off for some illicit tryst in the middle of the night, the least you can do is leave a note. That PI guy," he nodded at Andy who was three feet away from him, "he asked if I called the police. It never dawned on me but next time I will. He had a good idea."

Andy, perhaps embarrassed to be discussed as if he were not present moved to the far end of the counter, but not so far away that he could not hear.

Hilde could barely speak through her yawning. "I woke up on our floor this morning, Meg. No offense but that linoleum is really hard." I agreed that floors often are. "I feel crummy—like someone hit me over the head with a hammer. I was out for almost twelve hours. Then, I had to deal with my mother because I didn't let her know I'd be out all night." She pulled me aside. "I wish I knew that PI was coming today. I look awful. Don't you think he's cute?" Her dark eyes softened as she gazed at Andy. "I think he's cute. He came in to see Big Al and when he wasn't here he chatted with all of us. He's really nice. Do you think he likes me?"

"I'm sure he likes you, Hilde, but at his age he probably has a girlfriend or even a wife."

"He isn't wearing a ring." Hilde protested.

"Why don't you ask him?" Let Andy take care of this.

But Hilde didn't ask. While Andy came to the counter to ask if he could speak to me privately, Hilde watched him with adoring eyes. Seeing him through her big black glasses, I just didn't get it. Sure, I found Andy adorable but I was well past thirty. Hilde was nineteen. What did she want with a man who was pushing forty? Okay, not pushing very hard but pushing. In this decade.

Hilde seemed annoyed that Andy and I were leaving the

shop to talk. I was thrilled. After all the secrecy, I loved having an explanation for strolling down the Boardwalk with Andy in full view of anyone who passed. I fought the urge to hold his hand as I told him about my conversation with Sharmaine.

"Lynyrd was gone when she woke up. He told her he went out to get coffee." I sounded excited.

"But why would Lynyrd want to scare you?"

"Maybe he thinks I'll rat him out to the cops on the drug thing."

"You haven't actually seen him involved in any drug action, have you?"

I hadn't.

"He makes no effort to avoid you. He came to your place. I don't get it but I'll see what he has to say."

I showed Andy the paint ball stand where Lynyrd worked. Andy watched a few minutes before confirming my sentiments. "I'm hot just standing here in street clothes. How can he stand it under that suit? He's dressed like one of those scientists who work with the Ebola virus."

"Lynyrd has a lot of shortcomings but laziness isn't one of them. Sharmaine tells me he has three jobs. He works here during the day, on the pier on weekends, and I think he has some restaurant gig."

"Not to mention his sideline." Andy grimaced as the human target's effort to dodge the paint ended with a hard crash to the floor. "Oooooh." Lynyrd took a particularly hard hit. "I don't know if I'd be willing to work at that job. The guy works hard."

"He tells me he's going to quit the drug thing when he gets ahead. Maybe he already has. Quit that is. The entire time I've been around him, I've never seen any evidence of drug use or sales." My face fell. "Oh oh."

Andy followed my gaze. The human target removed his helmet and brushed a hand through his hair that was plastered to his skull by perspiration. His black hair. Lynyrd was not that day's human target.

"I thought he would be here now."

Andy waited ten seconds before he responded with a shrug. "See if you can find out anything about his hours from Sharmaine. Let's go back to the store and see if Big Al has returned."

"I can ask Sharmaine about Lynyrd's schedule but I have to be careful. When she woke up and he was gone, she thought he was with me. She was afraid Lynyrd and I had something going on."

Andy gave that idea consideration. "She thinks Lynyrd likes you?"

"She knows that he likes me but she worries that he likes me. But she worries that Lynyrd likes everyone. Every female at least. And she worries that every female likes Lynyrd."

Andy thought for a moment before he spoke. "I'm assuming she's wrong."

CHAPTER 54

"You're closing tonight."

"Me?" Had I heard Big Al correctly? My first reaction was pride. I, a lowly Little Dipper, was being asked to close. I, a lowly Little Dipper who was never allowed to work the register? Then, skepticism replaced pride. Was Big Al setting me up? Skepticism turned to fear. Was Big Al or his accomplice son planning on hurting me? I wanted, no I needed, Andy at the store by midnight.

Big Al didn't seem to be any happier about the news than I was. "I don't like it but I don't see no other way." He could have seen it another way forty-five minutes earlier when he sent two white wings home. "I didn't realize I got somewhere I gotta be." Sure, to establish his alibi. What about Ed? Sharmaine? Hilde? Why had he let them clock out within the past hour? I could see why Big Al wouldn't want to let the kids who blew in and out of the Heavenly Dips jobs on a weekly basis close. But was I any better? Not in Big Al's eyes. He, who never even let me near the register, knew that I hadn't earned the white wings on my back.

"Sorry, this just came up." He explained as he stuffed his wallet, cigarettes, and keys into his pockets. "You'll be fine." He reassured me. "I emptied the register. You'll only be alone for an hour if that. You'll just have a small deposit to make. Don't make no show of what you're doing. Put the cash in one of them bags." His instructions and accompanying demonstration were specific enough to be insulting. "Don't let this go to your head. You ain't keeping those white wings, ya know. I'm still getting those blue ones for you."

Al repeated the instructions – every word of the

instructions – before he stepped out the door. He made it clear that he was very worried even though he'd left minimal cash in thc drawcr.

"Ten five dollar bills. Twenty-four one-dollar bills. Twenty quarters."

I stopped listening. I got his point. He knew every bill and coin in the drawer. He wasn't worried about theft; he was worried about embezzlement. As if I'd risk that great job by skimming from the profits.

As soon as I heard the back door close, I pulled out my cell phone. Voice mail answered. "Andy, Big Al is letting me close. I don't like this, Andy. I am being set up. You were right. I should have quit. I will. I promise. I will. Just get here as fast as you can. Not the meeting place. Here. Come to the store. At midnight. Before midnight." I heard more than a hint of desperation in my voice.

Motivated less by my work ethic and more by the cameras hidden in the store, I greeted customers politely, dipped energetically, and worked the register as well as I could, which, without Big Al's scrutiny, wasn't that badly. Late at night, most families had departed from the Boardwalk. The customers were mostly groups of kids many of whom offered some variation of the tremendously humorous Uranus comment. I took no chances of incurring their wrath. I laughed every time. "Good one." "Very clever." "Never heard that before."

I was relieved when I felt the phone vibrate in my pocket. Andy was on his way. Between customers, I ran to the back and checked the time clock. The hands had never moved so slowly.

A half-hour before closing, I spotted Schyler Devereaux headed towards the stand. I felt surprised but happy to see her. She wouldn't rob me but, more importantly, she wouldn't ask me about my, excuse me, Uranus. My biggest worry was that she would bore me to death with tales of her great love affair with Jonas. I'm sure she would have, had she been sober. But, I realized as soon as she spoke, she wasn't. I scooped a Cherubic Cherry on a cloud and watched as the ice cream melted onto her hands. She didn't seem to notice. All she wanted to do was talk—after I gave her change for a twenty, a twenty she claimed Jonas had given her for ice cream.

I had nothing else to do. I listened.

"I remember you. You were nice to me when I came to ask about Jonas. The others aren't nice to me. Except for Ed but Ed, well Ed, Ed would pretty much do anything I asked."

So Ed's secret crush on Schyler was no secret.

"Like I could like him. I love Jonas. I still love Jonas. Did you know Jonas?"

As I shook my head I was very conscious of the planets orbiting about my head. Schyler wouldn't be caught dead in this getup but my outfit didn't seem to put her off. I was her new best friend. As she leaned across the counter to confide in me, her ice cream toppled off its cone and slid down the glass. That mess would slow me down at closing. "It's my fault, he's dead. If I had gotten to the bar earlier, he couldn't have left. You know how that feels?" She stared at me long and hard with the unseeing eyes of a drunk. "Choices I made, choices that seemed so unimportant. What route to take. Whether or not to run a light. Where to park. Those stupid little decisions were a matter of life and death to Jonas. They told me I missed him by a minute. One minute and my whole life could have been different."

I said all the appropriate things. "You can't blame yourself." "Hindsight is 20/20." "No one could have changed what happened." My platitudes didn't help. The tears that flowed down Schyler's cheeks flew into the air as she shook her head. "If I had been there earlier, he would not have dared leave." She slammed her fist on the glass with a ferocity that not only drove her point home but explained why Jonas had trouble breaking up with her. I didn't even want to ask her to step aside when a family of four who, if one could believe their shirts, all loved grandma, got in line behind her. I was relieved when a young woman who seemed to be a good friend rescued Schyler and, coincidentally, me.

As the little hand crawled towards twelve and I saw no sign of Andy, my apprehension grew. I had done every closing chore I could think of and was ready to run when the clock hit the stroke of midnight. I glanced up the Boardwalk. No Andy. In his message, he'd promised to arrive well before midnight. I checked my phone. No new message. I considered my options. Getting out of the store struck me as the best. I pulled down the metal shutter that provided overnight protection from all bad elements, human as well as natural, and locked it. After stashing the money from the register in the bag Big Al provided, I headed towards the time clock and the back door. That was when I noticed the freezer door standing open. Just like a victim in a horror movie, I did exactly the wrong thing. Did I have to close the door? Of course. Did I have to make sure that something hadn't gone awry inside the freezer? Of course not. But did I? Of course.

I approached the freezer door with caution. Then, just as I would in any B-movie, I felt the hands. Big hands. Big hands strong enough to propel me into the freezer. I fell through the door onto the wooden floor. The door shut behind me and I heard the lock click. The light snapped off.

Great. I'd fallen for this little trick once before. Okay, not in a freezer but in a confined space. A confined space that, shortly after I got locked in, caught fire. That's why when Ed first confirmed that Big Al didn't like me, I engaged Ed in a deep conversation about freezer technology. No manufacturer in this age of consumer litigation would make a freezer that could cause death, either accidentally or intentionally. I found the switch, turned on the light, and went to the spot where Ed had told me the emergency release was located. I barely felt chilled by the time I stepped back out in the store, which appeared empty and probably was. I wasn't sticking around to find out.

Going out the back door into a dark alley was not a viable option. With a manual dexterity I found surprising given my adrenalin level, I used the key to open the metal grate. I didn't waste any time. As soon as the opening door left enough room for me to slide underneath, I did. My fear was punctuated by a fleeting satisfaction that by doing so I ruined yet another set of wings – this time white ones. I wasn't worried about Heavenly Dips' uniform budget. I was worried about me.

A few people gawked as I shimmied out on my back. I spotted Mr. Smarmy standing among them. For once he wasn't flashing his big white teeth. "Are you okay?" He looked and sounded concerned but I had my doubts. For all I knew he had just tried to kill me.

"I'm calling the cops and I'm not going in that store until they come." I hit 911 on my cell and then I dialed Andy. He didn't pick up. "Andy, I think it's time for me to quit. Someone just tried to kill me."

CHAPTER 55

Mr. Smarmy and I sat at Big Al's desk talking to the two local police officers, one light, one dark, who had arrived on bicycles. The cops who wore shorts and helmets, and looked adorable in both, must have been nearby when the call went out. That or Tour de France cyclists. As I explained what happened to the two very cute and very young members of the Seaside Heights police department, the handsome twosome had a little trouble understanding my concern.

"So you locked yourself in the freezer?" The blonde asked.

"No. Someone pushed me into the freezer and locked the door behind me."

"But you let yourself out immediately?" The brunette took the follow-up question.

"Yes, but only because I knew about the emergency release."

"So someone played a practical joke on you." The blonde jumped to a conclusion.

"Some joke. I could have frozen to death. No one was aware that I could locate the emergency release."

"Then how did you find out about the release?" It was the brunette's turn to question me.

"One of my coworkers showed me where it was."

"So someone did know you could get out." The blonde again.

Cute or not, the twosome was beginning to exasperate me. Didn't they know the game was good-cop, bad-cop not bad-cop, bad-cop? "Someone tried to hurt me."

Mr. Smarmy jumped in. "I think that this was more than a matter of Ms. Daniels accidentally locking herself in the freezer. Your idea that it might have been a practical joke by one of her coworkers is a good one, except that the staff had gone for the day. My name is Bob Briggs. My stepfather is the manager of this store and he mentioned that he was worried that Ms. Daniels would be closing the store tonight. She was inexperienced. This was only her first time. I just happened to be walking by and thought I would check on her to see if she required help. I was too late, meaning the grate was down. I was a little surprised because it was barely midnight."

Tattletale. He just couldn't help himself, could he?

"You can imagine my shock when suddenly the door slid up and Ms. Daniels slithered out onto the Boardwalk. I think what we have here is a tasteless prank perpetrated by some of the less desirable elements who populate this boardwalk late at night. Someone saw Ms. Daniels alone in the store and seized on the opportunity. If they did intend to commit a robbery, unfortunately for them, Ms. Daniels had the money in her hand when they pushed her into the freezer. They got nothing."

I didn't agree with Mr. Smarmy's assessment. I couldn't see a stranger risking all for a few bucks. I did agree, however, that we should be on the lookout for someone. My opinion? Mr. Smarmy himself might be that someone. I just couldn't figure out how he got to the front of the store so quickly. The perp had to exit through the back door. If not, I would have heard the grate open and close, wouldn't I?

I could have told the young cops about the other scares I'd gotten over the past week or about the security cameras Maxwell Angel had installed. I could have but I didn't. I decided to wait for Andy. He was the pro. The local police wouldn't care about those incidents but maybe Detective Petino would. In the meantime, Mr. Smarmy and the police discussed the aborted robbery as if the alleged crime didn't have much to do with me. I sat on the chair and listened.

"Who are you?" The brunette cop yelled the question. I

glanced up to see Andy ducking under the grate.

"I'm here to pick up my girlfriend."

I glanced at Mr. Smarmy in time to see his eyes narrow. Did he know who Andy was? My guess? Yes. "What happened?"

"I was attacked."

"An apparent robbery attempt," the officer drowned out my response.

Andy turned to me and I shrugged as if to say whatever. He appeared more puzzled than concerned as he gave me a quick hug. "Are you okay? I got here as soon as I could." I assured him I felt fine. I guess he believed me. He joined the boys in the discussion from which I had long since been excluded. I could tell by the touch of a smile on his lips that Andy's view of the situation came close to matching mine, but the cops bought Mr. Smarmy's analysis.

Andy had no need to resolve the problem that night. He had no confidence that we could resolve the problem that night. He told the police that he would like to take me home. The cops said they had all they needed. Mr. Smarmy said he would close up. I said I would make the deposit at the bank. I had to get on my hands and knees in the freezer to retrieve the money from under the shelf where it landed after flying out of my hand. Mr. Smarmy, who claimed to have come to the store to help me, watched me without offering any assistance.

As soon as Andy and I hit the Boardwalk I spoke through gritted teeth. "You know that no passer-by assaulted me."

"I know."

"You know that it was no coincidence that Bobby Briggs—you know Mr. Smarmy—

happened to be outside the Heavenly Dips stand when it, the attack, the alleged attack, happened."

"I know."

"You know he convinced the police that the incident had nothing to do with me personally."

"I know."

"You know he's wrong."

"I know."

"You know I forgot my wings and halo in the store."

"I didn't know that."

"I thought you knew everything."

"I know that you're not going to need your wings and halo. I know you're not going to work tomorrow. I know you're not staying at your apartment tonight. Call Ed and tell him there's been an attempted robbery and that you have to . . . I don't know. Say you're shook-up and you want to notify him you won't be in tomorrow. That gives us a day to mull all this over."

"A whole day off?" A day off just might make my trip into the freezer worth it.

"Sound good?" Andy wrapped an arm around me.

"All but the part about calling Ed. He doesn't have a phone."

"After we make the night deposit, we'll drive by and you can run in and tell him."

We did drive by but Ed wasn't at home in my apartment. I left him a note.

CHAPTER 56

"This is where you're living?" My tone was more than slightly antagonistic.

"I told you I was staying in the house the Angels had built in Mantoloking. You know what the town is like. You know what the family is like. Why would they build something that wasn't nice?" Andy tried to sound perplexed.

"Nice is not the word to describe this place, Andy. Magnificent is the word."

Andy had told me the Angels had planned to abandon their ninety-year-old brown-shingled oceanfront Victorian for a brand new gray-shingled oceanfront contemporary home. Partial to old houses with traditional windows and covered porches, I wondered why they would move until I stood in the living area. Although not yet fully decorated, it was clear the same designer responsible for the Heavenly Dips store décor had not been involved. The space included not a single stuffed angel to mar the view through the wide windows. I felt as if I were on the beach. Gazing across low grassy dunes that allowed a view of whitecaps gliding through the darkness to the closest spot I would ever want the ocean to venture, it seemed unthinkable that the waters could grow angry and violent waves would wash through the room. Inside and out, the house appeared perfect. "I bet this house doesn't have harvest gold appliances."

"Odd you should mention that. The house does not have any appliances. The kitchen isn't finished yet."

As if I would care.

After a tour of many wings, Andy led me onto the deck that wrapped around the house. The sound of the surf was soothing. I'd seldom seen the stars twinkle as brightly as they did against the pitch-black sky. The ocean breeze made me feel as if the heatwave was happening somewhere else.

"I am living in a smoke-stained remnant of the sexual revolution and you are living in 10,000 square feet of oceanfront opulence."

"I don't know if it's 10,000 square feet," Andy spoke quickly and somewhat proudly before reconsidering. "The exact number wasn't your point, was it?"

I stared into his cool green eyes. They appeared somewhat amused by my hostility, at least my pretense of hostility.

Andy pulled me into his arms. "But you get to stay here tonight and maybe as long as we're on this case. I thought about this on the drive back. I don't think you should go back to that apartment. Or that job. At least until we find out what really happened tonight. Stay here."

"Let me think about this. I can either go back to standing on my feet in oppressive heat for a minimum of six hours a day. Or, I can lay on one of these chaise lounges I see all around me and spend the day reading and snacking while a gentle wind off the ocean . . . ." I interrupted myself. "This is a hard one."

His tone grew solemn. "I think we will prove that Big Al was responsible for pushing you into the freezer."

"Won't the cameras tell the story?"

"If the security cameras didn't catch the action it would be because Big Al adjusted them. He was the only one who knew where they were. But he didn't know about at least one other camera. We'll see if that covers the freezer. If he's the culprit, and I for one don't think that there is much doubt that he is, tonight marks the end of his career at Heavenly Dips. I feel comfortable stating that Max doesn't approve of managers locking employees in the freezer."

I had to agree. "I didn't see that specific offense listed in the handbook but if you read between the lines it's pretty much implied."

"If Big Al delivered tonight's warning, logic says he's responsible for your dive off the Boardwalk and your trip on the Ferris wheel. With him out of the way, you would be out of danger and could go back." He sounded as if he wasn't quite sure that would be a good thing. "That doesn't mean you have to."

I didn't argue. "So I just lie low until we see what happens with Big Al?"

"I don't think anyone would question that you want to take a little time off after the incident."

"Speaking of lying low. Is that a double chaise I see behind us?"

Andy turned to check out the porch furniture. "I believe it is."

"Why don't we lie low and watch the moon rise."

Andy had a better idea. "Why don't I bring out one of the lovely covers I purchased and we can lie low all night and watch the sunrise."

As I drifted off to sleep with the ocean breeze caressing my hair and Andy Beck caressing other parts of my anatomy, I had to admit that lying low was looking a lot better than going back to Heavenly Dips.

CHAPTER 57

The PI business was not a nine-to-five, Monday to Friday endeavor. Even on Sunday, Andy could not give up on locating Jonas's missing friend, Trent Barlow although the only questionable thing he'd ever done was be unavailable. The suspicious behavior was that of his parents who would not discuss his whereabouts. His inability to find Trent was eating at Andy so he was up and out early with a new plan to tie up the loose end. I was up and on the chaise lounge by eleven.

Not long after I settled in with my morning Coke and cookie, Amanda Angel appeared on the porch. I hadn't heard her footsteps. She simply appeared. But I wasn't startled, and not just because I recognized her. The beatific smile on her face was comforting. She was dressed all in white as Andy told me she had dressed since the day of her son's funeral. With her hands jammed in the pocket of her light cotton pants and the light wind lifting her shirt behind her, she appeared ready for a fashion shoot. She smiled, barely. When she pulled off her chrome-framed sunglasses, I could see the pain etched on her face. The radiance so clearly visible in the photos in Andy's files was nowhere to be seen. Still, Jonas's mother looked beautiful. Her eyes were the same pale blue as her older son's. Her hair was the same deep lustrous brown. The finer features of her face represented the feminine version of Jonas's perfect features.

"You must be Meg. I'm Amanda Angel. Jonas's mother."

I put two hands on the chair arms to push myself out of the lounger but she signaled me to stay put.

"I don't mean to disturb you. I heard you had a rough night."

"Not really. It could have been a very bad night but it wasn't. I just took a tiny tumble."

"I think you may be underestimating the situation. Max told me what happened. I wanted to stop by and thank you for what you did, what you are doing for us."

I couldn't say the first thing that came to mind, it was my pleasure. So, I stammered. Having buried both my parents before I reached twenty-five I could be expected to have a modicum of grace in mourning etiquette but I didn't. Not in this instance. What could I say to a woman who had just buried a son?

I didn't have to consider the problem for long. Amanda Angel jumped in. "I understand." Apparently she was gracious as well as gorgeous.

"Andy isn't here. He's working."

"That's one of the reasons that Max likes him." Her expression grew pensive as she perused the front of the house. "Are you enjoying staying here?"

"Who wouldn't?"

"We put a lot of thought into the design." She leaned back and stared at the roofline. "So many little touches. Did you see the apartments we built?"

I nodded. "It's a great house. Andy showed me around the whole place."

"Those flats were for our sons and their wives and children. We were going to have a happy future in this house. And now . . . ."

I read the slow shaking of her head as disbelief.

"We're never going to move in. I can't leave the house where Jonas lived. I can't leave my memories of him."

I expected her to continue. She didn't. So I spoke. "I've only seen pictures of Jonas. He was very handsome and seemed charming even in photos."

Joy rang clear in her voice when Amanda Angel spoke of her son. Her eyes gleamed as she stared out to sea. "He was always such a good-looking boy, a beautiful baby. A charmer. A cuddler. Of course, he was my first. I loved him to pieces."

"I saw your other son at the funeral. He must be a comfort to you."

Amanda smiled a rueful smile. "He tries. Edwin is a lovely boy but a bit awkward. I think it's a stage. He'll grow out of it." She had more to say about Edwin but she didn't say it.

"I made lemonade. Would you like some?" I felt like a domestic goddess offering homemade lemonade, albeit from a mix, to a guest on the deck of my palatial beachfront home.

Amanda demurred. "I just wanted to say hello. I don't mean to interrupt . . . ."

"I'm catching up on celebrity weddings." I pointed to an aged double issue of People magazine. "Most of them are already divorced. I think I can spare the time."

Amanda followed me through the living area into the kitchen that still offered expansive views of the ocean but little in the way of modern conveniences. I pulled the lemonade out of the dorm refrigerator Andy had bought and poured the pink lemonade into neon plastic cups. "I'd offer you something else but I don't think there is anything else. I finished the chocolate chip cookies for breakfast."

"You poor thing, living this way for us."

I gazed through the comfortably furnished living room across the deck, dunes, and beach to the surf and envisioned my apartment in Seaside Heights. Yep, living this way was tough. "This is part of the job. Andy's job really. I'm just helping out."

"Max and I want you to know how much we appreciate what you've done for us."

Despite the fact that we were in her house, Amanda waited for me to lead her back to the deck. I did and we sat across from each other at the table with an umbrella that shaded two of the chairs. I picked a seat in the sun. Amanda chose to sit in the shade clarifying why in fifteen years, when I reached her age, I would not have her porcelain complexion. Okay, I didn't have her porcelain complexion then let alone fifteen years in the future. But I felt happy in the sun. With a soft breeze off the ocean, the sunshine felt surprisingly comfortable.

"So." Amanda forced a smile. "Tell me about you and Andy."

I shrugged. "I don't know what to tell you. He's my boyfriend." I affected a scowl. "Am I too old to have a boyfriend?"

"Never." Amanda smiled. "At least one as nice as Andy. Is it serious between you?"

Again I shrugged. "We're kind of together. I mean neither of us would have time to see anyone else right now. So, by default, I guess it's serious. He's a really nice man."

"What do you like about him?"

I got the impression Amanda wanted to play counselor. I got the impression she needed to play counselor. I told her about Andy. "Let's see. I hate to be superficial but he is awfully cute. And I don't simply mean handsome, which he is."

"Clearly." Amanda smiled. "His eyes are an unusual color. Very appealing." So Amanda had noticed Andy's cool green eyes. "Sometimes I feel as if he can see right into me, my heart, my brain."

"Tell me about it. I don't think I fool him very often. But I don't actually try. I would never want to hurt Andy. He's kind. He's never defensive. He doesn't get angry easily. Even when we sail he remains calm. He doesn't yell. He's extremely even-tempered but not a pushover. He stands his ground. He can be surprisingly gentle when he wants to take care of someone."

"I know. He's been wonderful to Max. And to me. Max thinks the world of him. Between you and me, I think Max would like to hire Andy. I should say to bring him into the business. Now that Jonas is gone, Max sees no one who will care about it the way he did."

"Isn't Edwin interested in Heavenly Dips?"

"Edwin doesn't have the heart for business. Besides, he lived in his brother's shadow for so long. I don't think he'd want to step into Jonas's shoes. He wants, he needs, his own thing." Amanda sipped her lemonade and changed the subject. We made small talk about the house before she turned the conversation to Jonas.

"When someone kills another human being they think they are taking one life but they're doing much more than that. They're taking so many lives. I may still be breathing but the life I loved so much is gone. I know time will make it easier but will my first thought on Christmas morning ever be that Jonas isn't with us? I don't think so. If he can't be with us, and someday I will accept that he can't, I wouldn't want my holiday to begin any other way. I know we have to go on but part of me doesn't want to. Part of me wants to spend every day honoring Jonas's memory."

"What was Jonas like?"

"Not like they painted him in the newspapers. Did you read those articles?"

"Andy showed me." He had the clippings in his files.

"The headlines hurt the most. He's No Angel. Angel Was a Little Devil. As if his death was meant to provide entertainment. They only talked about whatever dirt they could dig up." From Andy's files I knew they had missed a lot, but rather than pointing that out to Amanda, I let her continue. "They didn't know what he was really like."

I didn't either. "Did he like to laugh? To dance? To sing? Was he funny? I don't even know what his major was in college." I asked.

A huge smile covered Amanda's face as she recalled her older son. "He was fun. Always. Even as a baby." The grief seemed to lift as she remembered Jonas from infancy to his teen-aged years. "He acted a bit wild over the past few years. College." She shrugged as if to ask what can you do? "I was worried, but I felt certain he would grow out of it. I had no illusions about what he could get into but I knew that he was basically a good kid. The drug stuff concerned me the most. Moral issues aside, in our society getting involved with drugs is one sure way to endanger your civil liberties and your future. But Jonas found a little drug use harmless. Until a few months ago." She paused and considered before she went on. She gazed out to sea and never met my eyes as she spoke. "I was never into drugs. I didn't even recognize the names of all the substances these kids have access to. They call them club drugs. I think they view them as aids to help them party. Like Ecstasy. They call it X or E. I think that's all the same thing. And then there's this other drug. You might have heard of it as the date rape drug. That's what cured Jonas. I knew he would be okay . . . after what happened."

I didn't ask. I suspected my silence would compel her to go on. It did.

"One night I found him on the porch at our house down the beach. Sobbing. I'd never seen Jonas like that. He couldn't stop crying. He had offered GHB to a friend. Kids use it like alcohol for a high but, as I mentioned, the press calls it the date rape drug. This kid put the drug in someone's drink. Jonas was livid. At the boy. At himself. He thought he knew the kid but clearly he didn't."

The episode Sharmaine had discussed. What Jonas thought when he gave the GHB to his friend I'd never know, but I did know that Sharmaine and Amanda Angel agreed that his contrition was real.

"He was angry with his friend. He was angry with himself for not seeing what could happen. He felt terrible for the girl. And he was scared. I'd like to say that my son was so morally upright that the incident turned him around, but that isn't what happened. He got scared straight." Again Amanda paused and again I remained silent. "His father handled the situation and Jonas dealt with it head-on. He did.

He seemed to be developing into a completely new person. An adult. I felt so happy thinking his wild years were over. That's why when he disappeared . . . ." Disbelief flooded her face. "His father thought he had fallen back into his old patterns but I knew something was wrong. Right from the start. I knew. From the first innocuous phone call from Max wondering why Jonas hadn't shown up at work, why he wasn't answering his phone. Dropping out of sight for a weekend wasn't unusual. We didn't have anything special going on at home so I didn't find that odd. He didn't always check in but when Max called me on Monday morning I knew Jonas was in trouble."

I sat silently because I had nothing to add. Could I dredge up some bromide to make Amanda feel any better? I didn't think so.

"You know, a mother is supposed to protect her children. I keep thinking that I should have been able to stop it, to prevent it. His death. Those thoughts haunt me."

"You know . . . ."

Amanda interrupted. "Yes, I do. I understand that there was nothing I could do. But knowing doesn't help. I can't help feeling that there must have been something I could have done." Amanda turned in her chair and met my eyes. "Thank you for asking about him. No one ever does. At the funeral, everyone said they were sorry. The next time I saw my friends they would ask how I was doing but they never mentioned his name. They never asked how the investigation was going. Never. Not once. Shopping with a friend one day in Bay Head, I ran into Schyler Devereaux. She's a cute young girl who dated Jonas on and off for years. I introduced Schyler as Jonas's friend. You should have seen Margie, the woman I was with. Her eyes glazed over. She said 'oh.' That's all she said. "Oh."

"People don't know how to act. I'm sure they care. They just don't know what to do." I believed what I said.

"Ask me about him. Ask me about my son. That's what

they should do. Ask me how the investigation is going. Ask if they are ever going to catch that arrogant cretin who thought he had the right to take another life, my son's life. That's what they should do." Amanda seemed embarrassed by the show of emotion that I found remarkably controlled. She slipped her sunglasses on to cover eyes that were filling with tears. Her voice was calm when she next spoke. "Thank you for asking."

CHAPTER 58

I didn't actually set out to see Hilde. I set out to take a walk. I will admit, however, that when it came time to pick a direction, the thought that Hilde's house was down the beach from our borrowed home did occur to me. So I strolled south along the water's edge searching for the shingled house that Andy had pointed out from the road. I'm not sure what prompted me to go up to the Bossick's door and knock. Okay, I am. I couldn't quite reconcile the image Hilde projected at work with the Hilde that Andy described. I was curious and a little bored. On my first day off, I didn't miss my job at Heavenly Dips but once Amanda Angel's visit ended, I did feel a little lonely all alone on the deck overlooking the ocean.

Based on what I saw when Andy pointed out the house, I was fairly certain the Bossicks owned the gray shingle Victorian that I would think earlier generations considered spacious. In deference to modern conventions, a monolithic glass addition, with architecture both oversized and overwrought, tripled the size of the house. I liked the new space. Just not as a wing of a classic summer cottage.

It took me a few minutes but eventually I found a stretch of wood boards that cut between the tilting fences that both protected the dunes and lent a rustic beauty to the scene. One stretch of path led me to a wide deck in front of a glass wall. If the Bossicks were at home, I expected one of them to appear, so I plastered a smile on my face and waited under the oversized American flag that snapped in the wind above my head. No one came.

I ventured up the steps to the porch that wrapped around the original house, the section that conformed to my ideal of a summer house. Every creak of the porch under my feet brought back memories of childhood summers in houses that were already old. As I pulled open the aged wooden screen door, the spring produced its unique creak, a sound I recalled hearing only before the age of twelve at my great-grandmother's house. I noticed a tear in the lower right corner of the screen. Doors like this one always had a rip somewhere. This door had many. Squares of spare screening were sewn on three out of the four panels in the wooden frame. I couldn't resist. As far as I knew, no one was home. Who would be hurt by a little noise? I pulled the door wide open and let it slam shut. The door behaved as I expected first with one loud bang and then a lower tone as the door fell into place. I loved that sound. Apparently, so did the woman who stuck her head around the corner of the deck. She had a smile on her face.

"I'm sorry. I was about to knock. No one saw me come across the deck I thought no one was home . . . ."

"I was on the phone. I saw you come up but decided that you were not dangerous. Am I wrong?" The petite woman grinned, something I had never seen Hilde do. The resemblance became more pronounced when she feigned a scowl. "I hope not."

"Not dangerous. Just hoping to see Hilde."

This time the woman did not feign a scowl; she scowled. When she did, I realized where Hilde got the cold expression that was the hallmark of her customer service demeanor.

"I work with her at Heavenly Dips."

"Oh. I was afraid . . . wondered . . . I didn't know . . . I was under the impression that only kids worked at Heavenly Dips." Mrs. Bossick had spotted me right away. I could fool the young ones with the sartorial equivalent of smoke and mirrors but no way could I fool the old ones. Not that Mrs. Bossick was such an old one. She could not have been fifty yet. "Hilde was in her room getting ready for work. I'll see if she's still here." Her expectant tone asked for my name. I gave it.

"Why don't you make yourself comfortable, Meg? I'll run up and see if she's available." Mrs. Bossick pointed to a wide selection of seating options on the deck. I was settling onto a chaise that faced the ocean when she stopped. "Before I do," she appeared embarrassed by her parental tone, but I definitely heard a tone I hadn't heard in twenty years. "I feel I need to get something off my chest."

I stopped my descent into the chair and stood in front of Mrs. Bossick feeling like a teenager.

"Am I correct in assuming you are the Meg at whose apartment Hilde stayed the night of Jonas's funeral?"

I nodded, feeling guilty although I did not yet know why.

"I was quite worried about Hilde that night. She doesn't usually stay out so late, virtually all night in that case."

That wasn't my fault, yet I knew Mrs. Bossick thought I should feel guilty.

"And when she came home, she seemed groggy. I suspected she had been drinking."

If that was true it wasn't my fault.

"I know that you are old enough to buy liquor."

"I don't." I interrupted. Suddenly, I saw myself through Mrs. Bossick's eyes. What kind of adult hangs out with kids? Aside from those with professional interests—teachers, coaches, and parole officers—the kind who appear on the news for a variety of reasons ranging from standing outside a liquor store giving liquor to minors to sitting in the Dateline kitchen trying to explain themselves to Chris Hanson. "I don't host parties at my apartment."

I like to think the sun shining in Mrs. Bossick's eyes made her frown, but, no matter what the cause, she was still frowning at me.

"I know it might seem odd, a woman who's a little older working at Heavenly Dips,"

She nodded. Her expression added that it certainly did.

"I just need to make a little money." I told her about

leaving my job to return to graduate school, but I left out the part about deferring school to sail around with Andy. "This job and the apartment nearby kind of fell in my lap. I hate the job and the apartment, but I have to get by until something better comes along. I am not part of the kids' social circle nor do I want to be. I have my own friends." Nowhere near Seaside Heights, but she didn't have to know that. "I think you can understand why I wasn't about to turn the Heavenly Dips staff away on the day of Jonas's funeral. Or any day. They are very nice to me." I couldn't imagine what she would think if I told her about my house-sharing situation with Ed. She'd probably call the cops even though he was twenty-one. At least I believed he was. Maybe I should have asked for ID. "I never thought of myself as acting in loco parentis. But I understand your concerns. Given that I am a bit older maybe I should think of myself as sort of an authority figure, or at least like someone who is older and wiser. Or should be."

Not a muscle on her face moved. I talked in an effort to elicit even the slightest trace of a smile.

"And the night of the funeral, we were just watching old sitcoms on television and we all fell asleep, one by one."

"That's what Hilde said."

"She was telling the truth. The funeral made for an emotionally draining day." Or a day when someone chose to drug us. I didn't bring up that theory.

"Thank you. I would appreciate you keeping in mind that Hilde is only a teenager and lacks your maturity."

Maturity. She thought I possessed maturity. I felt relief flood through my body.

"I'll get Hilde."

Although the sun was a bit strong and the breeze was a bit weak for my taste, I enjoyed the sounds of the beach while I waited for Hilde. I could not think of another situation where screaming and yelling sounded so joyful and soothing. When I heard a glass door slide open behind me, I turned to see Hilde with hair and clothes styled exactly as they were when she arrived for work. So much for the idea that she was a different person at home.

"Meg?" Hilde sounded confused.

"Hilde." I sounded thrilled to see her.

"How did you know I lived here?"

Now that was a good question. An obvious question. A question I should have anticipated. All the time I'd spent with Andy, and I didn't expect it or have a response. I tried the answer a question with a question routine. "I am visiting up the beach and took a walk . . . ." Unfortunately, I couldn't come up with a question.

Hilde could. "But how did you know to stop here?"

"I met Amanda Angel and when she mentioned that you lived down the beach, I asked her to describe the house so I could stop in."

"How did you meet Mrs. Angel?"

"A friend, the friend I am staying with, knows her."

Hilde sneered. "I'm sure he does." I'd barely made the wh sound in what, before she continued. "Don't lie to me, Meg. I've seen you with him. With Andy Beck. You're in the Angel house. I was taking a walk," she used air quotes as she parodied my explanation, "and I saw you."

Hilde was the one who should be a detective. I'd only been in the Angel house for sixteen hours. "Hilde, an incident took place at work last night and the PI thought I shouldn't stay in my apartment." That was true.

"I could tell what he thought." Her tone was bitter. "I saw you."

I wasn't certain what she saw but her intonation made it clear that Andy and I weren't playing scrabble at the time.

"Hilde, I know you thought he was cute . . . ."

"It doesn't matter." Her tone said it did, a lot.

"Hilde, Andy's almost twice your age. And I'm . . . older . . . we have more in common." I didn't mention that more meant sharing an underwear drawer.

"Whatever you say." Hilde was in a huff and wanted me to know it.

"Hilde, can I tell you a secret?"

"What?" She sounded petulant but petulance was a step in the right direction.

"I lied about my age by almost ten years. I'm not twenty-four." What the heck? Her mother would tell her if I didn't. "Ed guessed I was twenty-four and I felt so embarrassed. He didn't think a woman my age should have a job like this one. So, I let him believe I was twenty-four. And then I couldn't get out of the lie. Do you understand?"

Hilde did. I could tell. Her sour expression didn't exactly turn sweet but it did soften. She said she understood and I believed that she did. "I know what you mean. You say something or you do something and then you're stuck with the story. I know exactly how that is." Suddenly, her scowl resurfaced and I knew her mind had returned to the issue of Andy Beck. "But still, you knew I liked him. I made conversation with you. I gave you lots of opportunities to tell me you liked him."

"And remember how I tried to point out that he was too old. That's because I was interested in him too but I didn't know how to say it." Okay, that was true. More or less. "Hilde, please don't tell the kids at work about Andy. Then you'll have to explain how old I am and that would be embarrassing." I clarified. "For me."

I thought she offered her nod reluctantly but I accepted it as an indication of agreement, if not understanding.

"I don't talk at work. I've got to go." She changed to a pair of dark sunglasses she pulled from her apron and covered her eyes. "Why did you come here anyway?"

I shrugged. "Just felt like chatting. I'm not working today. I didn't know if you were. I thought we could hang out a little." I saw my face reflected in her glasses. I wasn't even lying and I had guilt plastered all over my features.

"Sorry, I'm on my way out. I'm covering swing shift."

She fanned out her skirt as if to confirm her destination. Just as she turned to leave, her mother reappeared—tray in hand. “I made lemonade for you girls.”

“I can’t, Mom. I’m leaving.” Hilde spoke only a few words to her mother but her attitude added plenty. You’re dumb. You never listen to what I say. You’re a great disappointment to me. You’ll probably get along fine with Meg.

CHAPTER 59

I didn't appreciate the way Hilde treated her mother or me, but I did appreciate the final words she tossed over her shoulder as she disappeared into the house. "I don't have time for lemonade. Maybe Meg does."

"I do. Do you mind?" I smiled and reached for a glass. The icy surface felt great. I might have been at the beach, but that didn't mean I wasn't experiencing the heatwave.

I gulped the lemonade, made not from powder but from actual lemons. "This is great." I held the cool glass to my forehead. "When you take a walk, you have to walk back. I always forget that part."

Mrs. Bossick smiled but appeared distracted. She went to the wall of windows and slid the door shut. She gestured for me to take a seat at a white wooden table under a purple umbrella. "Do you mind if I ask you something?" She slipped into the chair across from me.

Not if it gave me an excuse to sit and polish off the lemonade. I shook my head.

"I'm a little worried about Hilde. I know the Angel boy died and I realize she went out with him a few times . . . ."

That was more than I'd realized.

"But she seems so upset by his death. Has she said anything to you?"

"I know she, like a lot of people, had mixed feelings about Jonas but I think she felt terrible about what happened to him. Who wouldn't? I realized that she was upset. I've seen her get emotional. But I don't know any specifics. I'm sorry I can't help you."

Mrs. Bossick gazed into space, formulating her next question until the phone rang. She asked me to stay and rushed inside to answer the call. I finished my lemonade and Hilde's. After all, she wasn't coming back and I began to wonder if her mother was. She still hadn't returned. I put the glasses on the tray and carried it with me as I stuck my head inside the door. A very agitated Mrs. Bossick paced the wide tile living room floor discussing a shipment that never left Hong Kong. I gestured that I was leaving. She held up a finger and crooked it. The universal sign for come in and hang on a minute. I could tell the delay would be more than a moment but I nodded. I slid the tray on a tile-topped table and wandered over to a photo display on a long console under a wall covered with even more pictures.

Clearly, Mrs. Bossick loved photographs. She exhibited dozens. The wedding portraits went back three generations. I worked my way from them to current photos of the Bossick family. I found several recent shots of Hilde but more of Heidi. The twins were identical but Heidi's style was soft, friendly, approachable. I searched for a picture of them together. Call me crazy but if I had twins, at some point I would have photographed them together. I found photos that covered every year of the young Bossick girl's life. One Bossick girl per photo.

"I love pictures. I guess you can tell." Having resolved her business problem, Mrs. Bossick joined me in front of the array of photos. She pulled out her favorites to show me. "Hilde was such a beautiful child even with that worried expression on her face. I don't like that get-up she wears when she goes out these days. I think she looks much prettier this way." She handed me a photo of I assumed, Heidi.

"I thought Hilde was a twin."

Mrs. Bossick's expression said she found that thought amusing. "Whatever gave you that idea?"

"I think I heard someone mention Heidi."

"Oh, Heidi." She smiled at the mention of the name. "Hilde must have been talking about her childhood. When she was a little girl, she had an imaginary friend, actually more of an alter-ego. She called her Heidi. She was so cute. Sometimes she would be Heidi all day. She would dress up like Heidi and make us call her Heidi. Her little routine was adorable."

Adorable? I wasn't so sure Mrs. Bossick had the right adjective.

CHAPTER 60

After a few hours in a beach chair with the low waves washing over my feet, I returned to the house I had christened Scamelot and found Andy reading in the screened-in gazebo. "You're home early." I plopped onto a chaise lounge beside his. Plopping on the furniture in this house proved neither painful nor dangerous, a refreshing change from my place in Seaside Heights.

"Big Al cracked like an egg on ceramic tile. I think he felt relieved to confess and not simply about pushing you into the freezer. Big Al believed you had been sent by corporate to catch him skimming money, especially after the home office refused to let him fire you when it so apparent that . . . well . . . you weren't the best Little Dipper they ever had."

That comment hurt. I hoped they threw the book at Big Al.

"Jonas was right about Big Al. Too bad he didn't see him resign, seconds before he would have been fired and seconds after he was arrested. The guy's been stealing from Heavenly Dips for years. His trips to the bank included an extra stop at his own piggy bank, a lockbox in the trunk of his car. Jonas trapped him from beyond the grave. He'd given Schyler a wad of twenty-dollar bills and told her to break each one buying an ice cream cone at the Heavenly Dips store in Seaside Heights. The cops found three of them still in Big Al's private bank."

"Did Schyler know why he asked her to do that?"

"I don't know but I imagine she would do anything he asked."

I recalled Schyler's lanky build. "He should have asked

someone with my eating habits to do it. He would have gotten faster results."

"Speaking of you, Big Al maintains that he did not mean to kill you when he pushed you into the freezer. He believed one more scare might make you leave—which he wanted. Desperately. He thought you were on to him."

I had solved a crime—just the wrong crime. And okay, maybe solved was the wrong word. Maybe smoked out was a better term. My presence had simply forced Big Al Braddock into doing something stupid. "So because he thought I was investigating his embezzlement he decided to launch a harassment campaign to force me out? Why bother? I might be gone but the surveillance cameras would remain."

"He had those all figured out. Or thought he did. Max had told him there were two. He found them and blocked them. Unfortunately for him, he never considered that there might be a third." Andy shook his head. "He doesn't deny responsibility for last night. Not that it matters. They have him on tape. But that's all he takes responsibility for. He says he took advantage of the earlier attacks on you by adding one more."

"So I still have enemies out there? How many enemies can one Little Dipper have?" I was preoccupied with that thought but Andy continued with Big Al's story.

"Even though he denies any involvement in Jonas's death everyone wants to jump on the bandwagon that he killed the kid. Except Max. He feels betrayed by Big Al but he still can't believe that someone he's known so long would kill his son. Petino described how Big Al was spewing details of his crimes. Once he got started, he couldn't fess up fast enough. He thinks, and I agree, that Big Al would have confessed if he killed Jonas. I don't think the case is solved but I've been working non-stop since the day Max called me. I'm going to take a few days off. Just until we see what happens with Big Al."

"What about that kid Trent?"

"It seems that there was no real mystery surrounding Trent other than his family did not want anyone to know he was in rehab which is where he was when Jonas was killed." Andy shook his head. "I really thought Trent would be our man. It was so obvious. Too obvious."

I was anticipating some quality time with Andy when he broke the news that he had agreed to do a little checking around for Karl Elkins. "He's not going to give up. I don't know if I told you but I ran into him the other night. It couldn't have been an accident. Technically, he's stalking me. I might as well take advantage of this free time to check out what he wants and get rid of him."

"Why is he so intent on having you do the work?"

"I asked the same thing. He said he knew Max Angel would never settle for less than the best." Andy blushed as he shrugged off the compliment. "I talked to Max so I have a fairly good idea what I will find out. In many missing person cases, the missing person doesn't want to be found. Max intimated to me that was the case with Bunny. Unless she lied to Max for some reason, I don't think Karl will like what I come up with: Bunny Elkins does not want to be found. Nonetheless, I'll confirm his story with her friends."

"While you're talking to them, why don't you ask for some details on why Bunny hated Jonas?" I forced casualness into my tone.

Andy smiled. "I know you want me to tell them I've been hired to locate Bunny Elkins and nonchalantly add, 'by the way my girlfriend thinks she killed Jonas Angel so I'd appreciate your providing any evidence that might incriminate your good friend in his murder'."

"Bottom line, you've got my drift but you could be more subtle. Maybe she didn't kill him but she could have told them something that would hold a key to the Angel kid's murder."

"Possible." An unconvinced Andy returned to his reading.

"If you do have to go back on Jonas's case, I came up with another suspect this morning—if being a complete lunatic is grounds for suspicion." I told him the story of my visit to the Bossick house. "Her mother is worried about her. She wanted to ask me something. She hesitated and then the phone rang and she never got a chance to ask."

"For someone hanging out around the house, you had a big day. Want a drink?" Andy made no move to get up.

"I can serve myself."

"So then it wouldn't be a problem to serve me?" He handed me an empty glass.

Luckily, Andy Beck was very cute. Before I served both of us, I told him the details of my conversation with Amanda Angel.

"I leave you here alone for one morning and you uncover all this information. Instead of scooping ice cream in Seaside Heights, maybe we should have simply dropped you on this porch for the summer."

Now he comes up with that plan.

"I have two more pieces of information—good news and bad news from my visit to the Bossick house."

"Good?"

"You have an admirer."

"Bad?"

"Hilde knows that you and I are involved. I told Hilde that I met you at Heavenly Dips. Then I tried to convince her you were too old for her. Speaking of which. I never thought about how my summer activities would look to a responsible adult."

"Why would you? Aside from Big Al, I am the only adult observing you."

I noticed that he did not include the adjective responsible in his description. "Take a minute and view me from Mrs. Bossick's perspective."

Andy took a minute. "Yeah. I didn't view you from a parent's viewpoint."

“I think my days of fraternizing with the troops outside of work are over.”

“The whole experience will be over soon.”

Until then, we could enjoy the Angel house. Andy and I ate, drank, and stared at the ocean. “It’s hard to believe we can’t actually afford this.”

“Someday we will.” Andy sounded confident.

“Not if we keep living the way we are.” I hated to be practical but somebody had to be. When I am the more pragmatic half of a couple, that couple is in real danger.

“I like the way we live. You can’t complain about this.” Andy was right. I couldn’t complain. “So someday we’ll stop and get nine-to-five jobs but we can’t do that until we’re finished with this life. When we feel the need to settle down, when that happens, if that happens we’ll stop what we’re doing. For now, I’m off to get the story on Bunny Elkins.”

“Now?”

“I’d ask you to come along but I’m fairly sure you would spend all your time trying to prove she killed Jonas Angel.”

“Let me repeat, it wouldn’t hurt to ask the people you interview what they think on that topic.”

Comments like that explained why Andy left me at home.

CHAPTER 61

My cover was blown. Hilde knew. Big Al and his son knew. Soon everyone would know that I was the PI's girlfriend. Soon everyone could make a good guess at why I had come to Heavenly Dips. No one would confide in me. Maybe no one would even talk to me. Nonetheless, Andy and I decided I should work one more last day at Heavenly Dips. After all, what could happen to me in broad daylight on the bright Boardwalk? My goal? Observe the reactions of the others to Big Al's arrest and his attempt to warn me off with an eye to uncovering the perpetrators of the other attacks on me.

Andy dropped me in front of my apartment in Seaside Heights to pack up my meager wardrobe before I reported for work. Eventually, I would have to close the apartment and evict Ed but at the moment I focused on moving myself to Mantoloking.

As I came through the door, Ed greeted me with wide eyes.

"Why do you look so surprised to see me?" I sounded suspicious, perhaps because I'd just tripped over a gigantic cardboard box and a heap of bulging trash bags.

"I wondered if you would show up for work today, swing shift by the way. I only scheduled you for five hours. I didn't know what to expect. After all, you didn't come to work yesterday. You don't even know that the cops came and arrested Big Al. He is currently incarcerated." Ed's tone indicated he was excited by the news, although not excited enough to move from his reclining position on the sofa. I followed his gaze to a rerun of The Beverly Hillbillies, the episode where the Clampetts do something that their snobbish neighbors find appalling.

"No wonder he worried that you were a plant. Big Al has been stealing for years. Not big amounts. Just enough to stay under the radar. But over the years, the figures mounted up. Luckily, Big Al used the money to send his stepson to law school. He's going to need a good lawyer." Ed chuckled.

I knew more but didn't share with Ed. According to Maxwell Angel, Big Al's son hoped to work a restitution deal so his father would have to serve minimal time if any. According to Andy, Max would support the deal as long as Big Al had nothing to do with Jonas's death. Big Al denied that charge vigorously. Nonetheless, the cops continued to take a serious look at him for the murder.

With lots of pleasure and even more condescension, Ed informed me that with Big Al indisposed he would be managing the Seaside Heights store for the remainder of the season. Using a wide array of words I had read but never heard spoken aloud, he explained why he was up to the task. "I have been cogitating about the problematical reactions associated with my assumption of a managerial role. Although I have been an Angel for two years now, I have behaved in most ways like a peer. I will brook no disrespect. My first step will be to make that clear."

I didn't feel certain that he could make the directions to the restroom clear but Ed seemed determined to hold onto his GMAT talk. Having peeked at his prep book, I felt fully capable of telling him that his grandiloquence was recondite and could make employees perceive him as a popinjay who spouted taradibble. I kept my mouth shut. Why wouldn't I? He would never accept advice from a simple blue wing.

If Ed had guessed my motives for working at Heavenly Dips, he didn't say. He was so impressed with the news about his step up the corporate ladder that I wasn't sure he would have mentioned anything about me—even if he had learned my true identity.

"You know, Meg, I appreciate your letting me stay here

and all. But now that I am management I think the arrangement is inappropriate." His comment explained the piles at the front door. Ed was moving out. He didn't want to fraternize with the help. He didn't say Little Dipper but I knew what he meant. Big Al was gone but Big Ed had arrived. After all, Ed had learned management skills, or non-skills, from Big Al. "I'm moving back in with my friends. After all, I paid for the entire summer. I guess I should regret that I only got this promotion because Big Al is a murderer." His tone made it clear that he didn't feel bad at all.

"We don't know that. Big Al is being held for theft not for murder."

"Yeah, right." Ed snickered.

"Ed, there has been no resolution in Jonas's murder. You can't condemn Big Al until the proof comes in."

"Right, Meg. Jonas finds out Big Al is embezzling. Jonas stops coming to the Seaside Heights store, his favorite I might add. Why? Because he's afraid of Big Al. Are you telling me after that sequence of events somebody else just happened to kill Jonas?"

"Maybe." I heard the defensive note in my voice.

Ed shook his head as he grabbed the bags he'd piled in the doorway. "That limited way of thinking, Meg, is why you are not in management." His statement would have had more impact if he hadn't tripped on his untied shoelace on the way out.

CHAPTER 62

My biggest reservation about returning to Heavenly Dips, even for five hours, was working for Ed, or as he now viewed himself, Big Ed. He no longer sported gold wings. He had been elevated to a wingless wonder. A badge boy. He could barely stop fondling the bright blue tag that hung around his neck.

I knew that if he said one cross word to me, I'd be out of there. To avoid conflict on what I knew would be my last day, I obeyed all the rules. I went to the counter, got the key, went around to the back door and clocked in a few minutes early. Ed had my old halo and a new pair of wings waiting for me. Not a spare set of white from the cabinet, but blue wings. "I drove down to New Gretna to pick them up especially for you." Apparently, Ed worried that wearing white wings would go to my head. I didn't bother telling him my wings hardly mattered since I would soon shed them and vanish from Heavenly Dips just as I had arrived—without warning.

Sharmaine was on duty when I reached the front of the store. Lounging along the counter watching the daily parade pass by, but ready to serve. If she knew anything about my role in the events of the last few days, she didn't mention it. "So, how about Big Al killing Jonas?"

"We don't know that. Big Al hasn't been charged."

"Yeah, but it's only a matter of time." I noticed her bright brown eyes scanned the Boardwalk to the south as she spoke. Searching for Lynyrd? I assumed so.

"I'm sure the police are looking at Big Al but they haven't stopped investigating other possibilities. The crime is not solved."

She turned towards me and opened her wide eyes even wider. "Lynyrd says it's so obvious. I mean, Big Al tried to kill you. He pushed you in that freezer. He pushed you off the Boardwalk. And he put you on that Ferris wheel."

I didn't control the impulse quickly enough. I turned to Sharmaine with a frown on my face. How did Sharmaine know about the Ferris wheel?

"I think that was a really mean thing to do." Her voice sounded unnaturally high. "Ed told me about it."

I didn't tell her that Ed didn't know. Or did he? I couldn't figure out how the story of my sleepover at the traveling fair could have gotten out—to Ed or Sharmaine.

Sharmaine jabbered on about what happened the day before when the police arrested Big Al and led him away from Heavenly Dips in handcuffs. I should have listened but I didn't. My mind stayed focused on one thought: Sharmaine knew about the Ferris wheel. She wanted me to think that Ed had told her but I had never told Ed.

Was Lynyrd my victimizer? Had he told Sharmaine? He was the one who went out that morning and the one most likely to speak with Sharmaine. What possible motive would Lynyrd have to hurt me or scare me? His involvement in drugs was a non-issue, but maybe he didn't know that. Did he think I wanted to turn him in? I barely spoke to the customers as I reviewed every word I had ever exchanged with Lynyrd as well as with Sharmaine. My head was in the display case when the realization hit. I congratulated my customer on winning a Cherubic Cherry on a cloud and awarded him the first free cone in the promotion I invented. I got the ersatz winner on his way quickly so I could turn to my coworker. "Sharmaine, did you have a thing with Jonas."

"A thing?" She acted dumb but she knew what I meant.

"A fling? A romance? Sex?"

"No way." Her big brown eyes opened wide but not from surprise, from fear.

"Sharmaine, I won't tell anyone you slept with Jonas."

"No. No. I didn't. That's the truth. I didn't." I did not get the impression that she was lying but I did get the impression that she was frightened. "I never slept with Jonas."

Sharmaine sounded so earnest that I believed her. Still, her relationship with Jonas was all I could think about as I watched her scoop a triple-decker. As soon as she finished, I moved back to Sharmaine's side.

"But the girl you told me about." My intonation softened. "The girl with Jonas's friend. The girl he tricked."

Sharmaine stared across the Boardwalk but I could tell she didn't see the passers-by.

"That was you, wasn't it?"

Her eyes filled with tears.

"Did Lynyrd know?"

She nodded sending a few tears down her cheek. "Yes."

"And you think that's why he killed Jonas?" I tried the direct approach.

"No," she screamed so loudly that I expected Ed to rush from the back of the store to practice his management skills, but he didn't. "Lynyrd hated Jonas for what he did. He didn't hear the story from me but he heard it. He didn't know me then. He just knew the victim was a girl like me."

"A girl like you?"

"Someone that Jonas and his friends wouldn't normally hang with." She shook her head. "I should have known."

Two teen-aged girls with a hankering for Milky Way Mint kept me from finding out what Sharmaine should have known. By the time I finished dipping two scoops into black holes for them, Sharmaine had left for the day and Hilde had clocked in. When we had a break in traffic, I got right to the point. "Hilde do you have any idea who played those little jokes on me?"

I didn't expect Hilde to know but her guilty expression told me she did. "I heard things had happened to you, that Big Al pushed you into the freezer. I heard about the stage and the Ferris wheel."

"Who told you about the Ferris wheel?"

"I don't know. Ed or Sharmaine."

"Please try to remember, Hilde. It's important."

She said she would try but by the time I clocked out she hadn't. At least she claimed she hadn't. I doubted Hilde had any interest in helping the other woman in Andy Beck's life.

CHAPTER 63

I found Bobby Briggs, aka Mr. Smarmy, waiting where I expected to find Andy—at the end of the Sky Ride. When I caught sight of Briggs at the gate my face must have told my story.

"I'm not here to hurt you. I would never hurt anyone." The man appeared almost as earnest as Ed but not as convincing. "Can we talk for a moment? I didn't feel I had a right to come to the store." Mr. Smarmy seemed much more attractive—and much more believable—without his slimy grin. I said yes. I had to say yes. Talking to people like Mr. Smarmy was my job, my real job.

I let him lead me to the same bench where he had chatted me up what seemed like years ago but had only been a few days before. I didn't understand how Mr. Smarmy survived in his shiny suits. Despite the heat, his image was cool, crisp and, as always, slick. The occasional breeze that tousled my curls blew by Mr. Smarmy without disturbing a single hair. When he rested his hands on his thighs I recognized the really, really big ring that had amazed me in the arcade on my first day at Heavenly Dips. Big Al must have called him as soon as I arrived, if not before.

"I walked by earlier today and was surprised to see that you were back at work."

"Today was my last day. The kids at the stand don't actually know that."

"Do they know that you are Beck's girlfriend?"

I didn't single out Hilde. I shrugged. "They didn't mention if they do. I didn't tell them. I think the word might get out given all that's gone on in the past few days."

"It's odd. Big Al realized that something up when you

showed up. He never thought it had anything to do with the kid going missing. He claimed Jonas pulled that kind of stuff all the time. Big Al realized that Jonas suspected he was stealing. Then, Jonas stopped coming around and you showed up. Big Al assumed that you were there to spy on him. He said you made such a big stink about not knowing Jonas, he figured you must know him."

I made a note to ask Andy for additional training. Despite my proclamations to the contrary, it seemed that I was not a natural-born investigator.

I sat silently waiting for Briggs to continue. "You do know my stepfather hasn't been charged with the murder of Jonas Angel? If you don't count the court of public opinion where he's been charged, tried, and convicted. Have you seen the headlines? Heavenly Dips into Till. Heavenly Dipster Arrested."

I nodded and felt planets orbiting above my head. For the last time, I removed the halo. This conversation did not need punctuation by bobbing doodads.

"You know why he hasn't been charged? Because he didn't do it." Briggs grew agitated.

"I told people that all day today. I did. I don't know who killed Jonas Angel, maybe your father did, but I do know that he has not been charged. I try to say that but you're right. People do not differentiate between the theft and the murder." I could hardly believe it. I had something in common with Mr. Smarmy.

"There hasn't been an indictment and there won't be. The truth, my father's innocence will come out."

"If you're looking for a PI, Andy isn't available."

Bobby Briggs interrupted. "I'm not asking Beck to go to work for my father. I understand that would be a clear conflict of interest. Besides, my father doesn't need a PI. He is innocent. There is no physical evidence linking him to the murder." I didn't remind the guy that no physical evidence linked anyone to the murder. "There will never be enough evidence to indict him because he is innocent."

I agreed that there might not be enough evidence to indict but not necessarily because Big Al was innocent. "I am sure you believe in your stepfather."

"I know my stepfather. I know his limitations. I understand what he's capable of and I also understand what he is not capable of. Believe me, over the years no one has been more critical of Big Al Braddock than I've been. I don't doubt that he stole the cash. The amount wasn't that much; although the total mounted up over the years." His voice softened. "I didn't understand. I didn't even know the money my mother gave me came from Big Al." Bobby Briggs stopped staring into my eyes. He gazed over the ocean. "I feel responsible. Big Al wanted to help me with my tuition when I went back to law school seven years ago. He and I had been estranged for so long. By then my mother was dying and I think he wanted to please her and guarantee that he would have some family in his life for his old age. No matter why he did it, he got in too deep. He wanted to stop but he couldn't. The change in revenue would have aroused suspicions."

I don't know what my face said but I could guess from Briggs's next comment.

"He isn't an evil man."

"He tried to kill me."

Bobby Briggs's eyes met mine. In them, I saw an eagerness similar to the emotion I so often spotted in Ed's eyes. "He did not. He knew I would save you. He loved that store too much to let its reputation be damaged by anything as gruesome as a stiff in the freezer."

I found being dismissed as a stiff in the freezer insulting but I didn't protest. Bobby Briggs was on a roll.

"Big Al said he was suspicious of you. That's why he wanted me to get to know you. He'd tell me when I'd be able to run into you." So much for my incredible sex appeal. "But he didn't want to hurt you. Don't you find it a bit odd that he joked with me that some night he would let you close and push you in the freezer? Don't you find it odd that he phoned me and let me know that you were closing for the first time that night? He didn't tell me what he planned to do. He couldn't without making me an accomplice but in a way he did. He knew I wouldn't let it happen. And, I didn't."

"I got myself out."

"But if you couldn't, I was right there. With the keys. Spare keys he gave me for backup. In clear violation of company policy. You know what a stickler he was for company policy."

"He stole from that company, Bobby." I used the man's real name. Calling him Mr. Smarmy might have broken the mood.

"I'm not defending his behavior or my own. I feel responsible for what happened to you and not only in the freezer."

My eyes asked the question.

Bobby Briggs stared at the surf. "I waited for you the other night. I saw you stop to admire the view. I was waiting for the right moment to run into you accidentally when that kid ran up behind you and pushed you off. I didn't see him coming. I couldn't stop him."

"Wait a minute. What kid?"

"Some punk maybe fourteen or so. Kids all look alike to me these days. The hair. The clothes. The mouths. I heard him talking to his friends as they disappeared down the Boardwalk. He was saying something like 'I told you they couldn't fly.' I would have caught them but I thought helping you was more important. I ran to check on you but a family had come to your aid. I felt kind of annoyed. I didn't want you to fall but once you did I figured taking care of you would be a great way to bond. But I didn't move quickly enough. I didn't see any way to casually chat you up at that point. I left."

"You weren't responsible?"

"No, but I feel responsible for what happened with the freezer. I should have fought harder against Big Al's idea, that a good scare might be just what you needed to get you to quit. But after he heard about the Ferris wheel incident . . . ."

"How?" I interrupted. "How did he find out?"

"When you didn't show up on time, Big Al called corporate to see if he could fire you. I think Maxwell Angel told him to give you a break you'd had a rough night. He told him what had happened. Big Al believed there had to be a limit on how much you could take. He was gung ho about scaring you off. He and I didn't see things the same way. That's why when he mentioned you were closing I worried that he might do something . . . unwise. He was really frightened."

"Of me?"

"He thought you could cost him his job. He had already begun closing down his operation slowly. He got worried about Jonas's nosing around." He held up a hand. "Not enough that he would ever hurt him." He shook his head slowly. "I don't know why he kept skimming after I got out of law school. He never spent a dime on himself and I am doing more than fine. Surprisingly well." He wasn't bragging. He was thinking aloud. "From the minute headquarters told him you were coming, he started cutting back more quickly. That should have been enough but he wanted to know if the company, if Max, suspected. That's why he asked me . . . ." Briggs didn't finish the thought. I did.

"To hustle me?"

Briggs appeared if not ashamed, at least embarrassed.

I didn't force him to answer. "Why are you talking to me if you don't want Andy's help?"

"Because I think you need to know that my step-father is innocent. That means the murderer is still out there. Yes, if Beck finds the real killer, Big Al benefits, but you and your boyfriend nosed around in everyone's business. I think you could still be in danger." As he spoke, Bobby Briggs never smiled. His solemn face seemed much less threatening than his smile. "And, I want to make sure Beck keeps searching for the real killer."

I didn't see the harm in telling Bobby Briggs that Andy was still on the case. "If no one is indicted, he'll go on until he can't find any more leads to pursue."

Bobby Briggs shook his head and gazed out to sea. "For years I hated Big Al. I didn't want him taking my father's place. But now, just over the past few years, he has come to mean a lot to me. I didn't let him know for a long time. It's hard to eat crow. But I did. And now I want to help him."

We sat silently watching the day fade away. In my apron pocket, my cell phone vibrated. I didn't pick up. Bobby Briggs and I were having a moment. I wasn't sure what kind of moment it was, but I knew it was a moment. One that shouldn't be interrupted.

Finally, I spoke. "Big Al Braddock worked for Maxwell Angel for thirty years. He could have gone to Angel about the money. He could have explained. He could have made restitution. He didn't have to kill the kid. It makes no sense."

"Exactly." Bobby Briggs peered deep into my eyes. "It makes no sense."

CHAPTER 64

I was hurrying down the ramp from the Boardwalk and calling Andy on his cell phone when I spotted him pumping quarters into the meter with a speed that the mechanism could not accommodate. He stopped as soon as he heard my voice call his name.

"Where were you?" He sounded frantic. "I went to the Sky Ride to pick you up. You didn't answer your phone. I almost panicked." His intonation indicated that he had, in fact, gone ahead and panicked.

"You must have walked by me."

"When? Where? You should have called."

"I couldn't. Bobby Briggs stopped me on the Boardwalk."

"Well, that makes me feel better." His tone said it didn't.

"He wanted me to know his father is innocent. I told him we understood that there had been no indictment. I even told him that you were still working for Angel."

A car horn suggested that we move our discussion from the center of the street. Andy headed for his car but I grabbed his hand and pulled him toward the ramp to the boards. "It would be nice to spend some time together outside. It can't matter if we are seen together. I can't believe that my coworkers would be shocked."

We found a bench and watched the nighttime Boardwalk come to life as, speaking in low tones, Andy filled me in on his day. "The police are building their case. Petino told Max the evidence is largely circumstantial. Max feels the cops are not convinced that Big Al killed Jonas. I can see why. Yes, he had the motive. Since Jonas was killed with his own golf club he had the means. The timeline is so imprecise that he may have had the opportunity. However, the cops' current estimate is that the murder happened not long after Jonas was last seen around 7:30 PM and Big Al stayed at work until midnight."

"He didn't pull it off during one of his many trips to the bank?" My tone said I was asking a question, but I was making a suggestion.

"You know Big Al. Thinks the store can't run without him, so he never leaves for more than fifteen minutes at a time, never even takes a full meal break. Someone would have noticed if he was gone for a long period of time. No one did."

"Briggs insists that his father is innocent."

"He would, wouldn't he?" Andy stated the obvious.

The lights of Seaside Heights glowed even more brightly as the gray sky faded to black. The air grew cooler, which is not to say cool, and the breeze kicked up as I explained Bobby Briggs's position to Andy. "He feels the DA will never be able to get an indictment because the evidence just doesn't exist. He admits that his father was responsible for my trip into the freezer but swears that he had nothing to do with the other warnings I received. Bobby Briggs swears Big Al only capitalized on the earlier incidents."

"How did he know about them?"

"Everyone knew about the flight off the Boardwalk. It turns out that Max told Big Al about the Ferris wheel. I don't know if he told the others. Bobby Briggs thinks we could be in danger. I would assume from the person who dumped me on the Ferris wheel. This morning I was upset that Sharmaine knew but now I wonder if Big Al blabbed."

Andy's interest peaked. "Why would Briggs think we could be in danger?'

"His conviction that Big Al is innocent. I think he figures that as time goes by and no one goes on trial for the murder the killer, the same person who tried to warn me off, will get edgy."

Andy tried to emulate Petino's smirk but, on him, the snide expression was more of a sweet smile. "If we think the person who wanted to scare you off is the same person who killed Jonas, we have to rule out Bunny Elkins."

I sounded more disappointed than surprised. "So you spent today investigating Bunny and concluded she couldn't have killed Jonas Angel."

"I pretty much concluded she couldn't have killed a fly."

"She hurt Karl badly."

"Yeah, well, according to her friends that was the only way to get free of him. She would not even tell them where she was going for fear he would worm the information out of them. She sent one postcard to let them know she was okay. After that, she was going underground, at least until the end of the year. She is going to check in around the holidays to see if Karl has moved on. According to her friends, Karl gives new meaning to the word controlling. Did he tell you he got into shape for his wife? She worried he made all that effort so that he could control her physically. She was afraid that the new, stronger Karl would become violent."

If I were the wife of a controlling husband, I might have viewed his transformation that same way.

"Karl feels life has wronged him. Bunny watched him go from sad to angry. She wanted him to get help but he wouldn't. When she broached the idea of divorce, the control accelerated. She knew that he followed her, that he hid in the woods and spied on her at work. Karl believes he loves Bunny which is unfortunate for him because she isn't coming back. Her friends assume that she is somewhere she doesn't see the local news, because if she had heard about Jonas's death, she would have contacted Max somehow. They know she'll be devastated because she realizes how badly it hurts Max Angel."

"You don't think Bunny and Max . . . .?"

Andy interrupted. "No, I don't think. They did have a true mutual admiration society but the relationship remained strictly professional, or at least platonic." At the sight of my mouth opening, he continued. "Believe me. I considered that option. Really."

"If I were Karl I would try to convince the authorities that Bunny was a good suspect in Jonas's murder. Then, they would track her down for him. I mean they did try to reach her as a witness but they would have taken a whole different approach if she were a suspect."

"As your boyfriend, let me say, sometimes you scare me. That said, her friends convinced the police that she could not be in any way involved."

"If that's what they say."

"That's what they say, Maggie." The pet name. A signal that the argument was lost.

CHAPTER 65

Maxwell Angel knew Andy was going to talk to Big Al Braddock and his stepson. Detective Petino did not. We took the bridge across Barnegat Bay to Big Al's house in Toms River, this time in broad daylight. Andy pulled his plain white sedan behind Bobby Briggs's Mercedes. Big Al's old Chevy was nowhere to be seen. I suspected the vehicle, now considered evidence, had been locked away by the police.

Big Al's house was modest but worth enough to provide collateral for his bail. The interior went beyond modest to austere. The decor supported Bobby Briggs's claim that most of the money Big Al misappropriated went for tuition. My guess was that all the money he pilfered went into tuition. The funds certainly didn't go into decorating. Big Al's place made my place in Seaside Heights feel luxurious. What had the house looked like when his wife was alive? More of a home, I hoped.

Big Al had never lived up to his name physically. Now, he was not living up to it emotionally either. His frown had lost is ferocity. He appeared old and defeated. The network of red veins that spread across his cheeks matched an intricate web of red lines in each eye. His pained movements as he played host suggested he'd aged ten years since he'd walked away from the Heavenly Dips booth.

In a dining area off the living room, Big Al, Bobby Briggs, Andy and I sat on metal folding chairs around a card table covered with a stiff plastic tablecloth and drank iced tea in glasses from a fast-food promotion that had ended before Jonas Angel was born. Big Al's chain-smoking explained the wall color. Somewhere in the room there had to be a citrus air freshener that explained the aroma.

Even though he had recently tried to kill me—excuse me, warn me off—Big Al did not seem at all embarrassed to see me. No mention was made of my short trip into the freezer. No mention was made of Mr. Smarmy's project to deceive me. No mention was made of Big Al's position as chief suspect in the murder of Jonas Angel.

Actually, nothing substantive was said until Andy took the lead. "Big Al, I don't know what to believe. Bobby maintains you are innocent of Jonas Angel's murder. He thinks Meg and I could be in danger. I don't care for my own sake. I'm worried about Meg. How did you know that she had been threatened in two separate incidents?"

"Everyone knew the story about how she ruined her wings." After all that had transpired, Big Al still grew emotional at the thought of my crushed wings. The emotion was anger. He recovered quickly. "Then I heard the kids talking when they thought she got in trouble again. They all stayed at her house. When they got up she was gone. That kid, Sharmaine, worried that she'd run off with some loser she goes out with. I may be old but I knew that didn't happen." Big Al turned to me. "You might not be much of a Little Dipper but I knew that even you would be smarter than to hang out with the likes of that guy I seen her with." He grinned as if he'd just delivered a compliment.

I responded with a weak smile, actually more of a grimace. I didn't want to offend Big Al at this point. We needed information.

"So I figured something else had happened. I didn't ask, didn't want to appear too interested. But it got me thinking. If bad things kept happening why would anyone come back. That's when I cooked up the notion of one more little scare."

To my mind, that revelation marked the moment when Big Al should have turned to me and apologized, but his mind didn't work the same way as mine. He sat with his thin lips clamped tight together waiting for Andy's next question.

"After Max told you, did you tell anyone else about the

Ferris wheel?"

"Like I said, the kids knew."

"They knew Meg had been dumped on a Ferris wheel?"

Big Al gave Andy's question a lot of thought. "They knew something happened. Maybe I told them, but I don't remember when I would have done that. Or why. It ain't as if we sit around chatterin' all day."

Andy pushed Big Al to think it over, but Big Al did not produce a straight answer. Andy changed tacks. "You say you didn't kill Jonas." Andy sounded supportive. "Do you have any idea who did?"

Again Big Al spent a long time pondering Andy's question but came up with no alternative theory of the crime. He wanted his word alone to convince Andy and me of his innocence. "I swear to you that I didn't kill Jonas."

"Did you like the Angels?" I asked my first question.

"Very much. Max was always good to me." For the first time since I'd met him, Big Al's voice was modulated, his tone soft. "What I did was unforgivable. Mr. Angel trusted me. He treated me good and I betrayed him. That's what I feel worst about." His expression confirmed his words.

"Do you know his wife?" I asked.

Again anguish twisted Big Al's features into a portrait of pain. "Mrs. Angel is a lovely woman. I don't really know her. But when my wife, Bobby's mother, when she died Mrs. Angel, she came. She brought food and she gave me money to help with the funeral. She is a fine lady. I hate to see her so unhappy. It's not right what happened to her." Big Al's eyes filled with tears. "And she thinks I did it. That I killed her boy." He shook with sobs.

"But you didn't like Jonas, did you?" I kept my tone unemotional.

Big Al did not. His next emotion was disgust. "Kid was a snot." He sneered through his tears. "He wasn't good to his parents like they was good to him. I hated him for that but I wouldn't touch him. Hurting him would only hurt his parents." Big Al appeared earnest. I was willing to buy what he said. "I lost the most important thing in the world. My job. When my wife died that job became my life and now I can never go back." Big Al's tone suggested that he didn't realize whose fault that was. He turned to Andy with tears brimming. "Please, tell Mr. Angel, tell him that I didn't do it. I didn't kill Jonas. I would never hurt him. I mean Max. I could not bear to hurt that man." Apparently, Big Al didn't think that the theft he readily admitted was hurtful.

Andy assured Big Al that he would relay his message to Max. Big Al thanked Andy and then, suddenly embarrassed by his emotional display, said he had to use the can. He asked his son to see us out which meant walking us about ten feet to the door.

On the way, I asked Bobby Briggs. "You admitted your father asked you to run into me accidentally, but did you ever watch me at night? At my apartment."

To judge by his body language, Bobby Briggs was embarrassed. "If I were a better snoop I would have followed you home. I don't even know where you live. I just tried picking you up on the Boardwalk. Big Al would let me know when you would be coming and going from the store." He glanced at Andy. "Sorry, mate. I didn't know. But if you ever wondered she is a very faithful woman."

I am. Not that Bobby Briggs would be the person to test me.

CHAPTER 66

That afternoon Amanda Angel once again visited our deck. Her deck actually, but I was sitting on it. She wore white cotton slacks over a white bathing suit. Her white gauze blouse blew gently in the wind. I felt in awe of her pained, ethereal beauty.

"Max told me I could find you here. He said you and Andy went to see Big Al. What do you think?" She sat on the edge of the lounge across from mine and stared into my eyes. "I know the police are focusing on him but they haven't indicted him. I can't believe he did it. They tell us there is no forensic evidence. No hair. No fibers. How can there be no hair and no fibers? How can someone do a thing like this and leave no evidence? Whoever killed Jonas must have planned carefully." She gazed out to sea. "Why? The police delved into every little indiscretion of Jonas's. And, I will admit there were a number of them. But none that indicated a strong enough motive for murder." She shook her head. "If he hadn't learned, if he had been unfeeling, but I saw him." She released a deep sigh. "Jonas wasn't evil, just a little devilish. He could be devilish and kind at the same time." She smiled at the recollection. "Do you know Hilde Bossick who works at your store?"

"I work with her sometimes."

"Well, Jonas knew she had a crush on him. He had no interest in her romantically. She just wasn't his type. So Hilde pretended to have a twin sister that would be Jonas's type. I found the situation rather frightening. Jonas told me Hilde had a completely separate personality from Heidi, her imaginary twin. He thought it was a game for her. He didn't worry that she suffered from a multiple personality disorder.

He liked her when she played her twin. He even went out with her a few times. He never let on he knew she was playing a trick."

"That was kind?"

"You may see it as devilish, and I'll admit that if I had known at the time, I would have put a stop to it. But Jonas behaved very nicely to Heidi. I think Hilde called herself Heidi. In any event, he told her that he truly liked Hilde. So Hilde got to date Jonas and hear great things about herself."

Now Hilde's behavior made sense, at least as much sense as it ever would. "Did Hilde realize that Jonas knew she was pretending to be her twin?"

Amanda shrugged. "I don't think so. Why do you ask?"

"No particular reason." I changed the subject. "Have you seen Schyler recently?"

Amanda brushed a strand of dark brown hair from her brow as she shook her head. "I should get in touch with her. The police told us she helped Jonas uncover Big Al's thievery. Schyler is a nice enough girl. A little pushy. Jonas felt bad. After all, she had been his first real girlfriend. She couldn't believe their relationship couldn't last forever. Wouldn't believe. He wanted to make the break, but I don't think he ever found the opportunity to end things with her. If he tried, she certainly didn't get the message. After he died, I didn't have the heart to tell her what he was planning. I didn't know what to do. She seemed so distraught. The police had grilled her for quite a few hours. She couldn't believe they were accusing her. I explained that they spoke to everyone close to Jonas. When I think of what she went through . . . ." Amanda got lost in thought for a few seconds. "I told her they needed to know where everyone was when . . . during those hours. Of course, they were concerned that she couldn't prove that she was at home. She thought the police were attacking her. I couldn't subject her to more pain by telling her how Jonas felt or, more precisely, what he didn't feel. If it ever appears that she isn't moving on with her life,

I'll think of a gentle way to let her know the truth."

Amanda's released a deep sigh and stared into space. "I miss him, Meg. Every day. Almost every minute. I accept that he can't come back. All I want is to know what happened. I don't even know if he saw his attacker, if he felt afraid. He was struck on the back and the front of the head and I don't know which blows came first. Did the killer make him drive there? Did he even know the killer was there? Did he know his intent? Did he recognize the person? These are the things I want to know. Details. Did he roll over to flee or did the killer roll him onto his back when he was unconscious, or too weak to fight? I need to know."

I had nothing to say, no answers.

"I created a scenario that I try to believe. I told myself that he never saw the stranger who struck him from behind. Then, over a week after they found Jonas, they found his badge, twenty feet from his body. If the killer pulled it off in a scuffle, Jonas knew. He must have felt fear."

I didn't understand. "Maybe the badge just caught on something and fell off as he walked into the woods."

"The chain wasn't attached and the police didn't find it."

I had another suggestion that an animal had taken a shiny toy away to play but I kept silent. Amanda Angel didn't want to debate. She wanted someone to listen to her. The unspeakable pain on her face made me regret complaining about my life in Seaside Heights. This was why Andy and I made the effort we did, to find answers for this woman. All that work and what answers did we have? None.

CHAPTER 67

The week after I left work Andy interrogated, his word, Sharmaine about the incident on the Ferris wheel. Her story remained unshakable. She couldn't remember who told her what happened. Before, she had claimed Ed or Hilde had told her. This time, she threw Big Al into the mix. Andy questioned Ed and Hilde but they claimed they didn't know who was responsible. They couldn't remember if they told Sharmaine. Everyone knew. An exhausted Andy exhausted his leads. We accepted the possibility that we would never identify the person behind that episode.

Over the next few weeks, Andy continued to pursue the Angel case but found he was running out of avenues to explore.

I accepted that no one would be charged with the crime but Andy wouldn't. Andy couldn't. Neither could Maxwell Angel. He asked Andy to retrace his steps. Time and time again Andy reviewed every possible aspect of every possible suspect's story – including the ones told by the people I worked with. Going on the police's assumption that the crime happened not long after Jonas was last seen, he checked and rechecked their alibis. Lynyrd had been with Sharmaine and witnesses had seen them together. Big Al and Ed had worked until closing but had gone to their own homes after work. Big Al lived alone and Ed's roommates were out partying. Andy had verified that Hilde had been at home with her parents. Even given their alibis any of them could have found time to sneak out. So could Schyler whose parents assumed she was upstairs asleep. Andy's eyes kept turning to Schyler and her weak alibi. Mine kept turning to Bunny Elkins who had no alibi whatsoever.

After only a single week of idle pleasure, and no ice cream, I landed a consulting job from my old employer and pulled my computer out of storage. I spent my days sitting on the deck working. I pressured Andy into hiring a rent-a-wreck so I could make occasional shopping trips. On one trip to pick up some items from the sugar food group at Mueller's Bakery in Bay Head, I spotted a plain white sedan that I assumed belonged to Andy. When I peeked around the lid of the open trunk, I felt more dismayed than surprised to find Karl Elkins on the other side. I was also surprised that he had packed on a good twenty pounds since I had last seen him. That couldn't have been easy. I guessed he was coming from the bakery too.

"Ice cream angel." He recognized me immediately, even without my halo. "What a surprise." A smile would have turned that phrase into what a happy surprise. Karl didn't smile. He returned his attention to arranging tools and other materials in his trunk which was a veritable hardware store.

"Sorry. I thought you were a friend. Your car is similar."

"No, I'm not Andy." He stared at me with a gaze I found more than a little frightening although he paired it with a smile on his lips. "You never mentioned that Andy Beck was your boyfriend."

"You never mentioned you knew him." I didn't ask him how he found out I was involved with Andy. He could have gotten the info moping around the Heavenly Dips stand. Our relationship was common knowledge.

"He never told you about the work he was doing for me?"

"His work is confidential." I wasn't lying. I simply made a statement. "Weird coincidence, isn't it?" I smiled.

"Not really, but running into you is. I'm up here on a job. Just finished." He attempted a smile. "How are you doing? I haven't been up on the Boardwalk lately but I heard they arrested Big Al Braddock." He abandoned his organizational effort and slammed the trunk closed catching a latex glove in the latch. He pulled it out and molded it into a ball with a force that suggested he did not feel as calm as he tried to appear.

"Yes, for fraud not for murder."

"Yeah, but it's just a matter of time until they get him on that charge, right? I mean that would really be a fluke if someone else killed Jonas when Big Al was pulling all that crap." Karl expressed the popular sentiment.

I shrugged. "I don't think Big Al killed Jonas but that's only my unofficial opinion."

"But the cops do, right?"

"If they did, I think they would have arrested him on that charge and they haven't. God knows I'm not crazy about the guy but I feel for him being convicted in the court of public opinion for a crime he didn't commit." I didn't want to say more on the matter of the Angel murder. I certainly didn't want to hear about Bunny unless Karl was going to give her up for Jonas's murder. For the sake of politeness, however, I asked how he was doing.

"I'm doing okay. Better." He wiped sweat from his brow. When he spoke his topic was not his wife. "This drought is really getting to me. We've had a couple of sprinkles but that's about it. It's got to rain soon, don't you think?"

The guy always had been a bit obsessed with the weather. "I'm no meteorologist but the odds are we've got to see some precipitation soon."

"I hope you're right. You'd better be right." Karl lit a cigarette. "I can't stand the heat. I can't take too much worrying about this dry spell." He stared into the distance for a moment. "I want to thank you. You and Andy both helped me when I was . . . before I accepted my Bunny's decision. I'm doing much better now. I'm thinking of moving away, starting over." He must have caught the suspicion on my face. "No, not to the same spot where Bunny went. I don't know where she lives now but wherever she went I wish her well. Maybe she was right. Maybe we will do better apart."

Suddenly, I felt optimistic about the next rain. Karl

Elkins was moving on. Until then I expected that the two events would occur on the same day, a cold one in hell.

CHAPTER 68

Within two hours of running into Karl Elkins, I got another blast from the not very distant past when Hilde Bossick showed at our borrowed house. She arrived just as I was finishing a crumb cake. Not a piece of crumb cake, a crumb cake, one of the two I had picked up at Mueller's only hours earlier. I should have eaten the one with the glaze. Fewer crumbs to brush off. I couldn't get rid of the sugar covered crumbs before Hilde reached the top of the stairs. I greeted her with streaks of powder on my clothes and in my hair. She brushed her hand against her cheek to signal I might want to knock a crumb from the corner of my mouth.

For the first time, I saw her without her Heavenly Dips robe and I thought she looked lovely in her street clothes. Of course, the street clothes she wore, white slacks and a navy top, matched my taste. Her only eyewear was a pair of sunglasses that she slipped off. She wore no rings on her toes or her nose and, with the exception of one small, elegant rose, her tattoos were gone. She'd gotten me with the tattoos. I never suspected the elaborate designs were temporary.

"You quit." Her voice seemed thinner than I recalled. Her tone was tentative.

I nodded without offering any explanation.

"The store is really different now. Ed sucks as a boss." She leaned against the railing and studied her feet. The breeze blew her hair into a gentle frame for her face. She looked as pretty as her imaginary twin sister, Heidi.

"Well, he takes his job seriously."

Hilde sneered. "He's building a career. He's angling for a job in New Gretna. I wish he'd get it and get out of our lives."

I didn't wait for a subtle segue. I asked the question that still nagged at me. "Hilde, did you ever remember who told you about my night on the Ferris wheel?"

She replied without hesitating. "I'll tell you if you make a promise to me."

"What's the promise?"

"My mother told me . . . ." She paused.

For a moment I thought that Hilde was going to tell me that her mother told her about the Ferris wheel. Then I realized she wasn't finished.

Hilde had trouble spitting out the words. "My mother said that you know I don't have a twin. I'm not nuts, you know. I invented Heidi as a joke. A trick to play on Jonas. Really. That's all. I wanted to go out with him, but what could I do? Change my image to become his type. He would have seen right through that trick, so I resurrected Heidi. I made up a sister when I was little. I have been so frightened since Jonas died that someone would find out. I couldn't believe the cops didn't want to interview Heidi."

I could see how embarrassing the revelation would have been but wasn't convinced that was the only reason she was scared of the police. "Did you do anything illegal?"

"Well, making up a social security number might have been bad, but no one even noticed that I submitted the timecard with my number on it."

The switch must have been hard to pull off. "How did you get Heidi hired?"

"I knew what Big Al needed for documentation. So I just brought a mutilated copy of my social security card and my driver's license that I altered. A birth certificate was easy. Big Al didn't care. He barely glanced at it. He was happy to have a body to fill in while I was away."

"No one ever saw you and Heidi together. Didn't they notice?"

"Guess not. Ed did tell me he thought Heidi should have come to Jonas's funeral."

"If you see this as a joke, why are you so frightened?"

"I don't want to seem crazy. That's what people would think. But I knew what I was doing. I always know what I'm doing." She wrung her hands and let her eyes dart over her shoulder towards the beach and stayed there. Finally, she turned to face me. "Please, don't tell anyone about that. About Heidi and Jonas. Please. That's all I ask. Please." She stretched please to a five-syllable word as desperate people do.

"Hilde, I've known for quite a while. If I were going to tell, I would have told by now. I mean, I told Andy but no one at the store."

A twist of Hilde's upper lip told me that she wasn't happy that Andy knew. At the same time, I saw every other muscle in her body relax. No one else knew. I didn't actually say that. I could only assure her that if they did know, I hadn't told them.

"I don't want people thinking I'm nuts."

How could I tell her they already did? I couldn't. I confirmed my promise not to tell and followed the statement quickly with a request. "Now it's your turn. Who dumped me on the Ferris wheel?"

"Sharmaine told me." Hilde hesitated. "She was afraid, she worried that you suspected Lynyrd killed Jonas."

"Did he?"

"No. At least I don't think so. Sharmaine doesn't think he did."

I was confused. "Sharmaine told you that I believed Lynyrd was a killer. She told me she was worried that I was in love with Lynyrd."

Hilde smirked. "Yeah, she said that to throw you, and I guess the rest of us, off. She asked us all if we thought Lynyrd had really gone out for coffee or if he was involved with you. We all told her that was ridiculous. Lynyrd would never be interested in someone like you."

It was one thing for me to say that but I found the words

insulting coming from Hilde. "Why did she even say he went out? Wouldn't it have been less suspicious if she swore he'd been there the entire time?"

"Ed rolled over and opened his eyes at some point. Sharmaine needed a cover just in case he remembered."

I could accept that explanation.

"Anyway, after you got pushed off the Boardwalk, Sharmaine figured you would back off if you got another scare. On one of his jobs, Lynyrd used to run a Ferris wheel. I think he came up with the scheme but Sharmaine helped."

"So they left me stranded me on the Ferris wheel."

She shook her head. "Lynyrd took you."

"He's so skinny I didn't realize he was that strong."

"I don't think he is all that strong. He told Sharmaine you weren't as heavy as you looked."

Was Hilde this naively insulting? I didn't think so. I imagined she relished slighting the other woman, the one who had stolen Andy Beck from her. I ignored her barbs. "She told you this?"

Hilde answered with a nod.

When did Sharmaine start confiding in Hilde? I didn't ask that question. I had another. "Why would Sharmaine care what I thought? For all she knew, I was just some over-age Little Dipper."

"Well, that might have been my fault." Hilde seemed sheepish. "You know I liked Andy. I told you that I wanted to find out, you remember, I mentioned . . . ." Her conversation took a sudden turn. "I thought that maybe I could get to know him if I like ran into him by accident."

"Yes?"

"So I memorized his license plate number because his car is identical to hundreds of others on the road. You'd never notice it if you didn't know the tag."

"Yeah?"

"I didn't follow him or anything. But one day I went to Ocean City to visit a girl I know from home. I wasn't supposed to be there. I'd called out for the late shift and then I saw you working at the Ocean City store. I couldn't say hello because I called in sick. I said I had to stay in the house, the bathroom actually."

"Okay." I held up a hand in the hopes she would not provide any more details about her fictional medical condition.

"Anyway, you were leaving. And I saw you go down the Boardwalk and get in a car. And I knew the license plate. So I figured that maybe you worked for him or with him. I told Sharmaine what I thought." Her intonation was plaintive as she continued. "That's why she thought you might be watching Lynyrd." Hilde stopped and changed her approach. "Don't be mad. She knew you couldn't get hurt on the Ferris wheel."

I didn't think that was necessarily true, but I didn't argue. "So, Sharmaine thought a scare would make me go away. That's crazy." As I said the words I realized the scheme wasn't that stupid. Andy and I had talked about my quitting after each incident. Quitting would probably have been the logical thing to do.

Even Hilde knew that. "If I'd been pushed off the Boardwalk and dumped on a Ferris wheel, I wouldn't have come back."

I didn't say a word. I didn't know what to say.

"Don't tell the cops or anything. You promised." A hint of desperation crept into Hilde's voice.

I didn't think that was part of the promise I'd made but, at that point, I didn't care. "Why would I think that Lynyrd killed Jonas? Did he have a motive?"

"Sharmaine has this illusion that Lynyrd is in love with her and that he would kill for her. I can't imagine why she believes that but she does. His actions certainly don't convey that message. I don't think Lynyrd cares that much. Anyway, before she fell in love with Lynyrd, Sharmaine always had it bad for a friend of Jonas. Now, there is some bad blood between Sharmaine and the guy. I think whatever happened was Jonas's fault. I overheard him talking to Sharmaine one day. He sounded and acted all apologetic."

"They talked about the incident in the store?"

Hilde grew flustered. "No, they didn't see me on the beach one day. They were talking on a bench on the Boardwalk and I was just underneath them. On the beach. When I heard them talking, I couldn't help but hear."

I had my doubts. A reenactment would be needed to check Hilde's story, but I didn't care how Hilde got her information. My interest lay in the content: Sharmaine and Lynyrd's motive for hurting me and/or Jonas. "Let me see if I understand Sharmaine's viewpoint. Lynyrd is in love with Sharmaine. Jonas's friend did something to Sharmaine. Apparently, both she and Jonas agree that it was his fault. She thinks Lynyrd loves her so much he would kill Jonas to avenge her. If he were the killing type. Which she believes he isn't, but I might think he was if I figured all this out."

"Right." Hilde underlined her answer with one hard nod of the head.

"I can't even figure her behavior out after explaining it to myself."

"Sharmaine worried that you might tell the cops to take a look at Lynyrd. Even though she never thought Lynyrd killed Jonas, she realized if the cops did look his way they might not like what they found."

I could accept that line of reasoning. I couldn't accept that Hilde just happened to see Andy's license plate or to be in Ocean City the day I worked there or to be under the Boardwalk where Sharmaine and Jonas were talking. Coincidences did happen. I'd run into Karl Elkins twice. Once that day and once in Atlantic City. For all I knew, he only knew about one. But I certainly wouldn't want him to think I'd managed those encounters on purpose. Still, in one summer Hilde seemed to experience an unusually high number of coincidences.

She filled the silence. "I didn't mean to cut in on Andy. I kept asking you about him, trying to find out what was going on between the two of you. You aren't mad at me, are you?"

I knew the reason she asked which was probably the only reason she bothered to apologize. "Hilde, your secret is safe with me. If . . . ."

"If? No if. You promised." She took a step away from the railing towards me. Despite her narrow frame the move was threatening.

"Hilde, tell me. Did you kill Jonas Angel?"

The cold glare I'd grown familiar with, reappeared. "I knew people wouldn't understand what I'd done, playing Heidi. I wanted that entire episode to remain hidden. Would that happen if I killed Jonas?"

I got her point. If Hilde was concerned about her secret coming to light, she wouldn't want Jonas's life subject to intense scrutiny. Jonas's murder was the worst thing that could have happened to a girl with an imaginary twin.

CHAPTER 69

Andy and I had developed an evening routine of lounging on the deck of the Angel's oceanfront home. I began to forget, or tried to forget, that this was not our actual lifestyle. I got used to the perks of beachfront living. The sights, the sounds, the smells. I ignored the costs.

At night we sipped one of Andy's fruity rum concoctions and watched the ocean turn from blue to gray to black. I was the one who interrupted the sounds of ocean waves and cawing gulls. "For weeks, I didn't dwell on Heavenly Dips and today I had two reminders." I answered Andy's questions about Hilde Bossick and Karl Elkins.

"Don't tell me Elkins's wife came back! She planned too long and hard to get away from that man."

"No. He didn't ask a thing about her. I guess he saw no point in asking after you laid out the truth for him." I studied the surf for a few moments. "Andy, how do we know that Bunny Elkins is alive?"

Andy grinned. "Searching for another murder to solve? We haven't even solved the last one yet. Bunny Elkins isn't dead. She's following her carefully laid out plan. As promised, she sent a postcard to confirm she'd gotten away. She always said she wasn't going to call until the holidays. No one expects to hear from her."

"How do we know Bunny sent the card?"

"Because the police accept that she did. Her friend Sandy believes she did. Just because we have two loose ends doesn't mean we can tie them up together. Real-life isn't like that, Meg. Unfortunately. Sometimes we just never know."

My thoughts went to Amanda Angel. She had to know.

"Have the police thoroughly investigated the coincidence

that Bunny Elkins left her job at Heavenly Dips on the same night that Jonas disappeared?"

"I know they have been down every path including that one. I don't know what they concluded but I saw no evidence they considered Bunny a suspect. You know Petino. He doesn't share. You still think Bunny killed Jonas?"

I shook my head. "No."

Andy appeared relieved.

"I think Karl did."

Andy's smirk looked suspiciously like Petino's. "Why would Karl Elkins kill Jonas Angel?" Andy's tone stated that he knew the answer: he wouldn't. "He had no motive, or do you think he believed that his wife was having an affair with Jonas?"

I shook my head. "He believed that his wife didn't like Jonas."

"So he murdered Jonas? He loves Bunny but I don't believe he would be willing to kill everyone who crosses her."

"You're being snide."

"What do you want me to do? Confront him? 'Aha, Karl, we've figured it out. Clever plan but so obvious. You had no motive to kill Jonas. It had to be you.'" He chuckled. "Can you give me one reason he would kill Jonas"

Suddenly the truth seemed so obvious. "For his badge."

"Jonas Angel's badge was found in the woods. The police found it the other day. Maybe I forgot to tell you." Andy offered me the orange slice from his drink.

"Amanda Angel told me the badge was twenty yards from the body."

"The police assume the chain broke as he walked into the woods. Sure you don't want this?" He held the orange aloft.

I waved off his offer. "But they never found the chain and they even didn't find the badge at first. They found it later. How did they miss it?"

Andy threw out his hands, at least his free hand, palm up. I read the gesture as exasperation. "Maybe an animal moved it. An animal probably took the chain too. A lot of time passed." He bit into the orange slice.

"Presumably. But what if it didn't? What if the killer threw the badge there later?"

"But no one used it after Jonas did at 10 AM on the Friday morning he died."

"Andy, bear with me." I slid forward on the lounger and sat facing Andy. "Karl Elkins didn't know his wife was leaving him, right? But he suspected that he was losing her for months, maybe years. All his friends say that she had grown more and more afraid of him, that she accelerated her plans to leave because she didn't trust him. He goes home early that Friday night because he feels sick. His wife isn't there. He gets suspicious. So, he goes searching for her."

"In the woods along Route 9 where he comes upon Jonas taking a leak? I don't think so." Andy punctuated his thought by finishing off the orange slice with a flourish.

"Humor me, Andy. If your wife didn't come home from work, where would you check? At her office."

"She didn't leave the office until late. She made her last phone call after 9 PM and didn't log off the network until almost ten. If Karl called she would have been there which wasn't at all unusual on the last day of the pay period."

"Okay, so I haven't figured why he didn't simply call to see if she was there. But, what if he discovered her plan and wanted to stop her."

"So he waits along the road, not even the main road but a randomly selected side road, on the off chance that Jonas Angel has to relieve himself?" Andy's intonation told me that the obvious answer was no. His smirk rivaled Petino's.

"He saw him somewhere. By accident."

"And killed him for his badge. Right." Andy's right clearly meant wrong.

"It almost happened to me."

"To you?" Andy tried to keep a straight face but failed.

"Well, kind of. One day, years ago, I stopped at a grocery store on the way home from work. I didn't realize I'd forgotten to take off my badge until the check-out guy asked me. Actually, he didn't ask. He said, in a kind of creepy way, 'You work at Lakkland.' The way he stared at my badge scared me. I'm telling you, I rushed to my car and locked myself in."

"And made up a story that he was stalking a Lakkland employee and would kill for the badge to get close to her."

"Right."

"Just like you've made up a story that Karl Elkins killed Jonas Angel for his badge."

"Change 'made up a story' to concluded. I was right about the guy in the grocery store."

"He killed you for your badge?"

I ignored his remark. "That man thought about how he could get it. He wanted it. I could tell." I searched my memory for other clues that would point to Karl. It took me five minutes. Andy had probably relaxed, thinking I had dropped the topic by the time I spoke. "You know Karl said something odd given the circumstances of Jonas's death. He was talking about why Bunny didn't like Jonas. He mentioned one thing he didn't like about Jonas. He paid a fortune for his golf clubs, more than a lot of people spend on food in a year. The news organizations didn't have the information about the missing seven iron. They just said a blunt instrument, not a golf club."

"So Bunny mentioned to her husband that Jonas had golf clubs."

"Maybe. Or he saw them when he pulled it out of Jonas's golf bag and used it to bash in Jonas's head."

CHAPTER 70

I decided the following morning. As Andy was leaving, he mentioned that I must have stirred up a hornet's nest when I ran into Karl Elkins. "I have a voice mail from him. The usual message. 'Has anyone heard from my wife?'"

"I tell him Big Al isn't charged with the murder and suddenly he needs to talk to you? Give me a break. Karl thought he'd gotten away with murder. After we spoke, he realized he didn't. He needed you again because he needs to know what you know. You have my opinion about the night Jonas disappeared."

"And you know, although I admire your intuition, your scenario involves too big a coincidence."

"So are you going to call him?"

Andy scowled. "I have a busy day." He planted a kiss on my forehead.

I followed him onto the deck and waved good-bye without telling him that I intended to prove, or disprove, my theory. If I had, he might have hidden the file with Karl Elkins's address.

As I drove my rented wreck out of Mantoloking, I didn't have my plan finalized. Actually, I didn't have my plan started. I headed out armed only with my fantasy of how the encounter would end. Unfortunately, I had no idea how to convert that vision to reality. In my scenario, Karl believed that he had nothing to lose in confessing the details of Jonas's last minutes to me. Give me a break. It was a fantasy.

That fantasy was predicated on the assumption that I would not find the Elkins houses sitting alone in the woods at the end of a long driveway with no neighbors for miles around. When I found his street, I was happy to see many houses in the neighborhood and many people out and about. Karl lived in one of the uglier houses in a beautiful setting on the water in Tuckerton across the bay and down Route 9, but not quite as far as the Heavenly Dips corporate offices. When I hopped out of my dented, rented Ford Escort, Karl stood on the wooden landing outside the front door. I couldn't tell whether he'd been on his way in or on his way out. After a brief display of confusion, he raised a hand in greeting. He acted happy to see me. Acted.

"How did you find me?" Karl didn't move. He made me walk to him.

I explained that Andy had the address in his notes from when he worked for him. I didn't mention that I had waited for Andy to go out and then rifled through those notes to find the information.

"I have to say I'm kind of surprised to see you here." He forced a tentative smile. "What can I do for you?"

You can let me frisk you. Okay, I didn't say that although it had been my first thought. I went with my second thought. "I want to tell you a story, Karl. And, what I say might sound a bit ominous at points, but if you stick with me, it will all work out fine."

Karl had no idea what I was talking about. I barely did.

Beyond the sandy driveway, I saw boats chugging up and down an inlet and neighbors sitting on the waterfront patio next door. "Can we sit out by the water?" I pointed to two beach chairs set up beside a small motorboat tied up at a ramshackle dock. I wanted to speak to Karl in plain sight.

"Sure." Karl led me to the dock. He appeared confused but not worried. As I followed him, I marveled at the weight he'd packed on in the short time since I'd first met him. His rapid transformation gave going to pot new meaning. He pulled a fresh pack of cigarettes from his pocket and lit one as we walked to the water's edge.

"Sorry about the lawn. What with the drought the grass is

a little dry." Karl waved an arm at the brown vegetation surrounding the ranch house.

From my perspective, the grass was the least of his problems. Karl's garden offered many landscaping details: a doorless refrigerator, a bed of wheel rims, and a hedge of overflowing trash cans strewn along the side of the building. Beside the trash, a mound of sporting equipment appeared to be headed for the dump: tennis racquets, golf clubs, and a racing bike that cost more than I would make in a summer at Heavenly Dips. All the equipment was thrown in a heap.

When Karl waved to his neighbors, I was surprised they waved back at a man whose property was a blight on the neighborhood. I wondered if the place looked this bad when Bunny still lived there. I would have bet the current clutter reflected his personality, not hers.

"Like I said, I'm surprised to see you here," Karl asked as he headed toward two aluminum lawn chairs that faced the inlet. He took a green chair and directed me to the orange one.

The frayed plastic straps dug into my thigh as I sat down. "I think you'll be even more surprised when I tell you why I came."

My host stared at me expectantly but his expression said he had nothing to fear. Oddly enough, he did not ask if I had news about his Bunny. He sat silently and waited for me to speak.

"Karl, let me just say that I am not wearing a wire." As I stood up, the skin on the back of my thighs peeled away from the seat with a rumble. I pirouetted so he could see I had no place to hide a taping device under my T-shirt and shorts. Then, I settled back onto the plastic chair. "See. No wire."

Karl never asked why I might be wearing a wire. He was playing a waiting game. He expected me to continue.

I did. "You see, Karl, since Andy went to work for Maxwell Angel, I've gotten to know his wife. Do you know

Amanda Angel?"

"I seen her on occasion. At Christmas parties. Places like that."

"She's a lovely woman, don't you think?"

He shrugged.

"She's been so unhappy since her son died. Losing Jonas was a terrible tragedy for that family."

"Sure." Karl squirmed in his chair.

"Whether someone goes to jail or not for the murder of Jonas Angel doesn't matter. Well, it does matter but it is not the main thing. The main thing is that his mother wants to know what happened to him. That's all. If he felt frightened. If he suffered. I mean the cops say Jonas never knew what hit him but she doesn't know if that is true."

"Why are you asking me this?" Karl shifted his weight in the folding lawn chair.

I waited for the teetering seat to collapse but Karl regained his balance. I continued. "Because I don't think the police are ever going to charge anyone in Jonas's murder. I think whoever killed Jonas committed a perfect crime. I think the murder was carefully thought out and well-executed. I am telling you this because I believe that you are the person who committed the perfect crime"

Karl snickered. "Me! Why would I kill Jonas Angel? I have no motive." I discerned no trace of anger in his voice.

"I know that you had no obvious motive. That is what makes it such a great crime. However, I think you did have a motive. I think you stole Jonas's badge so that you could go into the Heavenly Dips offices to surprise your wife." I studied the man's eyes for movement. I saw them narrow. Slightly. A smirk remained firm on his lips. "I think you understood that you were losing your Bunny that night. How you knew, I don't know. Somebody may have slipped up. Said something. Whoever made the slip probably never even noticed. No one can ever prove that you knew. But I think you did know. At this point maybe you don't even remember what gave Bunny's plan away."

I watched a shadow make its way down the inlet in our direction. At last real clouds, dark, heavy and hanging low, were blowing into the area. The weatherman had called for rain but everyone had learned to ignore those predictions. They only led to disappointment. But suddenly I felt a chill in the air. Rain was really on its way.

Across from me, Karl seemed oblivious to the weather. His features contorted to confirm that he was deep in thought. "Let me see if I have this. Because I knew that my wife was leaving, what did I do? I don't remember." He chortled but he appeared nervous, self-conscious, unamused.

"I'm not exactly certain how it happened, Karl, but I think you ran into Jonas somewhere. I don't know where. I don't know how. I think you followed him and you grabbed his badge. Then you killed him."

"And why didn't the cops catch me when I used the badge to go see my wife?" He smiled.

I could have read the dark clouds as portending trouble, but I didn't. I plunged ahead with my theorizing. "Because you never used the badge. You never had to. You reached the office and you saw through the fence that she had already gone. You were too late. When you had the chance, you threw the badge back into the woods near the body and went home. No one would ever suspect you. You had no motive to kill Jonas Angel."

"This is an interesting theory. Can I ask you a question?"

"Fire away."

"If you believe that I killed Jonas Angel, aren't you afraid that I'll kill you?"

"Hardly. Number one, I told Andy I was coming here." I lied. "Number two, all these people have seen us here." I waved to a family of four passing slowly through the inlet in a small Chris Craft. "Plus, why would you kill me? So what if I make wild accusations? Can I prove one point? No. I'll never be able to. Why risk a second murder? This one they'd connect you to quickly."

"You're on drugs, right?" Karl eyed me with fear for the first time.

"I'm angry, Karl. I'm frustrated. I'm fed up. I see the pain on a mother's face and I can't help her unless I can tell her how her son died. That's all we can do for Amanda Angel. Revenge. Vengeance. They aren't worth much. Understanding, that is what counts. That is what could bring peace."

"Well, that sounds like quite a noble motive but I am sorry I can't help you. For one thing, I found out after my beloved wife left me that buying a new car was part of her escape plan. She planned her departure that carefully." The thought seemed to rile him but he brought his emotion under control. "So if I had wanted to find her, even if I went to Heavenly Dips, even if her car was there, I wouldn't have recognized her new vehicle."

"See. That proves my point. You got there and her car wasn't there. So you went home. You'd killed Jonas for no reason."

"Tell me again why I wanted to go to Heavenly Dips that night?"

"To see Bunny before she left. Maybe to talk her out of going."

Karl let out a yelp but not in response to my words. "What was that?"

I glanced up at the sky. All traces of blue had vanished. Dark gray clouds hung low. "Thunder. The pundits are calling for rain. Finally. After all the discussions of the weather we had this summer, are you the only one in the state who doesn't know that the dry spell is set to end today?"

"Thank God." He seemed preoccupied.

I continued. "Karl, I don't even know if the cops looked at you for the murder."

"Why would they? The cops only asked me about how

much Bunny hated Jonas, which was pretty much. But my Bunny could never hurt him." His tone grew angry. "She liked that father of his too much. They never even asked me where I was that night. Know why?" He leaned forward and spoke deliberately. "Because I had no motive."

"Well, we disagree on that one, Karl. What we agree on is that there can't be any evidence or the cops would have charged you. But there is nothing. No DNA. No murder weapon. You got away with it, Karl."

"I got away with it 'cause I didn't do it. If you ain't high, you're nuts." He started to get up. Should I have brought a weapon? The thought had barely formed when Karl simply settled back into his chair in a new position. "You talk about his mother but she didn't do such a good job. That kid was no great shakes. I mean from what Bunny said. Him dying ain't no real loss to the world."

I felt encouraged. Karl seemed ready to talk. "How so?"

"That kid had everything handed to him but Bunny said he acted like a no-good piece of crap. Bunny was a good judge of character."

I didn't ask how such a good judge of character ended up married to him.

"That Angel kid didn't respect his father or his mother. That mother who's missing him so much, she's fooling herself. That kid dying was the best thing that ever happened to her." He laughed. "Maybe I should say I did kill him and ask for a reward."

I should have been a psych major. Clearly, Karl's tongue was loosening up but I didn't know how to manipulate him. Seduction was out. Sympathy wouldn't work. Ego. That had to be the right approach. Play to his ego. Before I could, the clouds opened and we had to run for cover. I followed my host across the brown lawn to a metal canopy that ran along the side of the house sheltering container after container of junk, rusted despite its protection from the weather.

Even as I brushed raindrops from my hair, I kept the

conversation going. "So you agree that this was a perfect crime?"

"If no one's been charged, you have to admit it's a clever crime." Karl's smile struck me as unseemly. "But you can't put me away when I got no reason to kill the kid. Lots of people in the world have no motive to kill Jonas Angel. I don't know why you're looking in my direction."

I went back to the concept of the perfect crime. "Assuming you worked alone, you were in the physical condition to move Jonas's car and run back to your own. Even with a cold. The site where the body was discovered was clean. It's in the woods, yet the cops located no forensic evidence. For your business you keep protective gloves and slippers and who knows what all else in your trunk. I saw the stuff the other day. I think you used those items. That's why there's no physical evidence. And this is really important to his mother." I leaned forward and stared into his eyes. "I don't think you planned to kill Jonas. I think you just saw the opportunity and took it. I think Amanda Angel would like to hear that no one hated Jonas enough to kill him."

"Then why did the killer clobber the little bastard so hard?" Karl forced a nervous laugh.

"See, you're calling him a little bastard and you don't even know him. Maybe you resented what he represented. He was an undeserving kid who had everything handed to him."

"Hardly a motive. I do watch a lot of reruns, you know, Law & Order, NYPD Blue, JAG—even the old Perry Masons. So I know about this stuff. Someone who mutilates someone the way I hear that kid got worked over, he has a motive, that's personal."

"Or, it could be he has no motive and wants to make it seem like a crime of passion." Because he watches a lot of cop shows and knows that. I kept that thought to myself. "Remember the person who did this crime is smart. He got away with murder."

I expected the crack of thunder. Karl didn't. His eyes flew open and he jumped. Only a small delay separated the thunder and the lightning. He recoiled from the flash of light.

"That's a good one." I wasn't sure if he meant the thunderclap or my theory. "You got an answer for everything." A big grin spread across Karl's face. "So whatta ya know. I missed this one. I didn't know the rain was coming. You can wait here if you want, I gotta close the windows." He ran the few uncovered steps to the house.

The sound of the rain falling at full force was unfamiliar. I'd forgotten how loud the drops could be, especially on a tin roof like the one above me. I hadn't forgotten that under a metal roof was not the best place to be in a thunderstorm. I wished Karl would hurry. I used my time to check out the neighbors. A few had ducked inside to escape the rain but most of the potential witnesses still huddled on the porch next door. If Karl returned with a weapon he would not be able to use it. At least without going directly to jail. The downpour was heavy but not dense enough to conceal a murder.

Feeling comfortable that potential witnesses were in place, I perused the trash cans full of discarded household items and car parts that lined the side of the house. Searching for what? A written confession? What I found was almost as good. I had it in my hands when Karl came out of the house. "I have a friend who would love this. I don't think there are that many people searching for an orange and turquoise vase."

Karl thought long and hard before he informed me that the vase was not for sale.

"Too bad. I wanted to get something out of this visit. I thought coming to see you was worth a shot."

"Your efforts might work on the killer. Just not on me." Karl made that chortling noise again.

I sensed no anger. I didn't imagine I'd be so calm if someone dropped by my house to accuse me of murder.

"But before I go, tell me what you think about the crime. For Amanda Angel."

"Why would I do that?"

"You said you know a lot about this stuff."

I detected a softening in his tone. "The mother shouldn't worry about the kid suffering. Of course, I only know what I read in the papers, a little on TV, you know, about Jonas's death but anyone who watches a lot of television understands that there are many disadvantages in letting a victim comprehend what is actually happening and many advantages to taking him by surprise. My guess would be that someone sneaked up on the kid. Most likely, he never saw the guy coming. He might even have been humming a little tune right up until the moment the dude clobbered him. I mean he was a strong, healthy guy, right? He would have fought back if he knew what was coming. I mean I can't tell you what really happened because I wasn't there. But that would be my best guess. The kid never knew what happened."

"The tune. Any idea what it might have been?"

"The kid came from in New Jersey, so it probably would be a Springsteen song. That's about all the help I can offer."

I didn't know what to say so I simply said, "Thank you, Karl. Good-bye."

I turned my back. As I crossed the patio, in the seconds before I would have begun my sprint through the rain to my car, I heard Karl singing a refrain from a song on Springsteen's The Rising CD. I didn't know the title but I did know the refrain. "Let it rain."

I stopped and spun around slowly. My eyes met Karl's. For one second, I saw through his cynical amusement that Karl Elkins was telling the truth.

CHAPTER 71

Maybe things had not gone my way at Karl Elkins's place. Maybe he did not throw himself at my feet and confess the details of the murder of Jonas Angel. I wasn't surprised. I realized that I had a better chance of winning Mega Millions. If I'd done the equivalent of winning the lottery in the Angel case, I would have returned from Karl Elkins's house to Mantoloking and, after listening to Andy tell me that confronting Karl was the dumbest thing I'd ever done, we would have called Petino. He, after telling us that confronting Karl was the smartest thing I'd ever done, would have gotten a warrant to confirm that all ducks were in a row before he and his fellow officers swarmed the Elkins property where they would have uncovered the bloody golf club that killed Jonas Angel. As I told you, I didn't expect to win the lottery. And I didn't.

We gave Petino the information but had no idea what the police did with it. Petino wasn't the type to share. Andy and I both understood that it was a big leap, actually several leaps, from the presence of a vase from a Saturn dealer in Karl's trash to his realization that his wife was leaving him to his theft of Jonas's badge to get access to her office.

Andy refocused his efforts on linking Karl to Jonas Angel but came up with nothing. He resumed his pursuit of the elusive Bunny Elkins, but she had prepared her getaway meticulously. Andy searched for evidence that Karl had tracked his wife down and murdered her. He found nothing. The trail went cold. After Labor Day, he told Maxwell Angel that he would always work on Jonas's case but he had no active leads. He moved onto other jobs, I deferred graduate school and moved into another undercover job. We checked our finances and moved out of the Mantoloking house despite the Angels' offer of a good deal for Andy to go full time with Heavenly Dips.

We may have moved on, but I still believed in miracles. I always have. Okay, maybe not always but since the Saturday before Christmas when I got the parking space closest to Bloomingdale's. After that I had to believe in miracles. But only the small miraculous event: the check that didn't bounce, the train that didn't leave, the parking space that didn't disappear. I did not expect to win the lottery.

I am convinced that the little miracles in our lives are the result of many unconscious decisions people that we didn't know, and would most likely never meet, made days, weeks, or even months before the actual event. So it was on a Friday night in early May, long before Andy and I met Max and Amanda Angel, Carly Mims, a student at Rutgers University, agreed to accompany her friends to a bar near the campus. If Carly hadn't gone out on that night when she had a cold and felt like climbing into bed, she never would have met Todd Brinks and brought him to her family house for the holidays. If Todd had never introduced Carly to kayaking, her aunt wouldn't have given her a book on kayaking in Greenland for her birthday. If Carly hadn't shown Todd that book it is unlikely that the couple would have been training for the kayaking trip they planned to Greenland. If Todd and Carly had not been so intent on conditioning themselves for the trip, it's unlikely they would have taken their kayaks out on December 23 to a small lake near Carly's home and the Wharton State Forest in south Jersey. But they did and noticed a colorful object under the water. Carly stuck her paddle in as far as it would go. The paddle hit a hard surface. She jabbed the water several times, hitting the hood, the windshield and the roof of Bunny Elkins's Saturn. Inside the submerged vehicle divers found the remains of the car's owner.

In an effort to take the death penalty off the table in the

death of his wife, Karl Elkins had confessed that he had killed Jonas Angel. It had been an unpremeditated crime. He had simply stopped for a beer when he spotted the badge around Jonas's neck. Hoping for an opportunity to gain access to his wife's office, he followed him. The details came out in a book by Bridget Simkus.

Misunderstood: The Failure of Society to Recognize and Stop the Heavenly Dips Killer by Bridget Simkus was published on the third anniversary of Jonas's and Bunny's deaths. According to Bridget's account, society and Bunny had plenty of time to recognize what was bugging Karl since he had planned to kill his wife for over a year. He accepted that he could not keep his wife and realized he could not live without her, or, more accurately, he couldn't let her live without him. As Simkus explained, apparently without sarcasm, "he loved his Bunny too much."

The book confirmed what I believed to be the motive for the murder of Jonas Angel. The ice cream heir's charmed life had ended when he happened to be in the wrong place at the wrong time and Karl spotted his badge. And the worst thing about the unlucky coincidence was that, in the end, Karl didn't even need to go through Heavenly Dips security. He arrived at the gate on foot at the moment the replacement his wife had trained drove out. The wide gates slid open and he slipped in. A week later, worried that someone would tie a motive for Jonas's murder to the missing badge, he wiped it clean, went for a jog, and threw it into the woods.

Karl's account verified the story of Jonas's last moments he had imagined that day on his dock. The bulk of the new information in the book described his planning and execution of his wife's killing, preparations that allowed him to get away with the murder of Jonas Angel. For a time.

Karl had learned what he considered the most valuable lesson of his life from an outplacement counselor. "Chance favors the prepared" the facilitator of the class had said. Karl described most of what the trainer had to say as "useless yuppie crap" but that one idea took hold. For a solid year, Karl Elkins prepared—physically and mentally—to be ready in case the need to murder his wife became apparent. He feared that moment would come and did not want to miss his opportunity when it presented itself. Successful killers were patient. Karl was very patient.

Misunderstood described how Karl located a campsite on the fringes of the Wharton State Forest six miles from the Heavenly Dips corporate offices to use as a base camp to track his wife's movements, how he happened upon an abandoned boat ramp he kept in mind just in case he had to dispose of his wife's car with her inside, an idea he found very appealing until the drought started. The book talked about the rigorous physical training that allowed him to run to his surveillance location and, on the night of the murder, from Jonas's abandoned car back to his own, from his campsite to Heavenly Dips headquarters and from his wife's car back to the campsite. Even with the threat of a developing head cold, the runs had been easy for him.

Misunderstood included the text of an interview Karl gave Bridget soon after his conviction repeating the facts of the crime that Karl had given at his sentencing.

Bridget Simkus: What happened when you came home from work on the night your wife died?

Karl Elkins: Bunny wasn't there but that didn't surprise me. I was surprised by the flowers on the front steps of our home. They were from a car dealer and addressed to Bunny but not at our address, at her friend Sandy's address. At first, I thought Sandy had bought a new car and they had sent her flowers to us by accident, but the name on the card was Bunny's. I knew the flower shop so I drove by the florist to ask, casually, why the flowers had been delivered to our house. Bunny and I had been having problems, so I tried to do a lot of nice things for her, like sending flowers. So the florist, he knew us. When he saw the address he figured the dealership made a mistake. He wanted to know how I liked the new Saturn. I felt too humiliated to admit I didn't know we had a new Saturn. I had a whole conversation about how great Saturns are and I'd never even been in one.

I had to think things over before I confronted her, so I stopped for a drink. I probably saw the kid at a Christmas party or something, but I didn't recognize him. I recognized his badge. Those bright blue IDs are easy to spot. Bunny had one. It works as a passcard. Right away I knew I wanted it so I could surprise her at her office. Once you were through the entrance gate controlled by the key card, you could go wherever you wanted at Heavenly Dips and do whatever you wanted. There were no security cameras inside the fence.

Lucky for me, the kid glanced out the window and saw someone or something he didn't like. He bolted out the side door like a shot. I followed. The good thing about being a guy like me, middle-aged, ordinary, is that no one even noticed. I saw him climb into this car that costs more than I made in two, maybe three years. I got in my economy car and tailed him in his hotshot convertible. I didn't know how I was going to get that badge but I was determined. I followed the kid south on Route 9 and then turned behind him onto that dirt road. I pulled over and watched. He didn't go that far down before he parked. Nothing there so I knew what that meant. He was gonna take a leak. The kid didn't even turn off the car. All that money for a car and he doesn't even worry about it. I didn't even wait for him to walk into the woods before I drove closer. My car was nondescript. Even if someone saw the cars they would have seen a black Porsche and some other car. When you're treated as if you're invisible as much as I am you learn how to be invisible.

Getting the ID was easy. I came up behind the kid and hit him. He just dropped, fell forward without a peep. I rolled him onto his back and pulled the breakaway chain that held his badge. That was when I realized who he was but I didn't have time to think about it. I had the access I needed and was anxious to use it. But first I had a crime to cover up, one I had to make look like a crime of passion and, in a way, it was. That kid got everything I ever wanted. Hitting him felt good. I don't know how many times I swung.

I moved the car away from the body and stashed it out of sight. I hoped Mother Nature would do her best to dilute whatever evidence I might have left. I just had to keep the cops from noticing anything that night. I was in a hurry to get to Bunny's office. I knew I would succeed when I ran up to Heavenly Dips and saw the gate was opening. I just slipped right in. I didn't have much time to catch my breath. Just about 10 PM, Bunny turned off the light in her office and stepped out the door. She looked so happy.

Seeing me standing beside her new car wiped that smile off her face. Bunny seemed shocked to see me. Shocked and afraid – right up until the moment I shot her which I didn't do right away. I wanted her to know that the car dealership had sent her flowers to congratulate her on her purchase. I wanted her to know at the same time she had been planning to escape, I had been planning to stop her. I told her all of that before I shot her. I wasn't worried about noise. That industrial compound is isolated. Even so, I killed her with a single bullet through the heart. I didn't want her to suffer. After all, I loved her.

Karl described how gently he laid Bunny on the backseat of her new car and drove her to the abandoned boat ramp. Television dramas had taught him that the dark cedar water in the lake would obliterate any traces of skin, hair, or fiber he left behind. He lowered the windows, put the car in gear and released the emergency brake. He was surprised a light push was all that was needed to start the car down the ramp. The longest part of the night was waiting for that car to disappear below the surface. He said aloud that he felt bad that their marriage had to end that way. "The decision was yours, Bunny."

Karl hadn't watched all those crime dramas simply to waste time. He had a lot to do. Remove every item he wore or touched during the time period and, before he returned to his house, conceal it in a trash bag. Weigh that bag down with a cinder block and take it on a boat ride out into the Atlantic. Observe all the evidence sink to the bottom of the ocean floor. He knew all that from watching TV.

He disposed of all the evidence early that Saturday morning under the guise of a fishing trip. Things had gone his way. He even caught a few bluefish. He thought of offering a gift to the neighbors but since he was not typically so generous, he didn't. He simply made sure they saw him cleaning the fish on his return but only after he made the first round of frantic calls to Bunny's friends.

He practiced answers to the questions the police might ask. Did he notice Bunny was missing on Friday? No, she often worked late at the end of the month. She hadn't gotten home when, feeling sick, he went to bed early. He had slept in the spare room so she would not catch the cold he felt coming on. Yes, he wondered why Bunny had left the house so early on Saturday morning. No, he didn't worry. She was a busy woman with a lot to do. No, he didn't wonder why she did not leave a note. She seldom did. Yes, she always made the bed before she left the house. He had his story in order.

When Karl called the cops they dismissed his concern as unwarranted. No, he told them, he really couldn't swear that she had been out all night. He felt pleased he could tell the cops he had already called all her friends. The cops played right into his hands. They recorded his call and took no action. He never had to give the answers he prepared.

Bridget Simkus explained what had, until then, been the inexplicable aspect of the crime. The postcard. The police, who had a crime to solve and weren't looking for another one, wanted to get Bunny's perspective on Jonas's death. They let Karl know that Sandy expected a postcard from his wife. They wanted to make sure if he received any communication from Bunny that he notified them.

So, Karl took a trip to New York and bought a postcard with Bunny's favorite flower, an iris, on the front. He printed Sandy's address and found that imitating Bunny's big, childlike signature posed no problem. Gloves were out of the question in the summer heat, so he put a bandage on his hand to avoid fingerprints as well as a straw hat on his head to avoid cameras. Still, he kept his head down as he dropped the postcard off to guarantee a New York postmark. He waited until he was blocks away to discard the hat. He disposed of the clothes he wore on another fishing trip.

If he had been in Bunny's place, he would have devised a code but, apparently, she didn't. He assumed no one questioned the authenticity of the card he sent to Sandy because the police called to see if he too had received a card from his wife, the woman they saw only as a witness. "No," he choked back crocodile tears as he responded, he hadn't but he promised he would certainly let them know when he did.

Bridget Simkus quoted him in Misunderstood:

Karl Elkins: I said when. I wanted the police to understand that I knew my wife was alive, that I knew my wife would contact me, that I knew we would work out our differences. As I said those words I wished they were true. I did love Bunny. I always did. I always will. Killing her just proved how much I loved her. Sometimes we show our love in unusual ways.

Andy and I would not know those details until Bridget Simkus's book came out. We did not even know that there was proof that Karl Elkins had taken Jonas's life when we received an invitation to stop and see Max and Amanda Angel on their first Christmas Eve without Jonas. By the time we arrived at their big old Victorian in Mantoloking, however, we all knew who was responsible for Jonas's death. We had a subdued visit and tried to talk about topics other than Karl. When Andy and Max's conversation drifted towards football, I asked Amanda to step out on the porch with me. We huddled in a corner the rising wind couldn't touch. *

"When I went to see Karl Elkins in the summer, he told me a story about how Jonas might have died. Given today's news, I feel his story might be true. Let me just repeat what he said."

When I finished, Amanda's eyes glistened with tears. She said nothing. She turned and gave me a hug. "Thank you so much." Her intonation made her words one of the most touching experiences of my life.

When Andy and I were climbing into his car, she pulled a small package from her pocket. It was labeled Do Not Open Before Christmas. I said I'd wait until midnight but I didn't. As we drove up the ramp to the Garden State Parkway, I tore off the wrapping. Inside I found a smaller box. Inside that box I found a gold chain with a single charm dangling from it. Wings. Gold wings. I read the note from Max and Amanda. It said simply, "Thank you, Meg. You've earned them."

CHAPTER 72

Looking back on my summer in Seaside Heights, I clasped the gold angel between my fingers and watched the ocean waves break around the stranded roller coaster. "I feel so sentimental."

"Missing your old coworkers?" Andy asked.

"Hardly. They found me on Facebook. I am friends with them although they are not all friends with each other."

"Not surprising. They never really were. So, where are they now?"

"Ed got his MBA and has moved into the corporate world. He still lives in New Jersey and posts about all his successes."

"Sharmaine?"

"Puts up pictures of her kids."

"With Lynyrd?

"No idea what happened to him, but I think it might be good that he is not on Sharmaine's friends list. He might not have been as rough a character as I first thought, but his life was, to say the least, complicated."

"Hilde?"

"She friended me but never posts. Knowing Hilde she probably lurks out there watching everyone else. In her picture, she looks like the pretty girl you first met. Her profile says that she is in graduate school getting a Ph.D. in psychology."

"I don't suppose you're friends with Bobby Briggs."

I shook my head. "No, but you know who I found online. Remember Barry, the guy at the amusement park?"

"He found you?"

"No, I found him one day when I was bored. We

exchange birthday postings."

"See, your days at Heavenly Dips weren't that bad." He gave me a quick hug to confirm that he hadn't subjected me to a summer of horror. And, he hadn't. Not really.

"When I think about all the people who told me I wouldn't like Seaside Heights."

"Well, you did give the impression you liked quiet beach towns," Andy explained.

"People warned me that it would be honky-tonk as if that would be a problem."

"They didn't take into account that honky-tonk means junk food and Skeeball or maybe they just didn't believe how much you love junk food and Skeeball." He paused. "It is kind of hard to believe."

"Should we drive up to Mantoloking?" I alluded to the town with no touch of honky-tonk within its borders.

"To see what isn't there?" Andy asked. "I don't think the Angels are ever coming back. Max sold the business and Superstorm Sandy stole both houses."

I remembered when Amanda explained why they would never move to their new home. That summer we never imagined that the ocean would force her to abandon the century-old house that she had clung to for her memories of Jonas. "So much loss. Their son. Their home. And for Max the work that was his life."

"Max thinks that being forced to let go of the past might be the best thing."

I knew that the Angels had followed Edwin to North Carolina. It turned out Edwin was the son who inherited Max's entrepreneurial spirit. Max helped him in his new business and Amanda loved babysitting her grandchildren, including a baby boy named Jonas.

Andy wrapped an arm around my shoulder and squeezed. "We'll check back in the summer. I bet we'll be surprised at what we find. It's going to be great."

I nodded.

The rebuilding had begun.

About Seaside Heights

To hear the songs from Meg's summer in Seaside Heights, to learn about the old TV series that occupy Ed and for more information about the town and the storm that devastated it go to: www.Pinterest.com/JaneKelly80.

For information on all titles go to:
www.janekelly.net
www.facebook.com/janekellyauthor
www.amazon.com/author/janekellyauthor.
To follow Meg Daniels on Facebook go to:
www.facebook.com/MegDanielsMysteries

Jane Kelly

Book club discussion questions

1. *A Fear of Seaside Heights* is far from a historical novel, yet because Meg is looking back at least one decade, technological advances since that time would have changed the crime and the way it was investigated. These changes would have affected the search for Jonas and Bunny Elkins' reaction to the crime. Do you see any other ways the plot might have shifted based on technological change?

2. Would it be more or less difficult for Meg to go undercover in the current technological environment?

3. If you've read the *Meg Daniels Mysteries* available from Plexus Publishing, do you see a change in Meg's personality, expectations and goals?

About the Author

Jane Kelly is the author of the Meg Daniels, Writing in Time Mysteries and Widow Lady Mysteries. She holds an MS in Information Studies from Drexel University and an MPhil in Popular Literature from Trinity College, University of Dublin. She is a past-president of the Delaware Valley Sisters in Crime and has served on the board of the New York Chapter of Mystery Writers of America. She currently lives in the Philadelphia area.

Made in the USA
Middletown, DE
12 October 2020

21474251R00188